YP   Jeapes, Ben.
JEA   The xenocide
            mission

W9-AUJ-638

ALSO AVAILABLE FROM DELL LAUREL-LEAF BOOKS

Many thanks to the mostly-usual suspects for comments, critiques and coffee:

Tosin Ajayi; Chris Amies; Tina Anghelatos; Cherith Baldry; Neville Barnes; Jamie Barras; Janet Barron; Paul Beardsley; Jacey Bedford; Pauline Dungate; David Fickling; Liz Holliday; Tony Jeapes; Stephen Kilbane; Andy Lanc; Kat Patrick; Alastair Reynolds; Gus Smith; Jonathan Tweed; Liz Williams; Patricia Wrede

THE
XENOCIDE MISSION

PART I

One

Day One: 3 June 2153

Joel Gilmore's life was saved by a faulty component module, the vagaries of SkySpy's maintenance roster and a called-in favour.

The module in question was deep in the guts of the Big Scope and that was where he was wedged, hot and tired and even more hungry than when he had started. The Big Scope was one of the many items of surveillance equipment that hung in space around the SkySpy asteroid, trained permanently in-system, and Joel was surrounded by girders and strutwork and was not enjoying himself. It had taken five minutes to get this far and he wanted to go home. Not back to the base, and a meal and a shower – *home*, which had much more to offer.

In front of him, a quarter of a mile away through the visor and framed by girders, was the dull, dark rock of SkySpy. There was a much more interesting view if he squinted up through his helmet's top-plate: the Shield, a mighty gas giant, bigger than Jupiter, eternally trailed by SkySpy on its endless trudge around the solar system. The giant was fluorescent

1

with greens and yellows. A spectacular sight for eyes that were prepared to appreciate it.

Well, it had been one more useful lesson for life, he thought: don't give sarky answers to admirals at your lieutenant's exam. If you're right then they can't fail you, but they can take revenge in sundry other ways. For example, making your first posting in your new rank the most unwanted position in the Commonwealth Navy.

Something dark moved in the gap and obscured his view of the gas giant.

'Are you in position?' said a voice inside his helmet.

'Yeah, I'm here,' Joel muttered. 'Pass it through.'

'Here it is.'

No-one could mistake the pressure-suited form clinging to a girder ahead of him for a human. The fact that all four limbs pointed in the same direction was one clue. In gravity, Rusties were dumpy quadrupeds. In micro-gee they were amazingly agile, with all legs able to operate independently in any direction. Boon Round's forefeet held the replacement module – a cube the size of Joel's head, packed with crystal and electronics – and the Rustie passed it through the gap. The working space was so narrow that Joel could not have carried it in with him.

'Thanks. Component three-three-zero-three-nine-oblique-alpha,' Joel said. 'Right here.' In front of him, a row of similar modules poked their casing just proud of the innards of the Big Scope. He took hold of one and twisted it ninety degrees. It slid out smoothly and he passed it out to Boon Round, then pushed the replacement in and twisted it back to lock in place. It took thirty seconds.

'*Module replacement complete,*' said the Big Scope. '*All systems now optimal.*'

'Oh, good,' Joel said. He reminded himself for the thousandth time never to promise someone a favour. He had owed Sal Gedroyc one, and that was why he was out here right now while Sal enjoyed the first shift in the SkySpy canteen. Sal was less qualified for this work than Boon Round, so it would have been the Rustie who would have had to pull the contortionist act. But Joel was more qualified than Boon Round, and Rusties were absolute sticklers for concepts like hierarchy and precedence.

The Commonwealth was all about combining Rustie tech with human initiative, but Joel had joined the Navy to . . . well, the jury was still out on exactly *why* he had joined, but furthering his career and doing interesting things had definitely been part of it, and they both sounded better than 'because it was inevitable' or 'why not?' Putting up with Rusties, a naturally pedantic race at the best of times, had been a necessary evil and he was prepared to grin and bear it. He had even been quite sincere at the citizenship interview about his desire and ability to get on with them. But sitting out a six-month posting on a dull rock replacing components had *not* been part of the dream.

'I do not understand your flippant attitude to maintenance work, Lieutenant,' said Boon Round. 'It's very important.'

'You don't say?' Joel said. Only five months and three weeks to go . . .

'I have just said it.'

Now, that *could* have been a joke, Joel thought. Not a funny one, but a joke. He drew a breath to explore the subject further, and a glowing white spot appeared on the surface of the asteroid. It erupted a second later in a cloud of molten rock and vapour.

'What was that?' he exclaimed.

Other spots appeared next to the first, turning into matching superheated geysers, and then the spots began to move, scorching white-hot canyons across the rock. For a second, Joel just stared at the sight, aghast, his brain trying to make sense of the fact that SkySpy was being strafed by military-strength lasers. Then he swore and started to wriggle backwards out of the Big Scope, as best he could in a pressure suit intent on wedging itself into every nook and cranny.

'Go to general band,' Boon Round said urgently. A cacophony of voices and blaring alarms filled Joel's helmet. Words could be picked out of the gabble.

'*Negative radar lock. Negative radar lock.*'

'*Fire flares. Lock on visual.*'

No-one could have got close enough to SkySpy to strafe it without very good stealth tech indeed. The base had been built by masters at remaining unobserved, but now it seemed the masters had been surpassed.

Down below him on the surface of the asteroid, hidden hatches had moved aside and turrets had sprung up into space. Joel caught the brief flaring blur of torpedoes firing off. A bright white light, SkySpy's flares, glared through the mechanism of the Big Scope and he tried to move even faster. The flares might illuminate the attackers, but bright lights could shine both ways.

'Visual lock! Fire.'

More blurs, more torpedoes, more flashes. There was a battle going on out there in space and Joel couldn't see a bit of it.

'This is most spectacular,' Boon Round said. Joel gritted his teeth and kept squirming.

SkySpy had been built at a safe distance from the second world of this solar system and the creatures who lived there, but every year those creatures had pressed further outwards. They had helium retrieval bases on their moon. They had an ever-increasing space trade, with space habitats and space lanes to link them. And their mining operations had reached their system's first asteroid belt. It had always been inevitable that one day they would be out past SkySpy, but no-one had expected it quite so soon.

The Rusties called the natives of this system The Beings of Sample World Four. Humans called them the XCs. It was short for 'xenocides'. The inhabitants of the third world of the system, if any had still remained, could have said why.

'Got one!'

For the first time in his life, Joel cheered at the destruction of a spaceship.

And then the enemy lasers opened up again and Joel could only watch helplessly – with that part of his mind not intent on extricating himself from the second juiciest target in the war zone – as their invisible beams carved trenches across the surface of SkySpy and across the turrets. One by one they fell silent.

'I would advise speed,' Boon Round said.

'I'm going as fast as I can!' Joel shrieked.

'I'll go round behind you. I may be able to help you out.'

'You mean it takes this to make a Rustie have a good idea?' Joel yelled.

'You're quite new here, so you might not know we prefer the term "First Breed". "Rustie" is an entirely inaccurate human expression based upon our appearance . . .'

'Yeah, yeah, whatever.' In the dying light of the flares, Joel saw dark objects settling down upon the rock, no longer opposed by SkySpy's dead defences. Then he frowned as they vanished.

'Magnify,' he said to his suit, and the centre of his visor expanded the view. They hadn't vanished: they were burrowing into the rock, leaving neatly drilled holes behind them. 'Oh, no,' he muttered. Then, on general band: 'This is Gilmore. They're burrowing in. Look out for . . .'

And then the surface of the rock erupted, a fountain of vapour and debris blasting out from the first hole. And another, and another. Over the general band, Joel heard screams and shouts and the roar of explosive decompression.

'Power is out. Launch Lifeboat B. I say again, launch

6

Lifeboat B. All personnel to evacuate to Lifeboat B. I say again, all personnel . . .'

Boon Round's forefeet finally grabbed Joel's ankles and pulled him out of the Big Scope.

'We've been told to evacuate,' the Rustie said.

'I heard!'

'Then come on.'

The Rustie was already diving back down to SkySpy, propelled by his suit's thrusters. Joel set his suit to follow, and foremost in his mind was the absurd thought: My God, all those drills are finally going to come in useful!

There was a drill for everything . . .

His suit thrusters cut in, throwing him down towards the rock after Boon Round.

. . . including the very unlikely event of the XCs actually getting so far as to launch a surprise attack on the station without being spotted a light minute away.

A nudge from one of the shoulder nuzzles diverted him, edging him out into space. Two more nozzles cut in to swing him around the rock.

The surveillance gear on SkySpy was expendable – there was no tech there that would be any news to the XCs. More important was the destruction of anything that remotely hinted at how to open a step-through point. Or the precise whereabouts in space of the Commonwealth or Earth. Thermite charges were placed permanently against all computer equipment and memory banks in the station.

The dark, rough surface of SkySpy blurred past him.

What it came down to was: in the event of an attack, on-duty crew within SkySpy had to handle the defence of the station and, if necessary, go through a sequence of codes to set off the charges the moment an unfavourable outcome became evident. Off-duty crew and anyone outside the station got the hell out of there.

Joel and Boon Round came out the other side of the rock, side thrusters burning to cancel their outward momentum.

SkySpy had two lifeboats but Lifeboat A would have been too exposed to attack. Lifeboat B had emerged from its hangar and was floating just free of the rock, protected by the bulk of the asteroid. With Boon Round still ahead of him, Joel's suit fired a blast to put him on a final course. The airlock loomed, his suit retroed, and he and Boon Round touched down together. A suited human figure was already there.

'In, quick,' said the airlock master, pulling them towards the open inner door. By definition, if the lifeboat were needed then it would be a combat situation, so the ship was air-empty. She peered at the name patch on Joel's suit. 'Gilmore? You're most senior on board, sir—'

'What?'

'– so get to the flight deck.'

Joel got. The human pilot, Albarazi, and a Rustie that Joel couldn't put a name to were already there. 'Gilmore here,' he said as he dropped into the command couch. The autostraps wrapped snugly around him. 'What's happening?'

'M-main engines powered up, course laid into the

generator, standing by to burn, sir,' said Albarazi.
'Ready for your word.' He and the Rustie both stared
through their faceplates at Joel, poised over the
controls.

The lifeboat was too small to have a step-through
generator on board. All Commonwealth traffic
entered and left the system via a generator in Shield
orbit, which had pre-set orders to self-destruct if any
ship not beaming the correct codes came towards it.
The lifeboat would be there in ten minutes, it would
slip through into a far-off solar system and, short of
actually having confirmed proof that intelligent life
existed somewhere else in the universe, the XCs
would be none the wiser.

'Airlock master,' Joel said on the open band. 'How
many on board?'

'*Seventeen total, sir.*' Which left another sixty-three
unaccounted for.

'Where the hell is everyone?' Joel muttered.

'Dead,' Albarazi said. He looked at Joel from dark,
hollow eyes. 'You weren't in there. They dug in
through the walls, and then they drilled through the
bulkheads so we couldn't seal up, and people were
being torn to pieces and they're dead.'

Joel made himself picture the scene. The emergency
bulkheads would shut immediately there was a
pressure drop, but what good was that if someone
was digging tunnels all over the place? And the
bulkheads only protected the outer galleries; the
inner ones had always been thought to be protected
by the rock itself. And though all personnel should

have been suited up within seconds of the first alarm, what protection did a standard pressure-suit offer against explosive decompression all around you, with bits of rock and equipment hurtling about in hurricane-force winds?

'Command Centre . . .?' he said.

'Was the first to go after the generators,' said the Rustie. Joel made a last, desperate try on the general band.

'This is Lifeboat B,' he said. 'Calling all SkySpy personnel not on board. Respond. *Please* respond.'

Silence. Joel, the pilot and the navigator looked at each other.

'*Airlock master to flight deck. A three foot hole just appeared in the main section. We're under laser fire.*'

'We're getting out of here,' Albarazi said. 'Stand by . . .'

'Wait,' Joel said. All eyes turned to him and for the first time he understood what his father had meant when he talked about the loneliness of command. He was the most senior . . . 'Were the records destroyed?'

'Sir?' Albarazi's look suggested he really couldn't care about the records.

'Were the records destroyed?' Joel shouted.

'I – I don't know, sir . . .'

Joel shut his eyes, took a breath, made his decision.

'Boost to the Shield on full and get out of here,' he said. He unstrapped himself. 'Thirty-second countdown.'

'You – you're not coming?' said Albarazi, amazed.

Still suited, Joel could carry on the conversation as

10

he made his way quickly aft through the main cabin to the airlock.

'We don't know that the records were destroyed,' he said. 'I've got to check, and you need to get out of here now.'

'*But if we leave you . . .*'

'That's an order!' Joel was at the airlock, and he leapt out into space. He didn't need to be told what would happen if he was left, but he knew what he had to do. Bloody sense of duty, he thought bitterly. And no question of where he had got it from. Why couldn't he have swapped the inherited duty-gene for, say, eye colour?

His suit carried him swiftly away from the lifeboat and he took a final look back. Its laser turrets were in action, returning fire as good as they got. And then the main drive came on and it effortlessly slipped away from SkySpy, vanishing to a dot in a couple of seconds.

He wasn't alone. Another suited form drifted into his vision and he almost had a heart attack.

'What are you doing here?' he snapped. The Rustie braked to hang in front of him.

'None of my pride escaped to the lifeboat,' Boon Round said in a neutral, colourless voice.

'What's that got to do with it?' Joel said without thinking. Was he doomed to be plagued by this creature for ever? And then he bit his tongue because he knew the answer to his question.

'I might be able to die with them,' Boon Round said in the same voice.

11

'Right.' Joel swallowed. This time he had noticed the tone. Rustie translator units nowadays could convey colloquial speech and even different kinds of emotions, but there were emotions at the far end of the scale that still lay outside their programming, whereupon they would revert to this bland matter-of-factness. And that was how Boon Round spoke now. A human could lose both parents and all children, siblings, aunts, uncles and grandparents in one fell swoop and still not come close to understanding how the sole survivor of a Rustie – sorry, *First Breed* – pride would feel.

'Come on then,' Joel muttered, and they jetted down to SkySpy.

'It would be convenient to know your plan,' Boon Round said as they dropped down. Still bland, still racked by sorrow far outside the scope of his translator. He wasn't going with Joel to be helpful or out of a sense of duty; he was going with Joel because the sheer fact of association with another living being kept him sane. *Yeah, thanks for that responsibility*, Joel thought. *It's not like I've got anything else to worry about right now.*

'We enter SkySpy, we get to the computer centre and we set off the charges,' he said.

'SkySpy is without power.'

'The charges are self-powered.'

'What if we meet any XCs?'

We're dead. 'I don't think we will,' Joel said. He kept one wary eye on the heavens about them. 'It must have been automated. Think about it. Transporting troops all the way out here without being noticed would be harder than . . . well . . .'

'Sneaking up on SkySpy undetected in the first place?' Boon Round said helpfully.

'Look,' Joel snapped, 'at the first sign of any XC activity, play dead. They'll expect to have a lot of bodies floating around.' He winced as he said it, but it was true.

'And then?' Boon Round said. Joel entertained a vision of sinking a fist through the Rustie's faceplate. Probably bad leadership.

'We'll try and get out in Lifeboat A,' he said. 'If we can get on board and boost straight out of the bay, we'll be in with a chance.'

'If not?'

What is your problem, you stupid Rustie? 'There'll be sufficient power and air reserves to last us a long time,' Joel said with very forced patience. 'They'll send a ship, maybe a squadron, to investigate and pick up the pieces. I mean, they won't be worried now about letting the XCs know about us. And they'll pick us up.'

'How long do you see this taking?'

'In here,' Joel said, determined to change the subject.

They floated towards the bottom of the empty cavern that was the lifeboat bay. Without the lifeboat it looked larger than normal, and the vacant grapples and the blunt heads of the disconnected power feeds looked somehow forlorn. They entered the dark tunnel that led to the main complex.

Battery-powered emergency lighting gave the corridors of SkySpy a red glow. The two of them drifted slowly along the airless passages, boosted by small nudges from their thrusters. They came to a hole that crossed the corridor – a smooth, round tunnel, just wide enough for Joel to stretch out his arms. It came in from the direction of space, the top right of the corridor, and carried on towards the heart of the complex at the bottom left. Joel angled his head so that his helmet lights shone down it, towards the centre of the asteroid, and shouted in shocked surprise.

'What is it?'

'Guess,' Joel muttered. He had been expecting this, it *shouldn't* have been surprising . . .

He reached down carefully to take hold of the body under the arms and extract it from the tunnel. Chief Astronomer Annika Vogl was no doubt typical of what had happened to SkySpy. She had been in her suit, she should have been protected against loss of pressure, but the howling gale of escaping air had picked her up and dashed her against something, or something against her, and her helmet was cracked. The wind had carried her up the hole.

Vogl had been part of the station's scientific complement. Barely two hours ago, in what Joel had suspected was a vain attempt to chat him up, not knowing that he wasn't currently on the market, she had been sat at a console demonstrating the wonders of SkySpy's astronomical research. It was apparently very interesting to astronomers and very boring to Joels. And here she was now.

Joel peered back down the hole. This time he had an unobstructed view to the next level.

'This will take us straight there, almost,' he said. He glanced back at the late Chief Astronomer. 'There'll be more,' he said, and led the way.

There were more: most of SkySpy's crew had been in the deeper levels when the attack came. Human and Rustie corpses floated in the passageways, some still jostling very slowly, their momentum not yet absorbed by the walls and the other bodies. Smaller, loose objects, not secured when the air went, floated between them. Joel led the way and applied mental blinkers: he would get to the computer centre, set the charges, get out. Then and only then would he worry about what to do next.

'How are you, Boon Round?' he whispered.

'I am managing.' Still bland.

They came round a corner and Joel abruptly retroed, stopping dead. Then he yelled as Boon Round bumped into him from behind and he flew again towards the thing.

It had come to rest at the Y-shaped junction of three corridors, big, round and metallic. It lurked, alien and intrusive, the red lighting gleaming off its hull. The two jetted slowly up to it. One end was a blunt point, like a giant snub-nosed bullet, pitted with the openings of thousands of tiny nozzles. The surface was shiny but scored, and directly behind its cylindrical body was the tunnel it had carved through the asteroid. It was these things that had destroyed the base.

'It goes straight out to space,' Boon Round reported from the rear end.

'Uh-huh.' Joel had jetted round to the other side, and discovered something more urgent. 'Oh my God. Boon Round—'

'Behind you!'

The XC that had emerged from a corridor wore some kind of space armour. It had four arms and two legs that bent the wrong way and it was probably just as surprised as they were. It recovered first. Joel's muscles had frozen and he could only watch in horror, in terror, as it brought its weapon up . . .

. . . and three hundred pounds of Rustie cannoned into it, propelled by a single thrust of Boon Round's hind legs, and smashed it against the wall. Its weapon flew away and Boon Round wrapped all four limbs around the creature. The XC could only wave its four arms and hammer futilely at the Rustie's body as Boon Round went to work, pulling out every hose and every connector he could find. Air gushed out of the ruptured armour and the XC died.

Boon Round waited until the struggles ceased, then let go and drifted back to get a better view of the body.

His voice was conversational again. 'I'm sorry, what were you going to say?'

'Say?' Joel tore his gaze away from the dead XC and the memory of the frenzied Rustie. Rusties were normally so placid . . . And *XCs were on SkySpy*! It was a concept he would have to work up towards grasping . . .

'Oh, yeah, right,' Joel said. He pointed at the open

hatch he had discovered on the other side of the burrower. 'I was going to say, this thing's hollow, which means XCs probably came in on them.'

'Hopefully I got it before it could communicate,' said Boon Round. 'It depends on whether they are on a general band or have to initiate contact each time they speak.'

'Uh huh . . .' Joel leaned closer to study the dead XC's suit. The visor had misted up with a vapour he didn't want to think about. Some of the gear on the armour was completely beyond him, some he could hazard a guess at; and the glass-tipped tube, the size and length of a small cigar, that was mounted on the XC's shoulder was obvious. In fact, taken as part of the day he was having, it was entirely consistent.

'They're linked by video,' he said. 'Come on, quick.'

XCs were on SkySpy! Joel's neat little rationale about the impossibility of sneaking shocktroops out here unobserved had collapsed, but that tiny and irritatingly vocal part of his mind that insisted on being analytical regardless wouldn't shut up as they raced to their destination.

So, the XCs were here. What did they want?

Down one final level . . .

Well, a clean-up operation was one option. The XCs had got their name when a horrified discovery mission led by the Rusties' former masters had witnessed their extermination of their nearest planetary neighbours. So, there was plenty of reason to believe the XCs would strongly contest the sanctity of life of alien beings from beyond their own solar system. Once they detected SkySpy – somehow – then of course they would make sure they achieved total extermination.

Quickly down the corridor, past the canteen, through the gym . . .

But they would want the *knowledge* of those aliens. They would send in the troops to do what machines couldn't: retrieve that knowledge, intact.

Turn right after the living quarters . . .

In other words, the XCs were heading for exactly the same place as Boon Round and Joel. The only difference was their intent when they got there, and the fact that they didn't know which of SkySpy's many chambers or rooms it was in.

Fourth on the left . . .

Joel and Boon Round paused for a moment at the entrance to the computer centre, savouring the sight of the intact crystal storage banks and the absence of XCs. Then a group of five aliens appeared at the end of the corridor.

Boon Round jetted at full thrust down the corridor, spinning furiously and legs flailing, and just had to time to say 'take the banks' before he pounded into the XCs, sending them flying like skittles in microgee. Joel took one last look as they closed in on the Rustie, then jetted into the computer centre and shut and locked the hatch behind him.

The general band was still open and Boon Round's translator unit had finally given up on interpreting what its owner was saying: all Joel could hear was a single, monotone 'Ahhh-hhh . . .' He switched it off and searched feverishly for the charge control.

Got it: a black-and-yellow striped plate the size of his hand, set into one wall. He pressed it and it slid aside. Within were three switches, each under its own guard. Joel flipped each guard up in turn, then positioned a finger over each switch and pressed the three down together. He turned to look at the results of his handiwork.

Nothing: the banks were as intact as ever. Joel bellowed in fury and frustration. The central control had been broken or disconnected in the attack.

A red, glowing spot appeared on the locked hatch and Joel went back to work.

'Caution. Biometrics show imminent danger of hyperventilation,' said his suit, but he ignored it as he studied the banks. The charges were small black boxes, the front ends of dark rods that extended into the crystal, and a single light shone on each one to show that it was running off its internal batteries. Each box had a duplicate of the controls on the central switch: a cover for the three switches, a guard for each switch under that.

'Increasing CO_2 content to compensate for over-dependence on oxygen,' said his suit. The red glow covered half the hatch and was turning to white.

'Yeah, do that,' Joel muttered as he got to the first bank. Flip one; flip two; flip three; altogether now – flip.

The rod began to glow and the crystals shimmered as the heat distorted them, then frosted like shattered glass as their molecular structures distorted beyond recognition and their memory content was wiped for ever.

'*Yes!*' Joel shouted and went on to the next one. Flip one . . .

And another bank, and another. The hatch was almost incandescent.

The last two . . .

The hatch exploded into the room and XCs poured in.

The last one . . .

The XCs grabbed hold of Joel in their unbreakable four-handed grips and he didn't even try to resist, letting the force of their charge carry them away from the bank and across the room. All the better, because it gave Joel a proud view of his beautiful handiwork: a row of cracked, wiped, useless memory banks, their information gone for ever.

He glanced round at his captors. He could see through their visors: the maned heads and flat faces; the small, dark eyes, wide apart and perfect for triangulating on prey; the mouths with their bared shark's teeth.

A hundred and one lost memories flashed across his mind. Earth. His parents. Seeing the sun, holding a girl in his arms and kissing her, drinking a glass of good wine. These alien bastards were taking it all away from him.

He grinned and held up a single finger at them.

'And swivel,' he said. Then they came at him.

Two

Day Five: 7 June 2153

She awoke from the sleep that was almost death and every part of her being screamed the command: *Food!*

The faint, sweet tang of an animal drifted into the cave from outside, touching her olfactory pores, and she exploded into action; one moment a somnolent, curled-up ball, the next a ferocious predator with just one imperative on her mind. One bound got her to her feet; another took her to the mouth of the cave where she squatted on her legs and feeding arms, her hunting arms flexed out in front of her. A faint growl radiated from her vocal membranes as she scanned the forest ahead of her and her claws slid in and out by reflex.

A moment's pause. A faint breeze; leaves rustling; minute vibrations in the undergrowth that her hearing membranes picked up and amplified and turned into an image of sound all around her. *That* was two branches rubbing together. *That* was a nearby stream. But *that* . . .

That was the source of the scent.

A final bound took her flying into the centre of a

21

nearby bush, claws extended, teeth bared. There was a squeal from beneath her as she landed. A small, furry form shot out of the undergrowth, and the chase was on.

Branches slapped at her face as she raced through the trees, hunting arms outstretched; she barely noticed, her mind fixed firmly on the fleeing meal ahead of her. It dodged; she dodged. It ran faster; she ran faster. Every sense, every impulse she had was dedicated to catching this creature. Another instinct within her told her she was burning resources at a dangerous rate. They were already low after her sleep of half a year, and she had better get her prey soon.

The end came when the animal had to dodge a fallen trunk. It was too close to the ground to see it coming and it suddenly had to swerve to one side. But she had seen the trunk, and anticipated the move, and she made her own final sideways leap just before the animal. It gave a final squeal as the claws of her hunting arms sunk into it, and then her teeth tore into the flesh and hot, rich blood squirted into her throat. She finished it in a moment, threw out her arms and let rip a mighty blast of triumph.

The need for food was still there, but now much less urgent. She had her strength back; she could afford to relax just a little. Something was growing within her mind, a self-awareness that began to exercise control over her purely animal body. It told her to keep going, not to slacken off now. And then her pores picked up another prey scent and the awareness lingered just long enough to tell her to follow it, before withdrawing and letting her animal instinct do the rest.

Three hunts later, she was fully sated. The self-awareness was back and this time it grew and grew until it had taken her mind completely over, while the animal semi-sentience was pushed back into the darkness.

She stood up slowly and stretched, wiping her mouth. She knew who and what she was. She was Kin. She was Oomoing of the Scientific Institute; she had awoken from her latest sleep; it was time to get on with her life again.

She turned at a footstep behind her. A young male in the uniform of the Space Presence. His hunting arms were folded politely behind him and his feeding arms held out a robe.

'Wakefulness, Learned Mother,' he said.

'Wakefulness, Loyal Son.' She looked at him curiously while she took the robe and put it on. A quick scan through her Shared memories told her nothing about him. 'And you are?'

'Third Son of the Family Barabadar, Learned Mother. Will you come this way? We need to get to the Waking Hall.'

Oomoing made an amused tone as she fell into step beside him as they made their way through the trees to the edge of the bowl. 'You're a grown male. I can't call you Third Son.'

For a moment there was a note of shyness. 'My chosen name among my friends is Fleet.'

A questioning tone from Oomoing.

'I was always a fast runner, Learned Mother.'

'Then I would like to call you Fleet, because I hope we'll be friends.'

'Thank you, Learned Mother.' There was no mistaking the shyness. Oomoing made a mental note that this young male was not good at concealing; but then, pups never were. By contrast, it had already crossed her mind that if she were to think of breeding again then the Third Son of the Family Barabadar might be a good prospect . . . but she was controlled enough never to show thoughts like that at any level.

And speaking of family . . . She looked around and hummed with curiosity.

'None of your family were able to attend your wakening, Learned Mother,' Fleet said, as if reading her mind.

'Because?' Oomoing said in surprise.

'They're all on Homeworld, Learned Mother.'

This was one feeling Oomoing didn't even try to conceal. *'What?'* she bellowed. The surprise wasn't that her sons and daughters were on Homeworld. It was the implication that she wasn't.

Then they came out of the trees and Oomoing saw that this wasn't her usual waking bowl. The design was the same, but then, waking bowls were all similar: a crater or a natural hollow, studded with sleeping caves around its rim, and a forest carefully stocked with feeding animals to restore the sleepers' strength. But the bowl she always used, the one back at the Institute, was a natural crater. She could see at once that the rim of this bowl was artificial, though

24

sculpted to look natural. And the town they were heading for was completely different. And now she came to think of it, with her waking frenzy well and truly over, there were thousands of tiny differences. The smell, the taste of the air . . .

She bounced experimentally on the balls of her feet. Was she just a little bit lighter than usual?

'If I look up, will I see the sky?' she said.

'Of course, Learned Mother,' Fleet said, sounding surprised. Oomoing toned relief and looked up.

'And the ground above that, naturally,' Fleet added. But she had already seen the land where there should have been the horizon; it stretched up above the bowl, up through the wisps of vapour that passed for clouds, wrapping itself together to meet above the axial sun, with tiny little Kin and ground cars passing above her head like minute insects. She had looked up several times during the hunt, but then the trees had obscured the view. Now . . .

'I'm on a space station!' Oomoing roared. Several Kin paused in their to-ing and fro-ing and glanced at her, not concealing their amusement.

'This way, please, Learned Mother,' Fleet said quickly, and took her arm.

'Which one is it?' she muttered. She kept her head down, her eyes straight ahead, not attempting to disguise her fury. She was dimly aware of buildings and Kin around them. Fleet had got her out of the bowl and they were heading quickly for the Waking Hall.

'Habitat One, Learned Mother,' Fleet said with pride. 'The original.'

'Hmmph.' So, she was a very long way from home. Habitat 1 was a giant cylindrical space station with an orbit between the Dead World and the first asteroid belt. Out of the corner of one eye she saw a servor trundle along on its tracks, the air whistling in and out of its intakes. Servors derived their energy aerobically, without recourse to the inconvenience of nuclear power: you only ever saw them on space stations or in spacecraft, and if she had seen this one earlier she would have known immediately where she was.

'I've been on a habitat before,' she said.

'Indeed, Learned Mother?'

'It was for a conference. I didn't like it then –' she stopped, and swung round to glare at the young male – 'and I like it even less now! How dare you take me from my sleeping cave and bring me here, to wake up alone and friendless? By what right?'

'You are on the Reserve list, Learned Mother,' Fleet said, with just a touch of reproach. He was glancing anxiously from side to side and making vague, fluttering gestures with his feeding hands. He didn't want them to be overheard.

'That's for national emergencies. *National* emergencies, which by definition happen to nations. Which are back on Homeworld. So what am I doing out here? What nincompoop on the High Command decided it would be a good idea?'

Fleet's apologetic expression froze. 'My mother, Barabadar,' he said. 'The Marshal of Space,' he added, just in case the name itself didn't narrow down the range of Barabadars that Oomoing had heard of.

Oomoing subsided. 'I'm sorry, Loyal Son. But can you tell me anything at all about what's going on?'

Fleet gently nudged her out of the way of a groundcar and they fell into step together.

'All I can tell you, Learned Mother, is that my mother requires the services of the best forensic scientist we have. My orders were to bring you out here to await your wakening, then to escort you to our final destination.'

'I see . . .'

'And I have to tell you one more thing, Learned Mother. Habitat One is an international project with an international complement of crew, but for the time being this is a purely internal matter. In fact, my mother's orders are that you speak of this to no-one to whom I have not personally introduced you. Is this clear?'

Only the knowledge that he was just passing on orders kept Oomoing from biting the young snot's head off.

'I accept these conditions,' she said tightly.

'We're here,' Fleet said.

The Waking Hall was quiet, secluded, dark. It even smelt as it should: polished wood, the right amount of incense in the background. Someone had gone to a lot of trouble to make the surroundings familiar and comfortable. Not everyone in the Space Presence was an idiot.

27

A Sharer came towards them, white robe crisp around her, a welcome resonant in her tone.

'The Learned Mother has just awoken . . .' Fleet said.

'Of course, of course.' The Sharer's forehead wrinkled in a kind smile at Oomoing and she barged Fleet out of the way in her bustling eagerness to be helpful. She was good at her job; just the right level of reassurance, of motherly bonding. 'This way, Learned Mother, please.'

'The Learned Mother has some most important Sharing to do first . . .' Fleet began. The Sharer lashed out with the talons of her left hunting arm in a move that could have taken off half Fleet's face if he hadn't been quick enough to pull back. As it was she just nicked the tip of his nose.

'Later,' she said firmly. Oomoing was pleased to note that Fleet had enough self control not to strike back, and not to put a hand to the wound while the females were watching. He let the blood well and drip instead. She just had time to hear Fleet's courteously angry protest before she was whisked away into the female quarters and the door was shut firmly in the face of the seething young male.

Well, let the pup simmer a bit, she thought – she liked Fleet already, but one had to have priorities – and then she spent a glorious half hour being bathed, and having her fur brushed and her mane knotted in a manner appropriate to her rank.

When she was offered a proper waking meal she turned it down, deciding to meet Fleet halfway. He was pacing backwards and forwards in the Sharing area, a secluded passage with curtained alcoves down either side. His nose was already scarring nicely. He made a visible effort not to snap 'At last!' when Oomoing appeared, accompanied by the Sharer.

'I have Sharings from the Learned Mother's family,' Fleet said, stepping forward. 'Three of them.'

'Then you'll need a while to take them in, Learned Mother,' the Sharer said. 'Come in here.'

She led them into a cubicle halfway along the passage and drew the curtains behind her. Oomoing squatted down in the centre of the cubicle and the Sharer turned to Fleet.

'Well?' she said. Fleet squatted and drew a slim silver box from his tunic, which he laid on the polished floorboards in front of Oomoing. She opened it quickly and feasted her eyes on the contents: the three translucent, waxy nodules within.

Her children's Shareberries. Their memories of the last half year.

'They're in descending order of age, right to left, Learned Mother,' Fleet said. 'But first . . .' Oomoing shifted her hungry gaze from the nodules and looked up at Fleet. He bowed, and his tone was suddenly shy again. 'I have a Sharing of my own, Learned Mother, and I know my mother would want you to take it first.'

'Well, really,' said the Sharer, 'this . . .'

'Wait,' Oomoing said. Something in Fleet's tone had touched her, and she was having to face the fact that although the surroundings of the Waking Hall had done a lot to settle her, the whole scenario – being on the habitat, whatever mission Marshal of Space Barabadar had in mind for her – was most unusual. And as Fleet had pointed out, she was on the Reserve list, so she had responsibilities. She really should find out what was happening. 'I'll take his Sharing first,' she said.

Smothering a smile, Fleet sat down opposite her. 'I must tell you,' he said, 'that my own information was given to me over a radio link, but what I have, I'll Share.'

The Sharer had moved round to stand behind Fleet. 'And where is it?' she said.

'Lower left,' said Fleet.

The Sharer lifted his mane to show the back of his head and his Sharemass, the mass of dark, wrinkled spheres, hundreds of them and several layers deep, that covered it. She took a clip and pinned Fleet's mane back, then ran a finger over the spheres at the lower left until Fleet said, 'That one.'

'I have it.' She opened the small cupboard at the back of the cubicle and took out a small scalpel and a silver bowl. She turned back to Fleet with the scalpel in her hand and whipped off the Shareberry he had selected. A good Sharer could do this without even drawing blood, and she was a good Sharer. The nodule was small and dark and leathery. Then she held it carefully between two fingers of one hand and made a small incision in its rough surface with the top of the scalpel. She put the scalpel down and peeled away the surface of the Shareberry. All that was left was the waxy centre, which she put into the bowl.

She squatted next to Fleet and held out the bowl to Oomoing.

'Learned Mother, take this Sharing of your Loyal Son as your sacred duty,' she said. Oomoing reached out, took the Shareberry and placed it reverently in her mouth. She felt the saliva begin to flood around it, the Sharing enzymes starting to break it down and feed the information to her brain. 'Will you take the others now or later, Learned Mother?'

'Later,' Fleet said. The Sharer pointedly ignored him and continued to look at Oomoing.

'Later,' Oomoing agreed.

'Later it is, then,' the Sharer said brightly, packing her instruments away. 'Just call.'

She withdrew. Fleet studied Oomoing's face carefully, waiting for her to absorb the new memory she had just been given. Oomoing shut her eyes, sat back on her haunches and let it come.

Even though the Shareberry had come from the side of his Sharemass (acquired memories, incidental thoughts) and not the middle (personal information, to be Shared only among Fleet's family) there was the inevitable echo of Fleet's other memories – shades, textures, feelings – and she ignored these with a practised mental flip. Not only would it have been bad manners to proceed down that road, but she could sense the looming motherlode of far more interesting and relevant information that the nodule carried. She moved her mind towards it and began to drink it in.

A dark rock, no name, catalogue number 136750#48, half a mile long, a quarter wide, trailing the planet Firegod. Discovered by astronomers eighty-seven years ago, surveyed by robot probe twenty-four years ago, attacked five days ago by armed units of the Space Presence . . .

Oomoing convulsed with surprise, but even as one part of her mind was framing the obvious question, 'Why attack an asteroid?' further information was coming in.

. . . to reveal the presence of a base populated by intelligent, non-Kin lifeforms.

It was like a physical shock; she had to go back to it again. And then again. Non-Kin! *Extraterrestrials!* Her mind was divided. Part of it, the scientific part, the part that made her a reasoning, thinking scientist, crowed *at last*! Proof of all those theories. There were others out there. They were not alone.

The other part, the part that made her Kin, shuddered. Extraterrestrials. Outlanders. *Not Us*.

She kept going.

Subsequent to its capture, surveillance equipment was discovered orbiting the asteroid: painted black, floating free in space rather than tethered to the rock where it would be visible to any Kin who glanced that way through a telescope, disposing of its heat by refrigeration laser. It was virtually undetectable. However, it was the refrigeration lasers which had first hinted at the extraterrestrial presence: astronomers on Homeworld observing the first conjunction of the planets Firegod and Stormwind in nearly five centuries had noticed hot spots moving across the surface of the former. The hardest part of the subsequent investigation was speculating what might be causing these spots. Once the correct hypothesis had been devised then it was easy to trace them back to their source.

Neat: Oomoing loved to see science and logic being used properly. She also had to admit that the logistics of getting the soldiers there were quite clever:

Armed units were chosen from those about to go to sleep. They were launched into space on unpowered trajectories that would take them to within a few miles of the asteroid half a year later. Hence the ships carrying them could be small, light, and much harder for anyone on the asteroid to spot.

Utilizing the natural half-year sleep cycle was an elegant touch. But what about their waking frenzy? Launching a carefully planned attack on an asteroid would be the last thing on the mind of a recently woken soldier, so how. . .?

And again, with that question came the answer:

The waking frenzy can be circumvented by the introduction of certain chemicals into the bloodstream.

'Interfere with the frenzy?' Oomoing said out loud, aghast. 'That's . . . that's unnatural!'

'But doable,' Fleet said complacently. 'Incidentally, that's another military secret I must ask you not to talk about, Learned Mother, so please keep your voice down.'

Oomoing growled and went back to the memories, to learn the details of the attack: the lasers that took out the asteroid's defences; the burrowing machines that let out its air; the more than sixty bodies discovered.

Prisoners? she thought.

No quarter was given.

'Oh, brilliant!' Oomoing exploded. 'The first sign of non-Kin life and we go in with guns blazing . . .' Fleet was looking, well, stony. 'It was one of your mother's ideas, wasn't it, Loyal Son?'

'Indeed, Learned Mother.'

'I promise that from now on, if I'm to insult your mother I'll do it to her face.'

'You will have the opportunity, Learned Mother.'

She subsided into her chair again, but part of her mind was still whirling and it wasn't just with the surprise revelation. To attack without challenge or proper warning – even extraterrestrials deserved that most basic of considerations . . . didn't they? Not least from a reputable warrior like Barabadar.

Oomoing disciplined herself to take in the rest of the information; she could bother with her opinions of it later.

There were two survivors.

At last! Oomoing was transfixed by this final portion of the memories Fleet had given her. The mental images were fuzzy and indistinct: he had only seen them on a display and the camera images were obscured by the soldiers carrying them. They weren't moving.

The captives put up resistance but were subdued eventually.

They were dressed in spacesuits, that much was obvious. And at first glance they looked very different. One tall and thin with two legs, a rough analogue of the Kin shape but with not enough arms; the other shorter and apparently with four legs, nothing like a Kin at all. Two sexes? she wondered. Interesting diversity. . .

'Fascinating,' she said.

Fleet smiled. 'Your brief, Learned Mother, is to find out all you can about these things. My mother wants to know their strengths, their weaknesses . . .'

'Their level of threat?' Oomoing said sardonically.

'Most especially. And, if you can, to work out how they were able to reach our solar system.'

And hence, whether we can travel in the opposite direction. Oomoing read between the lines without difficulty. She searched carefully: there were no further revelations lurking at the back of her skull. 'There's still information I need,' she said. 'If Barabadar wanted to find out about them, it would have been a lot more . . . *constructive* to capture some alive. Why was no quarter given?'

'I know what I know, Learned Mother,' Fleet said apologetically. 'My mother is on her way – she's coming from the other side of the system – and she might allow you to Share.'

Might, Oomoing reflected. Naturally she would ask, but Barabadar would be senior enough to say 'no' if she chose.

'I look forward to meeting her when she gets here,' she said.

'Um, not here,' Fleet said. 'At the asteroid. We've had a ship on standby for two days, waiting for you to wake. We leave in two hours.'

Three

Day Eight: 10 June 2153

The airlock door slid into the hull and the asteroid was in front of her, a mountain in space that filled the constricted vision of her space helmet. Oomoing gazed at it hungrily, her eagerness conflicting with the conviction of her senses that the millions of tons of rock were poised above her, ready to fall on top of her at any moment.

Even her inexpert eye could see that the asteroid had been in the wars. She could see the furrows ploughed by the assault squads' lasers, the gobbets of molten rock left in their wake. She could see the three surviving assault craft; the attack over, they hung in space next to the rock, sleek and dark.

Her eyes settled on a particularly big hole. 'Mother of the Sky, that must have a big bang!' she said. 'I hadn't realized the battle was so fierce.'

'That was the launch bay for their ship, Learned Mother,' Fleet's voice said in her helmet speakers, with the kind of respect that only comes when someone says something very stupid. 'It's where we're going in. Colonel Stormer is keen to meet you.'

'And I him.' Oomoing covered her embarrassment with genuine feeling. Stormer, the male who had led the attack, would only have been obeying the orders of Marshal of Space Barabadar, but the unreasoning ferocity of such an assault still appalled her.

A line strung from the ship's airlock faded into the distance, merging into the colours of the asteroid, and Fleet clipped her suit's harness onto it. 'Just step out, Learned Mother. I'm right behind you.'

'You've got the equipment?' she asked.

'Right here, Learned Mother.'

So Oomoing jumped out into space. Her Reserve training came back to her and she didn't make too bad a job of going down the line. It only took a minute. Now she could see that the pit in the surface of the asteroid was indeed artificial, with smooth, regular walls and equipment around them embedded in the rock. It was dark, the only light coming from the end of the pit, and it was like sinking into the gloom of a deep pond with just a small, forlorn bubble of light and warmth at the bottom.

A crew of suited soldiers was waiting, and by the light of two emergency bulbs they unclipped her from the line and led her to a makeshift airlock set into the wall. It took two minutes for her and Fleet to be cycled through, and then they were in the asteroid, actually *inside* an extraterrestrial base, and two soldiers were helping her remove her suit. Her helmet came off and the familiar, slightly stale smell of ship's air came flooding into her olfactory pores. Oomoing looked up and down the passage; it was a circular tunnel bored into the rock and a floor was provided by a grating laid along it. The grating was completely redundant in the lack of gravity and it immediately set Oomoing to hypothesizing. Subdued red lights set flush into the rock emphasized the natural chill of the asteroid's interior. Colonel Stormer came out of the gloom to meet her, pulling himself with his feeding arms along a line strung down the passage.

'Wakefulness,' he said. 'And are we glad to see you.' He was a grizzled, middle-aged male and his expression was dour.

Oomoing was about to express surprise and delight at such a warm welcome, when Fleet spoke instead.

'The supplies are being unloaded, Worthy Brother.'

'Good. We can use them.' Stormer was older than Fleet and had much more prestige. His bow to Oomoing was almost equal-to-equal. 'Learned Mother, I'm instructed to place myself and my troops at your disposal, subject to security restrictions. We've already started trying to inventory the equipment we've found here but we will value your scientist's input.'

'Excellent,' Oomoing said. 'I suggest we start by Sharing. I'm anxious to find out everything you know.'

'I'm sorry, I was specifically told by Marshal of Space Barabadar not to Share.' Stormer didn't look all that sorry; he almost looked relieved.

'I beg your pardon?' Oomoing said.

'I was specifically told—'

'I insist on a Sharing!' Oomoing was outraged.

'How am I expected to do my job without proper background knowledge?'

'I gather it's a matter of clearance, Learned Mother.'

'Clearance?' The talons of her hunting arms slid out by reflex and Oomoing didn't know whether to laugh or cuff him for his insolence. Doing the latter in front of Fleet would be bad military discipline. 'Listen to yourself, Loyal Son. I'm cleared to be on a top-secret extraterrestrial base. I'm cleared to study their equipment and try to work out how they travelled faster than light, I'm authorized to study the creatures themselves, but I'm not cleared for the details?'

'Precisely, Learned Mother,' Stormer said, impassive.

Oomoing could see she wasn't going to get anywhere. She began to compose a blistering complaint to deliver to Barabadar. In the meantime . . .

'Then, let's start with the extraterrestrials,' she said.

'Of course, Learned Mother. That's why you're here. The *outlanders* are this way.'

Stormer pulled himself back down the passage, followed by Oomoing, followed by Fleet. Oomoing, still not used to this way of travelling, found that the trick was to use her feeding arms for pulling on the line, and her hunting arms for the times she pulled too hard, or swung away from the line towards the walls. Every time they came to a junction or passed the entrance to a room or a chamber, she looked yearningly down it, wondering what marvels of extraterrestrial technology lay that way.

'How much of the base have you explored?' she said.

'A fraction,' Stormer said, without looking round. 'It's a maze and it's big. We've sealed off this local area and repressurized it but we just didn't have the gear to do a full job. But now we've got the supplies, we'll be able to do it properly.'

Oomoing had already worked out that the plan had been for Stormer's men to sneak up on the base in small, lightly armed spacecraft, and for a much larger ship – her ship – to bring supplies after the base was taken. No-one seemed to have expected that the supply ship would stop off at Habitat 1 and wait for her to wake. It seemed a bit of an oversight.

'But you have troops exploring the rest of the place?'

'Of course. I can show you a map of what we've found, if you like. Those outlanders dug in deep.'

That word again. Oomoing remembered her own reaction upon learning of the extraterrestrials' existence. Stormer, a military male not given to scientific lines of thought, would have felt it all the more strongly. She felt the dislike, the loathing behind the word: to him, *outlander* was barely removed from Not Us, and it was probably only politeness in front of a female that kept him from using the ultimate term of contempt.

'Thank you, I will want to see it,' Oomoing said. 'My brief is to assess the entire situation.'

'Well, you can start here.'

They had stopped outside a doorway, and hanging by the doorway were two empty space suits. She could immediately tell which suit belonged to which extraterrestrial – a basic eye for shape told her that the wearer of one would have stood on two limbs and have two limbs free, while the other would have used all four for standing. Seeing the clothes that the creatures wore, but without the creatures inside them, somehow emphasized the sheer alienness of their species. She reached out a feeding arm and caressed the alien material, which wasn't unlike her own suit.

'Are you getting anything, Learned Mother?' Stormer said.

'You're the expert spacer, Worthy Son,' Oomoing said. 'They probably tell you more than they tell me.'

Stormer shrugged, as if to say, *whatever*. 'The tall one had this,' he added. From a box he produced a narrow circle of plastic. 'It was worn on one wrist.'

Oomoing took it in a feeding hand, turned it over and over. White, tough plastic; embedded in it was what looked like a headshot of its owner and a series of black and white parallel lines, probably some kind of computer code.

'An identity tag?' she said. Stormer's people all carried something similar. It occurred to her that if they could only read that code . . .

'Probably,' Stormer agreed, sounding surprised that he and the Learned Mother could agree on something. 'But press that red plastic square, there.'

Oomoing did, and a holo appeared next to the bracelet. It was a shapeless mass of colour that hung in mid air, the size of one feeding fist. It was a picture of something; but unlike a still photograph, which anyone could look at, it was attuned to the frequency of vision of an alien race. Eyes other than hers were meant to understand it.

'And that's all it does?' she said. 'No hidden keys, no access to computers, anything like that?'

'As far as we can tell.'

'I see.' She put it in her pocket. 'Well, looking at their discarded equipment is all very interesting but . . .'

'Through here,' Stormer said. He pulled himself through the door next to the suits. After a moment to collect her thoughts and control her excitement, Oomoing followed.

And she finally saw what she had crossed millions of miles of space to see.

'They're doing it again,' Stormer said without a lot of interest. The two extraterrestrials were kept in a large, circular room; Stormer had chosen it simply as a secure place to put his captives, with no idea what the room was for. There was only the one entrance and two armed sentries waited by it. The two creatures lay still and motionless against the far wall in what Oomoing recognized as freefall hammocks; apart from them, and a cubicle containing a freefall chemical toilet, the room was bare, though it stank. This would be the smell of unwashed extraterrestrial; she wondered if they found it as unpleasant.

Oomoing feasted her eyes on the two forms in the hammocks. She was already familiar with their general appearance and the facts of the case from reports that had been beamed to her on the way here, but actually to *see* them . . .

'Are they still keeping to the timetable?' she said.

'By and large. They do it less and less.'

The first time Long and Short, as she thought of them, had lapsed into this coma, there had been a major panic amongst Stormer's men and frantic, long-range, time-delayed calls to her on the ship, asking her advice. A Kin deprived of resources would lapse into the Small Sleep, but these two had food, so what was happening? Were they dying?

The fuss had died down abruptly when someone actually approached the two, and suddenly they started moving again. When it happened again, half a day later, Oomoing had given orders that they were not to be disturbed. The creatures always got into their hammocks before passing out, so obviously they were expecting it. She surmised it was indeed like the Small Sleep, some kind of resource-conserving coma – just one which happened on a regular basis. Or maybe it was just a way of passing the time when nothing was happening. It clearly wasn't life threatening, and that was the main thing.

'How are they eating?' she said.

'They drink the water we provide,' Stormer said. 'And you remember what we decided were emergency rations from their canteen? The tall one fell on them when we produced them, but since then it's gone off its appetite. The short one hasn't touched a bite.'

'That's worrying.' Oomoing gazed in concern at the unmoving form of Short in its hammock.

'As the Learned Mother pleases,' Stormer said, and

Oomoing remembered that Short had apparently despatched five of his soldiers before being subdued.

'Can I see this stuff you've been feeding Long? I mean, the tall one?' she said. Stormer nodded at one of his men, who handed Oomoing a slim, rectangular object wrapped in some kind of plastic.

She looked at it curiously, turning it over and over in her feeding hands. It was about the same size as two talons side by side and was covered in what she suspected was script. The plastic crinkled in her grip and a tab at either end practically begged, 'pull me'.

So she did. The plastic peeled away and revealed a dark brown, waxy substance. It was divided into rows of three squares and without any difficulty she broke an entire row off. A strange odour, pungent but very rich, tickled her olfactory pores. Embedded in the broken edge she could see what looked like some kind of dried fruit.

'Remind me why we decided these were emergency rations?' she said.

'They come out of a machine mounted on the wall,' Stormer said. 'If I'd built this place, I'd want emergency rations to be easily accessible to anyone who needed them. And smell it, Learned Mother! It's bursting with energy.'

Oomoing sniffed the dark slab and had to agree. And yet – she looked back at Long – the extra-terrestrial had gone off its feed. Maybe they didn't need to eat that much. Or maybe they needed a more varied diet.

She could try and second-guess them for ever. It was time to start using Barabadar's authority.

'I want the tall one let out,' she said.

'I beg your pardon?' Stormer said, so outraged he even forgot the 'Learned Mother'.

'It's the safer one, isn't it?'

'Well, I, I mean ... well, yes, the tall one hasn't killed any of my people, if that's what you mean,' said Stormer.

'Then I want it let out. Don't worry –' Oomoing held up all four hands to placate him – 'we won't give it free rein. I want to follow it, with an armed guard, of course, just to see where it goes and what it does. It might show us interesting things, and it probably has a better idea of how to look after its kind than we do. Now, please do it.'

'An armed guard? I'll follow it personally,' Stormer muttered. 'Well, as the Learned Mother pleases. We'd better revive them.'

'How do you do that?'

'Nothing simpler.' Stormer kicked over to Long and slapped his hands together loudly. 'Get moving! Come on! The Learned Mother has come halfway across the solar system to see you! On your feet!'

Long twitched, its eyes opened, and it recoiled at the sight of Stormer hanging over it. It may not have understood the words but it seemed to understand the gestures, and it slowly freed an arm and released the tabs that opened the hammock up. It came free and pushed itself gently off the wall. Even in free fall, Oomoing fancied she saw a measured caution about its movements.

Oomoing drank in the sight. The transmissions she had received on the way here still hadn't done the creature justice. It was long and lanky – a thin torso, small head topped by a short, fuzzy mane of dark brown hair, four feeble limbs; all part of a stretched body much taller than the colonel or any other male, though only a head or so above Oomoing's own height. Its skin was pale pink and looked clammy to the touch.

The eyes were recognizable – at least, Oomoing assumed that was what they were, though she had to remind herself to take nothing for granted. Still, they were in roughly the same place as a Kin's own eyes, and as the eye had evolved independently on Homeworld in a multitude of species, she didn't see why extraterrestrials shouldn't have something similar. She wondered how much of the spectrum they could take in. Between them was something else sticking out from the face – she presumed it was some kind of extraterrestrial organ and reserved judgement for the time being on what it might be for. Long was wearing two garments – one covering the haunches, with its legs sticking out below, and one wrapped round its torso with its arms and head sticking out of their respective holes at the upper end of the body.

Its limbs were drawn up together and it was rubbing itself. There was a very thin pelt on the arms and the legs, and the hairs there – but not on the head, for some reason – were standing upright. Oomoing could understand perfectly: it was hardly wearing anything, and it was very cold in here.

'The Learned Mother wants to see you, so move over here,' Stormer shouted, but Oomoing was already moving towards it. She looked into Long's eyes; each had a white background, a blue circle and a dark pupil within it. She wanted to feel the creature, see if the skin really was as clammy as it looked, learn the texture of that fuzz on the top of the head, so she reached out.

Long's pupils dilated and with an incoherent shout – *Where from? Which organ did it use for speech?* – it leapt across the room. It came to a rest with its back against the wall, the other side of the chamber.

'Stand to!' Stormer shouted, though his guards at the entrance to the chamber already had their guns at the ready.

'Don't worry,' Oomoing said. 'It knows better than to argue.' She looked at Long in fascination. That stance, that reaction reminded her of . . . yes, she had it. She studied Long with her stalker senses; amplified vision, smell, hearing. She could hear a fast-thumping heart beat. The smell of extraterrestrial was suddenly stronger. Its respiration was right up . . .

'I think it's frightened,' she said. 'Even terrified.'

'Frightened?' Stormer said scornfully. 'You think it's just an animal?'

'I didn't say that. Maybe its species kept the fear sense when they became sentient.'

Stormer plainly thought her on-the-fly theory was evolutionist nonsense, but he wasn't going to say so. 'What would it have to be frightened of, Learned Mother?' he said. 'We're not going to eat it.'

'Maybe it doesn't know that.' Oomoing decided to content herself with a visual inspection for the time being. 'Anyway, this is all speculation. Colonel, if you want to supervize this procedure, I suggest you get your gun out. Fleet, you've got the camera?' Fleet held up the device he had brought over from the ship. 'Then let's go. Are you recording? Good.' She looked into the lens. 'I am Oomoing of the Forensic Institute, present with me are Third Son of the Family Barabadar and . . .?' She looked at Stormer.

'Stormer, First Son of the Family Dadoi,' Stormer said.

'. . . and two other males acting as armed guards,' said Oomoing. 'I am about to release the tall extraterrestrial captured during the recent engagement . . .'

Joel studied the five XCs. The wall of the chamber was against his back and he was still poised for futile flight.

'Idiot,' he muttered to himself, but he hadn't been able to help it. Those taloned hands reaching out to him; those beady, calculating eyes . . . He had long ago worked out that if the XCs wanted him dead then that was what he would be. But maybe this newcomer had just fancied a bite to eat, or it had been time to start the inevitable torture session that would lead to him spilling the beans on every aspect of Commonwealth technology that he knew about, or . . .

Well, he just didn't know. He ran through what little

he knew of XC culture for the thousandth time. The soldiers, the guards, the one who had until now seemed to be in charge would all be males. But this big newcomer, who seemed to be giving orders, would almost certainly be female. Maybe even a mother, which made her most senior of all. He didn't really see having babies as being a sound basis for constitutional government, but it seemed to work for the XCs. So, she would be the one to make decisions. Perhaps he and Boon Round had been held pending the arrival of just this female. Maybe they were under sentence of death, and now was the time to carry it out.

But the XCs were standing back. Even the guards by the entrance had moved aside. One of the males had what looked like some kind of recording equipment held up to his face, and the female . . .

The female was actually gesturing at him, then at the door. He didn't understand the chirps and tones and percussive blows that were XC conversation, but the gestures seemed clear. They wanted him to move, of his own volition.

'Right . . .' he said. He glanced at Boon Round in his hammock, then back at the door. Then he kicked off from the wall and over to the Rustie.

Boon Round hardly twitched. Joel was getting worried about his companion. All the electronic equipment on them had been confiscated, which meant no translator unit, which meant he and Boon Round couldn't even exchange a few words. And he had seen how the loss of his pride had affected the Rustie; a shock no doubt exacerbated by the XCs' choice of prison. They were in the Commune Place, where the pride would come to meet, to gather together, to rub bodies and smell scents and bond. Or, in human terms, just to hang. It meant so much more to the First Breed.

Nor did it help now that Boon Round was almost starved. Humans and First Breed could both drink water, but Rusties didn't like chocolate bars and neither did Joel any more, after the first fifteen or so. He had had to start starving himself, or risk severely overtaxing the chemical toilet the XCs had thoughtfully provided.

So ... He looked at the door again, then at the female in charge. Was that what was going through her mind? We don't know how to look after you, so show us?

'Only one way to find out,' he said, and kicked off again.

Joel made his way through the dim passages of SkySpy with his retinue of XCs. They seemed to be giving him his head, so he would use the opportunity and see how far he was allowed to go.

Priorities were food and equipment. Anything else? He looked down at himself; grubby underwear and the need for a shower. OK, that was another objective. And if he was feeling naked, what must Boon Round be feeling? Yet another contributing factor to the Rustie's decline would be the loss of his harness, his decorations – yet more ties with the pride. Well, he knew where they were – the last place Boon Round had left them.

Joel had his first destination.

He didn't know how much of the base had been repressurized, so this was also an intelligence-gathering mission of his own. He pulled himself along, to a murmured narration from the female. He glanced back at the guards: they were plainly ill at ease, fingers itchy over their triggers, but they weren't interfering.

Conscious that every move could be his last if it was misconstrued, he reached the main airlock area.

'We'll go in here,' he said, and slipped into the changing room. He shivered at the sight of the rows and rows of lockers in the emergency red light, each belonging to a dead Rustie or human. 'God, it's like being surrounded by ghosts.'

Rustie lockers were arranged in First Breed alphabetical order, which Joel had never mastered, so he had to study the bilingual label on each door before he found Boon Round's. He tugged it open and grinned. There was the harness and – ta da! – a translator unit. Joel reached out.

With a roar, the senior male leapt forward. One of his lower hands snatched the unit and one of his upper clubbed Joel in the chest and sent him spinning across the room. Joel crashed into the wall with a force that knocked the breath out of him. XCs were small, but strong. The reaction bounced him back and he caught himself against a locker to steady his movement. The armed guards had brought their guns to bear on him.

This is it! He shut his eyes and gritted his teeth. Joel

Gilmore, born June 2130, Armstrong, Luna; died June 2153 in a changing room in a faraway solar system, the last sound in his ears the melodic chimes of arguing XCs.

Arguing? He opened one eye. The female had snatched the unit away from the male with her lower hands and they were definitely exchanging views. The one with the camera was still recording him and the armed guards still had him covered. Maybe they were just waiting for orders to open fire.

The male subsided while the female studied the unit. Then she tucked it away inside her tunic and gestured from Joel to the locker. She pushed herself back and the guards lowered their guns.

Joel cautiously moved forward and reached out for the harness. When he took it out of the locker, the female grabbed hold of his wrist and Joel's heart almost stopped, but she just wanted to study the gear. She must have worked out that there was nothing electronic or technological about it because she let Joel's wrist go again. Without taking his eyes off her, Joel wrapped the harness around himself and kicked off for his own locker.

Home sweet home! He grinned again at the sight of his dark blue shipsuit, two gold stripes on each shoulder, the insignia of his new rank that had cost him so much. And his aide, of course: even with his uniform back on, he would feel naked without that small box of electronics. He wasn't going to leave that behind.

'Um, I need that too,' he said. Sign language

seemed to be in vogue so he looked at the female, then pointed at the aide. She moved cautiously forward, then had a brief discussion with the senior male. Finally she picked it up and tucked it away with the unit.

'I know,' Joel said. 'You think I'll use it to set off the demolition charges or something, don't you? Well, it's a start. Now ...' He unfurled the shipsuit, then looked down at himself and wrinkled his nose. He put the shipsuit back in the locker together with the harness, retrieved a clean pair of shorts and kicked off for the showers.

There had never been any flowing water on SkySpy even when power was on: it was too precious a resource. Washing was done with jets of germicidal, perfumed powder, but even that wouldn't be possible without power. He had to use the next best thing – dry pads impregnated with the same stuff. Self-conscious under the watchful eyes of the XCs and that bloody camera, he swabbed himself down all over. Then he rubbed it into his hair, grateful that he had always kept it short and that he had had his facial hair follicles permanently zapped. At last, scrubbed clean, sweet-smelling and with fresh underwear, he felt capable of putting the uniform on again, and the familiar feel of the fabric against his skin was bliss. He was enclosed, he was comfortable, he could be warm once more. He zipped the shipsuit up the front and presented himself to the camera.

'004972 Gilmore, Joel, Lieutenant, Commonwealth Navy,' he said. 'Not that you lot have ever heard of the Geneva Convention, but I thought I'd mention it. And now I think we'll do the canteen. Why not?'

'Come on, Boon Round, let's be having you.'

Joel unzipped the Rustie's hammock and pulled Boon Round out. The Rustie didn't react.

'Look what I got you. You're a whole Rustie again,' Joel said. He unwrapped the harness from around himself, then paused. How the hell did you put one of these on a Rustie? It wasn't something he'd ever done before. He was pretty sure *this* bit went at the end; *this* bit wrapped round the body . . .

But whenever he tried to hold Boon Round steady, the slightest knock would send the Rustie tumbling in mid-air. Joel swore as Boon Round began to rotate for the third time.

But then Boon Round suddenly steadied. The XC male who had been handling the camera had come forward and was holding him still. Joel stared at him, then turned back to the female who must have given the order.

'Thank you,' he said, and finished putting the harness on. Rustie clothing wasn't the same as human clothing – it gave no protection, offered no modesty, but it did show rank and designation and all the other little things that gave a Rustie identity. A few straps, a few badges here and there, and Boon Round was complete.

Almost.

Joel turned back to the female. 'I need the translator unit, please,' he said. He unzipped the front of his shipsuit and mimed taking something out, then clipping that something under Boon Round's throat. 'Remember?'

The female paused, then reached into her tunic and retrieved the unit. The aide stayed where it was. The senior male expressed something forcefully again, but was obviously overruled.

'Don't worry,' Joel said. 'No funny business.' He made himself smile at the female and took the unit, then attached it to Boon Round's harness. One of these controls must be the on-switch . . .

A small light came on, and Joel hoped that was it. 'Boon Round, can you hear me?'

The unit would be sending vibrations direct to the Rustie's cochlea-equivalent. Mouthtalk only, not the fulltalk that was so important to Rusties, but much better than nothing.

A pause . . .

'Joel Gilmore? At last.'

The voice was flat, impersonal, but it was a voice and communication had been re-established.

'Yes!' Joel shouted. 'Boon Round, it's OK. You rest there. Look, I brought something for you to eat.'

They had brought back two boxes from the canteen, one full of food concentrates for humans and the other for Rusties. Joel calculated that if they ate sparingly, they should last about a week and then – hopefully – he would be allowed to go back for more.

Half an hour earlier, he had been resigned to dying; in the days he had been held captive, he had deliberately not given in to hope because he didn't think he could handle the disappointment. But now there really did seem grounds for optimism.

'Is there any water?'

'Right here.' Joel held the straw of a waterpack to Boon Round's mouth and the Rustie sucked it dry in one swallow. Then Joel picked a slab of Rustie food at random from the box and held it out. One of Boon Round's graspers, the tentacles on either side of his mouth, reached out and popped it into his mouth.

'Feel better?' Joel said.

'Strength is returning. Thank you.' Boon Round munched for a while. 'My harness is uncomfortable. You did not put it on properly.'

'Well, excuse me!'

'If that is your desire.'

Well, we're back to normal, aren't we? Joel thought. He picked out a pack of human food concentrate and bit into it. He looked up at the XCs. 'Now what?' he said.

Now, apparently, the XCs were going into a conference huddle. Joel looked dolefully at them and wondered if they were drawing up plans for an interesting execution. Somehow it didn't seem as likely as it had an hour earlier, but . . .

One of the XCs was coming towards him – the big female. She held out one of her several hands and Joel's eyes widened.

'That's my ident bracelet!'

The hand stayed outstretched. Joel reached out for it cautiously, ready to snatch his hand back at any moment; but still she stayed there, and so he took the bracelet and slid it onto his wrist.

'Thanks. Thank you! Very much. Oh yes. Very much indeed, thank you.'

The XC looked blankly at him, then withdrew for another conference. Joel withdrew himself to the far side of the room and looked at his wrist thoughtfully. A mugshot of his own features looked back, mounted on the white plastic next to a bar code.

Then his finger sought out and pressed the red plastic square on the white band, and an image appeared in the air next to it. 'Oh yes,' he breathed. 'Thank you, God.'

As well as the basic information stored on the bar code, the bracelet could store supplementary information, and if he had stuck to official procedure then the image should have been of his own face together with further details of blood group, allergies, religion, ethnicity, and last will and testament. Shortly before leaving for SkySpy, he had had a better idea.

Another face had appeared instead. Dark hair that could make the face look harsh when it was pulled back behind the head, or frame it to perfection when it hung loose. Bright blue eyes and a gaze that could blaze with fury or turn soft and tender. He had caught the picture just when the owner of the face was turning to him. It had been one of Admiralty Island's perfect equatorial evenings and they had been walking along the west shore, watching the sunset. She hadn't known what he was doing until she turned to say something and saw the camera, and in those eyes were irritation, amusement . . . and, just because he was there, that tenderness he knew so well.

Joel covered the image with his hand, and the warmth of the laser field suffused gently into his palm. For just a moment he had everything he wanted. He still didn't know what was going to happen to him, and he didn't have a plan for escaping – not even the germ of an idea for one. But right now, he didn't need to go home. He didn't even feel hungry. He had no idea if he would see her again, but at the moment small mercies were all he had, and the picture was enough. He wasn't alone any more.

'I cannot agree with your returning that item to the four-legged one,' Stormer said tightly. 'Learned Mother,' he added.

'Every one of the four-legged corpses had one of those around its neck,' Oomoing said.

'Exactly! It must be important!'

'Important to individuals,' Oomoing corrected him. 'Probably not important in the day-to-day running of this base. If it was some kind of computer that held the weapons codes, say, or other vital information, then probably only one of the four-legged ones would have it. Not every single one of them. Would you hand out a self-destruct button to each and every one of your men?'

Stormer glowered; Oomoing had no idea if he accepted her logic or not, but he wasn't going to argue. If he ever did, chances were he would go straight over her head to Barabadar.

'So, now what, Learned Mother?' he said instead.

Oomoing looked back at the extraterrestrials. One was eating, the other apparently worshipping some personal god contained in that bracelet. Oomoing congratulated herself on returning it; another calculated risk, but clearly it was safe and it seemed to have generated some good will.

'We continue to observe,' she said.

'With respect, Learned Mother, your brief from Marshal of Space Barabadar was to learn about them.'

'I've learnt a great deal already,' Oomoing said.

'Such as?' Stormer said sceptically.

'I'll make my report to the Marshal of Space,' Oomoing said, with a childish measure of satisfaction. Stormer wouldn't Share, so ... 'Ultimately, I'd like to take these two back to Homeworld.'

'You'd like to what?' Stormer exclaimed. 'Learned Mother,' he added again.

'I have to study them properly,' Oomoing said patiently. 'I can only make so many observations here. I'll never be able to learn anything definitive about their language, their biology, their culture ... Do you have a problem, Colonel?'

'Oh ... tell her, Worthy Brother,' Stormer said to Fleet.

The younger male looked abashed. 'I think my Worthy Brother means,' he said, 'that your brief from my mother was to assess their level of threat, their military capability, their technology—'

'*Definitely* their technology,' Stormer added.

'Well, of course,' Oomoing said. 'But there's the whole contribution to science to consider ...'

'That won't be relevant if my mother considers them a threat to the state, Learned Mother,' Fleet said. 'She'll only be interested in anything we can use to a military advantage.'

'And that won't include their mating habits and artistry,' said Stormer. 'If these two can tell us anything useful, we'll keep them. Maybe we'll learn how they Share. Maybe we'll have to extract the knowledge neuron by neuron, or kill them trying. But if My Martial Mother decides we're better off just observing the equipment on this base and drawing our own conclusions, then that's what we'll do.' He looked back at the two extraterrestrials. 'We won't starve them, don't worry. A shot to each head and they'll never know what hit them.'

'I see.' Oomoing looked sadly back at the two. There was so much knowledge locked up in those heads that Stormer had just so casually offered to blow apart for her, and Barabadar's orders would override her own. 'How soon does the Marshal of Space get here?'

'Her ship arrives the day after tomorrow, Learned Mother,' Fleet said. 'She'll listen to your report and then decide their fate.'

'Then I'll have to find out what I can, as quickly as possible,' Oomoing said.

'Indeed, Learned Mother.'

Four

Day Ten: 12 June 2153

Oomoing and Barabadar met in the Marshal of Space's cabin on her ship, shortly after it had braked into a parking orbit around the asteroid.

The cabin was in one of the ship's rotating sections. The return of weight, and going back to full white light and the familiar surroundings of a ship and other Kin, were most welcome.

And then they were at Barabadar's door. Fleet opened it without knocking.

'The Learned Mother Oomoing, My Mother,' he said.

'Thank you, Third Son,' said a female voice. 'Wait outside. Learned Sister, please come in.' So Oomoing entered.

'Learned Sister,' Barabadar said again. The Marshal of Space rose up from a squatting cushion and presented the Bow of Equals. 'How good to meet you at last.'

'Martial Sister,' Oomoing returned. Barabadar, she sensed, was a formidable hunter. Every movement was carefully controlled and spoke of the strength of her animal nature, lurking just below the surface of her conscious mind. Her talons slid in and out frequently and rapidly, all the way out to their quarter tips and then back again. Her eyes were shrewd and her gaze darted here and there, taking everything in. The muscles beneath the skin were tense and powerful.

'Please, sit down,' Barabadar said, indicating a cushion that faced her own across a work tray. Both females crouched. 'Keeping busy?'

'Extremely,' Oomoing said. The Marshal of Space's whole stance was putting her on the edge of combat herself. 'There are plenty of bodies to observe.' She emphasized the point, *to observe*. Barabadar had been explicitly clear that Oomoing could do what she liked with the extraterrestrial technology, run whatever tests came to mind, make whatever observations . . . but no autopsies. The bodies were to be treated with respect. Oomoing wondered if it was some kind of amends for the unprovoked, unchallenged attacked.

Barabadar's forehead muscles rippled in a smile, though there wasn't much humour there. 'I've read the preliminary reports you transmitted,' she said. 'Your assessments so far sound plausible.'

'Why, thank you, Learned Sister,' Oomoing said. She wondered how Barabadar would react if she complimented the Marshal of Space on being good at tactics.

'In fact, you've covered things so thoroughly it's barely worth Sharing,' Barabadar said casually. She picked up some notes from the tray in front of her and ran her eyes over the front page. 'They're clearly a long way ahead of us, but I'd already guessed that . . . You think they have control of gravity?'

'A hypothesis that fits the facts,' Oomoing said. The corridors in the asteroid were smooth, round tunnels with metal grids that provided a flat surface; there were no handholds, nothing to assist someone trying to get round in freefall, which was the base's current state. Something must have held the extraterrestrials against those grids. And she had seen the recording of the extraterrestrials' escape ship – even she knew that no conventionally driven ship moved like that. It had effortlessly bridged the space between the rock and Firegod, after which it had vanished behind the gas giant, never to reappear.

'And they must be able to travel at phenomenal speeds, to travel between stars at all. Any clues?'

Oomoing shrugged. 'There are two main theories amongst the scientific community as to how it could be done. Some think it should be possible to warp the local area of time and space in a way that seems to propel you faster than light . . .'

'Seems?'

'*You* don't feel you're moving at all; it would be as if the rest of the universe came to you rather than the other way round. But from everyone else's perspective you would just vanish. The other theory is about opening up small holes in space, which are predicted by some of the latest theories, and passing through them. For that, of course, you could just use a conventionally powered ship that just happened to have the means for opening a hole on board.'

'Not very convenient,' Barabadar commented. Oomoing paused; this was a practical point from a professional spacegoing Kin that had never occurred to her in her flights of theory. No, you wouldn't want to open up the hole on board the ship itself.

'Well, perhaps the means for opening the hole is *outside* the ship . . .'

'Much better,' Barabadar agreed.

'But either way would take a prodigious amount of energy, much more than we can easily produce, and as to clues here on this base – no, none at all.'

'All the information we could possibly need must be inside their heads,' Barabadar mused. She waved the notes. 'And yet I don't see anything here which suggests how they Shared.'

'I've no idea if they did Share,' Oomoing said. 'There's nothing that even looks like a Sharemass on the bodies that I've been able to locate externally.' No autopsies . . .

Barabadar went back to the notes and changed the subject. 'The energy weapons they used against us were formidable,' she said, 'and yet our stealth technology still seemed to fool them.'

'They probably use electromagnetic systems, like we do.'

'So they're not that far ahead of us?'

'Maybe. Or maybe electromagnetic systems will always be the best detection system to use at any level of technology,' Oomoing said.

'Maybe. When they did hit us, they hit us hard,'

said Barabadar. She flicked further through the notes. 'Your speculations on their home environment are less helpful.'

'I expect Stormer has told you I'm an evolutionist,' Oomoing said. Barabadar smiled again, with only a little more humour.

'Yes, he wasn't impressed. Anything that impugns his battle gods will upset him. I think you'll find that every time he's prayed to them, he's won a battle.'

'Has he ever fought a battle without praying to them?'

'Probably not.' Oomoing noticed Barabadar carefully withheld her own opinion on the topic, but thought she detected it from the tone. Then the Marshal of Space seemed to reach a decision. 'Learned Sister, from now on the outlanders themselves are of secondary interest. I want your absolute priority to be to find out how they travel faster than light.'

'I never thought you were that interested in expanding,' Oomoing commented. The entire direction of Barabadar's tenure as Marshal of Space had been towards consolidating, making things safe and secure.

'I wasn't. But it's just possible these creatures could strike at us. If they do, I want to be able to strike back.' Barabadar for a moment looked something between tired and disgusted. 'I've done this job for twenty years, Learned Sister, and I've been good at it. I've safeguarded our interests, which is all someone in my position should be required to do. And suddenly I have a whole new frontier to patrol.'

'And new interests to safeguard,' Oomoing murmured.

'Exactly,' said Barabadar, missing Oomoing's point entirely. *Safeguard our interests* was a safely neutral phrase which could mean a lot of things. In the case of extraterrestrials, Oomoing suspected it meant neutralizing the threat before it emerged. And that could only mean one thing.

'I'm sure you'll do your job well,' Oomoing said.

'I always have,' Barabadar said sourly. 'And look where it got me.'

'It's the scientific find of a lifetime!' Oomoing said.

'It's a political nightmare. Only a few people in our government know about this, so far. The question is, do we tell the other governments? Rather, *what* do we tell the other governments, since our interest in this place has no doubt aroused the curiosity of every mother on Homeworld with a good telescope? Or, do we kill the prisoners, blow up the base and pretend the whole thing never happened? Having, of course, taken as much of their technology as we can understand home with us.'

'That would be insane!' Oomoing protested.

'For reasons you have no idea about and aren't going to, it's an attractive option,' Barabadar said. Then the Marshal of Space sat casually back on her haunches. 'So far,' she said, 'you've made better observations than Stormer ever could, but there's nothing here any other bright female couldn't have worked out. You're better than that. Convince me you really were the right choice for this job.'

Oomoing paused to collect her thoughts. She had a feeling that Barabadar hadn't let her Share so that she could be tested more subtly. 'Ever since I heard of this place, I've rehearsed this meeting, Martial Sister,' she said.

'Really?'

'I've longed to greet you with something like, "So, you're the maniac who ordered an all-out attack on an extraterrestrial base."'

She could see Barabadar was amused. 'Well, here I am,' said the Marshal of Space.

'You also,' Oomoing said, 'went about it in the most unbelievably unprepared manner. You were woefully ill-equipped. The facilities your people have used to imprison the extraterrestrials are jury-rigged. You brought nothing with you that could have been used to make a more secure holding area. Your main supplies all turned up days later. You couldn't have planned this whole thing on the understanding that exactly two extraterrestrials would be captured. You weren't expecting prisoners at all.

'And,' she added. 'You did it without any kind of ritual of challenge. Not an honourable act by anyone's standards.'

The amusement evaporated and Oomoing knew she had struck home. 'Then what was I doing?' Barabadar said coldly.

This was a leap in the dark for Oomoing, but she only had one hypothesis that made any kind of sense.

'You were—' she began.

A call signal interrupted her. Barabadar waved her

to silence and took the call. 'Worthy Son?' she said.

Stormer's features appeared on the display.

'I'm sorry for interrupting, Martial Mother,' he said. 'I thought you'd want to know as soon as possible that we've discovered another ship.'

Four feet, Joel thought sourly. *What a bloody silly number.*

Of course, this wasn't an entirely worthy idea, and part of him was grateful that he still had this capacity for rational thought. But honestly, Boon Round could be so ... so ...

So.

Joel supposed he was glad to see Boon Round rallying. The Rustie was spending less and less time in his hammock, which unfortunately meant more and more time moving around the Commune Place and complaining about ... well, everything.

Which was what you'd expect from having two completely different species working side by side, Joel thought privately. You couldn't really have the Commonwealth without the First Breed, the Roving being their home planet and all that, but he sometimes thought there might be a case for having all the First Breed stay at home and let the humans do the spacefaring. Let both sides play to their strengths.

Joel passed his time doing exercises and thinking, which were really the only two options open to him and had the advantage that they could be done simultaneously. Escape was the main thing to think about, though exactly how was another matter. He kept hoping the big, friendly alien would return and let him out again. If he could somehow win her trust enough to get near a weapons locker . . . or *something* . . .

'I wish you'd stop that bouncing to and fro,' said Boon Round. Joel had devised the exercise of kicking gently off the floor of the Commune Place, doing a somersault in mid-air and landing on the ceiling feet first, to repeat the process indefinitely. 'It's deeply distracting.'

Joel stopped exercizing and sulked in one corner. For the thousandth time he triggered the image on his ident bracelet and gazed into those blue eyes. So freakin' typical. It had been as if every moment, every experience, every lesson of his life had been in preparation for meeting *her*. And before he had time to work out if he really was reading the signals correctly, he'd been sent to SkySpy.

'I wish *you'd* come up with some helpful suggestions,' he muttered.

'Why bother? These creatures murdered my siblings without pity and they greatly outnumber us. Our only hope is to die with glory, taking as many as we can with us.'

Boon Round sounded as if he approved of the idea. Perhaps he did. A Rustie in his situation would have nothing left to live for. Joel had a great deal to live for and he wore the proof around his wrist.

'Fine,' Joel said. 'Jump the next one to come through that airlock and die gloriously. Me, I'll hang around.'

'Humans are meant to provide us with leadership. Why do you not show moral support? The Ones Who Command would have worked out what to do long ago.'

'Oh, drop dead.'

They both knew the Commonwealth would react as soon as it heard from the survivors onboard Lifeboat B. Neither of them knew how long had passed since their capture but surely it would be soon. A starship would turn up, its translator banks programmed with what SkySpy had gleaned of the XC language, and their captors would be ordered in their own tongue to hand any captives over, or else.

Whereupon, quite possibly, the XCs would slaughter their captives anyway and then die their own glorious deaths. So, while sitting and waiting was a possibility, escape did seem the preferable option.

Hence, it was with a sense of detached reality that Joel saw a couple of XCs come in – Boon Round did not jump them as suggested – bearing bundles which they carefully left hanging in mid-air and then backed away from. Those bundles were Joel and Boon Round's spacesuits.

'Amazing!' said Oomoing. The cavern was well lit with lights brought in from Barabadar's ship and the object of interest took up most of the open space. She wasn't an expert on spacecraft but still there seemed something distinctly *extraterrestrial* about it, even though it was essentially a long tube, flat at the end that faced space, tapered at the inward end. It exactly matched recordings of the other ship, the one that got away.

The layout of the place confirmed her hypothesis about artificial gravity – there was quite clearly a platform of some kind running the length of the bay and down either side of the ship, with a safety rail to prevent anyone falling off. A rectangular hole showed dark against the craft's hull three quarters of the way down, and a small ramp led up to it.

Barabadar, studying the recordings of the attack, had noted that the asteroid's defences rose out of the rock from beneath hidden hatches. She had ordered a close survey of the asteroid's surface to see what else might be concealed there, and the entrance to this cavern had been found. From there, the searchers had located the inner entrance and backtracked through the maze of dark, airless passages to the occupied area of the asteroid. This was one of the unpressurized areas and everyone was suited up.

'It's the answer to my prayers,' Barabadar said. 'Loyal Son?'

Oomoing recognized Stormer's battle-fit shape in the armoured figure that approached.

'The area is secure, Martial Mother,' he said. 'As far as we can tell there are no outlanders on board.'

'You've been on board?' Oomoing interrupted. She caught his sour glance through his visor.

'There's an airlock and what looks like a simple control panel on the inner hatch, Learned Mother, but I don't want to start pressing buttons just yet.'

Oomoing could see his point. The extraterrestrials had been quite thorough about making sure none of their superior technology fell into Kin hands. The lifeboat was probably rigged to blow if any unauthorized entry was attempted.

'So how did you check for outland-extra-terrestrials?' she asked.

Stormer glanced at Barabadar, as if for permission, then back at Oomoing. 'We attached listening devices to the hull and we looked through the windows,' he said. 'There are lights on inside. I'd surmise it's under its own power.'

'And the inner hatch would have shut the moment it detected the pressure drop,' said Barabadar, 'so the interior is probably pressurized too.'

'So it will have their optimal environmental conditions.' Oomoing felt an ever-rising excitement. 'We could learn a great deal about their world if we could get on board.'

'Maybe,' Barabadar said. 'But if our two outlanders can operate it – and two Kin could certainly operate a ship of ours this size – then this could be the best way of returning them to their own people.'

Stormer and Oomoing both looked at her as if she had just renounced the battle gods. Stormer was probably thinking things it would be lethal to say out loud. Oomoing had no such compunction.

'Return them? You're . . . *returning* them?' she said, delighted.

Barabadar ignored them both. 'Third Son,' she said.

'My Mother?' said Fleet.

'Go and fetch anything that you know belongs to the two captives and bring it here. Stormer, have the captives and the dead bodies brought to this place at once.'

She turned away from the question in Oomoing's eyes.

Joel looked at the suits, then at the XCs, then back at the suits again. The nearest XC pointed at him, then at the suits, then back the way they had come. The two XCs continued to stand there, waiting.

Joel kicked over to the human-shaped suit, grabbed it in transit and ended up on the other side of the chamber. Then, though he saw one of the XCs flinch when he did it, he activated the control panel on the left sleeve. The suit ran a quick diagnostic and announced that it was intact, the breathing equipment had the same air reserve as when he was captured, the thruster unit was ready for use . . . in fact, it was fully functional, with one exception. The radio had been disabled, as Joel could see with his own eyes. The unit had been dismantled.

'Wow,' he said.

Boon Round glanced in his direction. 'It's a trap. They intend to lure us into a sense of false security and gun us down without mercy.'

Joel felt his exasperation rising. 'And that's why they don't just walk in here with guns at the ready and do it more simply?'

'They're sadistic animals. They like to play with our minds.'

'Fine,' said Joel. 'Hold me steady while I put this on and go out to my death.'

Boon Round airswam over to him and helped him suit up. As they connected the air hoses to the helmet, the Rustie said, 'Perhaps I will join you. We can die together.'

And so the two of them made their way under armed guard through the passages of SkySpy to a makeshift airlock. They passed through into the airless zone.

'Not that I have to explain anything to you, Learned Sister,' said Barabadar, in response to the question Oomoing had carefully not been asking. Fleet was off fetching the extraterrestrials' belongings and Oomoing's camera. 'But, as you surmise, I didn't expect to encounter outlanders here. Now, supposing your sons had planted an observation post in another solar system, and the natives there fell on it as we did here, without challenge, and a few of your sons got away to tell you about it. What would you do?'

Oomoing felt a sudden thrill as battle hormones started to flood into her bloodstream.

'Investigate,' she said.

'Exactly.' Barabadar's eyes still caressed the lifeboat and Oomoing suddenly sensed just how difficult this was for her. She *wanted* it, so badly. But ... 'I'm assuming the survivors have somehow left our solar system – I've got remote probes crawling all over Firegod's orbit and there's no sign of them. I don't know how long it would have taken them to get back home, but it seems a reasonable supposition that at some point we're going to get a visit from a well-armed, technologically superior outlander warship with vengeance on its mind. I would of course welcome a one-to-one battle, but a battle like this would by no means be certain.'

Marshal of Space Barabadar, thinking of defeat? Oomoing felt strangely disoriented. But, logically speaking, Barabadar was right, and just because she was a military leader didn't mean she couldn't use logic.

'Even worse,' Barabadar said as if reading her mind, 'we might bring them down upon Homeworld. And so, we'll remain here. If they come, they come; if we can communicate with them and convince them it was a mistake, then so much the better. If they want to fight then –' she looked Oomoing in the eye; Oomoing guessed she was still smarting from Oomoing's entirely accurate evaluation of her unprovoked, unannounced attack – '*then* I'll challenge them to the Ritual of Contested Land. Either way, we're going to stay here for the time being. But in the meantime, I hope to avoid even that much chance of a conflict we can't possibly win by returning their sons to them; the living and the dead.'

'The bodies as well?' said Oomoing.

'Naturally. They'll want to consume their dead.' Barabadar sounded surprised that Oomoing could think otherwise, and Oomoing refrained from pointing out that the customs of the extraterrestrials might be different. Indeed, consuming was part of Sharing and Sharing was an integral part of Kin biology, so why should extraterrestrials have the same features? For that matter, why should they have such a thing as the Rituals of Combat, which had surely arisen to meet the specific circumstances of life on Homeworld? But all that would be more evolutionist claptrap to the Marshal of Space.

'They still might kill us all,' Oomoing said instead.

'They might try, and if they try, we'll resist. I'm ordering all my people here to make Sharings to send back to Homeworld by message capsule. I expect you'll want to do likewise. And here comes Third Son, good. Make what observations you can of this vessel because it will be your last chance.'

Joel couldn't believe it. It had occurred to him that now might be a good time to try and make a break for the lifeboat bay, and he was so determined to get as close as they possibly could before making a move that it took a moment to sink in: they were heading there anyway. And then they were in, at the inner end of the rock-hewn chamber, and the smooth matte hull of the lifeboat was stretching away into the distance. A crowd of XCs still stood around.

Joel groaned and looked wistfully at the lifeboat's airlock. It was only a matter of yards away, but still somewhere he could never get with all these XCs about. As far as he could tell, the lifeboat was fully charged and untampered with, though an XC was clambering about the hull with what looked like some kind of recording equipment, maybe taking pictures. From the markings on the suit, Joel thought he recognized the large female that had supervised his brief moment of freedom, but he had other things on his mind and he turned his gaze back to the lifeboat. Just a few elementary commands were needed to make it whisk them away from here for ever.

A smaller XC, another one which Joel thought he recognized, came up to him and Joel almost yelped when he saw his aide in its hand. Then the suited figure held it out to him. Joel's mind seemed to detach from his body and it was as if a stranger watched him reach out and take it. No fuss, no XCs going for their guns. This was all official, kosher, above board. The XC ostentatiously let go of it once Joel had a firm grip; yes, it really was his to keep. Then the XC jetted over to the lifeboat to help the one with the camera.

'Thank you,' Joel said. He keyed in the command for a general self-diagnostic. The display lit up: *A-OK*.

Did XCs know these things could communicate? Well, he would have to find out. He changed functions and again keyed: *Open channel to Boon Round*.

Channel open, cue BR, said the display. So Joel keyed: *Tx BR: Do you read me?*

A pause, then: *Rx BR: Yes.*

Boon Round's suit radio was also out but the Rustie was wearing his translator unit; which, like an aide, doubled as a communicator.

More letters appeared on the display as Boon Round asked a question. *Rx BR: What are we doing here?*

Tx BR: Don't know, Joel replied.

Rx BR: Do they intend to let us on board?

Tx BR: Search me.

Rx BR: For what?

Joel glared at the latest message, then quickly looked up; how were the XCs reacting to all this longhand chit-chat? Still happy?

Still happy. The XCs were looking at him closely but they had made no effort to interfere. Yet they must have realized what was happening. Didn't they mind that their two captives were standing here, next to a fully functioning lifeboat . . .

It sunk in suddenly and took Joel's breath away. Were the XCs actually letting them go?

Boon Round was on again. *Rx BR: Can you interface your aide with the lifeboat systems?*

'I don't think we'll need to,' Joel said. More slowly: *Tx BR: I don't think . . .*

More movement out of the corner of his eye. Two XCs were entering the bay with – Joel swallowed – a body bag between them. A dead human. Behind them, two more with a dead Rustie. Behind them, more bodies.

'They really are sending us back!' he exclaimed. 'All of us!' Surely, even Boon Round couldn't complain about this.

The XCs towing the dead Rustie entered the bay and Boon Round went berserk. His suit thrusters blazed and he dived into the small cortège on full power, sending the XCs flying.

'*No!*' Joel howled. The dream scenario, the magical

answer to his prayer, was evaporating before his eyes. Boon Round ricocheted of the wall and flung himself at another XC. One of the Rustie's flailing limbs caught hold of the safety rail on the catwalk and he swung round to crash into two more of the XCs; two more out of the crowd that was converging on the disturbance.

And Joel, to his horror, saw weapons being raised.

He set his aide to audio pickup and pressed it against the visor of his helmet, hoping it could detect the vibration of his voice.

'Lifeboat systems command! Recognize Gilmore, J., Lieutenant!'

A couple of XCs with guns were trying to get a clear shot at Boon Round, but several more of them were grappling with the Rustie, trying to get him under control.

Words on the display . . .

Gilmore, J., Lieutenant, recognized.

'Lifeboat systems command!' His throat was already aching with the need to shout. 'All systems override, open inner airlock hatch!'

Complying.

A cloud of vapour erupted from the lifeboat entrance. A couple of XCs were picked up by the blast and sent spinning along with items of loose equipment and the unsecured contents of the lifeboat cabin.

Joel set his own thrusters to full and dived into the maelstrom of condensing gas. He cut thrust as he felt the artgrav field take hold of him and his feet touched down on something solid. He reached out blindly for the handholds he knew were there and hauled himself into the main cabin.

Tx BR: Get into the lifeboat! he keyed.

No answer. Joel repeated the command as he ran past the rows of seats, forward to the flight deck.

Rx BR: I am coming.

'Yes!' Joel shouted. He dropped into the pilot's seat and entered the commands that put all lifeboat systems on standby, ready for immediate launch. He felt the vibration through his feet, a distant hum as the flight systems powered up and the bars on the power displays moved up out of the red and into the green. The default destination, the step-through generator, appeared on the display and he punched another key to accept it and lock it into the nav computer.

He twisted round in his seat to look back through the hatch and down the cabin to the airlock at the end. His hand was poised over the flashing red 'launch' button on the pilot's desk in front of him. The hurricane was thinning out and the cloud of vapour was almost transparent now. The familiar shape of a Rustie appeared in the inner hatch, braced against the outrushing air.

Joel's hand came down. A slight vibration, the dizzy blur of the lifeboat bay rushing past the viewports, and the lifeboat was out into space.

'Your four-legged moron, what were you doing?' Joel shouted. He strode back down the cabin and the shout was futile because the lifeboat was still airless, but it relieved his feelings. 'They were letting us go! They were . . .'

The words dried up in his mouth. Behind Boon Round, he could see a spacesuited hand grasping the edge of the inner hatch. He moved slowly, cautiously forward, and angled round so that he could see into the airlock. An XC was clinging on for dear life with that one hand, and it was the upper arm – the one that didn't have fingers as such but did have claws. Only the XC hadn't been able to extend its claws, because that of course would puncture the suit. Its hold was precarious.

The other upper arm was stretched out into space and another XC dangled at the end, holding on with both lower hands. The air leaving the lifeboat was down to a light breeze, but Joel could still see that if the on-board XC let go, both would probably be pushed out into space by the remaining pressure.

How had they got there? Joel could picture the scenario. Say both were close to the hull when the drive field came on. The gravitational eddies would have caused chaos in the bay, but right close to the hull it would have been an area of almost calm. Maybe the gravitational forces had plucked at them, but not much, and the smaller one had been able to get a grip on the lifeboat itself.

All sorts of options ran through Joel's mind. Shut the outer hatch; that would deal with the second XC. Shut both hatches, repressurize the airlock and blow it again; that would deal with the first. But the markings on the suit of the dangling XC looked familiar, and the XCs *had* been trying to set them free, so he slowly walked forward, took hold of the inboard XC's arm and helped haul the pair of them into the cabin. Then he shut both hatches and set the cabin to repressurize.

The first thing he saw as he turned round was Boon Round about to attack. He recognized the flexing of the hind limbs, the poise to pounce, and he quickly positioned himself between the Rustie and the XCs.

'No,' he said. And there he stood for another minute, angling himself between Boon Round and the XCs every time the Rustie tried to get past him, until the display inside his helmet told him that the cabin was up to pressure again. He reached up and touched his helmet release.

'They're XCs!' Boon Round shouted.

'I know.' Joel half turned so that he could look at Boon Round and the XCs at the same time. They were looking at him and at each other and he suspected they were communicating furiously, but as XCs didn't talk through moving mouths it looked as if they were just standing there.

'They killed our siblings! Human and First Breed!'

'They were going to let us go, before you went mad,' Joel said. He put his helmet on a seat.

'I saw the bodies of my slain pridemates! What was I to do?'

Joel bit his lip and didn't answer, because there was no answer. If he was ever in the position of watching his entire family massacred then he might be in a position to judge Boon Round's actions.

He also had to admit he didn't actually *know* what the XCs' intentions had been; and even if they had been friendly, he doubted the mood would have lasted following Boon Round's outburst and the lifeboat's abrupt departure with two accidental passengers. Going back to drop them off wasn't an option.

But if he was to keep them, where to put them? The lifeboat's main cabin was just like the cabin of a normal passenger shuttle – rows of seats facing forwards, with an aisle in between and the flight deck at the end. Aft was the power compartment, the galley, the washroom . . . nowhere really secure to put the XCs. Even if they could be locked up somewhere, he didn't want them out of his sight.

So he crossed quickly to a wall locker, took an object from it and aimed it at the aliens.

'We'll be at the step-through generator in ten minutes,' he said. 'When we get there, we'll chuck 'em into space and let their people pick them up. Meanwhile we keep them covered with this at all times.'

'That is an optical fibre calibrator,' Boon Round objected.

'I know. They don't,' Joel said. He hefted the long, thin and suitably gun-like tool with what he hoped was armed confidence. Maybe the XCs were taken in, maybe not, but either way they didn't move. 'Boon Round, make yourself useful. Get up to the flight deck, confirm we're broadcasting the right signal to let the generator know we're friendly. And set the lifeboat to come to dead stop half a mile off.'

He was slightly surprised when Boon Round meekly obeyed. *Joel, you're turning into a leader*, he thought, and grinned. Who cared? They were alive and going home, and that was what mattered.

'*Martial Mother*.' Stormer's voice crackled with anger in Barabadar's headphones as the Marshal of Space's suit thrusters carried her back to the asteroid, a sheer rock face that filled her vision dead ahead. Her suit's computer was aiming her at the dark circle of the ship cavern.

'Tell me the worst,' she said.

'*Twelve dead, Martial Mother. Their armour ruptured when they were smashed against the sides of the cave. And two missing.*'

Twelve dead. Battle hormones doubled their rush into her bloodstream and she raged silently as she flew through space. She and Stormer and the others who still lived had survived only by chance. When that . . . that *thing* had taken off, everyone in the cave had been sucked out with it, as if caught in some kind of slipstream. Except that there could have been no slipstream in a vacuum – and yet, Barabadar herself had been flung far enough for her suit to take a couple of minutes to slow her down and reorient her to thrust back to the rock. Did it play with gravity? Had there been some kind of gravitational backlash as it fired its engines?

She put the speculation to the back of her mind as Stormer continued.

'Martial Mother ... I have to report that one of the missing is your Third Son. He is not among the dead that we have found but he isn't responding to calls.'

Third Son! Barabadar felt the sudden horror of loss. Third Son gone, and no body to take a full Sharing from ...

She gave no hint of it in her response, carefully vetting the harmonics of her speech for any trace of emotion. 'I see,' she said.

'My Learned Mother Oomoing is also missing,' Stormer said, and Barabadar cursed. Third Son was one thing; he would be mourned properly, she had old Sharings of his, and sons Four through Twelve would welcome the promotion. But the loss of Oomoing would annoy the Scientific Institute, which would annoy the government, which would all come crashing down on *her*.

Well, she would just have to take it. The fact was, infuriating and costly though the business had been and even though her plan to return the Not Us to their own people hadn't unfolded quite as she would have liked, the net effect was the same. She still had a load of dead outlanders on her hands but the live ones were on their way back.

A new voice spoke inside her helmet.

'My Mother, this is First Son.'

'Yes, First Son?' Her oldest offspring was on watch onboard her ship.

'We've been tracking the course of the outlander ship and using the probes in Firegod orbit to project ahead of its course. Now we know where they're going and where to *look . . . My Mother, the probes have detected something.'*

'Another ship?' Had the outlanders come in force already? Was it too late?

'Too small,' First Son said, to her relief, *'and it's just sitting there in space. It's small and dark and using some kind of stealth, but once we knew roughly where to look . . .'*

'I know.' Hidden in space, just like the outlander base itself . . . but that didn't mean it belonged to them. It could still be some covert probe from another Homeworld nation.

'One of our probes is in a position to do a flyby,' First Son said. *'I've already sent the orders.'*

Of course, if it *was* outlander . . .

'Tell it to abort,' Barabadar ordered.

'Very well . . . My Mother, the object is signalling the probe.'

'What's it saying?'

'Unknown, but . . . Oh.' First Son sounded almost despondent.

'What?' Barabadar said, not sure if she really wanted to know.

'The object has exploded, My Mother.'

Step-through generator has self-destructed following non-receipt of correct codes, said the display on the pilot's desk.

Joel stared at it in horror.

'Oh, crap,' he said.

Five

Day Ten: 12 June 2153

'Now what?' said Boon Round. Joel swung round to the Rustie, who was still holding his captive XCs at calibrator-point, but for once Boon Round's query sounded genuine, not sarcastic.

'I don't know,' he said. He turned back to look at the displays on the pilot's desk. The lifeboat was still heading away from SkySpy – no problem there. It was still heading towards the Shield, where at least one XC ship was in orbit. The lifeboat could out-manoeuvre any XC ship built and go anywhere in this system, but it wasn't a full-size starship and sooner or later he would have to start paying attention to its limited resources.

Boon Round was having similar thoughts. 'These two are a drain on our reserves and they are part of the armed forces that slaughtered my pride. We should execute them.'

'Sure,' Joel said without looking round. 'Set your calibrator to kill.'

'I meant—'

'Boon Round, they can't eat our food, we can

recycle the water indefinitely, and this boat was built for the full SkySpy complement, so two of us and two of them aren't going to drain anything.' Food: a good point. Joel fantasized briefly about force-feeding the captives with chocolate bars.

'We throw them out of the airlock and let their friends pick them up.'

'If you think you can persuade them to get into the airlock, go ahead.' Good will only went so far: Joel knew that his intentions were benign, but would the XCs guess? And would they care if they did? Or, if pushed too far, would these two just risk the calibrator and jump him and Boon Round? Better, he thought, to keep them where he could see them and not provoke them at all.

'So what do you suggest?'

'Keep them at gunpoint and let me think.'

He thought. As far as the XCs on SkySpy knew, two of their kind had been kidnapped, and Joel had an idea of what happened when XCs felt vengeful. Chances were that the XCs would come after them. They needed to lie low until the rescue ship – and there *would* be a rescue ship – got here.

Somewhere.

Joel called up the planetary display and immediately discounted the nearest planetary body, the Shield, as an option. The Shield had XCs orbiting it, so no lying low there. The lifeboat could outfly an XC ship but not necessarily outgun it.

So, next stop? He called up a display of the solar system. The optimum course for the lifeboat would be to continue its curved trajectory, on around the Shield and then downhill into the system towards the sun and . . .

He grinned. Then he laughed, a dirty, unpleasant chuckle. Oh yes. Oh yes! It was too perfect.

A century ago, the first mission to this system from the Roving had secretly observed the XCs' first go at interplanetary travel. The journey had been made to wipe out the non-technological inhabitants of the system's third world. The XCs now referred to the place as the Dead World, a name which humans and First Breed had picked up, and it was the one place that everyone knew XCs avoided like the plague.

The Dead World and the Shield were almost at perigee, as close together as their respective orbits ever brought them. With only a little nudging, the lifeboat could cruise there in a couple of days. The XCs would take much longer, if they followed at all. And the lifeboat could go into orbit and await the rescue ship.

Joel entered the necessary commands and turned back to give Boon Round the good news. He wondered if the Rustie would see the irony of sheltering there. Even Boon Round might find it amusing.

Still in her space armour but with her helmet under one arm, Barabadar entered her cabin. She leaned against the bulkhead while the facts whirled through her mind.

The outlanders were heading for the Dead World. Unless they deviated from their course, and making huge yet apparently reasonable assumptions about how quickly they could decelerate, they would enter orbit around the Dead World in a day and a half.

The Dead World! Barabadar could hardly believe how her bad luck had been compounded. What did they know about the Dead World? Did they know of the inhabitants' fate or was it all just a ghastly coincidence?

Every instinct shrieked at her to go after the creatures, even though the journey would take one of her ships almost a twelve-day and a lot of fuel. The outlanders had caused the loss of Third Son and honour demanded vengeance, and on general principle to have an outlander ship flitting at will around the solar system, *her* solar system, was untenable. But she still believed the outlanders would be sending reinforcements, and the chances were they would appear in this vicinity of space. She owed it to Homeworld to be here to meet and confront them.

With a heavy heart, Barabadar set her helmet down and activated the comms console.

'This channel to be assigned exclusively to me until informed otherwise,' she said, and keyed in her personal encryption code.

'Compose signal to commanding officer, *Chariot of Rightful Justice*, stationed Habitat One,' she said. Compared to this far-flung location, Habitat 1 was almost in the Dead World's hunting perimeter, and *Chariot of Rightful Justice* could make the trip in half a twelve-day. 'Proceed at once to the Dead World . . .'

It took only a couple of minutes to deliver the gist

of *Chariot of Rightful Justice*'s orders. Then Barabadar paused. She so desperately did not want to give the next order, but she couldn't send the ship in undefended and unforewarned against an unknown and potentially lethal danger.

'Upon approaching the Dead World,' she said, 'essential repeat essential that you enter along the following orbital corridor . . .'

Another minute and the orders had been finished, reviewed and delivered. There was a five-hour time lag between here and Habitat 1, but *Chariot of Rightful Justice*'s commanding officer was a niece and Barabadar had no doubt the ship would be under way in six hours, six and a half maximum. So, that was done.

It wouldn't get to the Dead World in time to intercept the outlander ship, but it might get there in time to pick up the pieces.

Now for the hard part. 'Compose signal to President Mother of the Scientific Institute,' she said. She made her tone as impersonal as she could. 'Pending verification of facts, regret to inform you of possible loss of My Learned Sister Oomoing . . .'

Oomoing nibbled carefully at the extraterrestrial food. It was dry and crumbly and tasted vile. She made an effort and swallowed it. She would see if the mouthful stayed down and if it did her any good; her hopes weren't high, but she was starving. If it stayed then, perhaps, she would eat the rest.

She took a swig from the waterpack. That much, at

least, the two races had in common.

Long, the two-legged extraterrestrial, had walked back down the cabin to the cockpit. *I was right!* It had been so difficult to tell in microgravity, but Oomoing had been sure, and now she knew. Long walked on two legs, Short on four. She was already forming yet another tentative hypothesis. Short had resumed his vigil over the two captives.

'Learned Mother.' Fleet murmured so quietly that Oomoing had to strain to hear him.

'You can speak up,' she said. 'I doubt they understand us.' Short looked up when Fleet started talking, but that was probably just because of the noises he was making. Short could tell Fleet was saying something, but neither of the extraterrestrials had made any attempt to communicate, so Oomoing doubted that they could.

'I think I can jump him,' Fleet said, still quiet.

'He thinks he can jump you,' Oomoing said to Short.

'Learned Mother!' Fleet protested, but Short didn't twitch. The gun he was holding – if it was a gun – was still aimed somewhere vaguely between them, in their average direction.

'He can't understand you,' Oomoing said, 'and you're not to jump either of them.'

'It won't be difficult.' Fleet flexed his legs experimentally, took a breath. 'The gravity's a little lighter and I'd guess there's more CO_2 than we're used to, but that won't be a problem. Learned Mother, these two are probably technicians, engineers, not

93

warriors. They won't have met one of the Kin in battle rage before. I can do it, Learned Mother.'

It was good to know Fleet was capable of deducing something; Oomoing had already drawn the same conclusions about the battle fitness of their captors.

'I don't doubt you're right, Loyal Son,' she said. 'On the other hand, Long does seem to be quite good at piloting this ship. Could you work out the controls?'

Fleet glanced down the cabin into the cockpit. Long was laid out in one of the couches there.

Those couches had attracted Oomoing's interest and they gave weight to her latest hypothesis. They seemed to be designed to accommodate either Long or Short, which made sense; at the touch of a button they reconfigured their shape. Long lay down on his back; Short lay prone on his front. It seemed unnecessarily complicated ... for two species from the same planet. Oomoing was more and more convinced she was correct, and it was a conclusion that she knew Barabadar and very probably Fleet would not want to hear. There wasn't just intelligent life out there; there were at least two forms of it, and who knew how many more besides?

'The ship seems automated,' Fleet said, bringing her back to the present.

'Long set the controls and now has nothing further to do. Could you override them?'

'I . . .'

'Do you know he hasn't set scuttling charges to destroy us unless whoever operates the controls uses a password? Can you work out their language and their writing so that you can interface with their flight computer?'

'I . . .' Fleet said again.

'Loyal Son, I commend your devotion, but these two are keeping us alive. We need to keep them alive in turn.'

Fleet subsided, doubtless thinking dark thoughts. It took a minute for him to speak again. 'Learned Mother, that so-called food was revolting and probably did us no good at all. If it turns out to be useless to us then we may have to go to sleep to stay alive.'

'That's a risk we must take,' Oomoing said 'You will *not* attack either of these two without my permission. Forgive me for making it an order.'

A concerted attack on an innocent planet; the calculated wiping out of an unarmed, Stone Age race. Like everyone else on SkySpy, Joel had seen the recordings of the XCs' attack on their neighbouring world. He had had the routine briefing for all SkySpy personnel. But no-one giving the briefing had ever thought that the briefee might one day end up in charge of two of the creatures. Now finding out as much as possible about the XCs seemed like a good idea, and as he bathed in the luxury of the lifeboat's powder shower he had the infofeed going in the background.

He very quickly found that no two 'experts' could agree on the available data and there were still huge gaps in the Commonwealth's understanding.

Tantalizing scraps of information swam around him. For instance, what the hell were *culling games*? The phrase was often referred to, but since they didn't seem to be televised, no-one from the Commonwealth knew what actually happened at them. But the phrase itself was telling. It was only the survivors of the games that rose to genderless sentience and then, at the equivalent to puberty, became an adult of a fixed gender, complete with the ability to Share. With that kind of start to life, perhaps the race could be excused for being naturally . . . uppity.

And when you had the teeth and hunting instincts of a shark, and the claws of a bear and the reflexes of a cat, and no fear of death because your soul would live on in the memories of your loved ones who would eat you after you died . . . it was a wonder the race had lasted.

But maybe not. On the plus side, their conflicts were conducted in a highly ritual and regulated manner. XC nations would never go to war because one of them had invaded the XC equivalent of Poland, because that kind of thinking was alien to the XCs. It was difficult for an XC nation to run short of resources and need more land, when half the population was asleep for up to half a year at any given time. And those friendly culling games seemed to take care of excess population growth.

On the minus side, when they did go to war it was at the drop of a hat, ritual or no, and a large part of the ritual was to go at the other side hammer and tongs until both sides were so depleted they couldn't go on.

They didn't target civilians, but that was only because there was no such thing. Warfare for the XCs had been such a constant that they didn't even give their wars names for future reference. There were theories, based on what little could be made of their dating system, that their outbreaks of war and peace and war and peace had been cyclical, somehow predictable; but they were only theories and mentioned in a footnote. Joel was after hard facts.

Another plus-fact was that XCs now spoke of the Era of War and there was no denying *it was in the past*. XCs hadn't had a decent, all-out scrap on a global scale for nearly a century. The XC leaders did seem to realize what their technology could do, and XC politics was a constant struggle between reason, the awareness of possible self-extinction, and their instinctive desire to eat their opponents.

All of which was overshadowed by the whopping great minus-fact of what they had done to the third world of their solar system.

But that had been nearly a century ago; certainly nothing to do with the lifeboat's two unwanted passengers. But at the back of his mind was the permanent knowledge of what their parents, or maybe grandparents, had done, and of what these two could easily do themselves if they so chose.

His stream of thought was interrupted by a beeping. It came from his aide. He frowned and looked at the display. The frown faded into a grin.

'Oh, yeah,' he said. 'Of course.' It was past midnight, SkySpy time. It was 13 June 2153.

He thought about letting Boon Round in on the secret, then decided not to. Boon Round reversed the old saying that misery loves company. Boon Round's company could easily *be* misery.

So Joel hummed to himself. 'Happy birthday to me, happy birthday to me, happy birthday dear Joel, happy birthday to me.'

When he came out of the shower, he went straight to the medifac and dialled up a couple of stay-awake pills. He wasn't going to sleep with the XCs on board.

Six

Day Twelve: 14 June 2153

The world was dead, and looked it; an ashen, powdery grey-black like the remains of a fire on a wind-swept hillside. Joel had stood at the windows of spacecraft and gazed upon the Roving and Earth, and he had basked in the warmth of the bright blues and greens reflected back at him. Looking at the approaching drab sphere before him, he shivered.

'How are our guests?' he said without looking away.

Boon Round glanced at the display which showed the interior of the airlock.

'Still asleep,' he said.

Eventually the two XCs had hunkered down on their haunches at the back of the cabin, rocking very slowly from side to side. Their eyes were open but a cautious hand waved in front of them produced no response. Joel had wondered if this was the long sleep he had heard about or just a kind of resource-saving semi-coma. But the advantage was that the XCs were right next to the airlock. He and Boon Round had been able to pull them in and seal the inner hatch; a

99

frantic, quick-as-possible manoeuvre that seemed to have lasted twice as long as it actually took, both of them convinced that the XCs would wake up at any time and revert to being mobile masses of teeth and claws. But they had done it quickly enough and the two were confined before they could wake up fully.

To curb any possible waking instinct to open the outer hatch, go round the lifeboat and attack the flight deck from the outside, Joel had kept the XCs' helmets in the cabin.

'Do we land?' Boon Round said. The Rustie had come forward and was looking out at the Dead World with interest.

'No need at the moment,' said Joel. 'We're way ahead of any of their ships. We'll sit in orbit and wait for rescue.'

'And these two?'

'We'll cross that one when we come to it.' *And who needs XCs anyway?* he added silently, bitterly, as the world came closer and filled his vision. The surface was obscured by roiling, dirty masses of clouds; not the fluffy white things he mentally associated with a sunny summer's day but masses of debris and dust thrown up from the surface. The planet had been subjected to a concentrated nuclear bombardment that had thrown it into a nuclear winter. Even before the attack, pictures showed it had been nothing to write home about; a cold, barren, rocky place. Yet there had been enough to support life, even a civilization of sorts. But now . . .

For just a moment, Joel felt very ill disposed towards the XC race in general. Then he winced as pain stabbed suddenly into the middle of his head and it felt like there was grit behind his eyeballs. He had been on the stay-awakes too long. The feeling passed after only a second and he could concentrate again.

Then the alarm sounded.

'Caution: target lock on. Caution: target lock on. Caution: target . . .'

Joel leapt for the nav computer. Locked on? Who was out here to . . .? An option was already flashing on the display.

Evasive manoeuvres recommended.

'So do them!' Joel shouted. Next to the recommendation, the world 'enable' flashed in a little box; Joel thumped it and in the viewports the Dead World swung suddenly away as the lifeboat went into its pre-programmed shake-off procedure.

'Explain,' he ordered.

'Analysing situation,' said the voice of the lifeboat. The planet outside swung suddenly past again as the lifeboat went into another spin. *'Evading lock-on,'* it said in a slightly different tone. Then it was back to the first: *'Tactical suggests planetary shield of armed satellites.'* A schematic appeared on the main display to make the point: the smooth curve of the planet's surface, speckled with an ever-increasing number of dots showing the location of satellites.

'What the hell is that doing here?' Joel shouted. What was the point of guarding a dead world? He could almost believe the XCs had done it purely to spite him, to foil his latest plan, just as things finally seemed to be working.

'*Evading lock—*' The lifeboat shuddered. '*Direct hit on power compartment. Redirecting severed power and command feeds. Defence fields activated, starboard field nodes severely compromised. Recommend implementation of combat . . . (evading lock-on) . . . status. Evading lock-on.*'

'Do it!' The lifeboat was swinging all over the heavens and every course it took just seemed to take it into the line of fire of another satellite. 'Why didn't you identify the satellites earlier?'

'*Satellites were identified. Level of threat was not assessed due to insufficient pilot information.*'

Joel swore. Earth had a network of satellites in orbit, the Roving likewise. The lifeboat saw nothing intrinsically wrong with a planet being orbited by satellites and expected its pilot to tell it different. Had SkySpy never noticed? Probably not, because it only looked where the XCs went, and they never came here. The XCs said it was a dead world, the explorers from the Roving who had actually landed there had concurred, and so the Dead World was of no interest to anyone.

'Get us into a higher orbit,' he said.

'*Higher orbit . . . (evading lock-on) . . . not recommended. Tactical analysis suggests this course will put us in line of fire of a greater number of satellites.*' A graphical display underlined the advice, showing any of the courses the lifeboat could take to get up and away. Each one showed the lifeboat being targeted by three or four satellites and each one ended with a well-rendered explosion.

'*Direct hit received on defence fields,*' the lifeboat added.

Red lights, many more than Joel knew how to deal with, were flashing on the control desk. The Dead World swept past his vision again and the lifeboat reported two more direct hits.

So, if *up* was out . . .

The pain stabbed again and the grit at the back of his eyes felt more like grinding boulders, but again it went as quickly as it had come.

'Then configure forceplanes for maximum aerodynamic effectiveness and dive,' he said.

Oomoing dreamt, and that itself was unusual, because dreams rarely came in the Small Sleep. And one part of her mind was fully aware that this *was* the Small Sleep, a measure forced upon her by the lack of food. Dreaming wasn't unusual at all in normal sleep, which lasted the usual half year, but now?

Still, it was a happy dream, so Oomoing sat back and enjoyed it.

She was with her family, and she was glad. It was her Waking Day and her three sons – she had never bred a daughter to be another mother, but her sons compensated more than adequately – were around her. There was First Son, proudly clutching the breeding contract Oomoing had negotiated on his behalf with her best friend's eldest daughter. Second Son, the day he joined her in the laboratory as her assistant. And her own Third Son, after gaining his pilot's licence. Chronologically it made no sense, but that aware part of her mind saw the connection – for each son it was the proudest day of his life.

She had fed in the waking frenzy, and then bathed, and now she reclined on a couch while they tended to her and brought her food and drink. Then they offered their Sharings to her and she took them in and lived the lives they had lived for the last half year. She shared in their joys and their sorrows, and the family was as one.

And someone else was there. Someone not of the family, someone Not Us, and Oomoing felt irritation, then anger that someone should gatecrash the occasion. But there was no-one there and she sprang up from her couch, and she could hear him but not see him, and smell him but not touch him; a presence all around, worming its way into the bonds between them.

And suddenly they were not her sons, they were rivals, they were impostors, they were after her for her name and her memories.

'It's not right!' she cried, but still it pressed down on her and now it was all around her, worming its way into her mind, into her body, into her being, stripping away her identity, her essence.

It's not real, said a small part of her mind, but that part of her mind felt itself rapidly receding.

She was *Oomoing*. Not Learned Mother Oomoing the forensic scientist, not My Mother Oomoing the mother of three sons, but *Oomoing*, the hunter, the fighter, the invincible.

You are not! shouted a small voice in her mind from a long way away, and she recognized it as the pretender Oomoing, the Oomoing of those other titles, the Oomoing that she was in her waking hours. *You are a captive on an extraterrestrial ship. Now is not the time to give up your mind. You must concentrate.*

Oomoing swatted the other, the impostor, the traitor away with an angry growl and sprang up, eyes open, fully awake. All her senses were confused. She didn't know where she was – a cave of some sort, but it was strangely light and dry. She breathed in deeply, but instead of the smells she would have expected of frightened food animals and moist earth and rotting plant life underfoot and trees and bushes, all that came in was a dry, alien scent that wasn't alive or dead. And where her ears should have been full of the rustling of plants, the passage of animals through the undergrowth, the wind through the leaves, all she heard was an annoying hum, a deep vibration through her membranes.

But she knew what was outside the cave. Two food animals, two prey. If she could get at them . . .

Her rival slammed into her, bowling her across the floor. A young male, smaller and weaker than her but just as hungry. Oomoing screeched in anger and swiped him across the face, hunting claws extended.

And yet they were not extended; something covered her hands. He fought back but all they could do was club each other with their fists where their claws should have been, landing heavy blows on the other's head and body. The same something that covered her hands extended over her entire body, as it did his, and the moment of puzzlement was enough to let that irritating voice back into her mind.

It's Fleet! He's a friend. You mustn't . . .

The male leapt for her, hissing. He wrapped his four arms around her and brought his teeth down to her neck. Oomoing had to strain her head backwards to keep away from the fangs while she pounded at his body with her feeding arms. She threw herself forward, and a solid-looking outcropping from the side of the cave dug a sharp corner into the male's back and made him yowl with pain. His grip weakened for just a moment and that was enough for Oomoing to get her feeding arms between the two of them and knock him away from her with a powerful shove. He lay at her feet and writhed in pain.

Oomoing held her hunting hands up in front of her, still covered with that annoying grey fabric, and *willed*. Black points appeared in the fabric at her finger points, and then with a sudden rush her claws were fully out, tearing through the obstruction.

The male cowered. He knew he had lost; he knew the greater fighter. Oomoing reached down with her clawed hands and grasped his head. Blood welled over her claws as she pulled him to his feet, head bowed, and opened her mouth wide . . .

It's Fleet!

Oomoing paused for just a moment to take the scene in; Fleet, cowed, standing before her ready for the death bite, his blood pouring out through her hands. Oomoing snatched her hands away in horror and Fleet collapsed.

'Loyal Son!' she exclaimed. She crouched down before him and cradled his head.

'Learned Mother,' he said in a whisper.

'Loyal Son, I am so sorry! I don't know what came over me . . .'

'I do. It was the waking frenzy. I felt it too.'

'But, the waking frenzy, after the Small Sleep? That's impossible.'

'Nevertheless, it happened. Am I bleeding badly?'

Oomoing studied his scalp wound. 'It may need bandaging. Perhaps the extraterrestrials have something I can bind it with.'

'Learned Mother, you don't have to . . .'

'I did this!' Oomoing said angrily. She welcomed the anger because if she let it fill her mind it pushed out the nagging doubts. *How* could she have done this? Asleep for no more than an hour or two and her animal self came out of the darkness and took her over? It was disgraceful. And she had hurt Fleet, not just one of her kind but a friend, an ally, a Loyal Son. 'I attacked you without need, without warning, without even a formal challenge.' She felt . . . dirty. Soiled. There were *rules* for fighting and she had broken every one of them. 'Let me make some kind of amends.'

The extraterrestrials had put them in the airlock. She didn't blame them, but it was inconvenient. She peered through the small window set into the inner hatch; she could see them in the cockpit at the end of the cabin, both looking towards her.

Behind them, the viewports were full of planet, dead and burnt, and suddenly she felt the presence of the stranger again; the one who had been there in her dream, the one who had taken her family from her, and now she knew who it was, because her every sense shrieked its name and it was as if a roar from a million throats blasted into her membranes.

Oomoing and Fleet screamed together.

'What was that about?' Boon Round said. He and Joel looked, appalled, at the display showing the scene in the airlock. The XCs had woken from their sleep and attacked each other. And how! They had moved in a blur of speed: hammer and tongs didn't begin to describe it. Joel had deliberately not let the two get out of their spacesuits, reasoning that they wouldn't want to extend their claws and puncture holes in the fabric; well, so much for that.

And just as suddenly as they started, they had stopped. Then that sudden blast of noise, and now the two were catatonic again. One was bleeding.

'Entering atmosphere,' said the lifeboat, and Joel shoved the problem of the XCs onto the backburner as he turned back to the control desk. The lifeboat was diving almost straight down into the atmosphere to get away from the satellites and a mighty layer of dirty cloud was spread across his vision, looking sometimes like a sheet hung just beyond the viewports and sometimes like what it was, a layer many miles away at right angles to their course. The lifeboat was surrounded by an invisible forcefield, shaped to streamline its passage through the atmosphere, but a flickering yellow glow ahead of him showed where the field was meeting the air. The glow spread across his vision, whitening and increasing in fury. The viewports tinted, then turned almost black so that just a gentle radiance showed ahead.

'We should perhaps pull up,' said Boon Round. 'We're probably out of range of the satellites by now.'

'Yeah,' Joel said. He studied the displays that showed the power available to the forceplanes, the strains being put on them and the added stress that would come if they tried to change course at this stage. The sums didn't add up. Or rather, they did, but it was the wrong answer. 'We're also committed. Sorry.'

The lifeboat ripped through the Dead World's atmosphere with an echo that dislodged rocks from mountainsides and rang across half the hemisphere. The blur outside the viewports gradually resolved into mountains and valleys and plains, as the lifeboat dropped down from hypersonic to supersonic and then to what Joel thought of as just bloody fast.

From beneath, the cloud cover was even less attractive than above; blacker than the blackest storm, it hung above them and seemed almost close enough to touch, a layer of rocks and debris poised to fall if someone sneezed.

Enormous snowdrifts and banks covered the land, blurring the outlines. It would have looked almost inviting, if it could only have been bathed with a decent yellow-blue light and not the drab, cold glow that made its way through the clouds.

Ground radar picked out the firmer lines below the illusion, and Joel's eye was suddenly caught by a mass of lines that couldn't have been natural. It was a giant grid of squares and plazas, lying in a hollow twenty miles across that was filled up with ice and snow. A town, maybe even a city. He could see where the main thoroughfares of the city had been, the open spaces, the winding trail of a river course. Size was harder to judge; how many people had lived here? Ten thousand? Twenty? Thirty?

But overlaying those shapes were a burst of lines radiating outwards from one point. And the radiation count was way up. This place had received a direct nuclear hit. He pictured those roads and parks and plazas filled with people. He imagined how it had been before the attack; the inhabitants going quietly about their business, those few who bothered with looking up seeing a bright star tear its way through the skies above them before blossoming into another sun, a sun that touched the earth and seared the ground and the people.

Or maybe the hit had come well into the attack, and the people had had a good idea of what was to come and been prepared for it. Shell-shocked, knowing the fate that had befallen their neighbours, perhaps already succumbing to the radiation, they had maybe looked up dully and waited for the mercy killing to come from above.

On the display, in the airlock, the XCs had woken up again. They were uncurling from their balls but not apparently making any effort to stand up. They seemed drained of energy, almost subdued. He found himself once again seriously hating each and every one of their race.

'Do you wish to land at the selected location?' The lifeboat's voice brought his attention back to the present and he realized he had adjusted the controls to keep the image of the dead city in the centre of the display. The lifeboat had noted his interest.

'No,' Joel said. 'Go back to hypersonic and head for the equator. We may as well go somewhere warm.'

Half an hour later, Joel had their landing place. It was equatorial, a valley which sensors said was a degree or two warmer than the average, which was to say merely very cold indeed. Joel surmised it was sheltered from the prevailing winds and he noted a chain of semi-active, smouldering volcanoes to the south. He wondered if there was something volcanic in the area, maybe hot springs, that contributed to the ambience. Whatever, it seemed the best place to go.

The inhabitants of the Dead World had also found the place attractive, it seemed. There had once been a major metropolis here, another grid, like the last city. An interesting place to touch down.

'We don't have to land at all,' Boon Round objected.

'I want to see what damage the satellites did,' Joel said. He glared back at the airlock and its inhabitants. 'And why do we want this completely empty,

111

uninhabited planet defended, eh?' he called. 'Afraid someone's going to find out what we did, are we?'

'Why else?' Boon Round agreed. 'We're safe. Surely these two have outlived their usefulness?'

Joel sighed and checked the controls. They were still half a mile up. 'Yeah, you're right. Let's just chuck 'em out.'

'At last you talk sense. Build up sufficient pressure in the airlock, then open—'

'We are not chucking them out, you moron.' Joel glowered at the two XCs. SkySpy had seen nothing to suggest their race's natural aggressiveness had declined one jot in the years since the Xenocide, and these two had just tried to eat each other, but he wasn't going to murder them like that. Strand them, maybe.

He glanced at the spread of ruins beneath the lifeboat, then at the display which was showing possible landing sites big enough to take them. He touched the display over one of them.

'Land here,' he said.

The lifeboat extended its landing feet and touched down along one side of a wide open plaza. Joel powered down the engines and, almost as a ritual gesture to show that they had indeed arrived, cut the internal artgrav. He immediately felt lighter, springier, and he bounced up and down a couple of times on the balls of his feet to get the feel of it.

Then he looked morosely through the viewports at what lay outside. It was dark – as dark as dusk on a dark, overcast day. Two- and three-storey buildings, the height of the lifeboat and more, surrounded the square. The stone was black and uninviting, the doors and windows were low and wide. Dust and debris gusted about the square in the wind, but no snow. It was cold but dry, though stains on the buildings and channels through the dirt suggested that water occasionally flowed here. Maybe snow did fall but got melted by warm volcanic breezes.

The architecture was solid and lumpish, nothing crude but nothing soaring and elegant either. This world was poor in metals and it was the opinion of Commonwealth experts that its inhabitants would never have reached a high level of technology; but they had still made it to a pretty advanced Stone Age, like the pre-Colombian peoples of South America. And what little they had had been taken from them.

'I said, the power and command flows have all redirected,' said Boon Round.

Joel jumped. 'Sorry, I was miles away.'

'I've been aft and inspected the damage,' Boon Round said slowly, as if to someone of feeble intellect. 'Remember, where the satellite hit us? We'll have to make repairs and I recommend an external inspection.'

'Good idea.' Joel didn't mention that Boon Round had been the one counselling against landing in the first place. He glanced outside and winced. It looked cold. More to the point . . . He called up the external environment display. 'Well, we can breathe the air . . . radiation . . . we'd get a dose of one hundred and fifty, one hundred and sixty millisieverts if we stayed out for a day. Which of course we won't.'

'That's higher than the recommended dose. We could wear our spacesuits for protection.'

'Pretty cumbersome, though. Don't worry, both our bodies can take the dose. We'll take a couple of antirads before we go out and never notice the difference.' Joel looked at the XCs. 'I don't know what their tolerance is, though.'

'You're going to take them outside?' Boon Round exclaimed.

'Well, I'm not going to leave them in here while we go out, am I?'

'We can at least agree on that.' Boon Round glanced at the airlock. 'I'm not sure I want to go in there with them.'

'You and me both,' Joel muttered. 'Get your calibrator really.'

And so Joel pulled on a weathersuit, and he and Boon Round swallowed a pair of antirads dispensed at the touch of a button from the medifac. Then, each armed only with instruments for fine-tuning an optical fibre network that they had to pretend were guns, Joel opened the inner hatch. The XCs looked up, but obediently moved back to let the two of them in when Joel gestured. Joel shut the inner hatch and opened the outer.

He sneezed as the air of the Dead World flooded into his nostrils and sinuses. It was bitterly cold and had a burnt, acrid quality that only lingered in his senses for a moment before the temperature anaesthetized his sense of smell. He tried not to think of all those decaying nuclei that were now entering his lungs and beaming their disrupting signals directly into his DNA. He quickly pulled his weathersuit hood up over his head, so that now just his eyes were exposed to the stinging cold.

Because he was nearest the outside he swung the ladder attachment out and released the catch that let it unfold. Then he climbed slowly down and became the first human to stand on the Dead World.

Apart from the ticking of the lifeboat's cooling hull and the moan of the wind, it was completely quiet. He was on a world where not another living thing breathed or moved. He shivered, with more than just the cold; it was an experience others could keep. He looked across the plaza at the empty buildings opposite. They were decayed and crumbling, and the empty holes that were the doors and windows in the bleak stone filled him with absolutely no desire to explore their dead secrets.

Boon Round and the XCs climbed down after him. The two unwanted passengers huddled close together, chirping quietly, and Joel again wondered what was going through their minds. Was it 'Damn, they caught us out' or 'My God, I had no idea'?

Joel had seen two-hundred-year-old archive film taken at the end of Earth's Second World War. In some areas, the allied forces that had conquered Germany had rounded up the civilian populations and forced them to walk through the Nazi death camps, to see at first hand what their late leaders had done. On the faces of some had been shame, some hardened resolve – it was no news to them at all – and some sheer, unwilling disbelief. If he could read XC expressions he wondered what he would see here.

'The damage is this way,' Boon Round said.

A dark outline in the ground around them showed where the lifeboat's fields were still on, intersecting with the ground. 'Field off,' Joel said into his aide, and they walked down to the stern of the lifeboat. Joel squinted up at the cracked hole in the hull, the charred scars of the blast.

'I'll need to stand on your back to get a look at it,' he said to Boon Round.

'Why should I have to carry you?'

Joel sighed. 'Because you're stronger than me. Rusties are stronger than humans.'

'I have lost count of the number of times you have used that term. You must know I prefer First Breed.'

'I'm sorry. The First Breed are stronger than humans and I, in my weaker natural state, must rely upon your superior physical prowess to get me up there to inspect the damage, oh wonderfully-strong and ever-so-slightly-touchy one.'

'I accept your reasoning,' Boon Round said. 'There's no need to over-elaborate upon your initial argument.' He reared up to place his forefeet against the hull. 'Climb up my back and stand on my shoulders.'

Joel scrambled up. He knelt on Boon Round's shoulders, braced his hands on the hull and slowly stood upright. The damaged section wavered in front of his eyes.

'It's clean,' he said. 'Nothing's going to short circuit. We can tie off—'

'Your right foot is too near my eye. Please move it.'

Joel growled to himself and shifted his right foot an inch.

'That hurt! You're scraping the skin off my shoulder. Can't you lift your feet?'

Joel tried to imagine balancing single-footed on the shoulders of a wobbling Rustie. 'No,' he said. 'Keep quiet, I'm trying to concentrate.' The damaged node that had almost compromized the forceplanes was just above him. He leaned against the hull and stood on tiptoes. 'Almost done, Boon Round. One more thing to check out.'

'You're much heavier than I first thought. I'm probably going to sprain something.'

'God, you're as bad as . . . never mind,' Joel said. 'Hold on just a minute longer.'

'As bad as what?' Boon Round's voice came from below him.

'A toy donkey in some stories my dad used to read me.'

'What's a donkey?'

'An Earth animal.' Joel peered more closely at the node. 'An unintelligent beast of burden,' he muttered to himself, and yelled as Boon Round suddenly dropped down on all fours and he fell to the ground. He landed with a blow that drove the breath out of his body.

'I heard that remark!' Boon Round stood over him. 'I've had enough of your constant stream of insults and petty slights against the First Breed.'

Joel wheezed. 'My what?'

'If you don't like us then I wonder why you bothered to join the Commonwealth in the first place. The Ones Who Command whom you were meant to replace at least treated us with respect.'

'But I . . .'

Boon Round pushed on. 'Ever since we have been incarcerated together, my every reasonable and subjective remark has been met by your sarcasm and lack of concern.'

'Your every what?' Joel had pushed himself up into a sitting position and to his surprise found that he wanted to laugh.

'And now you compare me to an unintelligent beast of burden.'

'Boon Round, I . . . I bet that when the Ones Who Command gave an order, you obeyed it and didn't drive them mad with whinging and whining!'

'We were bred to obey them! And that does it. I'll go no further. I'll not help or assist you in any way unless I receive your apology now.'

'Hmmph,' said Joel. The urge to laugh was growing ever stronger.

'That does not translate. Was it another insult? And don't give me the line about insults between friends being acceptable, because I've heard it before and we are emphatically not friends. Well?'

'I . . .' Joel sucked in his cheeks and bit on them to

keep the smile off his face. 'I apologize, Boon Round. I'm sorry I compared you to a donkey.' Then, because he couldn't resist it: 'I never meant to impugn your intelligence.'

Boon Round was silent for a moment. 'Your apology is accepted. Let's finish our work out here and get back inside.'

'Yeah.' Joel climbed back to his feet and took a step forward. 'Good idea.'

Something hit the ground where he had been sitting, and he looked down at it. It looked like a spear.

Time seemed to slow down; he was an outside observer watching the scene from afar. It looked like a spear, it was long and thin and had a point at one end and dammit it *was* a spear there was no getting around that but it couldn't be a spear because . . .

'Turn around, very slowly,' Boon Round said. Joel did, and saw the attackers.

There were five or six of them, approaching slowly from a small alleyway between buildings that opened into the plaza. They were the size of XCs – in fact, superficially they looked very like XCs except that they walked on four limbs, keeping what would have been an XC's hunting arms free for carrying things. Or, indeed, throwing them. They approached with every sign of caution, perhaps fear. Even with the four legs, it wasn't the smooth flowing walk of a Rustie but more of a scuttle, like a forward-facing crab.

Part of Joel's mind was screaming, *My God! Someone survived!* The rest was more practical.

'Can you get to the airlock quickly?' he said.

'I would recommend getting to the airlock slowly,' said Boon Round. 'We don't want to surprise them.'

'Yes we bloody well do. I want to surprise them with how quickly we can get into the airlock and fly away.'

'We mean them no harm.'

'Boon Round, we came out of the sky. How do you think they feel about us? Hold on.'

Joel's hand was moving slowly to the aide at his belt. He could send a command to the lifeboat to throw a defence field around them, and then they would be safe. But it would have to be quick . . .

The nearest local, now only thirty feet away, lifted its spear into a throwing position.

Joel dived to one side and the spear flew past him. It hit one of the lifeboat's landing feet with a dull clunk. Joel had his aide in his hand. 'Lifeboat systems command! Activate—'

Two XCs fell out of the sky in front of him and landed in a crouch, hunting arms extended towards the attackers, claws out. A low rumble, an ominous growl that set Joel's teeth on edge and vibrated in his ribs, came from both of them and it took a moment to realize it was the same two XCs they had brought with them, as if there could be more. The two had jumped clear over him and Boon Round to engage the enemy.

And engage they did. The big female sprang forward in a blur and flew into the nearest attacker, and they sprawled together on the ground. Her claws dug into its stomach area, and blood spurted as she lifted it up and flung it at another comrade. There was no screech from the creature, no high-pitched trill of agony. It was eerily silent.

Meanwhile the small male had wrested a spear from one of the others with his lower arms, which he reversed and buried in the guts of its former owner while his hunting arms tore the face off a second. A kick to one knee from the female shattered the leg of another attacker and it pitched forward into the dirt. Another swipe with those claws severed its neck while the female was already turning to deal with another. The male had leapt onto someone else and was gnawing at its shoulder, just one bite that almost took its arm off.

The one surviving attacker fled.

Joel stared at the XCs with a mixture of awe and horror. Their suits were spattered with native blood and they stood as if all the strength had drained out of them, like two exhausted prize fighters. Their shoulders drooped, their hunting arms almost trailed in the dirt.

'More are coming,' Boon Round said in a matter of fact way. Another group was lurking just outside the plaza, crowded into one of the alleyways and peeking out.

Joel gazed at them and his heart flooded with pity. He was getting tired of being the target of unprovoked aggression, but what could he expect? These were the survivors of a nuclear holocaust. Possibly the last survivors, ever. He couldn't set the XCs onto them and he didn't want to.

'Get back here!' Joel shouted. The female XC looked up and Joel gestured, pointing at her and then at the ground next to him with abrupt jabs. 'Get back!'

She understood that much at least, and took the male's elbow to lead him into the shadow of the lifeboat. Joel could see spears and arrows being raised and he finished the command to his aide that he had begun less than a minute ago.

'Activate defence fields now.'

A spear flew through the air. And another. Then a stone. Whatever the locals could find to throw. Meeting the field inches from Joel's face, they stopped dead and their charred remains fell to the ground with a crack, a flash of light.

'Get inside,' Joel said quietly.

'They won't get through the fields,' Boon Round objected. 'We can still do repairs.'

'Think what they've been through, Boon Round. Let's not rub it in. We'll take ourselves away and that will be that. You go first.'

'You want me in the cabin alone with these two?'

'Just do it.'

A still protesting Boon Round climbed back up the ladder and Joel indicated for the XCs to follow. He climbed up last of all and pulled the ladder attachment up. Then he sealed the outer hatch, opened the inner and headed for the flight deck.

He winced; the gritty feeling was back behind his eyes, stronger than ever. It was so strong that he was looking at the pilot's display through tears, but suddenly the feeling passed again.

'Aah!'

He jumped; the female XC had come up behind him. They looked at each other.

'Look,' Joel said, 'um, thanks for what you just did . . . um, I know you can't understand . . .'

He just had time to register that at least the claws were retracted before her club-like hunting hand whistled through the air and smashed into the side of his head.

PART II

Seven

Day Seven: 9 June 2153

The air was liquid and warm beneath the Roving's tropical sun. The gentle breeze played like a lover's touch over Michael Gilmore's face and arms and legs. The calm rush of the waves was in his ears, an invitation to run down the beach and dive into the clear blue water. The white sand caressed his bare toes and soles, soft and supple beneath his feet.

And *very* hot. He leapt back on to the veranda of the beach house, sat down quickly and rubbed his feet. Once they had stopped burning, he pulled his sandals on and stood up again to survey his realm.

Living out fantasies, he decided, was for people with high boredom thresholds.

Well, this was what he had retired for. He had always wanted to work his way through every fantasy that a man of his age and position could respectably get away with, and the tropical island had been an obvious starter. He was the only sentient being, human or First Breed, for hundreds of miles in any direction: Admiralty Island *that* way, the wistfully named St Helena – the last repose of the

Ones Who Command, the former masters of the Roving and the Rusties – *that* way. After five years as *de facto* head of the Commonwealth Navy, he had thought it would be good to get away from it all, be completely on his own and consider his options.

And bloody boring it was too. His skin was darker than it ever had been after a lifetime in space – mildly tanned, by more terrestrial standards. That was from yesterday's hard work. In the morning he had lain on the beach, cool drink by his side, reading a book from the pile of books he had always wanted to read and listening to music from the pile of pieces he had always wanted to hear. In the afternoon, he had wrestled not very successfully with his creative muse who was meant to be helping him write his autobiography.

After the first half hour, he had begun to suspect that the attraction of a tropical island was palling. By lunchtime, he had known with a dismal certainty that after a week of this he would be bored out of his skull. For forty-eight years he had thought he was the kind of man who could do without the company of other people, basing this idea on the fact that he didn't particularly like having other people around. Now, without the slightest chance of other people being around, he knew he was wrong. He liked the *option* of doing without other people. He loathed solitude enforced upon him.

Now it was Day Two and he wasn't in the least bit looking forward to it. Maybe he could vary the programme by doing the book in the morning, the drinking and reading and listening in the afternoon. Bloody typical, he thought, gazing out at the surrounding blue waters, that after a lifetime in space he had never learned to swim. He picked his aide up from the veranda table and looked at the result of yesterday's literary endeavours. The title was *Greatness Thrust Upon Him* and even that wasn't his own idea. Joel had suggested it.

Beneath it, in a last-minute dash of inspiration before going to bed, he had written: 'Chapter 1'.

'No,' he said, and deleted it all. The autobiography could wait, and the thought of Joel had given him an idea. He pulled up a chair.

'Letter to Joel,' he said to his aide. 'Joel, my boy, here's a hint. Never retire. Or if you do, make sure you've actually planned it out in some modicum of detail . . . Oh, bloody hell, what is it?'

The drone of an aircar had knocked his thoughts on to a completely different track. He looked around and spotted it, flying straight at the island.

They could have contacted . . . he thought, then remembered that he had set his aide simply to take calls and not inform him of them.

'Display calls,' he said, and whistled at the list that scrolled up on the display. All dated within the last twenty-four hours, all from the Admiralty and all tagged 'Urgent', which even with the Admiralty's general sense of self-importance was quite unusual.

He looked thoughtfully back at the aircar as it spiralled into its final approach, and held up an arm to shield his face as it touched down amid whirling sand. The door swung up and a four-legged form came bounding up the beach. He recognized Spar Mild, assistant to Arm Wild, who had been Senior of the First Breed nation and co-leader of the Commonwealth for the last four years. Spar Mild would only be here for one reason, representing its master. Gilmore was so glad of the break that he didn't even remind the Rustie that he had come here, among other reasons, specifically to get away from Arm Wild.

The Rustie hurried up to him, its breath whistling through the ring of nostrils at the crown of its head.

'You won't like this,' it said, and the words 'Don't bet on it' died on Gilmore's lips as it went on to deliver its news.

Admiralty Island grew in a few moments, but not few enough, from a black blur on the horizon to a sizeable landmass, serene amid the ocean blue with a beauty that was quite lost on Gilmore.

And there was the Admiralty Building, a series of white terraced structures set into the side of a hill that overlooked the sea. Somewhere in there the meeting was being held to discuss the SkySpy crisis. Gilmore already knew as much as Spar Mild; he knew of the attack, and of the lifeboat's escape, and there was the garbled report of Joel jumping off the lifeboat before it stepped through.

That was all he needed to know.

Seven days! he thought. *Seven days!* That was how long ago the attack on SkySpy had been. Anything could have happened since then. Anything at all.

The lifeboat wouldn't be at the Roving for another week; it had stepped through from the XC system into a solar system that was completely empty but for two gas giants and another step-through generator on the far side of the sun. It was a set-up dictated by the rules of step-through and astrophysics. It was also a quarantine measure in the unlikely event of the XCs getting hold of SkySpy's step-through generator and making it work.

Getting to the second step-through generator, and hence to the Roving, through normal space would take days. However, the lifeboat could transmit a report ahead for the generator to relay beam ... but first it had to be far enough around the quarantine sun so that it was in line-of-sight with the generator in the first place. And it had taken seven days to do it. *Seven days!*

The aircar swung round in a tight curve over the old launch promontory, with its disused gantries and museum-piece launch vehicles, and came to hover beside the Admiralty Building, setting itself down in front of the lowest level. Gilmore was out even before the door had finished opening and he ran up to the main entrance, taking the steps two at a time. Spar Mild ran beside him.

The sentries – one human, one Rustie – drew themselves up smartly.

'Commodore,' they said by way of acknowledgement, and he was in too much of a hurry to correct them.

The sentries outside the main conference room were more switched on. They too drew themselves up but it was Spar Mild that they were acknowledging. The human blocked Gilmore's way.

'I'm sorry, sir, may I see your pass?'

'I don't have one,' Gilmore said impatiently, and tried to push past. The man blocked him. 'Do you know who I am?' Part of him was instantly ashamed at trying to bluster on the basis of rank – he had always despised the habit in others – but right now he had more important things to worry about.

'I know you resigned, Commodore, and I also know this meeting is for approved personnel only.' The man at least had the grace to sound genuinely regretful. 'I'm very sorry, but . . .'

'The commodore has been reinstated *pro tem* and is here on my authority,' Spar Mild said. Gilmore and the sentry both looked at the Rustie; Gilmore knew, and the sentry probably suspected, that Spar Mild couldn't actually do that.

But the sentry stood back. 'A pleasure to have you back, sir,' he said. Gilmore grunted and followed Spar Mild in. What sounded like angry voices were ringing around the meeting chamber and his ears immediately pricked up.

He had to take one of the public seats around the edge of the chamber, which was easy because most of them were empty. This meeting really was for approved personnel only. At the head of the central table were Arm Wild and Valerie duPont, the co-Seniors of the Commonwealth. Arm Wild had his usual entourage of Rusties. Along from duPont were the Rustie Space Minister and John Chase, First Admiral of the Commonwealth Navy. Chase was speaking. Next to Chase . . .

The shock of seeing the man there was like being drenched in cold water. James Windsor – King James – met Gilmore's glance briefly, gave a cool nod and looked back at the First Admiral.

Gilmore became aware out of the corner of his eye that someone further along the row was also looking at him. A man and a woman sat a few seats down from him. The man was tall, broad shouldered and blond, straight out of a recruitment poster; the woman was more slender, less brutally Aryan. She would be about Joel's age, he reckoned; the man a bit older, late twenties or early thirties. The woman sat nearer to Gilmore and the quick blur of her face as she looked forward showed she had indeed been looking at him a moment ago.

Their uniforms almost made Gilmore laugh out loud. Dark trousers, with a gold stripe running down each leg; bright scarlet jackets; white belts; gold buttons that were a purely decorative adornment to their clothes' sealseams. The uniforms said exactly who they were and who they worked for.

'Madam Co-Senior,' Chase was saying, 'I'm baffled by this lack of security. The news came on a secure channel from the lifeboat—'

'It's spilt milk, Admiral,' said duPont. She waved a hand at a number of document images hanging over the desk in front of her. 'The fact is, they know, and I have had messages from all the Earth ambassadors, ranging from polite enquiry to a demand to be represented on any mission that we send to SkySpy. We'll have to accommodate them somehow. If the XCs learn about step-through then they could reach Earth just as well as us, so I can see their points. Please, Admiral, back to the briefing.'

'Very well,' Chase said, and it sounded as if he were saying it through his teeth. Gilmore could sympathize. Civilian diplomats getting involved? The situation was difficult enough as it was. 'As I was saying before Madam Co-Senior dropped her bombshell, we are agreed that the first priority is to find out exactly what has happened to SkySpy. We know no-one else was able to make it to the lifeboat but that doesn't mean no-one else is still alive. There may be pockets of resistance on the base, holding out against the invaders. There may not be. We can make guesses until we're blue in the face but we'll never know until we go there.

'And that,' Chase finished, 'is why I asked King James to be present. He has a suggestion that may be useful. Sir?'

'Thank you.' King James had aged. Still a slim man in good trim, but the hair and the moustache were greying. The original mission that had brought humans to the Roving and led to the foundation of the Commonwealth had been four years ago, and the then Prince James had inherited his throne unexpectedly in the course of events.

The mission hadn't gone quite as James and his father had hoped, but the man couldn't complain. His kingdom, UK-1, orbited the Roving and acted as the official port of entry to the planet. Plan A, rebuilding the British Empire on the Roving with the First Breed as its loyal subjects, hadn't quite worked out for the Windsors but as far as Gilmore was concerned, Plan B was a bloody good second best.

'Before we came here to the Roving,' James said, 'UK-1 had very little in the way of a defence force. We had the Royal Space Fleet, a small space service, but nothing much. Nothing demanding.'

As if by accident, his eyes met Gilmore's as he said that; or at least, his gaze drifted past Gilmore. Gilmore, of course, had been a captain in that small, undemanding Royal Space Fleet.

So had John Chase, and from the way James blinked, Gilmore suspected James had suddenly remembered this fact. The king hurried on.

'Our main defence was our isolation and the fact that no-one had any particular need to attack us. That changed when we came to the Roving – we became a far more desirable target and, due to the decision of the Commonwealth to make its technology available to the nations of Earth, our enemies suddenly acquired the ability to attack us.' Another lighthouse-beam glance around the room again caught Gilmore's eye. James was blaming him.

Well, what was I supposed to do? Gilmore thought. Everyone knew the nations of Earth would soon catch up with the Roving technologically, and if they were left to do it in secret then they would get there without the Roving knowing it. Far better to have it all out in the open; and so, admittedly with qualms, he had decided the Navy should make the principles of its ship technology generally available. None of the Earth nations had put that technology to use yet, but it was only a matter of time.

'And so,' James said, 'we decided to build up a proper defence force, should UK-1 ever come under attack. We now have two troops of marines, a couple of hundred men and women in all, and we intend to build up a complete regiment in time.' He looked up, not this time at Gilmore but at the couple sitting by him. 'Stand up, please, you two.'

They both stood smartly to attention.

'May I present Captain Bill Perry, two-i-c A-Troop, King Richard's Regiment of Royal Marines and officer commanding Able Platoon,' said James. 'Next to him, commanding Baker Platoon, Lieutenant Peter . . .'

The king trailed off, realizing that the marine next to Bill Perry wasn't a Peter at all. 'Lieutenant, ah, *Donna* McCallum, officer commanding *Charlie* Platoon,' he said. Donna McCallum gave a small nod. Gilmore took a brief moment to work out, from the swirl of names, who was commanding which phonetically named platoon, then turned his attention back to the meeting.

'Sit down, please,' James said, and turned back to the meeting. 'We're willing to lend Able and Charlie Platoons to the Commonwealth for the duration of this mission,' he said. 'Captain Perry is a veteran of the European Marine Force and Lieutenant

McCallum saw service in the Pacifican conflict, and their men and women are likewise experienced. That's two platoons for you, sixty marines, experienced and trained for combat in all conditions and gravities . . .' (*And that's quite a range* . . . Gilmore the spacer mused.) '. . . ready and raring to go. How is that for you, Captain McLaughlin?'

Andrew McLaughlin, whom Gilmore knew, sat across the table from James. Like many other human personnel of the Navy, McLaughlin was a veteran of the original Roving mission from Earth; he had commanded the North American Federation's *Enterprise*. More to the point he was also the recently appointed captain of *Pathfinder*, the first of the Navy's joint First Breed/Human starships and the nearest thing there was to a flagship. Next to McLaughlin was a Rustie which Gilmore suspected was Sand Strong, the First Breed Senior on *Pathfinder*.

McLaughlin had his back to Gilmore and hadn't noticed him.

'It would suit me just fine, sir,' McLaughlin said, looking not at James but at Chase, 'if only *Pathfinder* had the berths for sixty extra crew.'

'There's more than enough room on *Pathfinder*'s hangar deck. Our people can bivouac there, with your approval. They don't mind slumming it,' said James, a man who had never willingly slummed it in his life. 'Their supplies and equipment can be stored in the hold.'

'Sure,' said McLaughlin. 'What happens when we get there?'

'That is for the meeting to decide,' James said, and made as if to sit back down. Halfway there, he stood up again. 'Point of order,' he said, and finally he was looking directly at Gilmore. 'Is it in order to be discussing this in front of civilians?'

'Civilians?' Chase said. Then he realized. 'Oh, of course. Hi, Mike.'

'John,' Gilmore said.

McLaughlin twisted round in his seat and smiled. 'Hey! Commodore!'

'Ex-Commodore,' James said.

'Do you have an objection to Mr Gilmore's presence?' said duPont.

James gave a small, wintry smile. 'I do understand he has no official connection with the Commonwealth Navy. He officially handed in his duties.'

'The Comm— Mr Gilmore built up the Commonwealth Navy from scratch,' McLaughlin said.

'But I understand he was never formally a member. Everything he did, he did on ... what was it ... a *consultancy* basis.' James almost spat out the term. 'And I repeat, he no longer has any official connection at all. It was all over the nets. Didn't you see it?'

Arm Wild finally spoke. 'Michael Gilmore has offspring on SkySpy.'

James's regret was very well acted. 'So do many men and women. I'm sorry, Madam Co-Senior, Arm Wild, but if you are to employ the services of my marines, this meeting will have to discuss matters that are officially classified as secret on UK-1. We have no objection to sharing these secrets with highly placed individuals in the government and Navy of the Commonwealth, but we do object strongly to sharing them with civilians.'

Arm Wild may have been about to speak, but Gilmore had already got the message. More important, he sensed that the other Rusties around the table had got it too. James was appealing to hierarchy, to precedent, to the Proper Way of Doing Things, and that was how you swayed a Rustie's feelings. And Arm Wild, like any good First Breed Senior, would be swayed by what his juniors felt.

Anyway, if James's marines could get to SkySpy and maybe help establish whether or not Joel was still alive, and use of those marines depended upon Gilmore's withdrawal, he wasn't going to stand in their way.

'Forget it,' he said. He stood up abruptly and nodded at duPont and Arm Wild. 'I apologize if I've inconvenienced the meeting and I withdraw.'

He turned and walked out, seething, and was only dimly aware of the renewed gaze of Lieutenant McCallum, RM.

Gilmore leaned against the balustrade of the terrace, his back to the white layered bulk of the Admiralty Building, gazing out to sea. It had been four hours. How much longer?

Does it matter? said a still, small voice. *It's not as if you'll be able to do anything.* Gilmore scowled. That voice was an old, old friend. He had thought he had bid it goodbye four years ago.

All his life, he had been plagued with self-doubt, but at the end of the Roving Mission, he had thought he had finally laid the ghost. He had had four years as head of the Navy, full run of the roost, able to do as he liked. And he had set up his own chain of command so that the Navy could be run with due procedure: an Admiralty, with a proper hierarchical structure, and a Space Ministry to advise the leaders of the Commonwealth on space matters and to link the politicians with the Navy under their command.

All well and good, except that Arm Wild, being a Rustie, far preferred to deal with people he knew. That was *Rustie* procedure. He would happily bypass every mechanism Gilmore had set in place to advise him and approach Gilmore directly. It was annoying for Gilmore, who was acutely aware of the sensibilities of the people Arm Wild was ignoring, and it was frankly insulting for the Space Minister and Admiral Chase, so Gilmore had forced the issue by resigning. As far as he had heard, Arm Wild now toed the line, going through the appropriate channels. It was too early to tell if Gilmore had lost a friend in the process.

Now he was out of the chain of command and powerless, just when he badly needed power. He hadn't just shot himself in the foot, he thought, he had blown his leg off below the knee.

He wasn't going to move from the terrace until he found out what was happening, and his mind was racing with alternative plans of his own. He looked over at the launch promontory and the assembled detritus of the Roving's old space programme. And there, the centrepiece of the collection and its newest addition, was *Ark Royal,* the ship he had commanded when he brought Prince James to the Roving. One ship among the many sent by the Earth nations in a quest, it had turned out, to provide the Rusties with new masters following the extinction of the Ones Who Command. Gilmore never liked to overplay his own role in events, but it had to be said he had had a hand in persuading the Rusties not to take on *any* human nation as their new masters but instead to recruit their services on, yes, a *consultancy* basis, and to set up the Commonwealth instead. No wonder King James had a dislike of consultancy in general and Gilmore in particular.

But *Ark Royal,* Earth's technological state of the art, had been bought by the Navy so that the technicians of both species could work out how to integrate their respective technologies. *Ark Royal* was the spiritual parent of *Pathfinder* and every other Human/First Breed vessel in the Navy. He remembered the day it had been brought down from orbit, supported by antigravity generators, lowered down to ground level as gently as an elevator car to touch the surface of a planet for the first and last time.

And now he was fantasizing. If *Ark Royal* could be lifted back up again, it might still be spaceworthy. The fuel tanks were still there and just needed topping up somehow. The fusion engine could be made serviceable. There would be a few miles of optic cabling that needed re-laying ... but if he could get that and if some other ship could open up a step-through point for him and if he could find a crew then he could get his old ship to SkySpy . . .

God, he was desperate, he thought with a wry smile, and then the smile vanished. He *had* to get to SkySpy. It wasn't a joke.

'Commodore?' said a woman's voice behind him, nervous, hesitant. He turned and saw the woman marine there. One part of Gilmore's mind mentally appraised her: hair so dark it was black, cut short enough to fit into a helmet; blue eyes; not bad looking, though the profile could perhaps look a little severe.

Another part of his mind added that she was indeed about Joel's age, which meant she was young enough to be his daughter. She took a half step forward, stopped.

'I'm, um, I'm Donna,' she said. He detected a faint Kiwi tang in the words.

Marine formality certainly isn't what it was, Gilmore thought. 'I'd guessed you weren't Lieutenant Peter,' he said.

'No, he's Baker Platoon.'

'And what happened to him?'

'Broken leg. He fell down some steps.'

'Must have been a bad fall,' Gilmore said sympathetically.

'Two flights of them,' she added. 'He, um, just kept on falling.'

She still seemed hopeful, as if he should be responding in some different way. He couldn't work out what.

'So,' he said, 'is the meeting over?'

She hesitated for a beat more, then suddenly drew herself up to a far more formal pose. 'Yes, sir. *Pathfinder*'s still in the middle of a refit, but they're bringing it forward and she leaves day after tomorrow with official observers from the Earth nations and us. And I, um, I just wanted to, um, pass on my, um, sympathies regarding your son on SkySpy, sir.'

'Thank you,' Gilmore said mildly. 'But as your employer pointed out, I'm not the only parent in this situation.'

'You're the only one who knows about it, sir. Officially, SkySpy is simply out of contact, possibly due to a failure in the step-through generator, and *Pathfinder* is going to investigate.'

'Sixty marines should certainly be able to fix a faulty step-through generator,' Gilmore agreed. 'Tell me, Lieutenant—'

'Donna? We'd best get to the boat. We've got platoons to mobilize.' Captain Perry had come up behind his subordinate and he was looking at Gilmore with something not far removed from hostility. 'Don't worry, *Mr* Gilmore. We'll find your son for you.'

'That's very kind,' Gilmore said with a fixed smile and not the slightest friendliness. 'What makes you think I'm not coming with you?'

Perry's answering smile was condescending and equally unfriendly. 'Your friend Arm Wild will tell you all about that, sir. His Majesty laid down certain conditions for our inclusion on this mission and, well, people like you featured in the small print.'

Perry, Gilmore deduced, was the king's man.

'And what sort of people am I like?' he said.

'Civilians,' Perry said.

'Oh, that sort of people.' Gilmore boiled inside but his tone was bland. 'Out of interest, if your platoons have yet to mobilize, what are you doing down here wasting time when you should surely be with *your* people?'

'We were required at the meeting,' Perry said frostily.

'I saw.' Gilmore couldn't help grinning and he hoped Perry found it offensive. 'King James just loves to show off his officers, regardless of how much it interferes with their actual duties. Perhaps we can get together some time, we could share a beer and I'll tell you about the number of times he shoved his oar in during the Roving mission . . .' He suspected strongly that Perry agreed with him completely, but wasn't going to say so if it involved criticizing the king. 'Anyway, give my regards to His Majesty, and tell him how delighted I am we actually see eye to eye on something at last.'

'Oh?' Perry looked immediately wary.

'Sending a gunboat,' Gilmore said. 'The definitive answer of the British Empire whenever the natives started getting uppity.'

'Oh.' Perry seemed to lose interest in the matter. 'Come on, Donna.'

They turned away and Donna McCallum gave Gilmore a final glance so intense it could have been a telepathic signal. Gilmore was left with the lingering feeling that he had an ally, and he couldn't for the life of him think why.

Well, he could worry about that later. Joel was worry number one at the moment and, as a kind of sub-worry, there was the matter of getting onto *Pathfinder*.

He took his aide from his belt and looked at it.

'Don't do it to yourself, Mike,' he muttered. 'You're miserable enough as it is.'

But what the heck . . .

It was pleasantly shady beneath the trees but Gilmore wasn't there because it was cool. He just wanted somewhere where the display of his aide wouldn't be wiped out by the glare of the sun.

'Retrieve report,' he said. He screwed up his brow in thought. 'Can't remember the name. Report is pre-Commonwealth, about ninety years ago, details contact with the beings of Sample World Four.'

'*Please wait,*' said the aide. A moment later: '*Two reports are found matching your criteria. Author: Sigil Measure Lantern of the Ones Who Command. Full report and digest are available.*'

'Digest,' said Gilmore. He sat on the ground and read.

The story he knew so well: he could have recited it like he could once have recited a nursery tale to Joel. A squadron of prideships entered an unexplored solar system and noted signs of intelligent life on two worlds. Hope flared in the hearts of the Ones Who

Command who led the squadron, and of the First Breed who crewed the ships. The mission to find a replacement for the Ones Who Command, to be new masters for the First Breed, was running out of time. Even the best candidate race they had found so far was far from ideal.

The two worlds were the second and third planets of the solar system and they were dubbed Sample Worlds 4 and 5, respectively. Sample World 4 was detected first because it was emitting radio signals. Sample World 5 was radio-silent, and from orbit the ships detected signs of a pre-industrial civilization. The world was metal-poor and they didn't see it ever developing a decent level of technology, so they decided to concentrate their attentions on Sample World 4. The Pre-Contact Team began the task of deciphering their transmissions and learning their languages. They soon worked out that Sample World 4 was recovering from a near-catastrophic war.

The first nuclear explosion on the surface of Sample World 5 took the team completely by surprise. Their first reaction was to reassess the technological capability of the inhabitants: had they somehow managed to be a stone-age but nuclear-capable society? But the next twenty nuclear explosions, scattered at random over the surface, showed what was really happening. A stream of primitive liquid-fuelled missiles was heading from Sample World 4 to Sample World 5. The missiles had taken years to reach their destination and must have been launched before the prideships arrived. They took one on board to study it and found it to be quite unsophisticated.

Should they intervene? Should they stay unobserved? They debated at length, but the problem was solved for them when the stream of rockets suddenly ceased. Sadly it was only because the inhabitants of Sample World 4 were refining their rocket technology to a higher degree.

The new rockets were bigger, faster, multi-stage devices that made the journey between worlds in half the time. However, they did *not* have nuclear bombs on board. Their payload was observation satellites. The rockets reached Sample World 5 and deployed their load into orbit so that a network of satellites covered every inch of Sample World 5's surface.

And then Sample World 4 launched another salvo of nuclear warheads. Faster, better, they took only months to reach their target and it was clear that the satellites were guiding them onto the cities of Sample World 5.

This time the observers had no compunction about interrupting the stream of missiles. They took out as many as they could with lasers before they could get anywhere near their target, and the leading One Who Commands authorized the First Breed to send down landers to Sample World 5 to offer what assistance they could.

Unfortunately, the people of Sample World 5 by now were extremely suspicious of anything coming out of the sky. They mobbed the landing parties, and one lander was actually disabled by a rock flung from a catapult. The crew was massacred. The First Breed quickly pulled out and resolved to limit their well-doing to intercepting any more bombardments.

If only. Now Sample World 4's attention was given to building a fleet of crewed ships, and their destination was all too clear. The Ones Who Command had no choice but to withdraw and watch, or be discovered.

The crewed vessels took half a year to reach Sample World 5. The fleet of ships arrived in orbit, waited until they were in position, then began a systematic bombardment of every centre of population they could find. Even when the clouds of debris thrown up by the bombardment obscured the surface of Sample World 5, they kept firing until their stocks were depleted.

The attack fleet seemed to have been on a suicide mission, as the ships all blew themselves up once their job was done.

The Ones Who Command quietly crossed the xenocides off the list of possible candidates to replace them. Ever hopeful, they sent one of the prideships down to make a thorough survey of Sample World 5. Its crew spent a week on the surface and its One Who Commands commander pronounced the planet lifeless. The inhabitants of Sample World 5 were extinct.

It was like hearing the Easter story again: a familiar, oft-told tale but ever able to deliver a punch. Glumly, Gilmore finished the report.

Recommendations

Technologically, Sample World 4 is not far behind us. We expect them to be able to leave their solar system within another century.

A permanent observation station is to be left in the solar system of Sample World 4 so that we can continue to observe and assess their technological capabilities. A list of possible sites for this station is included in the attached Appendix. The First Breed should be capable of crewing this station on their own until such time as our replacements are found.

We recommend that *no contact* be made with Sample World 4.

Sigil Measure Lantern
Senior, Replacement Mission

The report ended. Gilmore blanked the display and slowly stood up. He strolled to the balustrade and looked out across the white sands to the sparkling sea. It was a magnificent scene and he wasn't seeing any of it.

After the failure of that particular mission, the Ones Who Command had decided to concentrate on one of the runner-up races. A by-far second-best choice, but one that was forced on them. A race of bipeds called human beings. So, without the xenocide, he wouldn't be here now . . .

'Sweet Jesus.' It was a murmur; half addressed to God, half to anyone who might be listening. 'They've got my son.'

And then, almost as an afterthought: 'I have *got* to get on that ship.'

Eight

Day Nine: 11 June 2153

Two First Breed were squaring off against each other in the front yard.

The one had been trotting across the flagstones, sent on an errand it wasn't to know was entirely bogus. The other had come round the corner from the observation tower at exactly the expected time. That was the First Breed for you; obedient to a fault, so eager, so easy to control.

Stand-off.

The watcher was inside the main residence, comfortable in the cool, dark interior. The First Breed were out in the bright sunlight and the watcher was invisible. No-one saw its amusement.

It was too far off to catch everything they said, but the observed bodytalk was easy to read, and as the watcher had provided the grounds for dispute, it was easy to fill in the blanks.

[Challenge]<<My quickening parent never even went into space>>

[Innocence]<<Did I say it had?>>

<<I've heard what you have to say about alleged

radiation damage in my DNA . . .>>

[Innocence renewed]<<I never said anything about your DNA, but I have questioned some of your actions>>

<<You know I passed all the tests! Why do you keep on about this?>>

<<If you would lead the pride then we have a right to know. And if it wasn't radiation . . .>>

[Incandescent fury]<<I have no desire to lead the pride!>>

<<Just as well . . .>>

A nice leadership challenge was brewing. Another couple of days, three at the most, and the pride would have a new Senior.

One day, someone in Capital might notice the rapid turnover in the garrison prides of the island that the humans called St Helena.

This particular dispute had been easy. The First Breed's masters had been wiped out by viral warfare gone wrong, and now to impugn the viability of another First Breed's DNA, especially implying viral action, was the worst insult. The DNA of the First Breed who was now on the wrong end of the exchange was quite healthy and sound, but it *was* at the lower end of the acceptability parameters due to some purely harmless retroviruses. Immediately the watcher had read its file, it had known that the subject would be sensitive. And given that this First Breed was so vehement about *not* having radiation damage . . . well, the natural suspicion of the other pride members did the rest. If the damage wasn't caused by radiation, it must be viral.

March Sage Savour, last of the Ones Who Command, turned away from the window with a sudden surge of self-disgust. Its life-support bubble carried it back into the building's interior. It was reduced to playing on the natural fears of its servants when once it had led a planet.

The bubble entered the emptiness of what should have been a Commune Place. There should have been others of March Sage Savour's kind with whom it could bond, socialize, be with. But there were no more and it had the place to itself. Statues and sculptures lined the walls, of which it was quite proud. March Sage Savour couldn't leave the bubble but it had got quite proficient at directing the carving remotely, with lasers. It was a new style. When did any First Breed create a new style? A half-finished work took up the centre of the room.

But now the bubble carried March Sage Savour over to the nearest comms console. It wasn't in the mood for art. Maybe there would be a friendly voice to fight off the sudden depression.

March Sage Savour wasn't a natural politician. Its first inclination, its first talent as a cub, had been towards sculpture. As the Ones Who Command died off and the mission to replace them became more and more urgent, no-one could afford the luxury of an artist's life. So it had been drafted into the Space Service, then discovered to its surprise that it was quite good at the job. It ended up as the Senior of a prideship with a crew of First Breed.

Then there hadn't even been enough Ones Who Command left to spare for space duty and they had all withdrawn to the Roving. When there were only five remaining, and March Sage Savour was most senior, the humans had been invited to this world.

Now there was only one left, and the humans were in charge.

Contact with the outside world was heavily regulated – things hadn't quite developed as the Ones Who Command had planned, and the Roving's new leaders had no intention of letting March Sage Savour try to rectify the situation – but possible. Messages were allowed, the last of an intelligent species couldn't just disappear into the darkness without a lot of people taking interest. And because March Sage Savour wasn't naturally political, it had taken a while for the fact to sink in that some of the messages had more than one level of meaning.

Friendly greetings, innocent correspondence ... yes. But something else too. The slightest of hints, heavily veiled offers of help ... March Sage Savour wasn't entirely alone. Even the First Breed weren't entirely united behind their new friends – though most of their opposition was in the form of grumbles followed by shrugging obedience – but the humans! A more back-stabbing race March Sage Savour had never seen in all his years of space duty.

So, there was a long way to go from where it now stood to reclaiming the planet, but help was there if only ...

Then, two days ago, March Sage Savour had stood

just here by the console and a glyph on the display had caught its attention. *SkySpy!* The word had seemed to blaze, to fill the display with urgent, screaming fury.

Oh yes. March Sage Savour remembered SkySpy.

For a moment, now, it just stood in reverie, remembering its space days. The mission to Sample Worlds 4 and 5. The attack. The xenocide. The landing on the Dead World, and what they had found there.

March Sage Savour had really hoped to die before this day.

But, who was that human artist? Apparently quite a famous one, whose work had never really appealed to March Sage Savour, but whose philosophy had? The human had taken a discarded, twisted chunk of marble, saying that there was some kind of supernatural being within it. Or something. Well, March Sage Savour could look at this problem like that. An out-and-out mess to the untrained eye, but to one who could see what lay within . . .

The next problem had been to work out how to send some coded messages of its own. It had managed, and plans had been laid. Contact was made with a couple of these strange, anonymous friends-though-they-hadn't-said-they-were. A situation was evolving that it could use. The angel was emerging from its block.

Allowing for antennae, turrets and other bits and bobs that Donna couldn't immediately identify, *Pathfinder* was essentially a hexagonal tube, the length of a thirty-storey building. It stretched from one side of her vision to the other, framed within her visor against the glowing backdrop of the Roving and decorated with items of data projected by her suit computer. The entrance to the boat bay was a rectangular opening in one face of the hexagon at the bow of the ship, and their suits carried them there automatically, homing in on the ship's beacon.

Their equipment had gone on ahead, but for the practice – and, Donna suspected, for the spectacle – Able and Charlie Platoons crossed the mile of space between UK-1 and *Pathfinder* in their space armour. They had been told to stand off while the boat carrying the diplomatic observers came and went, but now they could come in.

'Able leader to all marines,' said a voice in her helmet. 'Deactivate homing sequence, we're going in manually. Able Platoon will take the lead, Charlie Platoon to provide support.'

Oh Perry, you're so predictable, Donna thought. She had already guessed what Bill Perry had in mind and she wondered if you could take medication for an excess of testosterone. 'Charlie leader to Able leader,' she said coolly, 'Roger. Charlie Platoon, implement plan *entrée*, go, go, go.'

Suit thrusters blazed as her platoon's number two section cut their velocity by half and spun round, still approaching *Pathfinder* but more slowly and with their backs to the ship. Shoulder-mounted guns clicked into position on their armour and each marine became a small, armed spaceship, poised to repel any marauders that might try to come up from behind.

Numbers one and three sections accelerated to twice approach velocity and blasted past Able Platoon towards *Pathfinder*. They dropped down onto the ship around the entrance to the boat bay and their gripsoles latched onto the ceramic compound that was the ship's skin. They made a rough circle around the entrance, weapons readied against any foe that might appear from around the outer hull.

A small party of marines faced inwards, weapons pointed into the bay itself.

'Boat bay clear and secured,' said Sergeant Quinlan in Donna's earphones. She grinned.

'Charlie leader to Able leader: boat bay cleared for your arrival,' she said, careful to keep the satisfaction out of her voice.

'Thank you, Charlie leader. Come in after us.' Perry's voice was calm and couldn't be read, but Donna suspected that he had set what was meant to be a surprise test and Charlie Platoon had passed. So, would he be pleased or would it be an affront to his macho pride? Time would tell.

They settled onto the elevator and it carried them down into the light and air and gravity of *Pathfinder*'s hangar. They cracked the seals on their helmets and breathed ship's air; canned, tinged with propellant, essentially what you would expect a hangar deck to smell like. Donna welcomed it. Most of her active military service had been in hot, sweaty, insect-ridden jungles and there were distinct advantages to sterile, controlled environments.

The ship's hexagonal cross section could clearly be seen in the six walls of the hangar deck. *Pathfinder* was the first human/First Breed ship built, and both it and the ships that came after – *Explorer*, *Adventurer* and the somewhat desperately named *Climber* and *Scrambler*, which were still on the builder's blocks – had been built with two purposes in mind, exploration and defence. They were well-armed, well-equipped, long-range starships. Donna knew from inside information that although voices within the Commonwealth had pushed for the development of purely military starships, Michael Gilmore had held back. There was only one known alien race that gave any cause for concern, and they didn't have step-through. And while those voices said, yes, but the Commonwealth might meet someone else, Gilmore had said yes, but there again it might not. But it did need a defence force, and it did need exploration ships that could look after themselves. The Pathfinder class was the ideal compromise, to be used for either purpose simultaneously or separately.

The hangar deck was large enough for four landing boats, but because this wasn't a mission of exploration, only two were in place. Maintenance teams of humans and Rusties were working on them, and Donna watched them idly as the elevator came to a rest.

Two Rusties were waiting for them. Bill Perry said a few words to them, then nodded and saluted, and turned to Donna.

'This half of the deck is ours,' he said. 'Before we start unsuiting, get your people fallen in.'

'Yes, sir,' Donna said, and passed the order on to Sergeant Quinlan.

Two minutes later, fifty-eight marines were standing in neat ranks that faced Perry and Donna. They were unhelmeted but otherwise still in their space armour.

'Well, here we are,' Perry said, with pride in his voice. 'There's a lot of things I'd like to say, but stand by for someone who can say them a lot better than me.' He nodded at Able Platoon's sergeant, who touched a button on his wrist. A lifesize image of King James appeared in front of them. The sergeant touched another control to make the image turn to face the marines, then set it to 'play'.

'Congratulations, men and women of King Richard's Regiment of Royal Marines,' the king's image said. 'This is a proud moment for me, as it would have been for my father, after whom you are named. This is the regiment's first operational assignment and I have no doubt you will be a credit to us all. We enjoy good relations with the Commonwealth, and this is our chance to show them—'

The staccato buzzing of an alarm filled the hangar deck, drowning out the king's voice. It wasn't an alert, just a warning of moving machinery. The boat elevator was in action again, rising up into the boat bay through which they had come in.

'Cut it off, cut it off,' Perry shouted angrily at the sergeant. The king's image froze in mid-speech and the marines waited until the elevator had risen completely into the ceiling of the hangar. Perry looked suspiciously up at it, then over at Donna.

'No-one else was expected, were they?' he said. She shook her head.

'*Pathfinder* was due to cast off ten minutes after we came on board,' she said. 'No-one else was due after us.'

'So what was that?'

'Maybe that's its stowed position.'

'Maybe . . .' Perry glared up at the elevator for a moment longer. Then: 'OK. Sergeant, take it from the top again.'

'Yes, sir.' The image of King James flickered briefly, then:

'Congratulations, men and women of King Richard's Regiment of Royal Marines. This is a proud moment for me, as it would have been for my father, after whom you are named. This is the regi—'

The staccato alarm warned that the elevator was starting down again, and Donna didn't have trouble reading Perry's lips or the single syllable he uttered.

'Cut it!' he shouted at the sergeant, making a slashing gesture across his throat This time the descending elevator had a small landing boat, a pinnace, on it. It came to rest and a single figure carrying a bag jumped out. Donna's eyes widened when she saw who it was.

A human lieutenant had entered the hangar and hurried over to where Michael Gilmore stood, bag by his side. Gilmore handed the woman a crystal which she plugged into her aide.

'Do you accept my credentials as Commonwealth observer of this mission, acting for Co-Seniors Arm Wild and duPont?' Gilmore said.

'Yes I do, sir! Welcome on board.' The lieutenant's hand twitched in a salute, then she remembered.

'*Civilian* observer,' Gilmore reminded her cheerfully. 'No salutes. Where do you want me?'

'I'll show you to your berth with the other observers, sir. Mr Gilmore. This way, please.'

Gilmore shouldered his bag and started after the lieutenant. He slowed down as he drew near the marines. 'Captain Perry, Lieutenant McCallum, how nice to see you again,' he said. Then he noticed the frozen image of King James and gave a twisted smile. 'Ah. Of course. Speech time. Well, don't let me stop you. I'll no doubt see you around.'

He turned on his heel and followed the lieutenant out of the hangar. Donna had to bite her cheeks to stop herself smiling and at least try and match Perry's look of outrage.

'Carry on, Sergeant,' Perry said through his teeth, and as King James started his speech for the third time, Donna let her mind go into neutral while she pondered how even more interesting the mission had suddenly become.

She also wondered if the commanding officer of Baker Platoon had recovered consciousness yet, and whether any wild stories he told about being tripped at the top of the stairs by a fellow officer would be believed.

Nine

Day Fifteen: 17 June 2153

Sixty marines tramped round and round *Pathfinder*'s hangar deck at a slow jog. At a shout from their captain they broke into a fast charge. Then the artificial gravity cut out.

Michael Gilmore gripped the rail of the observation gallery and watched sixty bodies and 240 flailing arms and legs react to the loss of gravity. Those who got it right kept their heads and managed to stay on the floor, held in place by their gripsoles. Those who got it partially right lost contact with the floor but managed to airswim to another surface – floor or ceiling – to latch on there. Those who got it wrong were left flying through the air, occasionally colliding with each other to the sound of swearing.

Artgrav came back on, slowly, to give those who were now fifteen or twenty feet up in the air a chance of coming down without broken bones. They landed with a not very gentle bump.

'That was pathetic!' Bill Perry strode into the middle of the bay and glared around him, hands on hips. His face was flushed from the exercise and his

T-shirt was stained with sweat. 'Maybe we didn't make it clear to you that you are *space* marines! And space marines are just as good in freefall as they are on terra firma. And it's quite possible that SkySpy is still without power, and that means if we have to fight our way in, we'll be doing it in micro-gee and you useless bunch of tossers will be cut to pieces by the enemy.'

Gilmore had watched their manoeuvre as they boarded *Pathfinder*, from a distance, and thought it was pretty obvious that they *weren't* a useless bunch of tossers. Why did so much of standard military practice seem to consist of belittling people's proven abilities?

Someone muttered something that Gilmore didn't hear but Perry obviously did. He spun round on the miscreant. 'Yes, Private Jarnegan, you'll be in space armour and you'll be able to use its thrusters, but to use them properly you have to have a feel for what freefall is like in the first place, and so far I'm not seeing much evidence of that. Lieutenant McCallum!'

'Sir!' Perry's opposite number in Charlie Platoon drew herself up.

'Get your platoon fallen in. Sergeant Cale, Able Platoon will fall in. And we're going to do it *again*, until we all get it *right* . . .'

'He asked if we could stop off in the Outer Belt to practise attacking an asteroid,' someone said behind Gilmore. He looked round when he heard the Georgia drawl; he hadn't heard *Pathfinder*'s captain come up behind him. Andrew McLaughlin leaned against the rail next to him and watched the scene below. 'I had to disoblige him,' McLaughlin added.

One corner of Gilmore's mouth twitched; it wasn't much but it was the nearest he had come to a smile for a long time. His mind ran on two tracks: either/or. Either worry about Joel, or entertain the old feeling of helplessness, that there was nothing he could do, that he had bitten off more than he could chew . . .

A whistle from below, and the marines started their slog around the bay again.

'They keep going,' he said. 'I'll say that for them.'

'You were always against having marines in the Navy, weren't you?'

'Couldn't see the need for them,' Gilmore agreed. *Ships attack ships – who needs hand-to-hand combat in this day and age?* 'Feel free to keep reminding me I was wrong.'

They watched the marines for a moment longer.

'How are you getting on with your fellow observers?' McLaughlin asked. Gilmore grunted.

'How are *you*?' he said. 'You've got a group of men and women who know nothing about spaceships . . .'

'Exactly, and so they're happy to stay in their cabins and talk each other into states of advanced paranoia, and not even try to run my ship for me, which suits me just fine. Apart from the guided tour, you're the first to make it this far for'ard.'

Gilmore smiled, a bit more widely. 'Just making sure the ship's being run properly.'

McLaughlin chuckled. 'On the other hand, I have to

involve them with anything concerning SkySpy. Maybe you could take them a message? We'll be ready to step through to the lifeboat in half an hour. We'll pick it up, interview the crew and get a fuller picture of what happened.'

Finally! Gilmore thought. To step-through to the quarantine system, they had to be at right angles to the Roving's sun and at a point of equal gravitational potential with their destination. Once in position, they could travel light years in an instant, but to get to the starting point in the first place had taken nearly a week.

'I'll pass the word,' he said.

Another silence.

'Mike . . .'

'Andy . . .?'

McLaughlin looked as if he were swallowing a pill. 'Don't take this the wrong way, Mike, but . . . you're a civilian observer, naturally I extend you every courtesy but . . .'

'I have nothing to do with the way you run this ship or this mission,' Gilmore said. 'I understand, Andy, don't worry.'

'It's more than that, Mike. I have to treat you like one of the others and there may be areas I just can't let you in. Do you know, I've got sealed orders?'

'You've got what?' Gilmore said in disbelief. The Commonwealth Navy was run openly; he had always made sure of that.

'John Chase gave me sealed orders, to be opened once we've picked up the lifeboat. I understand they contain various options for how to proceed, based upon what we actually learn. And they're specifically labelled, eyes commanding officers and Captain Perry only.'

'Ach.' Gilmore made a noise in the back of his throat. John Chase was First Admiral and if he wanted to play Hornblower, that was his privilege. 'How bad can it be? I know what this ship can do, I've got a reasonable idea of what the marines can do . . . you're not going to surprise me.'

'Sure.' McLaughlin looked relieved. 'Thanks, Mike.'

'God, they're a shower. Half of them are just in it for the kicks.' Donna looked up from rubbing her face with a towel when Bill Perry spoke; she assumed correctly that he was addressing her. 'They wanted to get out into space, the marines seemed a nice short cut. An interim step for those who can't get into the Commonwealth all in one go.'

'They'll do their job, Bill,' she said, and went back to rubbing. 'They've all been through selection. We didn't just take anyone.' Besides, Perry's summary of why half his marines had joined up quite closely matched her own motives.

'Don't bet on it. Private Jarnegan, master of over-reliance on space armour? I asked the man why he joined up. "To kill aliens, suh!" He thought it was what I wanted to hear. And look at *them*!' Now he was glaring up at the gallery. 'Thick as thieves.'

She followed his gaze and saw the captain and the ex-commodore, side by side.

'Are you surprised, Bill?'

'I suppose not,' he said. 'These Navy types stick together, I understand that. Though why anyone can stomach that man Gilmore . . .'

'You've got a problem with him, haven't you?'

Perry looked aslant at her. 'Donna, the man sold out the UK.'

'Oh, Bill . . .'

'I've heard it from the king himself, Donna. During the Roving Mission he totally screwed up our chances of—'

'Bill, he made sure the Rusties stayed free. Why is that bad? The king and a bunch of fascists were all set to replace the Ones Who Command in their entirety, and they were not nice people.'

'He . . .'

'And he could have persuaded Arm Wild to throw us out altogether; but no, he let the UK stay in orbit and be the port of entry for the Roving, and as a result we've grown rich enough to start a marine corps from nothing. Do you have a problem with that?'

Perry grabbed his own towel and pummelled his head with it. 'You know his problem? He's an idealist and he does what he thinks is right, bugger what's best for everyone else.'

'He . . .'

'He's not a friend of the UK, Donna. He stayed with us for exactly as long as it suited him, he took everything the UK gave him, then he moved on. And because he's the precious *commodore*, McLaughlin's eating out of his hand.'

Donna let him have it. 'You should study your history, Bill.'

'How do you mean?' Perry looked at her suspiciously.

'I mean that on the Roving Mission, McLaughlin was captain of the American ship. He was stuck on the surface during the orbit battle, and Gilmore had to take command of the allied ships and fight off the baddies. So excuse our captain if he's got a soft spot for the guy.'

'Oh, bloody hell!'

'You didn't know?'

'Yeah, well . . . I knew the captain was on the mission and I knew Gilmore was in the fight . . . I didn't put two and two together.' Perry's clamped jaw suggested it was the last time he would make that mistake. 'It just means that if I need the captain's help, I'm going to have work twice as hard to get it.'

'He's not Gilmore's lap dog, Bill. He'll do what's right,' Donna said. But Perry just grunted in answer.

The diplomatic observers were berthed in a cluster of cabins around a central common area, well aft, on the last inhabited deck before the power levels. The idea was that when *Pathfinder* was exploring, its complement of scientists could be closeted out of the way of the crew and be safely scientific to their hearts' content. The observers had been told they were in a special apartment reserved for special passengers, and they probably believed it. Gilmore knew full well that it was generally referred to by the crew as the granny annex.

The atmosphere as he ducked through the hatch was tense and bored. Some of the observers were seated at the central table, ostensibly working on their aides, but the general set of their faces and the silence suggested that maybe they were beginning to wonder if this trip was a good idea.

Oh, it had *seemed* like one; their masters, the ambassadors to the Roving, had jumped at the chance to embarrass their good friends the Commonwealth. Squeezing observers onto *Pathfinder* had been the obvious step, just because they could. But the observers themselves were all too aware that they were civilians who were possibly headed into a war zone. They had seen the reports on the XCs. And there wasn't much they could do about it, or to pass the time in the meantime.

They listened while Gilmore delivered his message.

'The captain couldn't tell us himself?' Toshio Shintani, the observer for the Pacifican government, grumbled.

'Of course not.' Rhukaya Bakan smiled, first at him and then at Gilmore. She was observer for the Confederation of South East Asia. 'He's got better things to do than waste time on us. Thank you, Mr Gilmore. Coffee?' She was sitting nearest to the drinks dispenser.

'Thanks.' Gilmore pulled up a chair and sat down.

'And of course,' she said as she handed the cup over, 'we all have a duty to keep busy writing up-to-the-minute reports for our governments, whereas Mr Gilmore's government can get its information just as well from the captain when he returns. So that leaves him at liberty to wander about in the ship and wish he was still a captain himself. Is that an accurate assessment, Mr Gilmore?'

'It passes the time,' Gilmore agreed. It also spared him from going stir crazy. He saw that Bakan was still smiling but there was sympathy in her eyes.

'I hesitate to put myself in your shoes or to say anything so facile as "I know how you feel",' she said, 'but I have been in a similar situation. I've been cut off from loved ones by war, and . . . it's the not knowing, isn't it? If the worst came to the worst then that would be terrible but at least you'd have something to make your peace with in due course. But this way . . .'

'Exactly,' Gilmore said gratefully. 'You don't know, and you dread finding out.'

'It happened with me during the Rangoon Insurrection,' she said. 'My brothers were the other side of the fighting line, all communications were down and then the city was bombed.' Rangoon had infamously been destroyed by a nuclear blast. 'A horrible thing. It had been threatened but no-one thought it would be done. Thousands killed. Were my brothers among them? I just didn't know.' There was a faraway look in her eyes that told of the anguish of that time.

Gilmore's cup stopped on the way to his mouth. It had been the Confederation, her employer, that had nuked Rangoon, in an entirely dog-in-the-manger act when it became obvious that they had lost the city. Whose side was she on?

'And you work for . . .?' he said.

The faraway look was replaced with patient condescension, as if he had asked a very stupid question. And maybe it had been stupid, or at the very best out of place, but he wanted to know.

'Rangoon was destroyed by the extremists,' she said. 'You have to remember that the extremists were totally discredited by what happened on the Roving Mission.' Gilmore remembered: his small part in that was one of the triumphs of his life. 'The moderates are well and truly back in power. I made my peace with the Confederation years ago; my parents were Indian and Indonesian and I was born in Burma, and that mixture of races and cultures was only possible because of the Confederation. I made the Confederation my country because I could see it was the only way ahead for Asia, and now I'm proud to serve it and help it recover from the effects of madmen like Krishnamurthy. Surely you can understand that?'

'I can understand,' Gilmore said mildly. R. V. Krishnamurthy had made his own unique impact on the Roving Mission, but that was all in the past and Gilmore firmly believed in letting the past lie. 'And yes, you can understand what it's like for me. Thanks for letting me know.' He lifted his coffee cup up in a silent toast, and Bakan returned it.

Four years ago he had been on *Ark Royal* and staring down the torpedo tubes of the Confederation ship, *Shivaji*, while two of his crew were incarcerated by the Confederation on the Roving below and two more faced possible execution on *Shivaji* itself. And now he was sharing a drink with a Confederation official, and finding her quite attractive and pleasant. He hoped his old crew would understand. Or maybe he would play safe and just not mention it to them the next time he saw them.

Pathfinder stepped through to within half a light minute of SkySpy's Lifeboat B – an impressive piece of navigation and guesswork as to the lifeboat's precise position. The cries of joy over the radio as *Pathfinder* closed the gap suggested that the survivors of SkySpy were glad to see them. It didn't last.

'You're *not* taking us back to the Roving?' Lifeboat pilot Albarazi looked around the wardroom as if trying to find sympathy on one of the faces: McLaughlin, Bill Perry, Donna McCallum and Sand Strong, senior of the First Breed on *Pathfinder*. The decision-makers for the SkySpy mission. Around the edges of the room stood Gilmore and the rest of the observers. Some were taking notes, many were leaning forward to catch every word. Gilmore tried to keep his own face impassive. 'We hoped . . .'

'No, son, we're off to SkySpy,' McLaughlin said.

'We've been on board for days.'

'Son, you're almost at the generator anyway. And we have to find out—'

'Didn't you hear me?' Albarazi sounded desperate. 'The XCs showed us no mercy. They tunnelled in, thousands of them, and . . . they're animals, sir!' He leaned forward. 'Trust me, sir. Everyone left behind is dead. Everyone. They won't have—'

Gilmore spoke for the first time. 'The report you beamed ahead said Lieutenant Gilmore and—' he checked his aide – 'Boon Round of the First Breed got off the lifeboat and re-entered SkySpy.' McLaughlin shot him an annoyed look but kept quiet.

'Well, trust me, they're dead too,' Albarazi said. Gilmore hadn't been introduced and it seemed Albarazi didn't recognize him. 'The XCs won't have spared them, bloody idiots.'

Gilmore raged. 'Did you see them die?' he shouted.

'Um, no, sir . . .'

'Then we'll make our own minds up,' McLaughlin said, with a warning glance at Gilmore. Gilmore subsided in a fit of trembling that he fought to control.

'Why did they get off?' Donna McCallum spoke up.

'To make sure the banks had been destroyed.' Albarazi sounded surprised she should ask.

'Wouldn't you say that was the right thing to do?' She was presumably speaking to Albarazi but Gilmore could have sworn she glanced at Perry.

'Well, technically . . .'

'Mr Albarazi,' McLaughlin said, breaking into a rising level of tension, 'I'll want a full copy of the lifeboat's log and your personal report.'

'You've already got them, sir. Nothing's changed since I beamed the first report through to the Roving.'

'Better and better. What's your supply situation?'

'Supplies? No problem,' Albarazi said.

'Damage?'

'We took some hits but we've patched them up.'

'Is there anything to stop you getting safely back home as you are?'

Albarazi finally took the hint that the crew of the lifeboat weren't about to transfer to *Pathfinder*.

'No, sir,' he said sullenly.

'Then that's dandy. Our people will check you over but then you're on your own again till you get home. Captain Perry, do you require any further information?'

Perry looked up from the notes he was making on his aide. 'I'd appreciate a look at the log and the report, sir, but no further questions here.'

'Fine. Mr Albarazi will be escorted back to the lifeboat and we'll open our sealed orders.' McLaughlin looked apologetically around at the observers, but spoke in the general direction of Gilmore. 'And we'll be doing that on our own.'

'Commodore?'

Gilmore stopped in the passageway and looked around. 'That's Mr Gilmore,' he said, 'as your superior likes to point out. Um –' *well*, he thought, *while she's here* – 'that point you made about my son . . . thank you.'

Donna McCallum looked abashed. 'I just thought it needed saying,' she said. 'I'd be proud of him.'

Gilmore really didn't need advice on paternal feelings and his gratitude only stretched so far. 'I've been proud of him for a long time,' he said shortly. He might screw up everything else but he could at least *feel* properly. 'Anything else I can do for you, Lieutenant?' *She's only trying to be friendly*, said a little voice inside him, but he told it to shut up.

She flushed. 'No, sir. Nothing else. Sorry to have bothered you.' She turned and marched down the passageway, and Gilmore stared after her in frank bewilderment.

Andrew McLaughlin, Bill Perry and Sand Strong were left together in the wardroom, their aides on the table in front of them. Statistics extracted from the lifeboat log flashed in front of them.

'Thousands of 'em.' McLaughlin was derisive as he recalled Albarazi's assessment of the attacking force. 'A couple of hundred, tops.'

'True.' Sand Strong looked up from the display. 'But they have had two weeks to bring in reinforcements by more conventional means. Big ships, uncamouflaged.'

'SkySpy would have noticed a large force building up and there's nothing here to suggest it did. Assuming this is a reasonably accurate assessment of big ship deployment at the time of attack . . . there's no more than two or three at the most that could have got out to SkySpy orbit in the time they've had. Assume three ships, assume max crews of two hundred and a further, oh, one hundred fighting force equivalent to your marines on each . . .'

'Six hundred crew, occupying force of three hundred on the rock,' Perry said. 'But that's still a lot for my sixty marines to contend with. And three ships could have a lot of firepower.'

'Even so. SkySpy's a big place, it's unpowered, they don't know the layout; if I were them I'd be paranoid about booby traps so I'd be proceeding slowly and our assessment of numbers is probably way on the generous side. I doubt there's that many and I doubt they've secured half of it.'

'So we take the other half, sir?'

'Possibly.' McLaughlin drummed his fingers twice on the table and looked Perry in the eyes. 'Activate log, input audio. Captain Perry, is it your opinion that we have gained as accurate an assessment of the situation on SkySpy as we are able from available data?'

'I suppose so. Yes, sir.'

'Sand Strong?'

'I concur,' the Rustie said.

'Then we open our orders.' McLaughlin took a small box from his pocket, put it on the tabletop, opened it. Two data crystals. He inserted the one with a 'priority' tag into his aide. 'Copy to aide of Captain Perry and console of Sand Strong file "SO1", authorization my voice print.'

'*Order executed*,' said his aide.

'File SO1 and duplicate files SO1, open,' McLaughlin said, and their orders appeared on the displays.

The two men and the Rustie were quiet for a

moment as their eyes scanned the text. Then Perry whistled.

'Paragraph three?' Sand Strong said. Perry nodded.

'Keep going, son,' said McLaughlin. 'It *really* gets interesting further on.'

Ten

Day Eighteen: 20 June 2153

One moment there was nothing beyond the asteroid but black space pricked with a million little points of light. Barabadar was pulling herself down the line that connected her ship and the rock, and then a sphere of nothingness blossomed out of the nothing beyond the asteroid. It was like a mouth opening in the fabric of space itself.

Voices were already shouting in her earphones and battle hormones flooded into her system. *This is it!* The thought was intoxicating, and here she was halfway between either of the places she could actually do some good. She quickly began to climb back up the line, never taking her eyes off the sphere. It hurt the eyes to look at it; they registered *something* and yet there was nothing there to register. It might be very large and thousands of miles away, or much smaller and right in front of her eyes.

Then a cluster of small objects shot out of it. The sphere vanished behind them and Barabadar's immediate thought was, *Missile attack!*

'Take countermeasures,' she said, but even as she

did she saw she was mistaken. They weren't aimed at the asteroid, they were bracketing it on all sides. Barabadar's suit reported it was unable to get a lock on any of them and so it was impossible to tell how far away they were, but her hunter's eyes had already made the calculation. Perhaps a mile away but on a course that would take them past the rock. Definitely not an attack.

But one of them was heading directly towards her ship. The defences automatically opened up and fiery plasma erupted all around the intruder. It swerved – *swerved*, Barabadar noted – to dodge the gunfire and carried on. The ship's guns reacquired it, someone with initiative predicted its course and aimed slightly ahead. The gunfire connected and it vanished in an explosion of debris.

The others remained and a small nuclear burst from a torpedo flashed next to one. It began to spin, its system disabled by the electromagnetic pulse, and laser fire converged on it, tearing it to shreds.

'No nuclear torpedoes!' Barabadar shouted. 'There are unshielded personnel in the vicinity including me!'

Now the probes were abreast of the rock but showing no sign of changing course, apart from dodging the fire of the other ships.

'*My Mother.*' First Son, on her ship, spoke in her earphones. '*They're sending out signals. They're spying on us.*'

Of course they are, idiot. It was what Barabadar would do herself if she was in the position of the coming outlander commander: first get intelligence, and use unmanned probes to do it. And if you could open holes in space, intelligence-gathering entered a whole new dimension.

Every fighting instinct screamed at her to let loose with everything she had against the enemy and she had to remind herself angrily that she *wanted* the outlanders to come. And she wanted them to come peacefully. She didn't want to provoke them and bring their anger down on Homeworld.

But she did want to challenge them to the Ritual of Contested Land – *this* battle with the extraterrestrials would be done properly – and there was no point in making their lives too easy.

'Jam them,' she ordered. The probes were over the rock's horizon, heading towards the sun, and Barabadar could no longer see them. 'Relay radar image to my suit,' she said, and the picture appeared in her mid-vision. 'All guns, plot the convergence of their trajectories and target. Fire on my command.'

The probes had come out of that sphere thing and then moved apart. So, if they were going to be picked up again, they would presumably go back through another sphere, which would mean moving back together . . .

Sure enough, they were converging, and then another sphere opened in space in front of them.

'Fire!'

Most of the probes exploded in balls of flaming gas and fragments and only one made it into the sphere just before it closed up again. It had taken just seconds, but the battle had begun and Barabadar felt herself charged, ready for action. It would be good.

'All ships and soldiers to battle stations,' Barabadar said. 'First Son, I'm coming back up.'

The observers sat around the table in the granny annex and waited. Every now and then someone would open their mouth as if to say something like, 'Surely it must have happened by now,' but the hostile glares from their neighbours would make them stop before they started.

Michael Gilmore willed his fingers to stop drumming on the chair arm. The nervous twitch transferred itself to his left leg, and to keep that still he started drumming his fingers again. *Pathfinder* had moved forward a mile and opened another step-through point. The surviving probe had shot out into space and the point closed behind it. Data had flooded into *Pathfinder*'s computers. Now it just needed sorting out, tabulating, classifying . . . and acting upon.

The hatch opened and Andrew McLaughlin ducked into the cabin.

'I wanted to say this personally,' he said. His face was impassive and he wasn't meeting anyone's gaze as he held up his aide. 'OK, from the top. All but one of the probes were destroyed. The surviving probe received response to its hails from thirty-eight translator units and twenty-five aides, all in standby mode. It did not receive responses from the translator unit of Boon Round of the First Breed or the aide of

Lieutenant Joel Gilmore. Add that to the fact that Lifeboat A didn't respond either . . .'

McLaughlin stopped, looked up and grinned at Gilmore. 'I think we can assume they got away. Congratulations, Mike.'

It was as if a mighty pressure he hadn't known was there burst inside him, and relief flooded throughout his system. Gilmore realized to his horror that his eyes might be blurring and he blinked once, hard, to stop them. He didn't dare meet anyone's gaze but he heard a murmur going around the table, a pleased mumble from those observers who actually cared.

Rhukaya Bakan was holding out a hand. He took it and shook, and looked up into her smiling eyes.

'I'm very happy for you,' she said, and sounded it.

'In terms of alien presence,' McLaughlin said, 'probe detected three ships matching the description of the kind that attacked SkySpy, and two larger, conventional vessels.'

'So, what next?' said the observer for the South American Combine, who obviously couldn't care less about Joel.

'Since Lieutenant Gilmore and Boon Round aren't being held on SkySpy, so far as we can tell, that gives us more freedom of action. We still need to ascertain that the memory banks were destroyed and there's equipment on SkySpy that needs retrieving.' Gilmore brought his head up suddenly at the latter announcement, and it was noticeable – to him – that McLaughlin wasn't looking at him any more. 'So,' McLaughlin finished, 'we send in the marines.'

'Action!' said the Slavic Commonwealth observer. She seemed to approve.

'What equipment?' Gilmore said, and the pained look on McLaughlin's face almost made him regret asking. *I have to treat you like one of the others and there may be areas I just can't let you in . . .*

'Equipment vital to the interests of the Commonwealth, Mr Gilmore.'

'What equipment?' said Bakan.

'The precise details are restricted to the higher levels of the Navy, ma'am.'

'Since when?' Gilmore demanded. He knew the SkySpy protocols inside out. The Commonwealth's greatest fear was that the XCs would discover stepthrough, and there was nothing on SkySpy that was going to help them.

'Since Admiral Chase said so.'

'Oh bloody hell, Andy . . .' Gilmore burst out, feeling sudden panic that there *was* something on SkySpy, something he *should* have known about . . .

But no, there was nothing. He'd swear to it. *Nothing.*

'I'm sorry.' McLaughlin touched his hand to his forehead in a vague salute. 'Ladies and gentlemen, we'll shortly be entering a likely combat zone. All internal modules on *Pathfinder* will be sealed off, this one too. Please do not attempt to leave and do obey any instructions from the flight deck immediately. We'll keep the datastream coming so that you can continue to observe from here. That's all.' And he was gone.

'I thought ships depressurized for combat?' The European observer was looking at Gilmore as the obviously available authority on spacecraft.

'We did in the old days,' Gilmore muttered. His head was in his hands and he was staring at the table top. *The old days; like five years ago, when I helped save McLaughlin's ship.* 'But it's a cumbersome method. *Pathfinder's* divided into reinforced, airtight modules and the space in between is depressurized. On a ship this size it's more efficient and faster.'

'Look!' One of the observers was pointing at the wall display. Previously it had just shown black space; now a step-through point appeared, expanding to fill their vision. And then it was gone and the SkySpy asteroid loomed large ahead. 'We're going in!'

'Able and Charlie Platoons, go go go!'

Donna had just one last moment to swallow her nerves, and then her suit's thrusters fired and she was out into space and dropping down to SkySpy.

'Able Platoon, make for primary entry point,' said Bill Perry's voice in her ears.

'Charlie Platoon, make for secondary entry point,' Donna said.

On her right, the thirty armoured forms of Able Platoon suddenly blazed away in a haze of thruster gas. They were going in through what had been the bay for Lifeboat A.

Now Charlie Platoon was halfway between *Pathfinder* and SkySpy, falling towards a massive rocky mountain or flying straight at a huge rocky cliff, depending which way you looked at it. She felt her own armour's thrusters come on again, nudging her and her twenty-nine subordinates to their own designated entry point into SkySpy, a maintenance lock just beyond the rock's lower horizon. Thirty seconds to touchdown.

In the Malayan jungles, Donna had developed an instinct for possible ambushes, likely dangers. It might be a Pacifican insurgent, it might just be a snake that had chosen this piece of ground first. This wasn't anything like a jungle but the old instincts could adapt.

'Engineers to the front,' she said. 'Check for booby traps—'

Something blasted into her earphones; a cacophonous crackle of static that made her wince. Shouts told her that the others were getting it too.

'*Able and Charlie Platoons, tell your suits to filter it out,*' Perry ordered. '*Don't take anything that doesn't come from one of us.*'

And there was the airlock. Charlie Platoon's suits retroed, they changed orientation to feet-first and touched down on the rock.

Pathfinder's computers were set to expect incoming radio traffic. They deduced the blast of static was a signal and analysed it. They ran it through the translator programs and, as a courtesy, they piped the result down to the observers.

I am (97%) / This is (88%) / Here is (62%) / Let's hear it for (43%) Marshal of Space/Space Marshal <<name cannot be translated>>. Do you wish to retrieve (93%) / redeem (79%) / extract (42%) / counsel (29%) your <<plural use, formal>> worthy sons? Two of them are not here (92%) / gone (81%) / vanished (72%) / eaten (64%) / forgotten (51%).

Gilmore frowned at the uncertain mass of probabilities and wondered what McLaughlin was making of it. The Rusties had observed Earth for years before making contact, and even then they had had to move among the population to get their translators working properly. The ambiguity in the XC translation was unavoidable but annoying.

He ran his eyes over and over that last line as if repeated effort would extract some last bit of information from the bald facts presented.

'Respond on their main ship frequency,' said McLaughlin's voice. 'First, this asteroid belongs to us; they are not to interfere with our operation. And second, where are our two missing worthy sons?'

McLaughlin had thought long and hard how best to speak to the XCs. The general opinion had been that, like an aggressive human, you didn't respond with platitudes and weakness. To get respect, you just got aggressive back at them. Gilmore shut his eyes and hoped it had been the right choice.

There was a long pause, then a response. McLaughlin must have told the translator to go with the most likely translation and cut out the probabilities.

This is Marshal of Space <<name cannot be translated>>. Is your mother in?

'*My what?*' said McLaughlin.

'His what?' said an observer.

'His mother,' Gilmore said through his teeth. Naturally, the XCs would assume a mother was in charge of the mission. Even he knew that much about them. *Tell us about Joel, tell us where my boy is . . .*

The message went on.

Why do you dispute our capture of this hunting ground? It is clearly ours. Your missing worthy sons crashed on the third planet orbiting our sun. Let us return your other worthy fallen sons to you.

'*Sir!*' The new voice was one of the comms technicians on the flight deck. '*Images coming in from Captain Perry . . . they're bad, sir.*'

Able Platoon had entered SkySpy through the deserted lifeboat bay, and in a cavern beyond it they found the dead of SkySpy.

The bodies had been laid out neatly, hanging in microgravity just above the floor of the small cavern. Able Platoon moved silently among them, the more careless ones bumping into a suspended corpse that would slowly begin to move and jostle another, which would jostle yet another and so on until enough marines had reached out to steady the bodies and stop the movement.

'*You getting this*, Pathfinder?' That was Perry's voice.

'*Affirmative.*'

'*Why would they bring them down here, sir?*' That must have been another marine.

'*Dunno.*' Perry's voice was taut with anger.

'Because they're trying to return our worthy sons!' Gilmore shouted. 'They said so!' Some observers looked at him, then turned away; the others just ignored him.

'*But bear this in mind, people,*' Perry added. '*Just remember what we're dealing with here.*'

'*Sir! We don't show mercy, because we can't expect any, sir!*' It was an unidentified marine who spoke. Gilmore thought: Perry, shoot that fool now.

'*You don't have to enjoy this, Private Jarnegan.*' To Perry's credit, he sounded as fed up with the bloodthirsty speaker as Gilmore felt.

'*Captain!*' someone shouted.

The image blurred suddenly. It swept across the bodies and fixed on an entrance into the cavern.

Two XCs stood in the entrance. The aliens just stood there and didn't have time to move, because with a triumphant cry of '*No mercy, you bastards!*' ('*Jarnegan! No!*') one of the marines had raised his plasma carbine and fired, and the left hand XC's chest erupted with gory vapour.

'The outlander soldiers have opened fire, My Mother.' First Son's tone crackled with battle readiness. Barabadar could read the displays with her own eyes; yes, the outlanders had indeed opened fire. More to the point, they had picked the fight.

So, a fight was what they wanted. Good.

Barabadar spoke the words of the Ritual into the microphone.

'We deny you this land. You may not eat the food here nor drink of the water. The food creatures are ours. The crops are ours. The sleeping and the waking places are ours.' The rush of battle hormones swelled within her as she spoke; the feel of the plains, the light, the wind through her mane. She was defending a barren and airless asteroid with the words that were used to defend fertile, well-watered land but the incongruity didn't bother her. 'We have taken this land and it will never be yours.'

It was done, she was committed. Perhaps she and all her people would die out here in space, but it should assuage the outlanders' anger and Homeworld should be spared.

'All ships, open fire,' she said. 'All troops, the outlanders are to be repulsed.'

'Hold your fire! Hold your fire!' The members of Charlie Platoon cocked their ears as the noises of Able Platoon came over the comms link.

'They've engaged the enemy,' Sergeant Quinlan murmured.

'Keep going,' Donna said tightly. She had heard how the fighting got started. She profoundly wished some XC luck in picking Jarnegan off. A slow, ritual execution would be even better.

Charlie Platoon were much further into the rock; they had entered earlier and they hadn't been distracted by dead bodies. The platoon moved as a unit, its members facing in every direction so that whatever kind of junction they came to, someone was facing that way. The rearguard faced backwards, their suits co-ordinating with the others to guide them on their way.

In some ways, Donna thought, it really was like the jungle.

They just had to cross one more junction and they would be at the computer centre. It was just ahead . . .

A plasma shot rammed into the rock just by Donna's shoulder and debris clattered against her helmet. Charlie Platoon quickly withdrew.

Donna extended her suit probe into the open area. The image it sent back clearly showed XCs lurking in the entrance to one of the other corridors. The one they had to go down.

One of them brought his gun up and the image vanished as it took out her probe.

'They let us get this far and then they pick us off?' Quinlan said.

'That will do, Sergeant.' Donna was crisper than usual. Quinlan had said exactly what she had been thinking. Another explanation was, of course, that the XCs had been prepared to be friendly until Perry's people went and opened fire . . . Well, who could say? They were here now.

She thought, hard and quick. 'I saw four; there may

have been a fifth hiding further back. They'll have sent for reinforcements and we're almost at our destination, so we take them now . . .'

Charlie Platoon came out of the corridor in cone formation, and they came out firing. They spread out into the corridor junction, each moving aside above and below to make room for their fellows, each pouring fire into the corridor that held the XCs. The corridor before them disappeared in a cloud of plasma propellant.

'Hold fire,' Donna ordered. She jetted cautiously forward and, now the probe was out of action, had to peek around the corner of the target corridor herself. Charred remains of XC floated away from her, quite clearly dead. And just beyond them, the hatch to the computer centre. It had been cut open by a high energy tool; someone must have barricaded themselves (himself?) in there.

'Wait here,' she said, and jetted forward. 'Cover me. Keep an eye on all exits and especially down this corridor.' Then she was at the hatchway, and she went in.

One look at the ruined crystal banks told her what she needed to know; there was no danger of Commonwealth secrets falling into enemy hands.

She looked at the ruined hatch and tried to imagine it. Had he come in here, locked himself in, set off the charges and then waited? No, of course not; he would have wanted to set them off and then head for the lifeboat as quickly as he could. So if he had been locked in, it must have been because the XCs were outside.

What had it been like? It might have been the last five minutes of his life, with that countdown getting shorter and shorter as the cutting beam progressed around the hatch. Donna had chosen a profession where she expected to be shot at from time to time; he hadn't. And he had done this.

If there had been any doubt in her mind at all, it was gone. She had waited a long time and looked hard to find the right man, and she knew who it was. She wasn't going to let the XCs get him first.

A renewed clamour in her earphones said that Able Platoon had encountered the enemy again.

'Captain Perry,' she said.

'*Lieutenant?*'

'I confirm that the banks have been destroyed.'

'*Well done. Pull back to the ship.*'

'Can we offer you assistance, sir?'

A pause; either for thought or to fire at an XC.

'*Negative. You've done your bit. Do as I say.*'

'Aye aye, sir,' she said. 'Charlie Platoon, stand by to pull out.'

Four of the XC ships, the four in direct line of sight with *Pathfinder*, opened up their fire on the Commonwealth vessel. *Pathfinder*'s defence fields took the laser energy and splashed it harmlessly out into space.

Gilmore's heart pounded. It wasn't like the Battle of the Roving – the ship he was on this time was far superior to the enemy and everyone on board was well prepared – but that feeling of going into combat was all too familiar.

And this time he was just a passenger. He didn't like the feeling of helplessness. He sometimes suspected that Andrew McLaughlin sneakily regretted missing the Battle of the Roving; now was his chance to shine.

The data feed was humming with information from the flight deck.

'Forward battery, target the lasers on those ships. Take them out.'

'Unable to lock on, sir.'

'Target manually. Go for their laser turrets.' Gilmore remembered that bit from the report of the attack; the XC stealth tech was good.

'Aye aye, sir.'

Three of the ships immediately fell silent. They were the three that had attacked SkySpy, and presumably lasers were all they had, lightly armed as they were for their stealth attack. The fourth ship, one of the conventional ones, began to manoeuvre the moment *Pathfinder*'s own laser hit it. So, the XCs didn't have defence fields; good. It was heading for the SkySpy horizon, and just before it passed over it unleashed a burst of torpedoes.

Someone squeaked; no-one looked round to see who it was. The torpedoes were designed along exactly the same principles as the grapeshot that *Ark Royal* had faced five years ago – chunks of debris designed to smash and damage spacecraft directly, in the airless medium of space where no explosions had any real force.

Pathfinder's lasers picked them off one by one.

'My God.' The Slavic Commonwealth observer sat back and looked around at the others, a huge smile on her face. 'They can't touch us. This is amazing.'

Gilmore had already seen the tell-tale data on the display. 'Andy! Stand by stern turret . . .' he shouted, forgetting for a moment that McLaughlin couldn't hear him.

There were two conventional XC ships in this vicinity of space and only one had just disappeared behind the asteroid. It would take a while for it to come round the other side, if it did at all.

But the other ship emerged just then from under the asteroid's horizon. It came up aft and pumped torpedoes at point-blank range into *Pathfinder*.

Pathfinder's defence fields flared and not one got through. The stern battery opened up and laser fire gouged along the XC ship's flank. Molten steel blazed the length of the ship and it began to tumble, its power knocked out. It fell out into space, away from the asteroid, and didn't open fire again.

The observers breathed again; Bakan looked abashed. She gave Gilmore a weak smile.

'Maybe Katia's right?' she said.

Gilmore grunted. 'We're doing fine,' he said, thinking of the sixty marines out there who weren't so lucky. He had had one man die under his command and he knew what it was like. It was one too many.

Perry and his surviving marines were war machines, their plasma carbines blazing away at their owners' behest and their shoulder lasers under computer control, aiming and firing at anything that moved and wasn't a marine. Perry's philosophy was simple; XC soldiers could work themselves up into a fighting frenzy, and the only way to get past them was to be equally frenzied.

They were deep within the heart of the asteroid. Another junction, another knot of XCs, another fire fight; searing bolts of plasma blazing across the vacuum and splashing into walls, tearing into suits, charring the flesh and fluids within.

And at last they were at the hatch whose markings matched the glyphs shown in Perry's orders.

'We'll have to cut through,' he said. 'Corporal, Private, set carbines to torch mode. The rest of you, spread out, mount guard . . .'

Another XC patrol came around the corner. More fighting while the two marines worked on the hatch. They got through just as the last XC was despatched. Behind it was a darkened room, unadorned by anything except three boxes secured to one wall. Each was a metal cube, four or five feet on a side. Perry checked the glyphs against the copy of his orders that showed inside his visor.

'This is what we need,' he said.

'Do we destroy them, sir?' said Sergeant Cale.

'No, we take them back to *Pathfinder*.' An immediate general mutter of protest. 'And I know they're big and bulky, so now would be a good time to start, wouldn't it?'

*

Barabadar studied the data from the probe that she had sent over the asteroid's horizon. The outlander ship just sat there, apparently not going anywhere. It could have finished off any of the three attack craft if it had wanted, but it hadn't. Nor was it coming for her. It was just sitting and waiting.

Well, it wasn't going to abandon its troops, was it? She wondered what they were doing in there. One lot had made for what seemed to be the computer centre; she could understand that. The other had disappeared into the lower levels. Were there scuttling charges down there, perhaps? Something to destroy the entire base? Well, that suited her.

She still wasn't entirely sure why the outlanders were so determined to contest her victory here. If only the outlander commander's mother was on board! Surely she would talk sense. Was it even possible that her First Son didn't understand the Ritual . . .?

Barabadar vaguely remembered Oomoing's report. It had speculated that the Great Hunt had gone differently on the outlanders' world; different gods, different societies. Surely not *that* different, though; maybe their mothers just stayed behind and gave orders from afar. It was what she would expect of an inferior species, especially one that would rather pick a fight than pick up its dead.

'My Mother!' Barabadar's attention was drawn back to the display; the outlander troops were returning to their ship. Rather, half of them were. Therefore, half the outlander mission was presumably accomplished. The other half was still going on.

Maybe *then* they would retrieve their fallen sons.

It was a hopeful train of thought. Her thoughts raced. They had fought her soldiers . . . but they had spared the three attack craft, and not damaged Oomoing's ship more than necessary to put it out of action, and they had not come after her at all. Maybe they weren't determined to visit their wrath upon the Kin. So much uncertainty; she had to determine their intentions. What better way than to ask? Surely even a motherless First Son would recognize a flag of truce.

'Order all troops to disengage the enemy and withdraw to prior positions,' she said. 'First Son, bring us – slowly – up over the horizon. Just enough to clear the antenna.'

This is Marshal of Space <<name cannot be translated>>. What are your intentions?

On the flight deck, McLaughlin scratched his head. 'What does it take to make you listen, lady? Reply: to retrieve what is ours.'

A pause.

Will you now leave our system?

'Ah, what the hell. Reply: no, we're going to pick up our worthy sons from the third world.'

Do not approach the third world. The place is forbidden to you. We have sent a ship to retrieve your worthy sons and we will deliver them to you.

'Yeah, and I'm Arm Wild. Reply: thank you for the offer, we'll do it ourselves.'

I am Marshal of Space. Approach may only be made to the third world with my permission. I cannot allow outlanders near it.

McLaughlin clenched his teeth. 'This is getting boring. Reply: sorry, we're going and you can't stop us. Captain Perry, how you doing?'

'Back on board in one minute, sir.'

'Peachy. Nav, plot a course to the third world. Engines, power up main drive, all hands stand by to manoeuvre. And keep the defence fields up until we're out of range.'

Barabadar stared at the transcript. The insolence! What gave them the right to roam at will within her solar system? It wasn't enough that they planted an underhand spy base, but to imagine . . . The outlander commander seemed to think he had won a victory, and open access to the inner planets was his by right.

And as for that last line . . . *you can't stop us?*

She was fully justified. The Ritual was still in progress; she could finish this now with the means to hand.

'First Son,' she said. She stared at the image of the outlander ship on the display. 'Open telemetry link.'

Thirty seconds; *Pathfinder's* boat bay loomed in Perry's vision. He had never seen a more welcome sight. Another moment and Able Platoon would be within the ship's defence fields, safe from anything that the XCs could throw at them. He glanced at the three XC attack craft, previously rendered useless by *Pathfinder's* lasers. At the moment they were the only visible reminder of the XC presence. *You didn't get me, you bastards, I'm still alive*, he thought.

Then he cast an eye at the boxes, each one suspended between four marines as they approached the ship. He knew what was in them, and it was frightening. Did the Commonwealth deserve something like that? What would King James make of it?

The good news was that it would be in safe, responsible hands.

A movement out of the corner of his eye, a glare, and proximity alarms went off in his helmet. He looked up just in time to see one of the attack craft, with its main engine on full thrust, smash through *Pathfinder's* overwhelmed defence fields and crash into the side of the ship.

Eleven

Day Eighteen: 20 June 2153

Pathfinder shuddered as the shockwave tore the length of the ship. Those standing were flung violently against deck or bulkheads. The screams of the passengers were added to the groan of the vessel.

Gilmore had been seated. His lap took the impact against the table and held him in place. He gritted his teeth against the assault on his eardrums: the alarms, the shrieking, the shouting over the intercom and all around him.

He pushed himself to his feet – unsteadily, the artgrav was fluctuating – and fumbled for his aide. 'Shut down alarm to this module,' he ordered, and that part at least of the background clamour stopped abruptly. He thought of calling McLaughlin, listened again to the noise from the intercom and decided against it. If the captain was still alive then he could do without the distraction. 'Shut down data feed,' he said instead, and now all he had to contend with was the noise coming from around him. He ignored it and abruptly pulled open a tall, man-sized locker.

'My God,' said Bakan. She stood up, slow and

unsteady, and looked around her. Several observers were sitting or lying on the deck. Some of them were clutching at their arms or legs or heads and moaning loudly. 'Does anyone have medical training?' She was breathing heavily but was looking calmer and calmer with every second; someone determined to get the situation under control no matter what. 'We're going to have to take care of ourselves.'

'First aid and autodiagnostic kit in that locker there,' Gilmore said. He had the pressure suit out and was wriggling out of his jacket. 'It'll handle everything up to and including broken bones, instructions are self explanatory.'

'And where are you going?' Bakan said.

'Flight deck.' He didn't add: 'if it's still there.' He judged that the impact had been almost amidships. The flight deck was amidships, equidistant from bow and stern and from the hull in all directions. It was meant to be the securest place, shielded by as much ship as possible in all directions. But *Pathfinder*'s designers hadn't taken into account the possibility of a midships ramming.

He also had no idea what he would do when he got there. But the fact was, he was a spacer. It was where he could do the most good.

'We ... we were told to stay here,' Shintani objected, and Bakan rounded on the Pacifican.

'Don't be an idiot, Toshio. That was to keep meddling civilians from getting underfoot. Mr Gilmore is a trained spacer and he can do us all a lot more good there than here.'

Mr Gilmore had one leg into the pressure suit. 'Thanks,' he said. 'Could you give me a hand?'

Three minutes later he was through the module airlock and into the ship's airless passages. The artgrav was still wavering and every other step was either too light or too heavy. The passageway was lit with red emergency light, empty and eerie, and the only sound in his ears was his own breathing and his suit's systems. Now he had time to think again, he told his suit to tap back into the data feed.

It was a little more orderly than before . . .

'Get attitude control back . . .'

'All main systems are offline . . .'

'Get external video back online! I want to know what they're doing . . .'

'Get the main drive back and get us the hell out of here . . .'

Not much. But at least the voices meant the flight deck was still intact.

'Marines, what is your status?'

Then a voice that he recognized: the New Zealander woman. *'Charlie Platoon is back on board. We got thrown around but we're OK.'*

'Able Platoon coming back in.' It was Perry, and his voice was taut with anger and a desire to commit violence. *'Three men killed in the impact.'*

The lifts were non-operational; Gilmore wasn't surprised. He resigned himself to a long climb up the ship's ladders.

Halfway up, he had to step onto the deck as a repair

crew of humans and Rusties hurried down past him. Apart from them, the ship seemed deserted. Everyone would still be in their modules.

Two more decks up, and he noticed a change in the light. He climbed one more deck and looked out into space.

'Bloody hell,' he breathed. *Pathfinder* had almost been snapped in two. An enormous chunk had been torn from its side, three or more decks worth. The outer hull had shattered, the inner structures that it was there to protect were torn and twisted.

With the missing decks would have gone optical cabling, command channels, a large part of the ship's integral strength. *Forget it*, said the voice of his old enemy at the back of his mind, as his appalled eyes took in the damage. *This ship isn't going anywhere, there's no way you're getting to Joel, let's just sit down and give up . . .*

For a moment the smooth, velvet black of space called to him. Mesmerized by the emptiness, by the void that so exactly matched his feelings, he took a step forward. He could step out of the artgrav, out of the ship, into space and his worries would be over. He polarized his faceplate so that he could see the stars; they were rotating. *Pathfinder* was spinning head over tail around its centre of gravity. And there . . .

His despair was forgotten, banished to the back of his mind with an indignant yelp. 'Perry!' he shouted. 'Perry, can you hear me? McCallum? Anyone?' The ladder led up through the wreckage; he started climbing with double the vigour.

'Pathfinder *is in a state of emergency. You are not authorized to engage with the command systems of the ship,*' said his suit's voice. Gilmore swore, but because he knew from experience how much chance he stood engaging an artificial intelligence in logical debate, he kept going. He didn't dare look behind him.

'*Caution,*' said his suit. '*Biometrics show imminent danger of hyperventilation.*'

He was at the right level. He swung off the ladder, ever mindful of the torn plating that reached out from all sides, ready to prick a gentle little hole in his suit's fabric. Bullseye; the airlock of the flight deck module was dead ahead, out (thank God) of the damaged area. Another minute and he was through, and into the flight deck. His suit was still wittering about hyperventilation as he twisted his helmet off.

Several still forms had been laid against one bulkhead, human and Rustie. One in particular caught his attention: he couldn't see the features but he saw the four gold rings on the sleeve. But McLaughlin had a crumpled shipsuit to pillow his head and the face wasn't covered.

Those humans and Rusties who were still mobile swarmed over the command desks, fighting to bring the ship back under control. A Rustie saw Gilmore come in. Sand Strong, *Pathfinder*'s second in command.

'Mr Gilmore,' it said, 'you should be—'

'Get Perry,' Gilmore gasped. 'There's a huge great hole around deck fifteen and there's XCs heading towards it.'

*

Colonel Stormer had been itching for action, his men fully prepared, and they swarmed out of the airlock towards the stricken ship seconds after the Martial Mother's order was given.

'Finish the Ritual. Finish the intruders.'

The wound in its side was the obvious entry point. From there they could work fore and aft, wiping out the intruders, removing the challenge to their conquest. It would be good.

Then plasma bursts erupted all around him. The Not Us had divined his intentions. They were inferior creatures but not stupid.

'Return fire,' he ordered. He could see the Not Us soldiers, armoured forms jetting down from the prow of the ship. There was no cover out here. Both sides were in plain view, and who lived and who died would be down to chance and the battle gods. But Stormer had no doubt in the superior prowess of his own gods over those of any outlanders.

Two worthy brothers perished alongside him, their suits torn open by the plasma fire, their contents exploding through the rents into the vacuum. Lives lost and gone for ever, no chance of Sharing, but the ship was too close and the battle hormones were too strong in him for any regrets. Two, three of the outlander figures exploded ahead of him; he would leave it up to the dead to thrash out their differences in the afterlife.

And then he was at the hole in the hull, through it, and in.

*

'Never mind us.' Perry's voice was harsh. *'You're already onboard. Get down to fifteen and provide back-up.'*

In other words, some of the XCs might get past Perry's people and be unleashed on to a defenceless human crew. Gilmore shuddered at the thought but he approved of Perry's thinking.

'Bill, we'll take for ever . . .' That was Donna.

'Just do it! Perry out.'

God, it *would* take for ever, Gilmore thought. The endless passages, ladders, stairs, all still in partial gravity so thrusters would be no use . . .

Gilmore reached for his aide, then remembered he still wasn't cleared to talk to anyone. He grabbed the aide of the nearest human crewman and ignored the automatic yelp of outrage. 'McCallum, where are you?'

'Who the hell's this? We're in the boat bay.'

'This is the flight deck. There's a hatch. A maintenance hatch. Marked . . .' Gilmore screwed his eyes shut, trying to remember. 'Marked something like "hull inspection" or "hull maintenance egress" . . . it's directly opposite the boat elevator.'

A pause. A frantic, horribly long pause.

'"Intra-hull inspection egress hash 407 dash 1?" What about it?'

'It takes you into an airlock, and then you're through into the hull space. You can get right down between the inner and outer hulls, no grav, free fall all the way.'

'We're on our way!'

Gilmore breathed out, then turned to Sand Strong.

'Close . . . I mean, Sand Strong, I *recommend* you close, seal and lock all bulkheads around the damaged area. And the systems down there are iffy so send maintenance crews to check they really are closed, sealed and locked. And you might want to cut the artgrav in that area – it'll save power and make it easier for Perry's people.'

'At once.' Sand Strong was no longer the second in command of a starship but a Rustie – a genetically bred servant. It turned to the rest of the crew and relayed Gilmore's orders.

And then, Gilmore thought, *leave it to the marines.*

It was like the jungle again. A shadowy mass of obstacles, every obstruction a potential threat. But at least it wasn't humid and there weren't any snakes.

Charlie Platoon spread out around the ship, between the two hulls, falling down towards the stern. *Pathfinder's* innards were a blur of support struts and infrastructure as their suit thrusters carried them down towards the enemy. And there were the XCs ahead. No time for finesse.

'Charlie Platoon,' Donna ordered. She would give the order she had always wanted to give in the jungle but hadn't dared: meeting the enemy on their own ground, you just could not afford to get into an anything-goes firefight. The enemy might have planned for that. But here a firefight was all they could afford: the situation was that desperate. 'Fire at will!'

She raised her own gun, eyeballed the commands to her shoulder lasers and let rip.

Plasma and laser fire blazed down the dark tunnel between the hulls. Donna kept her finger on the trigger and sprayed fire back and forth, only just remembering the thruster commands that slowed her down. Some of the squat, four-armed XC figures exploded, others poured back fire of their own. A section of the outer hull exploded right by her and sent her smashing into the inner. Her suit fought to control the spin. She collided with an XC and the two of them spun down sternwards, past the hole and through the firefight. Thruster gas flared in all directions, hers and his; her suit began to settle, and she and the XC fell away and came round to face each other. She sent the commands to her suit lasers just as it brought its own gun up. The front of its armour tore open under laser fire and it died messily, and then she was jetting back up to the action. She clipped a fresh charge into her carbine and opened fire again as she rose to the combat.

Stormer was almost killed by an outlander lurking behind one of the struts that linked the two hulls. The Not Us already had its gun up when he saw it and he was just bringing his own gun to bear when a shot from one of his lieutenants took its helmet visor away. Stormer nodded his gratitude to his colleague and repaid the compliment by taking out another outlander that had been half hidden by a torn section of inner bulkhead. But then the lieutenant was transfixed by shots from two other outlanders, one coming up from around the hull and the other emerging briefly from behind one strut before disappearing behind another. Stormer was dangerously exposed and with a curse he kicked off for a more sheltered spot. Part of his mind registered that he was out of the hull space and into the ship.

The outlander that the lieutenant had killed was hanging in space, its arms flung out, but its feet stayed attached to the hull. And that, Stormer thought grimly as he let rip with another clutch of plasma fire that took chunks off the outer hull and scared two more outlanders away from what had been an advantageous firing position, was the problem. The armour these outlanders wore, naturally enough, went with their ship. Somehow their soles were designed to grip onto whatever material the ship was made of, which wasn't steel. His own were not. He and his men could only manoeuvre with suit thrusters; the intruders could use thrusters and run around, which gave them far more freedom of movement.

Then the wall of what had been an inner cabin came up at him more quickly than he had expected and he had to spend yet more thruster fuel to stop himself crashing into it. It dissolved into plasma and he jetted to one side to get out of yet another outlander's line of fire. He sheltered behind a cluster of cabling and fired back.

Stormer prided himself on being able to get around in freefall; that near-crash had been inexcusable. The only reason could be that the outlanders were finally getting their ship under control, cancelling out the spin. And of course the outlander troops would have their suit computers (he sprayed fire at three more of them, killing one and hitting a second, sending it spinning out of control and maybe killing it) tuned into the ship's computers, so that they could adjust to the changed motion without even thinking about it.

All in all, the advantage was with the outlanders.

An explosion right by his head threw Stormer back out into the hull space again; a gale of fragments and expanding gas knocked him against the outer hull. His grip weakened for a moment and another blast shocked his gun from his hand. It span away down the length of the dim cavern that was their battlefield; back towards the bow, if his sense of direction didn't fail him. Stormer set his suit to follow it but the explosion must have damaged something. It could only manage a couple of desultory bursts that carried him away from the fighting, before the thrusters failed altogether.

Away from the fighting! Rage flared within him. They were his people, he should be leading them; he should be in their midst, to die proudly.

For die he would; he knew that now. The Martial Mother had issued the ritual challenge and, for all their strangeness, the outlanders had responded well. He, Stormer, had failed. The outlanders were on their home ground and they were fighting for their lives. They fought like ... *almost* like Kin, he grudgingly admitted.

'Martial Mother, this is Stormer.' Even to his own

ears, his voice sounded weak. Was he losing air? He couldn't tell. His suit's diagnostics had packed in too. 'I ask permission to withdraw my people.'

No answer.

'This is Stormer. First Son of the Family Dadoi. Can anyone hear me?'

Suit radio also gone. Stormer wondered how far back up the hull he had drifted. It wasn't important.

He had one weapon left to him. He would have to do it manually.

The fingers of his feeding hands plucked feebly at the access plate over his suit's thruster controls. He couldn't look down at what he was doing but he could do it by feel. He found the nozzle of the main fuel tube and opened it. Then he located the nozzle of the reactant feed – the added element that made the fuel combust.

Normally the two chemicals met in small quantities in the suit's mixing chamber, and the exploding gas was channelled into the thrusters. Instead he plugged the two nozzles together, connecting one reservoir straight into another.

His last regret was that though he had left a Sharing behind him, it had of course been before this last battle. His family would know nothing of how he had died, but perhaps they knew him well enough to guess.

His last act was to send a final thrust command to his suit.

The explosion blasted a hole in both hulls.

*

'*This is Perry.*' The marine captain's voice was grey with fatigue and a singular lack of triumph. '*The XCs are withdrawing.*'

Tension on the flight deck dissolved into whoops of joy, humans thumping each other and the Rusties on the back.

'Well done!' said Sand Strong. 'All marines pull back into the ship. Damage control parties make your reports.'

'Sand Strong,' Gilmore said, his eyes on one of the displays.

'Medics report to the flight deck.'

'Sand Strong . . .'

'Ops, get reports from all ship modules.'

Gilmore gave up on Sand Strong. 'Pilot, extend the drive field to include all marines and get us out of here!'

Sand Strong did finally register that someone else was giving orders. 'Mr Gilmore, you must—'

Gilmore grabbed the Rustie's head and thrust it in front of the display. 'Look!'

Sand Strong looked. 'Pilot, do as he says! One light second distance, go now.'

Pathfinder had been damaged by the sacrifice of one XC transport ship. The XCs still had two more in reserve, and one of them was manoeuvring.

It fired its main engine and darted towards *Pathfinder* just as *Pathfinder*'s own drive engaged.

Pathfinder hung in empty space. The Shield was a green globe in the dark; SkySpy and its attendant XC ships could only be seen with the telescope that was trained on them.

Sand Strong, Gilmore and the ship's officers were gathered together on the flight deck. Perry and McCallum had joined them, helmets off but still armoured up. Andrew McLaughlin and the other injured were in the sickbay. *Pathfinder*'s captain had yet to wake up.

'We've done what we came to do.' Perry's face was tired and drawn but his voice was steady and hard. 'Even though it cost us half our people dead and the ship almost blown in two, we've done it. We can step-through back to the Roving and send in a squadron. Or, what the hell, just leave them alone, why not? They know we exist but there's nothing they can do about it.'

'We have reason to believe there are two survivors on the Dead World,' Gilmore said, staring at the desktop, not looking up at the marine. 'We can't go yet.' *Pathfinder* had shown it could manoeuvre. It could still get to the Dead World. It could still retrieve Joel . . .

'Sure we can. We step-through home, another ship steps right through into Dead World orbit and picks them up. And what are you doing here?'

'I asked him to stay,' Sand Strong said. 'Mr Gilmore has proved most useful so far.'

'Thanks for telling us about the hatch,' Donna added.

'That was you?' Perry said. He still glared at Gilmore but there was almost a tinge of respect as well. 'Good advice. Thank you. But you have to see—'

'We are Navy, my son and Boon Round are Navy, we owe it to them to get them,' Gilmore said. A dispassionate, professional stance that surely no-one could argue with, he thought. 'You'd do it for your marines.'

'And I am really sorry about your son, but I lost half my men!' Perry shouted. 'Have you ever taken casualties in the line of duty?'

'Yes,' Gilmore said. Perry really, visibly, hadn't expected that answer.

'I'm sorry,' he said, more quietly. Still with great control. 'But you're incorrect. I wouldn't do it for my marines, and they wouldn't expect me to, if I didn't think we were up to it. And we are not up to it.'

'Captain Perry,' said Sand Strong, 'with respect, this is a ship matter. Orders were to cede to your judgement in matters concerning SkySpy. In your opinion, has the SkySpy aspect of this mission been completed?'

Perry glowered. 'Well, we've established that the memory banks were destroyed and we retrieved what we wanted. So yes, we completed it.'

'And we have a good idea where the survivors are . . .'

'The big momma said they crashed,' Perry pointed out.

'Then you are right. We're in no state to go after them.'

'But . . .' Gilmore said, aghast.

'I'm sorry, Mr Gilmore. Using Captain Perry's method, a fully functional ship can be with them within days. An undamaged *Pathfinder* could get to the Dead World in much less time, but we still don't know how much damage the ship has taken; we still have no idea how spaceworthy we are. We have to get back to dock; that is our priority. And we know that we can step-through straight away.'

Gilmore simmered, but . . . He was gratified to see a look of sympathy from Donna McCallum. In fact, she really looked like she was sharing his pain. 'Right,' he said. 'Right.'

'Nav,' Sand Strong said. 'Scan for a step-through point along the nearest line direct to the Roving. Power up main drive, all hands stand by for manoeuvre . . .'

'Um.' The Nav officer looked over from his desk. 'No response from the step-through generator.'

It took an external inspection to confirm that the step-through generator wasn't there. It was usually mounted on the outer hull, ready to be flown out on its sled ahead of the ship to open a step-through point. But it wasn't there now.

At some point in the battle, an explosion between the hulls in the vicinity of deck three, quite some way from the fighting, had knocked holes in both directions. The explosion had been beneath the gantry that held the generator sled. The remains of the gantry, with the generator attached, were back at SkySpy.

There was silence on the flight deck as the report was digested.

'So, how long until the Commonwealth sends another ship anyway?' Perry said.

Gilmore's question was more urgent. 'Is the generator returning a signal?'

The generator was indeed returning a signal. It was returning the fact that apart from not being attached to the ship it was otherwise in one hundred percent working order.

The XCs had one fully functioning example of the prize of Commonwealth technology, a step-through generator that could take them anywhere, and it was defended by an almost unscathed warship that could probably match anything the crippled *Pathfinder* threw at it.

Pathfinder wasn't leaving.

Twelve

Day Eighteen: 20 June 2153

'And that,' Gilmore finished, 'is the situation.' He paused for questions.

The observers had been invited up to the flight deck, at Gilmore's suggestion in a rare moment of observer empathy. He knew how it felt, being kept cooped up in the granny annex, out of the way and out of the dataflow. They stood in one corner with himself and Sand Strong. Behind them the watch crew hunkered around the central command desk, co-ordinating the repair crews that were working flat out all around the ship.

Rhukaya Bakan was the first to speak. 'So, they have a step-through generator.'

'They have *our* step-through generator,' said Peter Lardner, the Euro observer.

'The one we were going to use to get home with.' The Pacifican, Toshio Shintani.

'Correct,' said Gilmore, who had spent the last five minutes explaining exactly that. He forced a smile. If the great game of life had dealt him the hand of a diplomat, he would handle it.

'I'm impressed you take it so calmly,' said Bakan. 'Perhaps worry about your son is clouding your judgement. We, on the other hand . . .'

Gilmore stared at her. *You bitch!* 'Listen—' he said through his teeth.

Sand Strong spoke. 'Ms Bakan, please! There's really no cause for alarm. It's highly unlikely that the XCs will be able to use it.'

'Oh?' Something in Bakan's tone rang an alarm at the back of Gilmore's mind: it was the 'oh?' of an advocate who is giving a hostile witness rope to hang himself. But Sand Strong would not have picked up on it.

'For a start, a step-through point requires enormous power,' the Rustie said. 'The ships used by the XCs are similar to the Earth ships of ten years ago, pre-contact. Their fusion reactors could never provide enough energy.'

'UK-One came to the Roving using its own power,' Bakan said.

'But it required the output of all its reactors, working in series.' Gilmore added his support to Sand Strong. 'The XCs have nothing like that many out here.'

Lardner cleared his throat. 'Doesn't SkySpy get its power from vacuum energy, like this ship?'

'Yes,' Gilmore said.

'And supposing they get SkySpy's power back online . . .?'

Bakan shot him a satisfied smile, as if to say, 'exactly'.

'That is very unlikely,' Sand Strong said.

'But possible?' Bakan insisted.

'Not impossible,' Sand Strong agreed.

'They'd be starting from scratch.' Gilmore had never had any patience for remote hypotheticals; he despised the mentality which said that cleverly playing with words could alter the facts. 'It took us years to copy First Breed technology, and that was when the First Breed technology had been deliberately left lying around for us to find. They're not going to twig step-through any time soon.'

He could see that he was getting home, at least to most of the observers. A few faint smiles, less hunching of shoulders and crowding forward. They were being reassured.

Most of them. Bakan opened her mouth, no doubt to lay down another clever legalism, so Gilmore got there first.

'And there's much, much more to step-through than just opening a point,' he said. 'You know the two ends have to be at equivalent gravitational potentials, along a line straight out from the nearest star. Starting in our current position, even if they could open a point then they'd end up in deep space somewhere thousands of light years from Earth or the Roving. To be a threat to us, they'd have to establish the co-ordinates of our worlds, then position themselves along a step-through line and—'

'And they don't have those co-ordinates?' Bakan said.

'Of course not.' Gilmore gestured angrily over at

the navigator's position. '*There* are the co-ordinates. The generator takes instructions from here, the flight deck. The nav computers.'

Something about Bakan's expression told him he still hadn't made his point. 'The generator has no computing power of its own? No memory?'

'No, it—'

'Actually . . .' Sand Strong sounded apologetic and he glanced up at Gilmore. 'There is an in-built memory buffer, of course.'

'And would that retain the co-ordinates?' said Bakan.

'It would . . . yes. It would retain the co-ordinates of the last five or six step-throughs.'

Bakan's voice was smooth and deadly. It was almost fascinating to watch as she held up her hand and ticked off a count on her fingers. 'The last step-through was to this place. The one before that was from the Roving to rendezvous with the lifeboat. So the Roving's co-ordinates will be in the buffer. The one before that will have been from when *Pathfinder* last entered the Roving system. Where did it come from then?'

'From an observation station on Sample World Seven. We were bringing in some researchers from . . .' Sand Strong paused.

'Do go on,' Bakan said, very pleasantly.

'From Earth.'

'So Earth was four step-throughs ago?'

'Yes.' Gilmore almost expected Sand Strong to add, 'Your Honour'.

'So Earth's co-ordinates will be in the buffer too?'

'It is not impossible.'

Two minutes ago the observers had been showing signs of relaxing. No more.

'So,' Bakan said. She crossed her arms and looked at Sand Strong. Then Gilmore. Then Sand Strong again. 'What are you going to do about it?'

'Where the hell did she learn so much about *Pathfinder*? Or about step-through?' Gilmore muttered as the little party made its way for'ard, to the hangar deck. He couldn't shake the feeling that Bakan had engineered the whole conversation, to make it reach the point where it seemed a reasonable assumption that the XCs were poised on the verge of step-through. It was disorienting; even more so, when he thought how with a few choice words, she had gone from a sympathetic, pleasant individual – someone who understood about Joel, someone who could share his feelings – to being about as welcome as a leaky spacesuit. The woman still refused to admit that action wasn't possible and she had insisted on speaking to Bill Perry.

Well, good luck to her. Gilmore knew what Perry would say. Unfortunately, Sand Strong's orders were to be co-operative with the civilians so they had to waste time actually bothering the marine captain.

'Our voyages weren't classified. She could have found details on the public net,' Sand Strong said by way of answer. They came to the lift doors and waited. 'As for the technical details of step-through

218

generators, I believe they were made public in your tenure as commodore.'

Gilmore ground his teeth all the way up to the hangar deck.

The smell of fuel, the noise of charging generators – all comfortable and homely to a spacer. Gilmore and Sand Strong led the observers around the landing boats and over to where the marines were checking and stripping their equipment.

'Captain Perry, could we have a word?' Sand Strong called. Perry said something to McCallum – it didn't look like an expression of joy at being summoned from his tasks by a group of civilians – and came over to them.

'Sand Strong?' he said, curt but polite. The Rustie was after all his superior officer. Perry had never expected to take orders from a non-human but he would do it properly.

'Ms Bakan would like to know—'

'Ms Bakan wants us to recapture or destroy the step-through generator,' Gilmore said. 'Preferably before the XCs turn Earth into another Dead World.'

'I would value your military assessment of the situation,' Bakan said with a bright smile. 'Please.'

Perry frowned at Gilmore, at Sand Strong. *I was interrupted for this?* Gilmore did his best to say 'I know, but what can you do?' by means of a shrug.

'I expect my military assessment matches what you've already been told,' Perry said. 'If we were closer, within range, we could pick it off with the ship's guns and wait for the Commonwealth to rescue us. But we're way out of range, so we stay put. Ship's gunnery isn't my specialty but I know that much.'

'A retrieval mission?' Bakan said. 'You and your people go out in your armour?'

Perry snorted: he had yet to learn even to try and be polite to civilians and for once Gilmore was one hundred percent behind him. 'We're, what, a light second away from SkySpy? It's a little out of our armour's range.'

'How much by?'

'Oh, about a couple of years. A light second is a long way on thruster power.'

'Well, we do seem to be exhausting the possibilities . . .' Bakan said.

'Indeed,' said Sand Strong. 'Please trust my professional judgement. The chances of the XCs successfully operating the step-through generator are minimal—'

'But not non-existent.' Bakan looked back up at Perry. 'Captain, please can you tell us all about Device Ultimate?'

Time seemed to stand still. Gilmore, who had no idea what Device Ultimate was, still felt as if the air around him had frozen. Perry had instantly grown a layer of composure that Gilmore was certain hid a core of deep shock.

Even Sand Strong was surprised. Gilmore knew enough Rustie body language to tell that.

'Device Ultimate?' said one of the observers. 'Is he a Rustie?'

'It's not a First Breed name,' Sand Strong said. 'It is
. . . where exactly did you hear about it, Ms Bakan?'

Not on the public net, I'll bet, Gilmore thought.

'It's what Captain Perry and his people retrieved
from SkySpy,' Bakan said. 'Tell us about it, Captain,
please.'

Perry looked at Sand Strong. 'Your orders, sir?'

Even Gilmore was hanging on every word. He of
all people should have known what was on SkySpy
and he was sure Device Ultimate had never featured
in any briefing.

'It's a bomb,' Sand Strong finally said.

The observers breathed again. 'Well, what good
is—' someone said.

'It's more than that, surely,' said Bakan.

'Why don't you tell us?' Gilmore challenged.

Bakan blinked innocently at him. 'And spread
classified information around?'

'It was a safety device installed by the Ones Who
Command,' Sand Strong said. 'We learnt of it from
Captain McLaughlin's sealed orders that came from
Admiral Chase. Where Admiral Chase found out
about it, I don't know.'

There was a long pause. He obviously wasn't going
to volunteer more.

Bakan sighed. 'Oh, all right. I expect my government and the admiral had the same informant. This is
what we've been told by March Sage Savour.'

Another of those sudden temperature changes.
Sand Strong, Gilmore noticed with a sinking feeling,
had suddenly become much more attentive. Rusties

had been created as servants by genetic manipulation, before the Ones Who Command wiped themselves out, and old habits died hard. March Sage Savour in his time had been Senior of the Roving. March Sage Savour had spent the four years since the Roving Mission in exile on an island in the Roving's tropics, while his comrades died around him. But March Sage Savour still clung onto life and apparently he still knew how to shove his oar in.

'March Sage Savour was on the mission that discovered the XCs,' Bakan said. 'He witnessed the xenocide at first hand, and a worst case scenario for him was to have fleets of XC ships pouring through step-through points onto the Roving. He and the other Ones Who Command therefore devised the worst case solution. Device Ultimate contains a highly powerful grav controller. A miniature black hole that can be turned on and off at will. It could be put on board one of your landing boats operating under automatic pilot. It could be shielded and flown into the sun's interior. At full boost, the process could be accomplished in days. The grav controller would cause sufficient fluctuations there to destabilize the sun and cause it to explode.'

No-one spoke; everyone's mind was taken up with the vision. Bakan continued, almost as an afterthought: 'Naturally it has a lot of safeguards, it requires authentication codes and all that to operate, but March Sage Savour gave them to me before we left.'

Gilmore had once unexpectedly found himself in

command of a ship armed with nuclear weapons. That experience, he now found, was far down the scale of possible surprises.

'It . . .' he said. 'I mean, I . . . they never told us about it. It was on SkySpy all this time and they never told us.'

'No,' Bakan agreed. 'They wouldn't, would they? They weren't going to trust a device like that to the First Breed or to humans.'

'Isn't it a bit . . . drastic?' said Lardner.

'It won't cause a nova,' Bakan said. 'The XC race will survive. What will happen is the top one percent of the sun's outer layer will erupt. There'll be a blast of plasma and radiation and a magnetic pulse that will wipe out the XC civilization. Knock them back into the Stone Age.'

'And us?' Gilmore said.

'We shelter behind the Shield, appropriately enough. The planet would take a knocking but we'd be safe. Then we stay put and await another rescue attempt by the Commonwealth – one is bound to come. I have the exact specs to show you, Sand Strong, if you're interested.'

'Millions of XCs would die. All the ones in space and on the day side of Homeworld, for a start,' Gilmore said. He was so caught up with the horror of the vision that it even took a moment for the additional thought to register: *Joel, too.*

'What's wrong with you?' Bakan shouted. Her composure, the calm and quiet lawyerly tones, were suddenly gone. 'They could be studying the generator right now, working out how it works, sending its details back to Homeworld. Even if we recapture the physical item, the knowledge will have spread and they'll . . . they'll . . .'

She caught herself abruptly, took a breath, let some colour return to her cheeks. Gilmore studied her in fascination.

'My God, you're terrified, aren't you? The Commonwealth has always had a healthy respect for them but you . . . you are honest to God, pants-wetting *terrified*.'

'Half the XC population or the entire Earth,' said Bakan. 'It's no contest.'

'Prevent another xenocide by becoming xenocides ourselves?' Gilmore said.

'If necessary.' She glared at Sand Strong. 'You must see that!'

'Sand Strong . . .' Gilmore said.

'The decision is mine to make!' Sand Strong was unexpectedly vehement. Bringing the Ones Who Command back into the equation had been a powerful stroke. 'I am now Senior of this ship.'

And Gilmore had to respect that.

Bakan didn't. 'Your orders were to evaluate the situation and take appropriate action,' she said. 'You can decide to use Device Ultimate, with the full sanction of the Commonwealth government . . .'

'Ms Bakan, be silent or be removed from this group,' Sand Strong said. Then there was a very long pause. 'Captain Perry?'

'Sir?'

'Where is Device Ultimate at this precise moment?'

'Over there, sir.' Perry indicated the three large boxes to one side of the bay.

'Detail a twenty-four hour sentry watch. Armed.'

'Already done, sir.'

'Thank you. No-one is to approach it without the personal, signed approval of myself or Captain McLaughlin.' Sand Strong looked up at Bakan. 'Our orders were to retrieve Device Ultimate, to prevent it from falling into XC hands. We've followed our orders. Now, we will continue to repair *Pathfinder* and await rescue ourselves.'

'And if they work out how step-through works?' said Bakan.

'They will not.'

'But they'll have the knowledge,' Bakan insisted, 'which they could use at any time.'

'We're not a secret to them any more,' Gilmore snapped. His patience with this creature had stretched as thin as it could before holes started showing. 'The Commonwealth will open negotiations with them. We'll talk to them—'

'*You can't talk to these creatures!*' Bakan was all but screaming. She swallowed, gained some composure. 'Captain Perry.' Bakan turned to the marine. 'You've fought them. You've seen what they're like. You've lost men to them, good men, you've seen the corpses on SkySpy.'

Perry was stony faced. 'I have my orders, ma'am.'

Bakan paused. 'You take your orders from Sand Strong?'

'Of course.'

'Yes, of course.' It was obviously an internal struggle, but she mastered it. She bowed to Sand Strong. 'Thank you for considering my option. I couldn't have asked for more. Excuse me, I'm returning to my cabin.'

She turned and headed for the elevator, leaving the rest of the observers, Gilmore, Perry and Sand Strong standing in bewilderment.

Rhukaya Bakan was the first observer to get back to the granny annex. Apart from her it was deserted. She put a hand on the table to steady herself, took two or three deep breaths. She had almost lost it.

But gradually the heavy breathing died down; then her shoulders shook slightly, and then a chuckle crept out of her. In the secure solitude of the annex, it turned into a full-bodied laugh. Yes, she thought, a pretty convincing display of fright and terror. She hadn't expected it to convert Sand Strong there and then, but it should have planted seeds and that was what counted. It was already an unexpected bonus that *Pathfinder*'s human captain was out of the running.

Now for the next stage. In a way it was ... satisfying. To have all ambiguity removed, all alternative options rendered non-viable by a Rustie with a conscience and his liberal human sidekick.

Bakan went into her cabin, took her aide, turned it on. She called up a certain file, a certain program. Told it to execute.

*

'She's a forceful lady,' Sand Strong said. He and Gilmore had shucked the observers and now they walked slowly back to the flight deck.

'She works for the Confederation,' Gilmore said bitterly. *And I let myself forget it. Won't do that again.*

'True. And I must thank you, Mr Gilmore.'

'Thank me?'

'You didn't try to force my decision-making. You respected my seniority. I have to confess I'm insecure in this position – it was never what I expected.'

Gilmore forced a chuckle. 'Tell me about it.' Yes, Sand Strong had eventually come up with the decision Gilmore had wanted, but still the temptation to intervene and *make absolutely sure* it was the right decision had been strong. But the whole point of the Commonwealth was that humans and First Breed acted together. In a disagreement between a human and a Rustie of equal rank, the human won – Gilmore hadn't been happy with that proviso in the Navy Regs but the Rusties themselves had insisted. But to have a single Rustie commanding humans, even making decisions they didn't like – not at all a Rustie concept, guided as they were by group consensus – was something else. In fact, those five minutes on the hangar deck had been the test and proof of the whole Commonwealth concept. Gilmore was glad.

And he wasn't going to spoil it all by praising Sand Strong out loud. It would be too much like a master praising an apprentice.

'*Stand by for a general announcement.*'

Man and Rustie stopped in their tracks.

'I gave no such instruction,' Sand Strong said in surprise.

'First Breed of the Commonwealth vessel Pathfinder, *this is March Sage Savour.'*

The voice rang out throughout the ship, in the bland tones of an early-model translator unit. Underlying it, Gilmore could hear the original speech in the Roving's common language, sounding like someone constantly clearing his throat.

March Sage Savour's image had appeared on every display down the passageway. The head was larger, the muzzle blunter than a Rustie but the common ancestry was obvious. Gilmore had last seen the One Who Commands four years ago, and even then the creature had been decrepit. Now the rust-like skin flakes were worn almost smooth with age, the skin underneath looking dully polished.

March Sage Savour had the undivided attention of every being on board *Pathfinder.*

'I speak to all loyal First Breed on this vessel. You know that the First Breed/Human Commonwealth was not our original plan for the future of the Roving. If you are listening to this then the flaws of the Commonwealth have become evident.

'The xenocides of Sample World Four now have the means to leave their solar system and to advance upon the Roving. Through their inaction, the humans would allow this to happen. There is a device on board that can prevent this. It is called Device Ultimate. For the sake of the Roving and our prides, it must be used now, before it is too late.'

Sand Strong wasn't doing anything other than

listen, and Gilmore couldn't expect more. He snatched at his aide. 'Flight deck! What the hell is happening? Where's it coming from?'

'Tap on the internal comms system, sir.' The human speaker at the other end sounded almost panicked; Gilmore could see him desperately working at his desk, trying to override the override. 'We can't block it.'

'Keep trying.' Gilmore broke contact and listened to the message.

'The human Rhukaya Bakan has the details of Device Ultimate. All First Breed who are loyal to their planet and their prides must turn to her. Disregard the instructions of the Commonwealth; the Commonwealth has failed you. Take the ship and deploy Device Ultimate.

'For all our sakes, do it now.'

Thirteen

Day Eighteen: 20 June 2153

'Bloody hell.' Gilmore shook his head to clear it. March Sage Savour's announcement left an echoing silence around the ship. 'Are you all right?'

'I'm fine, and yes, I still support the Commonwealth.' Sand Strong took off suddenly down the passage. 'But I am not the one you should be worrying about,' he called.

'Oh, God.' Gilmore took off after Sand Strong.

Gilmore had discovered, five years ago on the Roving Mission, that a single, solitary Rustie could be as independent and intransigent as it liked. One Rustie on its own was a challenge to command. But the more Rusties you put together, the easier it became; body language, pheromones and basic loyalty to the pride meant that an idea could sweep through a group of Rusties and its collective mind almost at once. And the Senior was guided by the pride's consensus.

Sand Strong, alone with Gilmore, had been in no danger of being taken in by March Sage Savour's announcement. But it might be a different matter wherever there were groups of Rusties gathered together. The drive compartment, the hangar deck . . . the flight deck.

They turned the last corner to the flight deck hatch at the same time as Rhukaya Bakan stepped out of the lift. She turned towards them with a sweet smile and opened her mouth to speak.

'Get back to your cabin, you seditious bitch, or you'll be arrested for inciting mutiny!' Gilmore bellowed.

The look of surprise was one very small triumph – and it didn't escape Gilmore's notice that she hadn't denied the charge – before he and Sand Strong were on the flight deck.

They walked into a gabble of raised voices, angry gestures and the strong smell of agitated Rustie. The Rusties on watch swarmed in confusion, seeking counsel from the humans who were meant to be leading them. They saw their Senior come in and rushed towards him.

'What do we do?'

'We thought . . .'

'We heard . . .'

'The One Who Commands says we must . . .'

Several weren't even bothering with their translators. This was too important.

'*Quiet!*' The clamour died down and some of the Rusties stood with their heads lowered, in subservient pose. But the rest were taut, tense, ready for action, and they looked to Sand Strong for their guidance. The Rustie walked over to the command desk and one of his graspers pressed a control. His announcement rang throughout the ship and the translators automatically turned it into something the humans could understand. 'All First Breed on board will please report, now, to the Commune Place. There are no exceptions.'

Then, to Gilmore: 'I'll do what I can.' Louder: 'Lieutenant Nguyen, you have the ship.'

'Aye aye, sir.'

The Rusties filed out, leaving the humans looking at one another in confusion.

'Mr Gilmore?' Nguyen was a young woman but probably the most senior of *Pathfinder*'s command crew left fit after the crash. 'I'd, um, appreciate your analysis of the situation, sir.'

'First step, get the software officer to make sure no-one else can tap into the ship's systems like that,' Gilmore said. 'Carry on with repairs. And get a visual and audio tap on the Commune Place.'

'That's private!' Nguyen was shocked.

'Well, call me old fashioned, but I like to know about important decisions that affect me. You asked for my analysis, you got it.'

She looked uncertain for a moment, but then gave the orders. 'Do you think Sand Strong can swing them?'

'He doesn't have to swing them, just hold them.' Gilmore crossed to the nearest display where a security camera was giving a bird's eye view of the Commune Place. A large, circular room with drinking and feeding troughs, but most of all with space for the

First Breed to be with one another, bond as a pride, feel as one. And make decisions. The ship's Rusties were already filing in.

'March Sage Savour's speech was mouthtalk only. Not fulltalk,' he said. Fulltalk was what Rusties used to communicate face to face: body language, words and pheromones mixed together. Remove any component and the result was a lot less compelling. 'Sand Strong's been a Pride Senior for some time, and his clan was the first to declare support for Arm Wild. He believes in the Commonwealth.'

It wasn't like a debate or any public meeting of humans. The First Breed in the Commune Place just seemed to mingle and mill around. A human eye couldn't see any order or pattern in it. Gilmore ordered a computer analysis on what was going on, the gist of the conversation.

Premise 1: the Ones Who Command willingly abdicated their position.

Counter-premise 1: the Ones Who Command gave their authority to the humans, not to the Commonwealth.

Premise 2: we were made to serve the Ones Who Command.

Counter-premise 2: see premise 1.

Premise 3: the XCs may be able to operate the step-through generator . . .

And so on. A hashing and rehashing of the exact position as it now stood, no detail too boring or irrelevant to ignore. The Rusties on board *Pathfinder* were confused. None of them had particularly enjoyed being the servants of the Ones Who Command, none of them wanted to return to the old days . . . but they were unused to challenges to authority. They had accepted human authority in the Commonwealth because they had always expected to transfer their allegiance to *someone* – they had built up to it all their lives. But there was nothing to protect them from the re-emergence of the Ones Who Command.

But Sand Strong was holding ground. He stood in the middle, surrounded by concentric circles of Rusties all facing inwards towards him. It was almost as if his authority flowed out from the centre of the crowd. The pride was deferring to him.

The computer kept a running summary:

Accept authority of Commonwealth: 48%
Accept authority of Ones Who Command: 29%
Still seeking assurance: 23%

Given a simple show of hands, the computer analysis said Sand Strong would win. But Rusties didn't go by shows of hands.

Accept authority of Commonwealth: 54%
Accept authority of Ones Who Command: 22%
Still seeking assurance: 24%

Gilmore held his breath . . .

Accept authority of Commonwealth: 76%
Accept authority of Ones Who Command: 11%
Still seeking assurance: 13%

. . . and let it out again. The numbers were changing before his eyes. Every new convert added was strength to the argument, became another good reason why a doubting Rustie should change its own mind, and add its own strength, and so on. Sand

Strong was going to win, and once the mood changed, it would be a complete swing, exponential and unstoppable. The end came quickly in these things. Rhukaya Bakan, stick that in your—

'Look!' Nguyen said.

Gilmore blinked, stared, yelled: 'How the hell did that get there?'

The software officer was going frantic, hands flying over his controls. 'I don't know sir, I'm sure it's not in the system.'

March Sage Savour had appeared in the middle of the Commune Place.

It was a hologram, had to be, but it added bodytalk to the argument. It wasn't March Sage Savour as he really was, surrounded by his life-support bubble with tubes and equipment plugged into him. The last of the Ones Who Command stood free and tall, lifesize and larger than the Rusties, dominating them not just by natural authority and stance but by sheer size as well. Everyone would have known it was a clever computing trick, but it worked.

And it was talking.

'—another way. The Commonwealth has failed you, but only in this instance. I do not ask you to turn against it, though you know it is not what we wanted. But I do say this. Defend your prides, your friends, your world. Deploy Device Ultimate. Avenge the First Breed who died on SkySpy . . .'

'Got it!' The software officer was triumphant only for a moment. 'Um, it's a local holo projector, sir, must be hidden somewhere in the Commune Place. And I can't get at it remotely.'

'—*and after that, return to the Commonwealth with your heads held high. Return as heroes, and help the First Breed take their rightful place . . .*'

Gilmore set his aide to pick up the speech, and ran from the flight deck.

Clever, clever, clever. Sand Strong had naturally reduced the argument to two positions: support the Commonwealth, or support the Ones Who Command. But March Sage Savour had introduced a third element: support me in this, *then* go back to the Commonwealth. This was a one-off emergency, it wouldn't happen again, so . . .

'Summary?' he said to the aide. He had no idea what he would do when he got there but he had to move, do something. An impassioned, impromptu speech. Wave the holo projector under their noses, show them how they were being manipulated. Whatever it took.

'*Accept position of March Sage Savour: 44%,*' his aide said calmly. '*Accept position of Sand Strong: 45%. Still undecided: 11%.*'

The lift was too slow; he was pounding down the companion ways.

'*Accept position of March Sage Savour: 72%. Accept position of Sand Strong: 26%. Still undecided: 2%.*'

No! The count was changing too quickly, he wasn't moving fast enough. The door to the Commune Place was just ahead.

'*Accept position of March Sage Savour: 100%.*'

Gilmore skidded to a halt outside the Commune Place. '*No!*' He thumped his hand, hard, into the bulkhead. Then he hammered on the door. 'Sand Strong! Sand Strong, open up! You can't do—'

The door slid open. Sand Strong stood there, the apex of a wedge of First Breed.

'Thank you,' Gilmore gasped. 'Look, you have to—'

'I'm sorry,' Sand Strong said. 'I tried. We've decided. Mr Gilmore, I know you're against this move. Please don't impede us.' He walked forward, followed by the rest of the pride. They pushed Gilmore back down the passageway and he fought to keep a place beside the Rustie Senior against the press of bodies.

'For pity's sake, Sand Strong, there's no logic to this! You can wait for the rescue squadron and—'

Two Rusties peeled off and pressed against Gilmore, forcing him back from their leader. Sand Strong kept walking down the passage, not even looking back.

'We can have you restrained,' said one of the Rusties. 'We would rather not because you are a friend to the First Breed, but we can and we will if you interfere.'

Gilmore glanced down the passage. Sand Strong had disappeared into the lift. He looked down at the two Rusties and held up his hands.

'There'll be no need,' he said.

'Thank you,' they said. They turned away and left him standing.

He leaned against the bulkhead, put his hands to his head. 'Come on, come on, I can do this, I can do this . . .' There was a roaring in his ears and he stood on the edge of an abyss deeper, more profound, more final even than when he had stood in the middle of the damaged zone and gazed out into space. This was *it*, he had failed, everything was going to be a disaster from now on.

It was the familiarity of the feeling that saved him. It had been an old friend, once, before the Roving Mission, and had come close to ruining him on several occasions. But damn it, five years as commodore of the Commonwealth Navy had shown him he *wasn't* a failure, there *was* a way to beat it. He knew that old friend and he knew how to thwart it. Just *think*. Think, and the way ahead would crystallize ahead of him. Out of the storm would come a sure, steady path that led to success. That magical word, *success*.

Gilmore pulled his aide out, held it to his mouth . . . and paused. There was no doubt that Sand Strong was heading for the flight deck. He could call ahead, tell Nguyen to seal the bulkheads and not let anyone with more than two legs through . . .

In other words, instruct a junior officer to bar the way of her seniors. *No*.

'Get me Captain Perry,' he said.

'*Captain Perry is engaged*,' said the aide. Gilmore winced, guessing who Captain Perry was engaged with. Sand Strong moved fast.

'Get me Lieutenant what's-her-name. McCallum.'

Donna McCallum's face appeared in the display. She looked surprised. 'Mr Gilmore?'

'Sand Strong wants to use Device Ultimate,' Gilmore said without preliminary. Her eyes widened.

'He's probably giving Perry instructions right now?'

She looked away, then back. 'Yeah, Bill's talking to someone on his aide.'

'You know him better than me. Is he likely to go along with it?'

'He doesn't have to go along with anything. There are enough Rusties on board to work it without our help.'

'But there's a marine guard on it,' Gilmore insisted. 'Can you strengthen it? Bar access to anyone?'

'We could. I doubt . . . hold on.'

The view in the display blurred, then fixed on a skewed view across the hangar deck. It showed Perry from the waist down, approaching Donna. She had clipped her aide back to her belt but left it transmitting, sound and vision.

'Lieutenant.' Perry sounded as if he was sucking on a lemon. 'We've been ordered to vacate this half of the hangar deck. We may keep to our bivouac area but we may not approach Device Ultimate or any of the landing boats. Pass the word.'

'Bill.' Donna's voice was low, earnest. 'They want to use that thing. You can't let them . . .'

Was there the slightest pause? Some indication, any indication of conflict in Perry's thoughts? Gilmore could imagine the façade, the frozen expression, the stony stare of a man determined to obey instructions he didn't agree with.

'We can follow orders, Donna.'

'That thing could murder billions of creatures! Don't tell me those orders are legal!'

No pause this time; Perry wasn't going to take argument from a junior.

'We're not being ordered to do it, just not to interfere. Follow orders, Lieutenant McCallum.'

'Aye aye, sir,' Donna said sullenly. The display showed Perry's legs turn and walk away; then there was another blur and Donna was back on. 'Did you get that?'

'I got it. What else is happening?'

Donna looked away again, then back. 'Ten ... twenty Rusties just came in. Some of them are armed ... the human engineers are being sent off the hangar deck.'

Gilmore closed his eyes. The Rusties were going through with it. They really were.

Then he had another, horrible thought. 'Lieutenant, can you put an armed guard on Captain McLaughlin in the sickbay?'

Donna shrugged, taken by surprise. 'Sure. Why? You think he's in danger?'

'Maybe, maybe not. I do think, I do *know* that he's the only one on board who can legitimately countermand Sand Strong. And I know this whole thing has been engineered by a woman whose employers weren't afraid to use violence during the Roving Mission to get their way and who is prepared to wipe out millions of alien lives to protect her own. One human life isn't going to be a problem.'

'I'll see what we can do.'

'Thanks.' Gilmore looked her in the eyes. 'Lieutenant, the vibes I've got from you are that you're a person who likes to do what's *right*.' He remembered her comments when she attended the debrief of the lifeboat pilot. He had heard the emphasis in her voice when she said *right*. Not what was technically correct, not what was approved or acceptable but what was *right*. 'Using Device Ultimate isn't.'

She smiled, but not with her eyes. 'Nor's mutiny, Mr Gilmore.'

'I'm not talking mutiny. It would be mutiny if the crew of *Pathfinder* got involved . . . but you're not in the crew.'

She looked at him shrewdly. 'I've got duties to attend to. Meet me in the canteen in half an hour's time.'

Gilmore sat in the canteen and poked at the bits and pieces on the tabletop in front of him. Several small gas canisters and an item of electronic equipment. The canisters no doubt contained pheromones, the last piece was a holo projector. Gilmore had paid a visit to the Commune Place and found them secreted in vents, under the troughs, behind the décor – probably planted on the observers' tour of the ship and all part of the plot to let March Sage Savour sway the First Breed. On his second appearance, in the Commune Place, the One Who Commands had used not just mouthtalk, not bodytalk, but fulltalk; words and gestures and pheromones all in one persuasive package. The First Breed hadn't stood a chance.

Very, very clever. Bakan had known this was going

to happen. She had planned it. It had been an ambush. Well, for what it was worth, she wouldn't be influencing the Commune Place again.

Someone was standing over him. He looked up and recoiled slightly. He had expected a single marine lieutenant, not a delegation of grim-looking Navy personnel.

Nguyen was at their head. 'Say the word and we're with you, Commodore,' she murmured.

'I beg your pardon?'

Nguyen pulled out a chair and sat opposite him. The others clustered around, turned their backs, kept an eye on the rest of the canteen. *Hello, world, we're having a secret conspiracy*, Gilmore thought.

'We don't want to use Device Ultimate, sir. We know Sand Strong was got at. We can't accept orders like that . . .'

'You can accept orders from your superior, Lieutenant.' Gilmore's face and voice were cold.

'Sir, all the humans will follow you. You can . . .'

'That will do!' Gilmore snapped. 'If you don't like taking orders from the First Breed, you shouldn't have joined the Commonwealth Navy. When we get back to the Roving I'll be glad to pull what strings I can to effect your transfer to one of the Earth fleets, humans only.'

Nguyen looked as if he had slapped her. 'But sir . . . but . . . I mean, they want to commit another xenocide . . .'

'There won't be a xenocide.' Gilmore's voice was quiet and level. *Not in the Navy that I founded.* 'Now, you and your friends return to your posts before I'm forced to raise my voice and tell you in public that I won't be a party to mutiny.'

The look in her eyes was of pure condemnation. She slapped her hands on the tabletop and stood, which spoiled Gilmore's brief fantasy of yelling at her and perhaps leaning forward and grabbing her hair and punctuating every syllable by hitting her head against the table. *Why can't you see it? If we go back to the Roving with the news that the human half of a crew mutinied against the Rustie half then the Commonwealth dies, there and then.* 'Of course . . .' he said. She paused, looked back. 'I can't order you all to remain in good health. I can't order you to press the right buttons. I can't order you to do anything on the double. Things like that really are up to the conscience of the individual.'

She didn't look like she got it; well, maybe she would eventually. Some of the others obviously did because they looked a bit more approving as they left.

Gilmore put his head in his hands. 'Yi yi yi yi yi,' he muttered.

'Problems with the workers?' Donna McCallum sat down opposite him with two cups of coffee and pushed one of them towards him. 'If you're going to have a conspiracy in the canteen, you should at least look like you're engaging in canteen-compatible activities.'

'It's not a conspiracy yet,' Gilmore said.

Donna nodded at the equipment on the desktop. 'Counter-conspiracy, then. Is that what dunnit?'

'It's the culprit,' Gilmore said. 'Look.' He pressed a key; a miniature March Sage Savour appeared on the tabletop. 'His second speech, in the Commune Place, was pre-recorded with fulltalk bells and whistles. Very persuasive.'

'There's no way of manipulating it? Making the image say something else?'

'If we had time we could manipulate the image and get the chem labs to knock up some fake pheromones for us. But we don't have time.'

'So if we stop this at all, we target Device Ultimate.'

'Exactly.' He leaned forward. 'We need to—'

'Plan, think ahead, work out what to do. Done it.' She was smiling over the rim of her cup. It was an infectious smile, full of mischief; Gilmore felt she was enjoying this not so much because it saved millions of XC lives as because it would stir things up. And it wasn't the smile of someone who has exhausted all the options. There was cold steel in the blue eyes behind the smile that showed just how seriously she was actually taking this.

'And . . .?' he said, as was plainly expected.

'I did a run-through of the whole operation in my head,' she said. 'The device will be loaded into one of the ship's boats and a course will be hardwired into its nav computer to take it into the sun. Not hackable by remote means, so scratch that option if you were considering it.'

Gilmore had been considering, and obediently scratched it.

She took another sip. 'Device Ultimate is in kit form

and will take hours to assemble. A provisional launch time has been fixed for 07:00 tomorrow. That Bakan woman has the code required to activate it, so the key thing is that the data gets from Bakan to Device Ultimate. The crystal is vulnerable exactly twice. Once is when it's sitting in her cabin. If you've got any ideas of how to get into her cabin without anyone seeing, I'd like to hear.'

The ship's ventilation system chose just that moment to waft a gentle breeze across the table. An air vent opened into the canteen just above them and their combined gazes crept up to the grill in the ceiling. It was all of twelve inches wide. They looked down again.

'When's the second time?' he asked.

Donna smiled again and put her coffee down. Gilmore stifled the urge to throttle her. 'Did you do drama at school, Commodore?'

Fourteen

Day Nineteen: 21 June 2153

'This, First Son, is when I could really use the presence of Oomoing,' Barabadar said.

'Indeed, My Mother,' First Son commented. 'She is duly mourned.'

'That wasn't what I meant,' Barabadar said.

'As My Mother pleases,' he said complacently. First Son didn't even aspire to understanding his mother's thoughts. Officially he was meant to be in mourning for his younger brother but he didn't seem that upset. Perhaps he was still jubilant at the successful conclusion to the Ritual of Contested Land. They had challenged, they had fought and the outlanders had withdrawn; the contested land was clearly theirs.

But it's not just about the Ritual, First Son. The outlanders are still here . . .

Barabadar and First Son were in their space armour and they surveyed the busy scene in the cavern, the same hole in the rock that had previously held the outlander's escape craft. It had seemed large and empty after the craft took off, but now it was rapidly filling up again. Armoured Kin jetted hither and thither, each bearing tantalizing scraps of outlander technology. It all looked chaotic but presumably made sense to someone.

The outlander ship had been seriously damaged by the sacrificed assault craft, and large chunks had been knocked off in the fighting that followed. Space around the rock was aswirl with bits of outlander technology and Barabadar was having it all brought in for examination. Unfortunately she badly needed a good scientist or three to study it all and deduce what it was actually *for*. The bits ranged from unidentifiable fragments, probably part of the hull, a few handbreadths in width to . . .

'What is that?' she said. It was the first truly interesting thing she had seen. A team of engineers was manoeuvring what looked like an intact piece of machinery down into the cave from the open, spaceward end. It was a cube, each side twice the height of a Kin, attached to some kind of gantry.

'Team Three!' First Son bellowed. Barabadar winced; he was still on their shared band. 'Hold it right there! That thing might be dangerous. My Martial Mother will . . .'

He stopped as he realized his Martial Mother was no longer standing next to him. He glanced up and saw her jetting up towards the object. 'My Mother!' he yelped.

Barabadar ignored him. The cube filled her vision and her thoughts. Team Three had jetted to a halt at First Son's command and they hung in space, just inside the cavern entrance, while Barabadar jetted slowly around the thing.

Barabadar took it all in. The gantry it was attached to was jagged and shattered at one end; it must have been shot off the ship, or severed in an explosion. Thick, rugged cabling snaked from the object, down the gantry, and ended abruptly in a cluster that reminded Barabadar of some very large beheaded worms.

'What are you doing, My Mother?' First Son had caught up with her.

'Look,' she said. 'Deduce what you can from this.'

First Son looked. After about a minute, Barabadar began to wonder if she shouldn't just say it out loud.

'It was mounted externally?' First Son finally offered.

'Brilliant!' Barabadar snapped. 'Yes, it was mounted externally. But look at these cables, First Son. Would you say they were power leads?'

First Son peered close. 'That looks like optic cabling, presumably how the thing interfaced with the ship's systems. But the rest of it . . .' There was indeed one thin cable that looked like fibre optics. It was outnumbered and outmassed by the rest. 'Yes. It seems to have required an immense amount of power for . . . whatever it did. Some kind of weapon?'

'If it is, it wasn't used during the fight.' Barabadar resumed her jetting. The cube rotated in front of her. She was only putting half her mind into the conversation, the rest was occupied with far more important thoughts. 'They only used lasers and torpedoes, like us. This . . .'

A prodigious amount of energy, Oomoing had said.

Outside the ship, they had both agreed.

She made her decision.

'Well, I know who could tell us what it was for.'

'And I mourn her loss,' First Son agreed dutifully.

'I wasn't talking about Oomoing!' Barabadar snapped. Once again her thought processes had jumped to a parallel track and First Son had still to keep up. 'Get me a status report on the last two assault craft, First Son. We have unfinished business.'

Fifteen

Day Nineteen: 21 June 2153

'Going somewhere, Donna?'

Donna looked up. Her vision was obscured by targeting solutions and data feedback from her armour playing on the inside of her visor – and Bill Perry. On the far side of the hangar deck, rust-coloured, four-legged forms swarmed over the landing boat that was being modified to carry Device Ultimate on its one-way journey. It was the pinnace that Michael Gilmore had come aboard in – not part of the ship's complement, therefore surplus to requirements and safely disposable.

She reached up and lifted off her helmet, and the data display vanished. She stood there in her otherwise complete space armour and smiled brightly at her superior officer. The smile wasn't returned. Perry wasn't in a smiling mood.

'I thought some of my auto-aim was a bit glitchy during the fighting. I want to polish up its precision targeting,' she said.

'We do have people who could tweak it for you.'

'They don't have to wear this suit, do they?'

Perry shrugged. He probably felt she was making work for herself, but he also knew she was using the same principle that made skydivers pack their own chutes. If you want a job that could save your life done properly, you do it yourself. 'OK. Let me know if you come up with anything that can be shared.'

'Will do.'

'Might do some polishing myself,' he muttered as he turned away. He probably thought her activity was a coping mechanism, a way of taking her mind off what the Rusties on the other side of the hangar deck were about to do.

Donna put the helmet back on and the data displays swarmed back over her vision. She grinned and eyeballed the *target acquire* icon, then looked at Perry's receding figure. A pair of cross hairs appeared side by side over his kidneys, then merged into one over the small of his back. She heard the whine of the mini-servos that controlled her suit lasers as they treacherously targeted the vital organs of a superior officer.

Then Perry stepped out of the way, and the lasers were pointing straight at the pinnace.

Gilmore was back on the hangar deck, representing the Co-Seniors of the Commonwealth, just as Rhukaya Bakan was representing the President of the Confederation of South-East Asia and the rest of the observers represented their own leaders. Gilmore hadn't trusted himself to speak to any of them but he sensed that not all of them shared Bakan's blood lust. Still, they weren't going to miss this.

Bakan led the way like a shepherd leading her flock, Sand Strong padding along beside her. She strode confidently over to the chief Rustie engineer, who stood at the airlock to the bomb boat.

'Do you have it?' the engineer said.

Bakan delved into her pocket and produced the crystal. 'Right here.'

And, as promised by Donna, the data had become vulnerable. Device Ultimate was pre-human technology, built on the Roving's old protocols. Human systems couldn't interface with it. Instructions had to be downloaded from an old-style data crystal. And there it was.

Gilmore made his move. He lunged forward and grabbed the crystal.

'Stand back!' Sand Strong bellowed. Gilmore ignored him, turned to face Bakan. He was taller than her and he did his best to loom.

'I'm begging you, please, reconsider,' he said in a low voice. He had rehearsed it; low equals earnest, sincere, desperate.

'Give that crystal back, Mr Gilmore,' said Sand Strong. 'You are seriously out of order.'

Gilmore held the crystal up between thumb and forefinger. 'What's on this could murder millions. Billions. You once told me about your brothers – what would they think?'

He hadn't expected an answer; it was just something he thought someone playing his role should say. But Bakan did answer.

'One of them had gone over to the rebels; the other had gone across the lines to talk him into coming back,' she said. 'One of them died a traitor and the other died for his country. They made their choices, Mr Gilmore. I accepted that long ago. Now, this is my choice.'

Gilmore stared at her. The woman was a . . . a pit, he thought. A pit into which every scrap of remorse, of decent human feeling, had been dropped years ago.

'You don't have to provide it, though!' he said.

'We've already been into the mathematics.' *Where had that gun come from?* It was small, easily concealable; it fitted neatly into Bakan's small hand and it was pointed straight at Gilmore. 'The death of a lot of XCs for the lives of even more humans and First Breed. I could add you to the first half of the equation and it really wouldn't make much difference. So, hand it over.'

Gilmore stared down the barrel. A dark, cold circle that swelled to fill his vision. *Come on, Donna, come on, come on . . .*

And, finally, he felt the crystal suddenly grow warm between his fingers.

He let his hand drop, put the crystal into Bakan's outstretched palm. She bowed slightly and handed it to the engineer.

'Thank you,' she said. The gun disappeared back into her coat; Gilmore made a note of exactly where, for future reference. The engineer turned and climbed up into the pinnace.

A minute passed. Another minute.

The Rustie engineer climbed slowly down again. 'The crystal's corrupted,' he said, and he glared full at Gilmore as he said it. Gilmore looked blandly back, then remembered that under the circumstances he could hardly be blamed for showing some satisfaction. He gave a broad smile.

'That's a shame,' he said, and he sensed a wave of relief flow around the observers as well. It would take a very lucky guess to work out that the data on the crystal had been scrambled by a low energy laser pulse from Donna McCallum, standing the other side of the hangar deck.

'Isn't it,' Sand Strong said. He gave Gilmore a long, appraising look. 'How fortunate that March Sage Savour provided us with a copy as well. I'll go and get it; and you, Mr Gilmore, will remain exactly where you are until I get back.'

'Bloody hell.'

The Kiwi-accented words murmured in Gilmore's ear. He had backed away slightly from the group and was standing there with folded arms. Donna had come forward, her helmet tucked under one arm, apparently to watch the proceedings. She was over the halfway line that divided the marines' half of the hangar deck from the rest, but no-one seemed to care.

'I know,' Gilmore muttered.

'I can't pull the same trick twice.'

'You've done what you can.'

'Bill,' Donna said, more loudly. Perry was standing

a short distance away, the proper side of the line. A crowd of marines stood behind him watching in silence. 'We can stop this,' Donna said. There was a murmur of assent from the others.

'It's not our affair,' Perry muttered. Like many others, he couldn't take his eyes off what was happening with the pinnace.

'Like hell it's not! You really want to get back home and tell your girlfriend you let a new xenocide happen? Bill, we outnumber them . . .'

'Lieutenant . . .'

'And we outgun them.'

'Quiet!' Perry snapped. He glanced at the marines around him. Officers shouldn't argue in public. 'Don't make me . . .'

Gilmore shut his ears to their bickering. In his mind's eye he saw the pinnace coasting through space, a red glow appearing on its silver skin; the glow turning to yellow, to white, and then plasma streaming around it as the fields came on and helped it on its way into the heart of the star.

And then what? His mental gaze drew back a few million miles, a far-off view of the burning ball that gave life to this system. Maybe a slight darkening, a contraction . . . maybe no sign at all. But suddenly, the topmost layer – on the scale of his mind's eye it would only appear as a thin dusting of gas, but in reality a deadly blast – expanding outwards in all directions. A cocktail of super-searing plasma and hard radiation. The first planet of the system shredded to a burnt cinder in seconds. The occasional XC ship in close orbit; the crew torn apart by the radiation a few seconds before the blast reached them and they disappeared into the infernal glare and heat.

And then the prime target, Homeworld. The atmosphere rippling and streaming away from the planet, like a puddle of water blown away by a jet of warm air. Again, on this scale, quite innocuous; nothing to suggest the mega-hurricanes down below, tearing away the topmost layers of the planet. The cities razed to nothingness, individual XCs smashed against the hurtling debris and then flashed into vapour.

The blast carrying on from Homeworld, the atmosphere perhaps returning, the few dazed survivors picking themselves up from an assault a thousand times worse than the one their forebears had perpetrated. The shockwave carrying on, reaching the Dead World . . .

Which was already dead so it hardly mattered, except for the two lifeforms that might be down there. They would have a fifty-fifty chance, depending on which side of the Dead World they were at the time. A fifty-fifty chance on his son's life was not acceptable odds.

Gilmore jerked his head up, snapped out of the reverie. Sand Strong was approaching, a crystal held in one of his graspers. An escort of Rusties surrounded him until he reached the engineer, and the engineer held it cupped in both graspers as he climbed up into the pinnace. No, that crystal was safe. They weren't going to sabotage the plan that way.

Only one other way presented itself. If he stopped to think about it, he knew he would consider it madness, so he didn't. His heart pounded but otherwise he felt strangely calm.

'Thanks for your help,' he said. 'It was really appreciated.' Then, more loudly so that everyone could hear, 'No. No, I'm not going to watch this.'

He strode away and didn't look back.

Last minute nerves? Donna thought as Gilmore strode away. *I wouldn't have thought it.* She looked back at Perry. His arms were folded, his face was colder and he seemed to be breathing heavily. *Enjoy your conscience, Captain,* she thought with disgust.

She turned back to the pinnace. The airlock was sealed, the power leads disconnected. The Rusties and the observers backed away to a safe distance as the engines whined into life. A power trolley rolled up with a Rustie at the controls and hooked onto the pinnace's front landing wheel, then pushed the little boat backward onto the boat elevator. *This is it, this is it . . .*

Perry's breaths were getting shorter.

She was still in her armour, the only marine who was. She could pick off the driver of the trolley, she could—

Perry filled his lungs. 'Marines will stand to!' he bellowed. A microsecond's pause, then the marines leapt for their rifles. 'Sergeant Cale, Able Platoon will form a barrier in front of the pinnace and prevent anyone from getting near. Secure the remote controls and disable them. Lieutenant McCallum, Charlie Platoon will secure the pinnace, board it and deactivate all systems.'

The Rusties and the human observers stood transfixed at the sudden burst of military activity. 'You can't—' Bakan said, before she and the others found themselves surrounded by a wall of armed men and women and herded away from the pinnace.

Perry stood before her, teeth bared and a deadly glint in his eyes. 'And one more word from *you* and I'll—'

A crackle of plasma fire behind him and Perry convulsed, then fell into her arms. She staggered under the weight and fell backwards to the deck. Donna had time for one horrified, tragic look at the blackened and smoking pit between his shoulders before Rusties, marines and observers dived for cover as more plasma fire blazed out. And the fight was on.

'Ready, Lieutenant.'

'*Good luck, Mr Gilmore,*' said Nguyen.

Gilmore stood and looked at the outer door of the airlock. He felt his suit tighten around him as the air was pumped out.

In the ship's present state of emergency, someone using an airlock would immediately set off a variety of attention-seeking alarms on the flight deck ... unless there was a sympathetically inclined lieutenant there, operating the system for you.

The outer door slid aside and Gilmore stepped out into the rich velvet black of space. Suit thrusters carried him away from the ship and into the dark. Only a light second out from SkySpy, half the distance between Earth and its moon, the Shield was still big: a glowing green ball that dominated the sky. SkySpy itself and its attendant XC vessels couldn't be seen with the naked eye. In the other direction was just deep, bottomless space.

'Mr Gilmore, fighting has broken out on the hangar deck. Do you want to abort?'

Fighting? Gilmore didn't know whether to weep or rejoice.

'No,' he said. 'I'll keep going. Thanks.' Fighting could resolve things ... but he didn't yet know in which way.

The thrusters cancelled his outwards movement from the ship and blazed in a different direction. Gilmore moved up the length of *Pathfinder*, past the hideous gash of the wound in the ship's side and on up to the boat bay. Thrusters slowed him again and he drew level with the wide, rectangular opening in the ship's side that was the boat entrance. He moved in and waited.

'Stop this! Hold your fire!'

Sand Strong was hovering on the edge of the field of fire, hopping up and down with agitation, not daring to get any closer to the fighting. The hangar deck was smoky and plasma trails streaked through the air. A handful of Rusties, including the one that had shot Perry, were holding the marines off. Sand Strong was dangerously exposed as he tried to get one side or the other to lay its weapons down. No-one was shooting at him but no-one was paying him any attention either.

The armed Rusties were sheltered behind the pinnace and there was no cover between the marines and them. All both sides could do was exchange pot shots whenever someone showed. The marines were handicapped; the Rusties could shoot wherever they wanted, but the marines had to make damn sure they didn't hit a vulnerable part of the pinnace. An exploding fuel tank within the confines of the hangar deck wouldn't serve the interests of either side.

Bill Perry had been killed immediately by the first shot. Donna had compartmentalized her feelings on that, shoved them to one side and to the back of her mind, because now she was in charge.

Motion behind the pinnace immediately drew marine fire. The power trolley rolled slowly across the deck and plasma blazed off its metal sides. It wasn't being driven, just pushed by the Rusties sheltering behind it. It was a good choice for impromptu armour. The Rusties that remained behind the pinnace gave it covering fire.

'Get the wheels!' Donna shouted, which was easier said than done. They were covered by a metal skirt that came almost down to the floor. Donna chose a different strategy; where exactly were they pushing the trolley to?

Easy; the remote controls, mounted on a panel in the hanger wall. She took aim and fired, and the panel exploded.

The Rusties didn't stop. The trolley inched over to stand in front of the remains of the panel. Donna heard the whine of a power drill. They were unscrewing the hull plating beneath the panel, gaining access to the undamaged innards of the controls.

'Both platoons, concentrate fire on the trolley,' she ordered, and the trolley began to wilt and melt under a concentrated volley.

But then the elevator whirred into life and the pinnace began to lift up to the ceiling. The Rusties who had been sheltering behind it leapt for cover as their protection vanished.

'The elevator! Take the elevator out!' Sergeant Quinlan yelled.

But it wouldn't be enough. Donna could already see that. They still couldn't shoot at the pinnace, just the metal shaft that was pushing the platform up towards the ceiling. Solid metal, no vulnerable parts, and in about ten seconds the pinnace would be beyond their reach.

She was still in space armour; she did the only thing she could.

And there it was. It rose up on the boat elevator into the bay and stopped in front of him. Its landing legs retracted and thrusters fired to move it forwards.

Gilmore fired his own thrusters. He only had a few seconds here; the pinnace wasn't going to hang around. He had just long enough to attach a lifeline and get inside the range of its drive field so that when the main drive came on . . .

Pathfinder suddenly shot away. The pinnace was accelerating with that deceptive grav-drive ease away from its mothership. It had started on its kamikaze mission. It felt wrong, too easy; there should have been a countdown, a fanfare, drama.

Gilmore began to pull himself in. Get to the handholds, get to the airlock. Then he yelled and almost let go, because there was movement where there should have been none. Someone, something was coming round the side of the boat.

It was a marine, fully armoured. He peered more closely through the visor.

'What the hell are you doing here?' he shouted. No response. Their radios were on different frequencies and he couldn't remember which. So he jabbed a hand at the airlock; Donna nodded and pulled herself after him.

Inside the pinnace he repressurized and they took their helmets off. The boat was too small for artgrav so they clung to the bulkheads and looked at each other. He repeated the question, just as loudly. 'What are you doing?'

'Me?' Her tone blazed with a white-hot anger and he wondered what had pressed her button. Surely not his own quixotic gesture. 'I had this mad idea of disabling Device Ultimate. Something only a real idiot would do. And since Bill got shot in the back, I had to do it.'

And that explained the rage. Gilmore had only known one colleague killed in his time, and it hadn't even been someone he especially liked, but it had been a shipmate and it had left a big, big hole.

'I'm sorry,' he said sincerely.

'Right.' She peered past him. 'And that's it, is it?'

Device Ultimate seemed quite innocuous; a collection of black boxes that almost filled the cabin, linked together with thick, industrial-strength power cables. Here and there a light shone or blinked. There was nothing to suggest it was the most powerful, the most lethal weapon of all time.

The command unit was easy to find; a small sub-unit with controls covered with Roving glyphs and the data crystal sitting smugly in its port. First Gilmore yanked the crystal out and placed it against the floor. He braced his hands against the ceiling, raised a foot and deliberately crushed it. It exploded under his heel with a most satisfactory crunch and small particles drifted around the cabin.

'Too easy,' Donna said.

'I know.' He studied the sub-unit more closely. He wasn't good at Roving glyphs. There was a display and figures moved across it. They weren't flashing or showing any other sign of error or alarm. Device Ultimate had downloaded its instructions from the crystal and it was still working.

Now the shock of her presence had faded away, Gilmore realized it was being replaced by a quite unreasonable anger on his part that someone was intruding on his moment of glory. 'You can give me a hand,' he muttered.

'Suits me.' She stepped forward and looked at the device. 'What do we do?'

'Unplug it. Everything.'

'Right-o.' She grabbed one cable, braced and pulled. Nothing. 'It's screwed in.' She took hold of the cable end, where it met the box, in one armoured gauntlet and twisted. 'It's not screwed in. Hold on . . .'

Her armour joints whined as she started to apply the suit's power to the task. The cable stayed joined to the box.

'I don't believe it,' she said. 'Is there a toolbox?'

Gilmore was having similar luck with his own cable. 'Must be, somewhere.'

'It could be back on *Pathfinder* . . .' He glared at her. 'Hey, just pointing it out. I'll look for it, you turn this thing round.'

'Right,' Gilmore said, and moved for'ard.

Everything unessential had been stripped from the cabin, even the pilot's seat. He floated at the pilot's position and looked at the controls.

'Oh,' he said.

'Oh, don't say *oh*,' said Donna behind him. '*Oh* is a negative word.' Gilmore didn't react. She followed his gaze to the pilot's controls. 'That hole shouldn't be there, should it?'

'No,' Gilmore said quietly. There was a big hole in the desk. A nav computer-interface-shaped hole. Another hole next to it was where the main drive controls should be. 'They really weren't leaving it to chance. They gave the pinnace its course, then took out everything that could be used to override it.' He toggled a switch: it was dead. 'We can't even contact *Pathfinder*.'

'Not that way, no.' Donna toggled her own

armour's radio. 'This is McCallum. Sergeant Quinlan, any marine, do you copy?'

Nothing. She switched to *Pathfinder*'s main comms frequency and tried again. Still nothing.

'We're out of range,' Gilmore said quietly. Suit radios were only meant for short range; they were probably already a couple of light seconds from *Pathfinder*'s position. They were a small speck of light and air in deep space, very alone.

'So we can't talk to the ship and we can't turn round?' Donna was just as quiet.

'Nope. We're about as committed as you can get.' He tried the controls, one more time for luck, then looked up at her. 'Next stop, the sun.'

PART III

Sixteen

Day Sixteen: 18 June 2153

The Dead World loomed large in the viewports and on the main display on *Chariot of Rightful Justice*'s flight deck. Jajing prided herself on the speed with which the ship had got here from Habitat 1, and she gazed fondly at the three males who had made it possible; her three sons, the ship's sole crew.

'Orbit insertion in five minutes,' said Second Son. He sounded proud. They all knew they had excelled themselves in following Marshal of Space Barabadar's orders, promptly and to the letter. Barabadar had sent a priority order from the vicinity of Firegod, that suddenly strangely popular area of space which Jajing knew better than to wonder too much about, and *Chariot* had responded.

'Approach corridor is confirmed,' said Third Son.

'Transmit the codes,' Jajing said.

'Codes transmitted.'

Essential repeat essential that you enter along the following orbital corridor, Barabadar had said. The orders had been followed by precise co-ordinates – not especially fuel-efficient co-ordinates either – and a series of codes to transmit ahead of them.

Chariot's crew had worked out what the codes were for long ago, as soon as the Dead World had been close enough for the ship's scanners to pick up the satellite shield. An elaborate, a most intricate and no doubt extremely expensive defence system. But the codes had shut the system down so that *Chariot* could approach the Dead World in safety. Jajing could not help wondering, in a small and independent part of her mind which dared think thoughts that the Marshal of Space would rather she did not, what this system was for. She suspected that she was being let into a secret that should not be revealed. Well, her sons could keep quiet, and so could she.

Jajing looked out at the Dead World and suppressed a shudder. Even twinkling in the sky of Homeworld it was ominous, a bright light that set the senses all on edge. Long ago, centuries before space flight, the Dead World – they had called it that even then, long before the birth of modern astronomy could verify it really *was* dead – had been an omen of ill will and bad luck. To have it in your birth constellation had been a terrible stigma.

Those days of superstition were long over and Jajing thanked her battle gods for it, but the instinct remained. And now, to be so close . . .

'My Mother, the satellites are responding to our queries,' said First Son. 'We have a record of the fugitive ship and the path that it took.'

'Show me,' said Jajing, and a representation of the Dead World appeared on her personal display. The

satellites were green dots and the path of the intruder
was . . .

'That can't be correct!' she said. The intruder had
swerved all over the sky. She played the scene back
from the beginning and now a gold speck approached
the green specks. A green speck flared, the gold speck
turned red briefly to show the hit. And then it *turned*,
impossibly, and turned and turned again; sometimes
taking more hits, sometimes evading them. Finally, it
put its nose down and dived straight into the
atmosphere.

'So where did it crash?' she said.

'It didn't, My Mother.' First Son studied his
display. 'The satellites report that it pulled out at
latitude forty-five degrees, then turned south.'

'It must have crashed! Or burned up. No ship
could—'

'It then flew at hypersonic speed to the equator
where it came to rest,' First Son said. 'It's true, My
Mother.'

The secret that was the Dead World's defence
system was nothing compared to the secret that was
this remarkable ship. No wonder Barabadar wanted it
back. Was it some kind of prototype? Had foreign
agents stolen it? Was *Barabadar* stealing it? The nation
that had a ship like this would be unbeatable in space.
Barabadar's Space Presence had to have it.

'Display its last known position,' Jajing said, and
the gold speck appeared on – sure enough – the
equator.

'Shall I signal My Martial Mother Barabadar that

the ship is intact, My Mother?' First Son said.

Jajing thought. Barabadar was still out at Firegod, several light hours away. Whatever data they sent, Barabadar would not receive it for hours. Why send an incomplete interim report when, just a little bit later, they could send a complete one?

'Not yet,' Jajing said. She checked the fuel displays. 'Third Son, calculate the fuel penalty involved in changing our orbit so that we pass over the ship.' A complete report included a visual inspection.

'Yes, My Mother.'

'My Mother?' Jajing looked up in surprise at First Son's tone, a mixture of caution and annoyance. 'That will take us out of My Martial Mother's designated corridor,' he said. 'We were not to approach the planet closer than—'

'We will report,' Jajing said patiently. 'We will report everything we are to find out.'

'But the orders assumed the ship's destruction, so there'd be no question of our leaving the corridor. If My Martial Mother had wanted us to leave the corridor and report on an *intact* ship, she would have—'

'The orders, the approach corridor and the instructions plainly related to the satellites, and they've been shut down,' Jajing said, with ever-decreasing patience. 'I know what Our Martial Mother the Marshal of Space intended!'

'Yes, My Mother,' First Son said, but he didn't seem convinced.

*

It took half an hour for *Chariot* to change its orbital attitude, its crew strapped into their acceleration couches, but again Jajing was pleased with the smooth efficiency of her sons. She wondered whose performance she could most embellish in the log, without making her intentions too obvious – any one of them would make a good mate to the daughter of another family. First Son traditionally was the favoured prospect, of course, but he had already mated twice, and . . .

She should get on with running the ship. 'Second Son, stand by on the telescope,' she said. 'Try and get as much as you can on the first pass; save us having to go round again. You won't get anything visual through those clouds; use infra red and radar.'

'Yes, My Mother.'

Jajing glanced across at First Son and was puzzled for a moment by what she saw on his display. It looked like some kind of power readout.

'What are you doing, First Son?' she said.

First Son looked up and tried not to appear guilty. 'I was scanning the satellites for power surges,' the irritating runt said. 'Just in case . . .'

'In case what?' Jajing demanded. She sensed the first surge of battle pheromones from the traitor and battle hormones rushed into her own system.

'In case the orders were—'

'I have explained the orders!' Jajing shouted, barely hanging onto her maternal restraint. Then even that was gone and all she knew was *challenge*. This was an intruder, not even a female but a scrappy male, impinging on her territory. Her claws extended from her left fighting hand and she raked the side of his head. 'Obey!'

And then the male was out of his couch and hurtling towards her, flying impossibly through the air rather than bounding along the ground. Jajing raked his flanks with both sets of claws as he flew past her. Howls of rage filled the cave and to her surprise she saw that there were two other males, claws out, fangs bared. She tore at the annoying straps that held her down and then she was out and floating in the air with them. One of them grabbed her leg and sank his teeth in. Jajing yowled, and her talons tore off half his face.

The fighting went on for a few more minutes. Controlling the ship was the last thing on what was left of any of their minds.

Chariot of Rightful Justice began to tumble.

The fireball broke through the cloud cover and a few seconds later the distant boom reached Joel's ears. He stood in the doorway that overlooked the dim, barren plaza and squinted up. A streak of light seared across the heavy backdrop of the overhanging clouds and then was gone. A dim rumble reached his ears a moment later.

'What was that?' Boon Round looked up from his corner of the room.

'Looked like a meteorite. A big one.' Joel found himself almost wishing it had come right down on top of him, Boon Round, those bastard XCs and the sodding locals holding them captive. It would be a quicker and better death than the one that awaited them.

Unlike their captivity on SkySpy, food wasn't a problem. But Joel knew about radiation poisoning. Maybe it would have been better if he hadn't. Perhaps he was just imagining the symptoms; increasing nausea, hair and teeth falling out, cancers blossoming in a variety of interesting ways in essential organs.

He certainly wasn't imagining the hallucinations – a meaningless montage of scenes from his life, even things he had long forgotten as a small boy – and the headaches that accompanied them. Often his father or Donna would appear, though more usually the scenes were recent, since he had come to SkySpy. Meanwhile spears of burning white light would burn through his brain, sometimes coaxing out the most amazingly obscure memories. His life was literally flashing before his eyes. It was like someone was rummaging through his head, dredging up all kinds of stuff at random. Joel wished them luck in making sense of it.

All the anti-radiation treatment they could need, smart drugs that would seek out and repair the damaged cells and DNA within their bodies, was not far away in the lifeboat. But he had been brought here unconscious, to wake up with a splitting headache and an anxious Boon Round gazing into his eyes, and he had no idea where the lifeboat was. He had very little memory of the events leading up to the moment when, according to Boon Round, the big female had clobbered him. He had no memory at all of the clobbering.

It was a strange sort of captivity, here in this empty house overlooking a stone plaza. Food and water were provided once a day; the water in a jar carried by a local, the food by other means. There was no door, nothing to keep them in; but if he or Boon Round stepped out, within seconds a couple of weapon-bearing locals would appear from somewhere. Making a break for it wasn't an option.

The locals had taken his aide but left Boon Round his translator unit. Joel assumed they had been guided by the XCs as to how to proceed, based on what the XCs themselves had seen and heard. Joel could use his aide to get at the lifeboat; all Boon Round's translator unit was good for was talking to the Rustie, and that was becoming less and less fun as the days passed. The translator unit should have been able to contact the aide but Boon Round had had no joy when he tried. Both aide and translator unit were built for a society that was covered by an ever-present electromagnetic blanket; they didn't need a vast range because wherever you went, there would always be something nearby to pass on the message, even route it up to a satellite if needed. Here there was nothing. It was the Commonwealth's technological reliance against the electromagnetic silence of the Dead World, and the Dead World won.

Joel leaned against the doorpost and gazed gloomily out at the plaza. One corner was cut off by an open stream flowing through a stone gutter, and the water steamed gently. Joel remembered the evidence of volcanism that he had seen from the lifeboat; this was what kept these people alive.

Otherwise, the plaza was very like the one that the lifeboat had landed in. Same dark stone, same manic architecture. Occasionally he would see some of the locals. They usually scuttled by quickly, trying to keep out of the wind as much as possible as they went about their business. The exception was the processions.

The locals did a lot of proceeding, though it wasn't exactly carnival time. A parade would shamble through the square. They would enter and leave by any of the square's four main entrances, eyes on the ground, absorbed in what they were doing but clearly taking their time. Sometimes they would be in single file, sometimes double; sometimes there would only be a handful of them, sometimes so many it would take a couple of minutes for the procession to pass by. No doubt it made sense to them.

If it weren't for the dark stone and the squashed lines of the buildings then the whole scene would have been attractive in, say, a Mediterranean setting on Earth, or down the coast from the Admiralty back on the Roving. Here on this cold, barren planet in the depths of a nuclear winter, it was even more bleak and dreary than it ought to be.

He reached for his ident bracelet for the umpteenth time; his one, slightly desperate source of consolation. Sometimes, just seeing Donna's face would fill the gut-wrenching emptiness inside him and renew his determination to stay alive and see her again. Sometimes, it just made him think of his chances of actually doing so and would depress him still further. You never could tell until the picture was actually activated. He wondered what it would be this time.

But then a movement caught his eye and he watched the small party approach purposefully from the far corner.

'Food party,' he said. 'It's the little one.'

He knew the routine by now. He stood back from the door as the small group came near. The usual mix; four of the Dead World locals, scuttling on their four legs, with spears clutched in their two arms and swords strapped at what could reasonably be called their waists. Another local would be with them, unarmed; and then the only variable, one or the other of the XCs, bearing a pile of food concentrates from the lifeboat which had been formulated to be edible by both humans and Rusties. This time it was the small male.

The XC came up to the door, threw the food in without ceremony and turned away. Joel noticed yet more scars and slashes on its head and body, even tearing through its spacesuit, and he wondered what exactly the locals were doing to the XC prisoners. And when they were going to start on Boon Round and himself.

'Concentrates,' he said as he picked the pile up and dusted everything down. 'Gee, you shouldn't have.'

It made a change from chocolate. It was a balanced diet, for one thing. A very boring diet, but still balanced. You could only grow healthy on the stuff, if the radiation didn't kill you.

It was lucky the XCs had overheard him ordering food from the foodfac. XCs conversed through tympanic membranes and they could probably imitate any sound they chose, and now they would just deliver the command verbally to the equipment on the lifeboat. Another verbal command they must have overheard was 'field off', and Joel bitterly regretted that he hadn't used the controls for that particular one. They could never have got him off the lifeboat otherwise.

He hadn't used voice interface to get the antirad pills; he had pressed a button, and the XCs hadn't even been in the cabin at the time. So they had no idea how to get them; they probably had no idea of the need.

Boon Round came forward and picked up a food slab. 'What do you think the XCs eat?' he said.

Joel shrugged and took a savage bite out of a slab of his own. His head sometimes still throbbed from the female XC's knock-out blow. He was possibly concussed and probably dying of radiation poisoning. And he knew who had got him into this.

'Whatever I'm doing that makes you think I care,' he said, 'tell me what it is and I'll stop.'

Oomoing knew the procedure and she drew back from the grill as the party approached. It swung open and the locals held their spears poised, like a bizarre honour guard, as Fleet walked in. He stood in the middle of the small room and the grill shut behind him. Oomoing jumped forward to catch him as he buckled.

She laid him down gently. There was nothing that could be used as a bed or a mattress, one part of the floor was pretty much like any other, and so she just put him down where he was.

'Fleet?' she said. She peered into his eyes, waiting for the return of intelligence.

'Learned Mother.' When it came the tone was weak, the membranes barely vibrating. 'It gets worse every time.'

'I know,' she said. The enemy didn't alternate them on these occasions, or pick the one who was nearest the door, or apparently use any kind of pattern. Sometimes it was Fleet, sometimes herself, and that was all she knew.

But she knew the feeling of helplessness, the creeping paralysis, the way that every part of your mind screamed defiance and swore that this time it would be different . . . but it never was. And then you would come to lying on the floor of the cell, and you would remember everything you had done, as if from a great distance, like watching a stranger in your own body.

The worst times were when they *both* woke up on the cell floor. Then they didn't need to remember because the cuts and the bruises and the bite marks and the slashes were testimony enough. But mostly it was just a food-gathering trip for the extraterrestrials.

Much to her surprise, she and Fleet could both eat the scraps that the enemy gave them.

Something else Oomoing remembered very clearly was arriving on this world. The shock of discovering that there was life here; and not just the primitive organisms that might have been expected but an entire culture, which surely no-one had ever suspected. It had hurt, to discover new life and then seconds later to have to fight it, but there had been no question about the hostility, and she and Fleet needed Long and Short alive. It had hurt, but it had at least been a decision they could make as *rational* beings.

Unlike the bitterest of those long-distance memories, which was clouting Long around the head, and then going back to help Fleet subdue Short, who didn't seem so susceptible to blows to the brain box. And then they had let the enemy on board and meekly walked with them to this place, deep within the city.

She wondered if forgiveness was a concept that featured large in extraterrestrial society. She hoped someone could forgive her because she wasn't sure she could herself.

Seventeen

Day Eighteen: 20 June 2153

'Hello,' Joel said. 'Visitors.' And it wasn't even feeding time.

He straightened up from his usual position in the doorway as the locals approached across the bleak paving of the square. An armed party of four, and one in the middle, unarmed. They scuttled towards him on four legs, like the rest of their kind, but there was a purposefulness to it that suddenly made him nervous. Was this the long-awaited execution? Was this finally, *It*? His heart began to pound.

But the group just came to an abrupt halt. The unarmed one stared at Joel, so Joel stared back. It came forward.

'Oh, no,' Joel said. His heart was slowing down, he was breathing more easily but he felt the tell-tale tickling at the back of his eyes. One of his headaches was coming on again.

But then he blinked, because the desolation outside in the square suddenly faded away. The ruins took on shape. The stark buildings suddenly seemed light and inviting. The battered, hustling survivors became healthy, well dressed citizens; still locals but no longer alien. Friendly, familiar; *Us*. And instead of millions of tons of rubble swirling about in the atmosphere, there was a clear dark blue sky and a sun that shone brightly down.

And he could *feel* it. The light was warm on his upturned face. The air was crisp and clear in his lungs, no longer charred and burnt but new and fresh. But it was more than that. He could feel, he could *sense* the community, the health, the goodness of the gathering. This was a happy place. A well-to-do place. A community of units that lived in harmony with itself.

A procession was passing through the square, and now Joel saw it for what it was. It was clearly the begetter of the occasional shuffle that Joel had witnessed, but it was grander and much more purposeful. Still a curiously low-key parade, heads held low, the sense of obedient duty strong in their movements; but there was joy and satisfaction because this procession was what life was about. A sacred duty. The walkers filed silently through the square, one side to the other, then out again.

Joel was just getting into the vision when the pain struck.

It was the headache again; the headache he had been getting ever since they landed on the Dead World. Sometimes it was like a handful of grit rubbing together behind his eyes. Sometimes . . .

Joel screamed. He only dimly knew that he was curled up on the floor, hands clutching at his head, face buried in his knees. Grit? This was huge grinding slabs of stone, crushing his optic nerves, sending sparks of agony deep into his mind.

Then it was over and he was lying on the floor in his curled-up position. Boon Round was crouching next to him, supporting Joel's head in his forehands.

'Another headache?'

'Yeah . . .' Joel gasped.

'Are you better?'

'All the more for your asking,' Joel muttered. For a glorious moment he thought the pain had vanished, but no. It was back to a twinge, but it was still there. He had to move his head very carefully as he pulled himself up and glanced up at the locals through the doorway. The plaza was back to its old, desolate self.

• *(It was not always) this way.*

'I know,' he said. 'Is that meant to be some consolation?'

'Consolation for what?' said Boon Round.

• *(You saw) how (it was).*

'How do you know what I saw?'

'I don't. Are you sure you're better?'

Joel gazed at Boon Round; Boon Round gazed blankly back at him. 'I saw the city,' Joel said. 'I saw how it used to be. How did you know?'

'I have no idea what you—'

- *(We have established) contact. Good.*

'– are talking about,' Boon Round finished. And this time, because they spoke at the same time, Joel knew the other speaker wasn't Boon Round. He also realized he wasn't exactly *hearing* it. A succession of ideas, of images, of concepts would flash through the back of his mind. Some part of him would take them, extract the ideas being conveyed and turn them into speech.

'You . . . you don't hear anyone else talking?' he said.

'Of course not.'

Flash flash flash . . .

- *(We have) tried and failed (to establish) contact with (the four legged one).*

Joel felt something feeling around in his mind. It went from concept to concept; it matched the ideas with his memory of how to speak; it paired up the ideas with the words, and it turned the whole thing into speech that he could understand.

- *(The four legged one is)* Boon Round. *(You are)* Joel Gilmore.

Joel slowly pushed himself to his feet, with Boon Round's support. The unarmed local was just outside the doorway.

'Raise your right hand if you can understand me,' Joel said.

'Why ever . . .' Boon Round said, but Joel poked

him and pointed at the local, which was raising its right hand to point up at the sky.

The cold cut into them like knives. It had been cold in the house, but at least it had been out of the wind. The four armed locals draw back slightly but they had their spears at the ready. Contact had been established; trust was yet to follow.

Joel and Boon Round stood facing the unarmed local, and shivered. The flakes that covered Boon Round's body tightened up into a windproof covering. Joel reached for his belt and turned his weathersuit heater to max.

'Can you really talk to him?' Boon Round said.

'It's not ... it's not talking. The knowledge just comes into my head and I know what he's just said.'

- *(My name is) Meewa. (I am a) Processor.*

The concept of *Processor* was very clear, though Joel couldn't see how it could possibly be so. It must be a term from his own memory that was being applied out of context.

'He's called Meewa and he's a Processor,' Joel said. What did it *mean*? Did Meewa join in the processions? Did he process something? Information? Words? Food? Or did it mean both?

'Is that good?' Boon Round asked.

'He got us out, didn't he?'

'Why?' Boon Round said darkly; Joel had been wondering the same thing.

- *(We need to) know whether (you are) our friends or our enemies.*

Joel thought of their arrival; they had stepped down from the lifeboat and been attacked.

- *(That was a) misunderstanding; (we are) sorry. Once the Processors learnt (of your presence), (we took) steps to remedy the situation.*

'Yeah. Right.' Joel rubbed his head and suddenly he knew Meewa had sensed the pain that stabbed into the depths of his mind. And Meewa knew what was causing it.

- *(I am sorry for) the pain. (It is not) like this (when) (we talk with) the* malesna. *Our minds (are not) made for full communion. (It took) (a lot of) time and experimentation (to make) contact. (But) (I have to) know – (are you our) friends, and (will you) help us?*

Joel got most of that, except for the *malesna*. There was only a vague suggestion of meaning attached to the word; rather, there was a great deal of meaning, but only a little that his own mind could comprehend. Something to do with animals, some sort of sacrifice, some sort of feeding or source of sustenance. He put it to one side.

'Help you how, exactly?'

He glanced at the weapons and suspected what might happen if the answer was 'no'. And then he remembered that he was talking to a mind reader.

But he actually sensed amusement. The mind reader understood.

• *(We have been less) hospitable (than we might). (Let us show you) something better.*

'This way,' Joel said, as the Processor led on.

'Where are we going?' Boon Round said.

'Better hospitality, apparently . . .'

They entered a building in the corner of the square across from their previous dwelling, next to where the stream of hot water entered a tunnel under the buildings.

Joel stopped dead at what he saw, and encouraging images in his mind from Meewa confirmed his impression of what it was for. Boon Round bumped into him and protested.

'Tell me,' Joel said, 'that this isn't the most beautiful sight you've ever seen.' He was already fumbling for the release tags on his weathersuit.

In the centre of the room was a square hollow, about three feet deep and ten feet on a side. A small flight of stone steps led down into it and it was full of steaming, hot water.

Joel wore just his boxers and floated blissfully, arms and legs spread out to hold balance and just his face and toes breaking the surface. Every part of him felt *warm*. Not the dull, dry heat of his weathersuit's heater but proper warmth, the glow that comes from within.

'Are you going to take for ever?' said a familiar voice. Rusties didn't have the same worship of hot baths that humans did. Boon Round had dunked himself briefly, then climbed back out to shake himself dry.

'And a day,' Joel said without opening his eyes. 'You bet.' He tried to remember the last time he had felt this good. This mellow, this warm, this happy . . .

Actually, it wasn't difficult. The last night on Admiralty Island, before setting off for SkySpy. He had stood behind her, her back pressing into his front, his arms clasped around her waist, chin resting on her shoulder and the smell of her hair in his nostrils. And they had watched the sun going down. Billions of tons of flaming gas forced into nuclear fusion by its own gravity, taken from view by the natural rotation of the planet they were standing on, but the most romantic and idyllic moment of his life. The realization that there would never be another sunset quite like it; never again to be watched at *that* moment and with *her*, and that it wasn't often he held a trained killer in his arms.

Two hours later, he had been on the shuttle that took him to the prideship that took him to SkySpy.

Oh, no, not again!

The headache was back, and that meant, so was Meewa the Processor. He touched his feet to the bottom of the pool and crouched, still keeping as much of himself as possible submerged in the delicious warm water. Meewa and escort stood on the edge of the pool.

- *(Is this) of use?*

Joel yelped. *'Yes!'* Meewa was holding out a packet of antirad pills. Joel leapt out of the bath and grabbed it. Unopened, untampered with. Perfect. He tore it open and tipped out two orange pills (First Breed) and two blue (human). He and Boon Round gulped them down. Joel knew the instant feeling of health and vitality as the smart drugs went to work on his radiation-damaged cells was pure illusion, but still a pleasant one.

'Thank you,' he said. 'Thank you very much. How did you know?'

- *(I saw them) in your mind. (You wanted them) badly.*

'Damn right!'

- *(We need to) explain (our) situation (more fully). Come (with us). (I am) authorized (to) show (you).*

Joel glanced at his discarded weathersuit. The thought of getting back into it was not pleasant, but he had declined the offer to have it washed. Its proper maintenance would be beyond these people.

'I'll be right with you,' he said. 'Ah . . . got a towel?'

They were led outside again, into the cutting, cold wind, but this time it met the warm inner radiance left over from his bath, and it wasn't half as bad as it could have been. Still, Joel and Boon Round put their heads down and trotted at speed behind Meewa.

They went out of the plaza through a dim tunnel in the wall, which had dark doorways opening off it, and then into another plaza. The pattern of tunnel and plaza was repeated twice more – each plaza was a variation on the same theme. The whole city seemed to be built like this, almost like a series of interconnected modules. In its glory days it must have looked spectacular.

Halfway down the fourth tunnel, they took a right and went into one of the doorways. Out of the wind they could slow down, and their way along the worn stone passage was lit by lamps. They passed locals who looked at them, perhaps with curiosity or hostility, but who stayed back.

Then it was up a narrow, curving stairway in single file. The Processor took the lead, followed by Joel, Boon Round and the guards.

Occasional windows in the wall let in the Dead World's cold light and bitter wind, and Joel saw that they were climbing up inside a tower. He even began to pant a bit with the climb and he quickly turned down his weathersuit heater. The last thing he wanted was to produce a sweat which could evaporate from his skin in that cold breeze.

As they passed one window Joel turned his face away to avoid the blast – and stopped dead in his tracks when something caught his eye. He looked. He stared. He got a prod in the back, and reluctantly started walking up again.

They came out into the tower's top room – a

circular chamber of dark stone with a high, domed ceiling and tall, wide windows that gave no protection at all from Dead World weather. Joel tried hard to keep his sense of direction, work out in which direction he had been looking on the stairs. Before anyone could stop him he ran over to the window in what he thought was the right direction . . .

'Yes! The lifeboat!'

Boon Round appeared at his side. The lifeboat sat serenely where they had left it. From up here they could see the grid pattern of the city, the endless series of plazas. The tower grew out of the corner of a square and, two squares diagonally along, was the lifeboat.

'North-west,' Boon Round said.

'Sure, you've got a compass?'

'We landed with the nose pointing due east. If that direction is east then it is to our north-west. We approached this tower from the south. We now know where the lifeboat is.'

Before Joel could think of a face-saving answer to the elementary display of compass reading – *pain*.

• *Please.*

Meewa took his elbow and turned him gently away from the window. Joel reluctantly looked around him, as was obviously expected. His attention was caught by the tables around the edges of the room and he wondered if it was a children's nursery. Hundreds, thousands of bright stones in strange patterns. Weird clay models of amazing intricacy, dark grey slates covered with scribbles which he suspected were writing; maybe not a nursery after all. An avant garde art museum?

• *Once, (a place for) watching the stars.*

Joel hadn't even noticed the return of the headache, but now he got a quick flash of locals standing at the tall windows, looking out at a clear, starry sky. Other locals played with the stones and the clay. Making notes? Models of constellations? Calculations?

Then he looked up at the domed roof of the chamber. He didn't understand everything up there – a lot of writing, curves, lines – but he recognized the basic idea. It was stars. He presumed it was the Dead World's night sky, from a time when you could actually see the sky at night. And there were a lot of stars up there – more than he would have expected, from what he remembered of the view from SkySpy.

'Boon Round,' he said, 'this place is an observatory! These people ... these people really were advanced. Just as much as Earth or the Roving, a few centuries back . . .'

'So I had deduced,' Boon Round said, 'from this.'

The Rustie had wandered forward into the centre of the room. Set into a pit was a circular wooden board, perhaps ten feet across. There was a golden ball at the centre and painted, golden rays blazed out of it. Joel suddenly had no doubt that this was a model of the solar system. It might even have been clockwork.

Three planets orbited the central sun – small wooden balls that moved along elliptical tracks. Presumably, they were the uninhabitable first world, then the home world of the XCs, and finally the Dead World.

'Odd they didn't know about the outer planets,' Joel said. 'You'd have thought they'd put in the Shield at least. It should have been visible from here.'

'Perhaps they aren't interested in what lies beyond this world,' Boon Round said. 'Only what's between here and the sun.'

'They don't have either of the homeworld's moons,' Joel observed.

'Perhaps they didn't have telescopes. This is naked-eye observation only.'

The headache . . .

- *(I must) cause (you more) pain. (The explanation is) nearly complete.*

Joel gritted his teeth. 'Go on.'

- *(This is how our) worlds (are) now.*

Meewa opened a flap in the floor and turned a small wheel. The model began to move; the XCs' world and the Dead World crept around their tracks until they were as close together as they would ever be. Both worlds had to make several orbits of the sun to get there; their years were of quite different lengths and the XCs' world lapped the Dead World several times before the two made the right conjunction.

- *And this is the . . .*

Another of Meewa's information dumps, straight into Joel's head. He saw more than just the two planets at perigee. He saw . . . it was like a feast day, a celebration, a religious event; every festival of every one of Earth's religions rolled into one, plus Winter Solstice, New Year, Carnival.

On the level above this room, on the roof of the tower itself, the Processors gathered. It was a scene repeated all across the world, at the tops of mountains and towers like this. Their necks craned upwards, their gaze was fixed on the blue star gleaming bright in the dark. And they were taking *something* from the sky.

- *(At these) times (we would) reach out (to the) . . .*

[That sacrificial animals idea. The *malesna*.]

- *. . . (and we would be given) life.*

The pain, the pressure was building up inside Joel's head, worse than ever before. More pictures, more images . . .

'Stop it!' he screamed. His hands were clasped around his head, trying to hold it together, to stop it bursting. He was on his knees and Boon Round was holding him up.

The pain stopped abruptly. Joel breathed a sigh of relief that spread throughout his body, better even than the warmth from the bath.

'You're bleeding,' Boon Round said. Joel felt the trickle from his nose, put a finger to it, saw the blood on his finger tips. 'What did you see?'

'Hard . . . hard to say.' Joel pushed himself to his feet and leaned on the rail that surrounded the model. He tilted his head back and pinched his nose. Meewa was turning the wheel again and the planets were returning to their previous positions. 'Something about . . . something really important happens when the planets are close. They get . . .' Joel curled his fists up tight, frowned, tried to squeeze the concept out of his brain. 'Guidance. Information. *Stuff*. They get it from the sky.'

'Astrology?' Boon Round sounded scornful.

'No, not astrology! It's more important than that. I . . . I need to think about it, get it straight . . .'

But Joel couldn't quite picture it. These *malesnu* were involved, somehow. And the XCs' Homeworld.

- *(We need) malesna. (We have) some (but not) enough. (After) you, (some more) (came from) the sky (but they were) lost (to us). (Can you) (help us get) more malesna?*

The question took Joel by surprise.

'Um . . . how?' he said.

- *In this.*

A clear image of the lifeboat.

'Um . . .' he said again. The doubts were back in his mind, and again he knew that the Processor knew

293

them. Joel knew exactly what the Admiralty would say if it learnt he was hiring the lifeboat out to a non-technological species for their errands. Maybe an arrangement could be made, but it was something that could only be done at the level of admirals and politicians. Or his father. Not a mere lieutenant.

On the other hand, he and Boon Round between them were the ranking Commonwealth officers and sole government representatives on this planet.

But again, Meewa seemed to understand the hesitation.

• *(Please consider) the request, (and) (in the meantime) (let me show) you more.*

'Does it still hurt?' Boon Round said as they followed the Processor.

'Yeah.' Joel rubbed his temple. 'I think he's keeping what he says short, though. He knows it hurts. He's guessed humans aren't built for telepathy.'

'I haven't received any pictures at all.'

'No, that would be . . .' Joel bit his tongue and stopped. Now really wasn't the time to start antagonizing his companion again.

'Do go on.'

Joel sighed. 'No offence, but the Ones Who Command designed you not to have any imagination or initiative. And maybe that means no telepathy either.'

'There's no offence. That's how it is. And it's a reasonable hypothesis.'

'Well, believe me, you're damned lucky.'

'Incidentally . . .' Boon Round took a step closer, as if passing on a confidence. 'Your aide is in this tower somewhere.'

'What?' Joel stared at the Rustie. 'How do you know?'

'I just heard its contact tone in my translator unit. It is definitely nearby; probably on an adjacent floor. Its signal is strong. Shall I contact the lifeboat through it?'

'God.' Joel glanced out of the window. 'You could, couldn't you?'

• *Please come.*

Meewa was watching them. Was he picking up on the exchange? There had been no headache apart from a brief flash with that last message, so maybe not.

And things were getting interesting. Meewa had made the attempt to communicate; they hadn't been killed . . . They ought to find out what was happening.

'No,' Joel said. 'But file it away for future reference.'

'Very well.'

'And now . . .' Joel gestured for Boon Round to precede him. 'Let the lesson continue.'

'Learned Mother.' Fleet lay on the stone floor of the cell, his back propped up against the wall. He sounded, and was, weak. Worn out. Oomoing wondered if she caught a note of despair.

'Loyal Son?'

'I've been thinking.'

Unwise, Loyal Son, Oomoing thought. 'Go on,' she said.

'My Mother raised me to serve the battle gods unswervingly.'

'Of course.'

'And they've brought me here. They've brought us here. Why?' Now there was no doubt about the despair. 'I am Third Son and so my chances of shining in combat have always been limited compared to Second and First, but . . . I can't have angered the gods this much? And you, Learned Mother! What have you done to anger them? What *could* you have done? I know we may not see eye to eye on certain matters concerning them –'

For example, their existence? Oomoing thought.

'– but I know you are a good mother to your children, you serve the nation dutifully – how can they be angry about that? How, Learned Mother, how?'

Fleet paused. Then: 'Learned Mother,' he said, as if about to impart a terrible secret, 'the battle gods I have been taught about cannot be so unreasonable. Either I have been taught wrongly or . . .'

You've worked it out too, then, Oomoing thought.

'Tell me, Learned Mother. Please.'

Oomoing heard the raw appeal in his tones and leaned back against the wall on her side of the cell. Where to start?

'Loyal Son, I'm surprised at you,' she said. She deliberately put anger into her tone, hating herself while she did it. There was a time and a place to deconstruct ancient superstitions, and this wasn't it. Fleet needed something to believe; she couldn't say what he might become otherwise.

But she wasn't going to turn into a didactic priest either.

'Do you remember the hurricane two years ago, back home? All those coastal towns, flooded out?' she said.

'Of course.' A hint of surprise.

'Thousands of Kin, forced to cling onto roofs and treetops in the dark and the rain. One weak moment and they would have been swept away. What do you think they felt? I expect it was close to despair. I expect it was close to what you feel. And of course, many of them never felt anything else, because they died. But others survived and now serve their country and their battle gods with distinction.'

A pause.

'Your point, Learned Mother?'

'You are one Kin, Loyal Son. The battle gods are immeasurably older and immeasurably greater than you or me. We can only judge from our own limited experience; they have the full scope and range of Kin history to draw upon. We can't stop believing in them because we're having a hard time. Don't presume to generalize from your individual experience.'

In other words, be scientific. If you're going to stop believing in the battle gods, do them the courtesy of having a good reason.

Oomoing knew full well that she hadn't answered his question, but she hadn't not answered it either.

'Thank you, Learned Mother. I'll – I'll think about that.'

So, she had done her duty as a mother to a son. She had helped him continue, though how much longer they could continue *for* was another question. The natives patched them up but they couldn't replace lost blood. They couldn't heal damaged and battered bodies. But, she had helped him, and would continue to until they reached that point when their damaged and battered bodies just gave up.

It was some consolation, as the numbness crept back into her mind again and she knew that once again their captors were taking her over.

Meewa's tour continued according to some itinerary that only Meewa knew. Every time Meewa made contact with Joel, every time their minds came close, Meewa seemed to understand more about Joel ... and Joel found out more about Meewa. Every time he sensed further depths, more complexity. And to his surprise he was liking the Processor. He sensed a loneliness. Meewa was young for his position; his talent at Processing (whatever that was) had put him in the unexpected position of First Contact specialist.

Joel knew that Meewa knew he too was still reckoned as young amongst his own people, and that he was in a situation of much more responsibility and gravity than could reasonably have been expected from his vocation in life. Well, Meewa knew how that felt. They both had things in common.

Joel knew that Meewa was daring to let himself

hope that, well ... who knew? They might even become friends. Never one to turn down an olive branch, Joel found that he hoped so too.

And then they came out onto a balcony. It was a circular gallery around a central pit, and several other locals were already here. Meewa introduced them as the other Processors. The Processors were staring down at the creatures standing in the middle of the pit. The *malesna*.

Joel and Boon Round stiffened in surprise. Joel exclaimed, 'What are they doing here?'

The two XCs just stood there, facing each other. Their arms hung limply at their sides and they didn't move.

Boon Round relaxed a little. 'So, these are the *malesna*? I'd say they're not as well looked after as we are.'

'How can you tell?' Joel slowly sat down where Meewa indicated, ready to leap up at any moment if the XCs got nasty. He had seen them move before, and boy, could they move.

Come to think of it, the locals had seen them move too, but there was no evidence of extra guards, other than the ones on the top ledge with him and Boon Round.

'I can see several new wounds that were not there when we last saw them,' Boon Round said. Joel growled in irritation; the question was meant to be sarcastic.

A door opened down below and some locals staggered in, carrying ... other locals. The ones being carried seemed to be asleep. They were curled up, their legs drawn up to their torsos and their arms wrapped around themselves. The sleepers were placed around the edge of the pit.

And Joel had another painful vision from Meewa. Somewhere, under this city, were catacombs full of sleepers. Miles of tunnels, thousands of locals. They were . . . not dead. Not alive. Not in a coma. They just *were* – there was nothing there except the bodies.

Until they received that vital infusion – lifeforce, intelligence, sentience. This was how the survivors of the xenocide had stayed alive. A few had stayed up here on the surface to manage things, the rest had gone down to sleep and wait for—'

The XCs pounced, straight at each other. Arms out, claws extended, they clashed. The female slashed the male across the face and blood spattered out on to the sand. The male leapt back, then crouched and sprang low at the female. He wrapped all four arms around one of her legs and sank his teeth into her haunches. He tore out a chunk of dripping flesh and blood spurted into his face. The female screeched and clasped both hunting hands together. She clubbed at the back of the male's head. He collapsed face down into the sand and the female gathered herself up to jump down on him.

But suddenly she stood back, all arms hanging limply at her side, and a couple of locals scuttled into the arena. They swarmed around the female and the still form of the male, bandaging and tending to their injuries. Then they ran back through the doorway.

Slowly the male picked himself up, turned to face the female, and pounced again.

• *(An excellent) waking session!*

Joel turned to stare at Meewa, then reluctantly looked back at the fighting, drawn by an irresistible fascination. The pattern was obvious: pounce, fight, come close to killing each other, then the sudden time-out for the tending of wounds. Boon Round seemed to find it equally fascinating, perhaps in exactly the same masochistic way. What was going through the Rustie's mind Joel couldn't guess, but in his own mind he just *knew* that this wasn't right. XCs would fight at the drop of a hat, but *this* . . .

He could see their strength, their life energies, in the same way as the Processors. He could see there was no intelligence there, nothing to make them thinking, sentient beings. They were just two fighting and killing machines.

When they fought, the Processors weren't controlling them, guiding their actions; quite the opposite. The Processors were taking their sentience from them; their self-control, the mental forces that defined them as conscious, thinking creatures. All that was left was their fighting instincts. Put two XCs together without that self-control and this was what happened.

Meewa turned to look at him: it was a moment's warning to prepare for the abrupt return of the headache. And he *saw* it. He saw how it was. It was horrible, hideous, but to the people of the Dead World it was *right*.

'My God,' he breathed.

Meewa was basking in the lifeforce coming off the two *malesna*. In his mind's eye, Joel could see it being channelled from the Processors, out of the *malesna* and into the sleepers. Some of them began to twitch. They had been sleeping since the Great Death, the name these creatures gave the xenocide. Now they could awake again.

Joel looked back at Meewa. 'You . . .' he said. 'You sick bastards!'

Perhaps the words hadn't been understood, but he knew that Meewa had got the emotion. Joel sensed hurt, confusion.

Like he cared.

Eighteen

Day Eighteen: 20 June 2153

'And . . . and the xenocide, the great attack,' Joel said, 'was just . . . just self-defence! They're the good guys. Don't you see it?'

They were back in their house-cum-prison. The guard had been relaxed; they could leave and walk around the plaza, if they so desired (They didn't – not in that wind). Now Joel looked anxiously into Boon Round's expressionless face and wished Rusties didn't look so *blank*.

'No,' said Boon Round.

'Oh, for God's sake!' Joel leapt to his feet and paced round and round the room. 'Which bit don't you get? Look.' He crouched down in front of Boon Round again. 'We have the XCs. The xenocides. The race formerly known as the xenocides . . .'

'They are xenocides. No-one disputes that.'

Joel ignored him. 'Their world is constantly racked by war and fighting. But somehow, through some miracle, they drag themselves up by their bootlaces each time, each time they make themselves just a little bit more civilized than before, and then, wham! Another war, and they get wiped all over again.'

He leapt up and paced about again, illustrating his points by waving his arms wildly in the air. 'Only it's not them fighting. I mean, it is, but they aren't doing it because they want to. It just happens that the two worlds are close and the Processors . . .'

This was where it broke down. He didn't have reasons, just results.

'Look, I don't know how or why, but the people on this world seem to take their . . . their *minds*, their *awareness* from the XCs. Not all the time, but they need . . . recharges. They need to top up. And when they did that, in the past, at the other end of the line the XCs were being reduced to animals. No self-control, no awareness . . . and when you put two XCs together in that state, they fight. It's how they are.'

'That—' said Boon Round.

'I *saw* it, Boon Round. I've got that information in my head and . . . I'm working it out. There were millions of locals here, once. Hundreds of thousands of Processors, sucking the XCs dry. But now . . . well, the xenocide knocked them down to below some kind of critical mass. The few that were left were able to keep going without the XCs, which is lucky for them 'cos there aren't enough left to reach out like they used to. But now . . . now, they're going to milk the two we brought with us for all they can. They'll wake up more and more of their own kind, until they have enough to start all over again. They'll wake their race up and the whole XC homeworld will . . .

'Look, maybe the XCs knew all the details, or maybe they just pieced things together, but they knew that their wars were being caused by the Dead World. Somehow. So they launched their attack. Which the Ones Who Command saw. And we've been afraid of them ever since.' More subdued, he said, 'Now, what don't you understand in all that?'

'It's all quite obvious,' Boon Round said. 'That wasn't what I meant. You quaintly describe the XCs as the good guys. I remind you that they weren't under anyone's influence when they attacked SkySpy and wiped out my pride. That was all their own work.'

'Well . . .' Joel had to rein himself in. 'Yes, yes, I know that, Boon Round. XCs are naturally contentious little sods, but that's just . . . just their nature.'

'You lost friends on SkySpy too,' Boon Round pointed out.

'I know!' Joel bellowed. 'I know and I hate them for it and . . .' He clutched his head. 'But . . . Look, I've got to forgive them, Boon Round. I've got to, because hanging on to hatred might make me feel better here and now, but it won't do any good in the long run. Hang on to that hatred and the only justifiable course is another xenocide, wipe out the XCs before they wipe out us, because with the amount of hate that we have there won't be any middle ground. And as we know that wouldn't be justified, we've got to let go of the hatred first.' He kicked the wall. 'If you want to hate anyone, hate the merciless little pricks that run this place.'

'But what *they* do is in *their* nature,' said Boon Round. 'You wouldn't blame a raptor bird for feeding on some defenceless rodent. Exactly the same principle applies here, even though the two parties are on different worlds.'

'And the two parties are intelligent!' Joel sat down in one corner and put his head in his hands. Did they know what they were doing? Did they know that at the other end of the line, their *malesna* were having their identity and dignity stripped away and being turned into brutal, feral animals? Did they *care*? 'Maybe the Dead Worlders don't know that. Maybe the XCs didn't know about the Dead Worlders . . . those two could tell us. God, I wish we could talk to them! If only we had a translator, or—'

'We do,' said Boon Round. Joel lifted his head up slowly to look at the Rustie.

'Where?'

'On the lifeboat.'

Joel snorted. 'Yeah? So how did it get there?'

'Both lifeboats were constantly updated with information in SkySpy's banks,' Boon Round said. 'It was to save downloading time in the event of an attack. SkySpy had a working translator model; therefore, so does the lifeboat.'

A vast pit seemed to open under Joel. He couldn't believe he had really been that unbelievably stupid. He knew the evacuation protocols. He knew how SkySpy worked. And he hadn't thought . . .

'The life— . . . a trans— . . .' Joel glared at the Rustie to cover up his own feelings. 'You mean . . . we had them on board . . . all that time . . . why didn't you *say something*, you stupid Rustie?'

'I assumed you knew, you stupid human. And what would you have wanted to say to them?'

'I'd have wanted . . . I'd have . . . oh, I don't know!' Joel was pacing around again. 'Look, we have a problem. Meewa wants us to use the lifeboat to collect more XCs for their little games.'

'I see,' Boon Round said. 'Yes, that could be a problem.'

'Thank you!'

'The lifeboat on its own could never get through their homeworld's combined defences. On the other hand there are isolated space stations which we could probably raid . . .'

'We are not abducting any XCs!' Joel said through his teeth. 'They . . . I'm sorry, Boon Round, I know their kind killed your friends and mine, but they just don't deserve this. We're talking about an entire race.'

'Your attitude is entirely unreasonable,' Boon Round said. 'We're in these creatures' favour, now. We can play along and regain the lifeboat. We could even capture a few more XCs to show our good will, build up some trust. I'm *not* talking about the entire race, just a few. A space station crew, say, would keep the locals happy for years to come, and in the meantime we could make our escape. Once we're back in the lifeboat we can do what we like.'

Joel shook his head. 'For one thing, it wouldn't work. Boon Round, I can't afford to have the slightest duplicity in my mind, because Meewa will see it. We can't plan a single surprise, because he'll know about it. And for another thing – no! We are not going to abduct a single XC! Not one! It's not . . . *right!*'

'You are—'

'Put yourself in their place!' Joel shouted. 'Two aliens have just kidnapped us and delivered us to a bunch of sadists who need to make us kill each other to keep their own race alive. How do you feel about that?'

'My feelings are irrelevant. This is the situation that we must work with. We have two choices: do what they want, or work out how to get to the lifeboat without them. We know its position, now.'

'But we can't get to it,' Joel groaned. Yes, they knew where it was, and they could walk the distance in ten minutes. They'd just have to get through several hundred spear-toting locals *en route*.

'We must think of a way.'

'I've already told you that Meewa—'

'In that case,' Boon Round said simply, '*I* must think of a way. They can't read my mind.'

Joel snorted. 'Oh, yeah, right! We're reduced to you having a good idea.'

'I see no reason to stand here and be insulted,' Boon Round said, and paced out of the room. Joel strode to the door after him.

'Good luck!' he called. 'Maybe you could fix up a perpetual motion machine while you're about it!'

No answer. Joel sat down again in his corner. 'Ladies and gentlemen, I give you the Commonwealth. A place where humans and Rusties, sorry, *First Breed*, can live and work together in perfect harmony. Like chalk and cheese.' *I mean, just because he's absolutely right and we don't owe the XCs anything and . . .*

But he carefully steered his thoughts away from that direction. There was another direction to go in, far more fun and just as hopeless.

'Is this seat taken?'

[A whole bunch of information objects from the sound of the voice alone. The accent is from a place called New Zealand. The tone of the voice is warm, friendly and female. Associated information objects: desire to look good, possibility of procreative activity not to be ignored.]

He looks up. His view is darkened by the glasses he wears but the outline of a female shows against the background aura of the sun. It is hot [so hot! So luxuriously hot . . .], *the sun shines bright with light that reflects off the blue sea* [so much water!], *the sand and the white stone of the promenade. He is sitting at a table in shorts and a T-shirt; the clothes are baggy, plenty of room for the gentle breeze to get in and caress his skin with a cooling touch. Self-image: relaxed, sexy, attractive. He sits in the shade of a large parasol and sips at a pleasantly cool drink. The table is at Alf's, properly known as the Alfresco Bar on Admiralty Island* [a whole cascade of associated information objects, to be explored later].

'It's all yours,' *he says.*

'Thanks.' She sits down in the chair and breathes relief. 'This gravity! How do you get used to it?' Her

skin is not highly tanned, which suggests she has not been here long. The tone of complaint amuses him. He recognizes a newcomer to this world, which combined with her gender means there are two reasons to be interested in her.

Gravity on the Roving [many associated information objects] *is slightly higher than on Earth* [many, many, many associated information objects] *but he is used to it. This world is his home, now. He is a citizen of the Commonwealth* [a term laden with emotion and pride].

Different imperatives run through his mind, all stemming from the fact that she is an attractive female, pleasant to look at: engage in conversation; spend time with her. There are also more negative ones: don't be a jerk, don't put her off. He hardly knows they are there but they guide his actions, his mood, his words.

'It just takes practice,' he says. 'Sitting down a lot helps.'

'Yeah, I noticed. If it doesn't kill me . . .'

'It'll make you stronger.'

'Kind of a default medical exam for citizenship,' she says. They smile at each other, a moment of shared understanding. 'You a Commonwealth man?'

'Yup. Four years.'

'So you were in at the start? I suppose that gives you time to adjust.'

'Well, I . . .' *A sudden reticence, a non-desire to speak of his father; a fear she might think he's bragging.* 'I was on UK-One when it came. I decided to stay.'

'That so? I'm with UK-1 now. It was meant to be a

stepping stone to the Commonwealth but now I wonder.'

'Yeah?' She's probably thirsty; he wants her to stay longer; he signals a waiter. 'Doing what?'

'Well, the king's decided he wants to start a defence force . . .'

Hardly relevant, the Abbot Processor's thoughts pulsed. *The female unit is high in his affections. So what?*

The Abbot Processor had been Meewa's sponsor all his life, ever since Meewa's latent ability had been detected as an infant. His opinion was doubly important to Meewa now; not just as his superior but as a loved and respected senior figure. But Meewa had to suppress his irritation at the casual, dismissive tone of his master's thoughts.

His master's fingers ran over the sculpture, the piece of retrieved memory that Meewa had put together. The clay to give meaning and shape to the information that ran between their shared minds, the stones to show the links between the information objects that his finger tips were uncovering. Meewa had enjoyed making that model. He had sensed a friendliness, a sympathy in the tall visitor and it had been a pleasure to map out his mind. Then had come that slap, that rejection when they watched the *malesna* fight. Meewa still smarted from it.

It was only slightly less irksome than the Abbot Processor's scepticism.

With respect, I must point out the connotations with the Commonwealth *information object*, Meewa pulsed back. *This is the first time he's thought of himself as a member of the Commonwealth in the presence of an outsider that he wishes to be close to, which makes the meaning he attaches to it more apparent. And I cross-link these thoughts to his father information object. A unit he greatly admires.*

Your conclusions?

This Commonwealth was designed to help two species live together. Meewa was thinking carefully as he pulsed back. This was the crux of his argument. *He's proud that it was formed to save one species from slavery. He's proud to be part of that entity.*

Just as Meewa was proud to be a Processor. It was another common point between them; something else to make Joel Gilmore's anger personally hurtful.

There's also a lot of self-interest here, the Abbot Processor observed. *He's in the Commonwealth for what it can do for him, just as much as, if not more than what he can do for it. His belief in the Commonwealth is more theoretical than practical. Note that he does not particularly like these* Rusties.

Meewa would rather the floor opened up and swallowed him, but he had to contradict.

The dislike of Rusties is a surface thought based on day-to-day experience. It doesn't run deep. His deep layers have a strong element of compassion and a desire for what he perceives as justice. His approval of the Commonwealth is based on theory, but it is a grounding theory. And I remind you again of his father. He craves parental approval even without realizing it. He will never do something that he thinks would hurt his father.

The Abbot Processor was impatient.

And where does all this take us, Meewa?

Meewa had to say it.

He doesn't approve of our treatment of the malesna *and he won't help us gather more.* His tone was reluctant, but firm. This was how it was. Facts were facts and not worth arguing about.

The Abbot Processor had taught him that.

Now the Abbot Processor stood and walked to the window. He looked out at the visitors' sky vessel.

I see. Compassion, you say. There's no compassion for a dying race?

There's plenty! He greatly feels for our predicament and despite his distaste he feels more fondly towards us than he does towards the malesna. *But I say again, he will not help us acquire more of them.*

Very well. We need his knowledge; we don't necessarily need him. The Abbot Processor turned back from the window. *You are authorized to recover that knowledge, Meewa. Go deep into his mind and do it.*

Meewa almost demurred, but he had contradicted his master enough for one day.

Boon Round may attempt to interfere, he pointed out instead.

Boon Round will be dealt with. You cannot read him and the pair have rejected our friendship; he is therefore unnecessary to us. I will have him dealt with; you do as instructed. The Abbot Processor left.

I'll start at once, Meewa pulsed. And he apologized mentally to Joel Gilmore for the pain he was about to cause. *But,* he added silently, *you brought it on yourself.*

*

Boon Round trudged moodily around the plaza and his thoughts, though he didn't know it, mirrored Joel's. *So this is the Commonwealth.*

Ridiculous, really. An agreement to co-exist, to help each other ... even though everyone knew it was really the humans in charge. But they at least *pretended* the First Breed were their equals and partners – until it came to the crunch.

A small part of Boon Round's mind pointed out that the humans could have taken straight over from the Ones Who Command. It had been the original plan. The First Breed would still be slaves, just slaves to different masters. The Commonwealth had come about because some humans – the father of that idiot Joel Gilmore, for one – hadn't been able to trust certain other humans with that kind of responsibility. And, all things considered, Boon Round preferred freedom to slavery; a constitution that guaranteed certain rights ahead of the arbitrary whims of the Ones Who Command.

But he would rather be mistreated by a One Who Commands, which was in his nature, than be insulted by a human, with whom he was meant to be an equal.

Trudge, trudge, trudge. Boon Round had come to the end of one wall. He turned right and walked along the next.

Humans! Who needed them? Sometimes he could just ...

Boon Round stopped in his tracks. Had he really been so stupid? Had even he, proud member of a race which (as Joel Gilmore had pointed out) was not renowned for its imagination, really not thought of something so obvious? He knew how to get to the lifeboat.

Then he heard the screaming.

The picture of Donna hovered in front of him, generated by his ident bracelet. Joel studied it gloomily. Eventually he took his finger off the tab and the image vanished. Memories. Fond memories.

Joel stood up and wandered over to the door. Boon Round was pacing along the far wall of the plaza. He wondered if he should go over and apologize. In fact there was no *if* about it. None of what had happened was Boon Round's fault and he had been taking it all out on the Rustie. If they were meant to be equals then he had been inexcusably rude; and if he was meant to be Boon Round's superior officer then he had been venting his frustration on a subordinate. Even more inexcusable.

A twinge in his head. 'Oh, come on!' he said to the air. 'Not again!' He looked around, but saw no sign of Meewa. In fact, the square was deserted – the only sign of life, one pissed-off Rustie. The pain came back and grew stronger.

And stronger. And *stronger*. 'Hey!' he yelled, but to no effect. Surely he could manage it, he had been here before . . . but never as bad as this. His vision blurred. Something was growing inside his brain which must explode soon. His head would burst but it would be over.

But it kept growing *still*. His balance was gone. He

toppled over, unable to take his hands away from his head to break the fall. His head banged against the door lintel. He felt the shock, he felt skin break, he felt blood trickle down his face. But there was no pain because he didn't have any pain to spare from the torture going inside his head.

Joel screamed, shrieked, shrieked again. His throat was raw. He wanted to faint, wanted the blackness to come, but he stayed obstinately awake.

Then he saw the images. He recognized Meewa's touch in his mind, and it was delving. Delving deep. He sensed the connection between them, saw the stream of information flowing from his mind to Meewa's.

An image of the lifeboat. The pilot's desk. Thoughts and ideas and concepts from his basic training. Meewa was learning to fly the lifeboat.

'No you don't!' He didn't know if he said it, shouted it, just thought it. But he fought back. He closed his mind. The flow slowed down, slightly, and then the pain and the pressure built up again.

And still Joel fought.

Boon Round pelted across the plaza. Four locals were running towards him, reaching for their swords. He put his head down and charged through them.

Then he was through the door and in the front room of the house. Joel Gilmore lay on the floor, his body locked rigid in an agonized backwards curve that should have snapped his spine. Blood streamed from his nose and ears, and his face was as red as a sunset. His mouth was wide open, wider than Boon Round had ever seen in a human before, and his face was contorted, but the screaming had stopped. Boon Round had a horrible feeling he had reached the stage where even screaming wasn't enough. Or perhaps he had simply scraped his vocal cords raw.

Joel's mouth moved. 'Th . . .' he breathed. There was no volume in his voice, no power left in his lungs to provide it. Boon Round moved closer, cocked an ear. 'They . . . they're . . . getting . . . lifeboat . . . info.'

Boon Round turned quickly as a local loomed in the doorway. It held a spear at the ready and it looked warily at him. Presumably it only saw what it thought Boon Round was – a four-legged creature whose only means of manipulating objects were two grasping tentacles, one either side of the mouth. It began to advance.

Boon Round flicked his graspers at the local, let it think that was all he could do. The local edged closer. Then Boon Round reared up on his hindfeet and his forefeet grabbed the shaft of the spear. He twisted it free and in the same movement clubbed his assailant with the blunt end. The local staggered backwards out of the door. Boon Round quickly spun the spear so that the business end was aimed at those clustering outside. The door was narrow; only one could come through at a time. For a minute or two, he was safe.

How long before they fetched an archer?

'Help . . .' Joel breathed.

Boon Round made up his mind.

'No!' he shouted. 'I have had enough of your

endless complaining!' He studied the spear grasped in his forefeet: a wooden shaft and a sharpened stone point. His forelegs tensed and the spear snapped. Boon Round dropped to all fours, held the point in one grasper and jabbed it into Joel's side. The point went through the weathersuit and into his skin, and Joel gasped. 'On your feet, human!' Boon Round snapped.

Joel looked at him blankly, his pain clouding his mind. Boon Round grabbed Joel's head with his graspers and looked straight into the human's face.

'Meewa, I expect you can hear me,' he said. 'I have had enough of your hospitality and I am leaving. You can keep this pathetic human if you like; I have had enough of him too. However, *I* am now going to walk to the lifeboat and I am taking this creature with me. If I see a single one of your people along the way – ' he waved the spear point in front of Joel's eyes – 'the human gets it.' He jabbed Joel again. 'Now, human, *get up!*'

It took several more jabs and blood was beginning to seep through the tears in his weathersuit, but Joel managed to stagger to his feet. Dazed, barely coherent, but the pain seemed to have stopped.

'Now, out,' Boon Round said. Another jab. They shuffled out into the square and started for the lifeboat.

Meewa had followed instructions and the way was clear. Boon Round was grateful for his First Breed's 200-degree-plus vision as he scanned rooftops, arches, hidden corners for the ambush he was sure would come. One plaza down. Two plazas down . . .

'Look . . .' Joel protested.

'Silence!' Yet another jab, and they kept walking.

Boon Round knew where the lifeboat was from the tower, and the tower was an obvious landmark, so that was where he headed. Now the tower was one plaza ahead of them.

A flicker of movement ahead; a local just vanishing around a corner.

'I warned you, Meewa!' Boon Round held the spear point over Joel's stomach. 'I said I don't want to see anyone! Get everyone back, *now*!'

They paused; no more movement from ahead, so they cautiously started walking again.

Five locals jumped from behind a pillar and fell on them. Two bumped into Joel and knocked him away from Boon Round and the spear point. Another swiped at the point itself with a sword and Boon Round barely missed having his grasper severed. The last two jumped on Boon Round himself.

Boon Round didn't bother contesting the issue. He ducked down low between their legs and scarpered.

He was tensed for a spear, an arrow, *something* in his back and he darted from side to side as he ran across the plaza, but nothing came. The locals thought he could be dealt with later; they had Joel, Meewa could go back to work. The tower was just ahead. So close, so close . . .

And the tone sounded through his translator unit. *At last!* He was back in range of Joel's aide. And that meant . . .

He switched to comm mode. 'Lifeboat systems command. Activate secondary engines. Take off. Rise to altitude two hundred feet. Stop. Await further orders. Acknowledge.'

'*Acknowledged,*' said a neutral voice from his translator unit. '*Complying.*'

In the distance, he heard the engines whine into action. A beautiful sound.

Locals were pouring out of the buildings ahead. Boon Round swerved, weaved his way between them. He would run round in circles if necessary, but he would stay close to the tower.

Some of the locals were slowing down, stopping, gazing upwards. The lifeboat had come into view above the rooftops. Its landing feet were still down, the ladder still out. Boon Round hadn't told it to compensate for wind movement and it was drifting slowly like a giant metal blimp.

'Spin around vertical axis towards starboard,' Boon Round ordered. It turned. 'Stop!' as it came to face him. 'Move forward, descend to fifty feet . . .'

It was a brave local who could stand still while the monster came down from the sky. Boon Round ordered the lifeboat to set down in front of him and the sight of its landing feet touching down in front of them, the shock absorbers compressing, the whole spectacle of it settling into place was the happiest sight of his life. He glanced over to where Joel had been.

Joel was gone. Well, he would just have to hope Meewa could take a hint. He ran to the ladder, climbed up, shut the inner hatch and took a deep breath.

Safe. He was safe. He could put the defence fields on and be untouchable. Or just take off, why not?

Why not – for a very good reason. He walked more slowly to the flight deck, looked out through the viewports. Joel had been in *that* direction *there*, so . . . he looked away . . . *that* direction over *there* would be safe. At least for Joel. He reached for the controls of the laser turret.

A few more commands, and high energy laser fire ploughed into the square outside. He waited for the smoke to clear and peered out. He had cut a smoking black trough clear across the square from one corner to the other. He had deliberately stopped it just short of the buildings.

They couldn't have taken Joel very far; he would give them thirty seconds. He sat back and waited.

Because Joel Gilmore was actually right. Boon Round could argue, and had, that the Dead Worlders using the XCs as they did was part of the natural ecosystem in this solar system, a strange symbiosis between two worlds. On that basis, he and Joel had no business preventing the locals from acquiring more *malesna*. But then Joel had cunningly used that ploy of inviting him to put himself in their position. That changed things, because Boon Round could very well do that.

It was natural for a First Breed to be the slave of a One Who Commands, but that didn't mean he liked it. Boon Round took the argument one step further. If he had lived all his life in complete ignorance of the Ones Who Command, and then they had turned up out of nowhere and claimed his service, would he have tolerated it?

No.

So, Boon Round's mind was made up. They couldn't, wouldn't capture any more XCs, and they had to get the lifeboat away from the people who wanted them to.

Thirty seconds was up. He aimed up at the roof of the building across the square safely opposite where Joel had last been seen. Another laser burst made the roof explode in a cloud of vaporized masonry. Panicked locals swarmed out into the square. Boon Round aimed low and ploughed another laser trough, shepherding them away from the lifeboat. How many hints did Meewa need?

Joel finally appeared. He was alone, walking unsteadily out of an archway, but his head was held high and there was a big smile on his face. Boon Round held his breath and tracked him as he crossed the flagstones, then disappeared underneath the lifeboat. Boon Round ran back to the airlock and opened the inner hatch.

Joel was slumped across the bottom rungs of the ladder. Human and First Breed gazed at each other across that impassable vertical distance of ten feet.

'Can't,' Joel gasped. Boon Round swarmed down, grabbed Joel in his forefeet, propped him against the ladder.

'Quickly,' he said. 'I'll help.'

'You . . .' Joel took hold of the rungs, lifted a foot with obviously a great expense of energy. 'Not going to stab me?'

'I never was.'

'You did, though.' Another rung.

'Not properly. I had to make them think I was sincere, so I had to make *you* think I was sincere.'

'Blood . . . bloody good acting,' Joel muttered. The next rung. The back of his weathersuit was stained red.

Boon Round's peripheral vision caught movement. 'Joel! *Move!*'

The *malesna*, the XCs, had entered the square. Boon Round recognized the steady, stilted walk. They were under the control of the locals.

He leapt for the ladder and climbed as far as he could before Joel got in the way.

'Quick! *Quick!*'

Joel's top half was inside the airlock. Boon Round shoved him the rest of the way with his forefeet, then swarmed up the rest of the ladder himself.

Joel lay on the floor of the airlock. Boon Round slapped the outer hatch control.

The hatch slid half shut, then struck the ladder attachment and stopped. Boon Round bellowed in frustration. The ladder needed to be raised manually and they didn't have the time. Boon Round grabbed Joel and dragged him into the cabin, shutting the inner hatch behind them.

Boon Round dragged Joel over to a seat. 'Lifeboat

systems command, stand by for lift-off to orbit, power up main engine . . .'

'No,' Joel whispered. 'Not yet. Get me to the front of the cabin.'

'What?' Boon Round exclaimed. 'You surely don't claim to be any condition to fly this thing?'

'No.' A faint croak. 'I . . .'

'I've just rescued you, human! Do you still think I'm incapable of . . .'

'You've . . . you've done . . . bloody well.' Joel managed a smile. 'Please. Got to . . . rescue . . . the XCs . . .'

'You're mad!' Boon Round raged. 'Even if what you say about them is true, at the moment they're under control and the outer hatch is jammed open.' Boon Round glanced out of the viewports. A small crowd of locals had gathered around the lifeboat and the two XCs were at the base of the ladder. 'We have to take off. They'll work out how to cut their way in eventually.'

He looked down. 'Joel?'

Joel had passed out.

A thump, another one. The XCs had bypassed the ladder and leapt straight up into the lifeboat. They peered through the porthole at their quarry. As far as Boon Round was concerned, that did it.

'Lifeboat systems command,' he said. 'Override airlock safeties and take off for orbit.'

The city fell away outside the viewports and the lifeboat tumbled into the sky.

*

It was the usual dazed awakening, but with a thunderous roaring in her ears and bone-scraping agony in her arms. Her body felt as if it was being split down the middle.

Oomoing hung by one arm to a support within the airlock; the rest of her was half in, half out, and Fleet clung to her other, outstretched hand. It was a bizarre reversal of the way they had come on board in the first place.

Fleet was hanging on to her with his hunting claws. They dug deep into the flesh of Oomoing's hunting arm; it was an animal self-preservation reflex that had kept him from death when the vessel took off. The tips of his claws grated against bone and Oomoing's blood streamed out of her. With an effort, Oomoing shut down the pain reflex.

Half a mile below him, maybe more, and receding, Oomoing could see the city. She was standing upright, even though she could see the ground in front of her as the ship arced into orbit. She was held in the ship's artificial gravity and Fleet was dangling away from her, pulled by the gravity of the planet. No wonder she felt she was being torn in two.

'Fleet!' she called over the roar of the wind. The invisible shield that surrounded the ship kept the air in its vicinity completely still, but the noise of it moving past on the other side was deafening. 'Let me get you.' She reached out with a feeding arm, trying to get a grip on his wrist. It was shorter than the hunting arm he clung on to and she couldn't quite reach.

She glanced up; how long till they were out of the atmosphere altogether? Her lungs were tightening, her vision spotting.

She looked back at Fleet and he looked straight into her eyes. 'I'm killing you, Learned Mother,' he shouted.

'No, Fleet, wait, just a moment longer . . .'

But she had already seen the resignation, the knowledge of duty, and the pain as he retracted his claws and they slid out of her was ten times worse than their going in. The gravity of the planet drew him away from her with deceptive grace and ease, and then he was gone.

Meewa approached the body slowly. It was shapeless and broken but there was no mistaking the *malesna*. The force of the impact had made a small dent in the stone beneath it and its innards had splattered in a messy circle. It had fallen much further than the other units, the ones swept up into the air when the vessel took off.

He gazed up from the body into the sky and pulsed a blaze of pure, righteous *anger* at the heavens. He didn't feel it connect with anything. The other *malesna* was out of range.

One of the guard-units with him asked a tentative question.

How should we dispose of the remains, Processor?

Meewa transfixed the hapless unit with a glare.

However seems best, he pulsed. *Bury it. Use it as fertilizer. Do what—*

He stopped. There was something . . . it was like the subtlest scent, the vaguest hint of colour. It was tantalizingly familiar.

It was the feeling he had got from the *malesna* as they surrendered their force to the Processors. Surely this creature couldn't still be alive?

No, one look showed that there wasn't the slightest chance of that. Meewa crouched down by the corpse, tentatively reached out a hand. The legs, the body . . . nothing. But as his hand moved up he felt it more and more strongly.

His fingers brushed the *malesna*'s mane. He pushed it aside, gazed in wonder at the mass of dark nodules that had been hidden there. Hundred of little spheres that seemed to call out to him, beseeching him to take them . . .

Give me your knife, he pulsed urgently at the guard-unit. The guard handed the knife down and Meewa inexpertly cut at the cluster. Eventually he stood with the dark mass held in his hands, like a quivering jelly. He reached into it with his senses. It pulsed with vitality. It was everything they wanted from a *malesna*, and more.

He looked back up at the sky and pulsed: *Thank you!*

Nineteen

Day Twenty: 22 June 2153

Laser fire splashed across the connected boxes that made up Device Ultimate.

Donna kicked the nearest box angrily and bounced slowly back across the cabin. 'I'm not even scratching it. This is made of strong stuff.' She braced against a bulkhead to stop her movement.

Gilmore gradually uncurled from his ball, took his hands away from his eyes. The laser light had been blinding.

'Look.' He pointed. 'Seams. Joints. This stuff has been worked. It was put together in a factory somewhere. It was made, it can be unmade.'

'Maybe, but not with a suit laser. Something more industrial strength.' They had tried everything they could think of. Donna slammed a fist against the bulkhead. 'This boat armed?'

'Nope. Civilian transport only.'

'So,' she said conversationally, and as if it were his fault. 'We're screwed.'

Gilmore gritted his teeth. '*We* are,' he said, 'but not necessarily the XCs.'

She looked at him. 'Oh God, this is where we get heroic and suicidal, isn't it?'

'There's probably fuel in the thrusters,' he said levelly. 'We can't *use* the thrusters without the controls but we can get into the tanks. Your lasers are powerful enough to ignite it. We blow the boat up.'

Her eyes blazed. 'That is only slightly less stupid than my own bright idea.'

'Which was?'

'We have air. We pressurize as high as we can, then blow the hatch. The reaction will knock us off course.'

'Not a great deal,' Gilmore said. 'Chances are good the sun will still catch us, and hence, Device Ultimate. And, um, what happens to us?'

'Oh, we still die.'

'Well, that's all right then.'

They looked at each other.

'Funny thing,' Donna said. 'Maybe your way has a greater chance of success but either way, I'm extremely disinclined to do anything that actually results in taking my own life.'

'Odd, that.'

'How long till we reach the sun?'

'Three days, I think it was.'

'The boat can support us that long, can't it?'

'All the way to the bitter end,' Gilmore confirmed. 'We'll get a grandstand view of what it's like inside the sun and we'll be able to watch this thing go off without any kind of obstruction.'

And then . . .

'Shielding!' they said together. To survive getting

329

that close to the sun, the pinnace's fields had been heavily enhanced, to direct the light and heat away from the hull and not have both boat and Device Ultimate vaporize before the latter could do its work.

They could certainly disable the fields. The pinnace and Device Ultimate would be destroyed before any harm was done.

'Well, that's that, then!' said Gilmore.

'And the great thing is,' Donna said, 'we *still* die!'

'That's a relief.'

They looked at each other again for a moment.

'So here's the plan,' he said, more soberly. 'We disable the fields. We coast into the sun and we let it do all the killing for us.'

'That sounds about it. And in the meantime we get religion and pray earnestly for a miracle.'

'While there's life, there's hope,' Gilmore agreed piously. 'Or so I'm told.'

'Oh, it's true,' she said. 'Believe it.' She worked her way into a clingstrap against the bulkhead; it saved floating around. She seemed quite calm, now, and Gilmore wondered how much of it was a façade. For that matter, how much of his own calm wasn't entirely real either?

'Voice of experience?' he asked. There was another clingstrap opposite her, across the cabin, and he pulled it around himself.

'Five years' service in the Anzac Marines, two of them spent in the Pacifican Campaign,' she said. 'Taught me everything I know. Two years trudging through hot, sweaty, insect-ridden jungles. I saw a lot of action if you count the sheer number of five-minute firefights.'

'That so?' Gilmore was impressed. He was still well aware of their impending death but to his surprise he found he could push the subject away with a conscious act of will; the final act of defiance by a rational man against overwhelming fate. He had lived his life; if anything distressed him now, it was that Joel would be upset to hear of his death. But if the universe wanted him to give in, to depart his life a gibbering, sobbing wreck, he wouldn't give it the satisfaction. So he made conversation instead. 'Aren't you, um, over-qualified for King James's toy marines?'

'Am I ever! But I *wanted* to get to the Roving,' she said. 'When the Campaign ended it was still pre-Rusties and space wasn't a very interesting place. So I tried the mercenary lark – I mean, the Confederation was nearby and it had so many enemies that there was always work – but my heart wasn't in it. I didn't want to fight someone else's wars. But then the whole Commonwealth thing happened, and I finally figured that the Roving was the only interesting place to be. Only they didn't have any openings for someone with my, um, skills. UK-One did, so I reckoned, why not join UK-One and spy out the Roving from a distance, see if this great Commonwealth thing is really worth joining?'

Gilmore grinned. He enjoyed talking about the Commonwealth, one of the few things in his life that had his unequivocal approval. 'And was it?'

'Eventually. I pretty soon worked out that UK-One –' she pulled a face – 'was a mistake. I joined the marines because it was new and exciting and I got a commission and more pay. The first retrograde step was being junior to Bill . . .' She paused and Gilmore knew what the montage of thoughtful expressions meant. Perry had been nothing but a pain to him, but to Donna he had been a friend, a colleague, someone she had worked with and fought alongside. It forged bonds that didn't just vanish with death. 'Bill, who was a nice guy if you got to know him but, let's say, limited in his outlook and let's be frank, the teeniest bit of a dork at times. And then, *then* I learnt what it means to work for King James. That was when I hit bottom and began to dig.'

Gilmore laughed. 'I could have told you, if you'd asked.'

'I mean, my supreme commander was a man whose idea of good soldiering is to dress up in smart uniforms. Whose idea of good leadership is to wear a slightly smarter uniform with a fancy hat. Oh, and he'd quite like us to be good at our jobs too, but buggered if he'd show the way at all.' She smiled and a faraway look came into her eyes. 'I was ready to chuck it before very long, but then I got my first leave, and I went down to the Roving, and I met someone who persuaded me it was worth staying.'

Her gaze, her tone made Gilmore smile with a faraway look of his own. 'I know that face. Sounds like he was special.' He *assumed* it was a he.

'Yeah, eventually. Background completely

different from mine, but opposites attract and we agreed on . . . well, the basics. He'd been brought up not to take nonsense, to be straight. Like me. And you see, all my life I'd been on the move. I found I was really in a place where I could settle, put down roots, give a meaningful answer when people ask me where I'm from. And I saw that with this guy I'd never be lonely. Apart from the times he disappeared into space for months on end, but you know what I mean.' Gilmore knew. 'Still took me some time to realize he was the one, though.'

'What changed it?'

'Time, and getting to know him. But the best bit was when he took his lieutenant's exam. Normally it's a panel of captains who conduct the exam –'

'I'm familiar with the procedure.'

'– but this time Admiral Chase himself sat in on it and the admiral asked him about navigating an EVA pod near to an asteroid. What could cause it to develop a spin? He trotted out all the correct answers; gravitational anomaly, over-emphasis on one or other of the thrust controls, misjudging the distance visually without referring to the instruments. The admiral asked him, supposing you misread a decimal point on the display? Now, bearing in mind that the decimal point is fixed on the display and the size of a grapefruit, he replied – and I quote – "What kind of idiot would do that?" And the admiral said, "I did when I was a middie." And he said, "I'm sorry sir, but I wouldn't." And the admiral said, "So you think you're a better pilot than me?" And he said—'

'"Too bloody right I do. I mean, sir."' Gilmore stared at her. '*He*'s your boyfriend?'

Donna shrugged, looked almost apologetic. 'Anyone who can speak to an admiral like that is my kind of guy.'

'There . . .' Gilmore trailed off, quite taken aback at this sudden revelation. He wasn't quite sure why it put him out – like, his son's love life was any of his business – but it did. 'There were some, like the commodore of the Navy at the time, who would have said that an answer like that was hot-headed, indicative of a certain immaturity in a grown man of twenty-three, not at all best suited to someone in a position of command over subordinates.'

'I was given too many orders by too many idiots during the Campaign,' said Donna. 'His kind of attitude kept me alive.'

'It got him sent to SkySpy.'

'Yeah, that was a drawback.'

'Joel . . .' Gilmore said. 'He, um, never mentioned you.'

'You know, I'd gathered that. I'm still trying to decide if I should take it personally or not.'

Gilmore thought for a moment. 'Not. Twelve to eighteen, he lived with his mother and we were on opposite sides of the solar system. I think he got used to telling me what I needed to know and keeping the rest private. If you didn't come up in casual conversation, that means he doesn't think of you as casual. You're more important.'

A pause, while Donna worked through this slightly

inverse logic. 'Right. Thanks.'

And after that, there didn't seem to be any more to say for a minute or so.

'We heard about the Pacifican Campaign,' Gilmore said eventually. 'Never really understood it. At the time I was commanding an asteroid sweep. HMS *Australasia*. One thousand tons, one hundred feet long, crew of fifteen. I thought it was as far as my career would go and we'd never heard of the Rusties.'

'Happy days,' she said.

'No, not really.'

'Never thought you'd end up as the founder of a great nation, did you?'

'I didn't found a nation. It was just an idea that worked at the time.'

'But you believe in it, don't you? I've seen the look in your eyes when you talk about it.'

Gilmore paused for thought. 'Yes. I'd been running myself into the ground for my entire life, trying to conform to other people's patterns. Then the Rusties came and everything changed, but people just kept on in the same old ways. Look at the Roving Mission.' He snorted. 'Look at this one. The Commonwealth was the first ever *totally new* thing in . . . in *anyone's* life. The Commonwealth could change all the old ways. Still can, if *Pathfinder* can get back home with a united crew and no act of xenocide on its hands.'

'And you're ready to die for it?'

Another pause. 'Apparently,' he said.

Die. Donna was the first to use that word, though they both had it at the back of their minds. No reason,

Gilmore thought, why the universe's entire quotient of Gilmore DNA, father and son, shouldn't pass from the gene pool in roughly the same area of space. Nicely tidy.

And a third voice spoke into the cabin. A Rustie's voice from a translator unit.

'This is SkySpy lifeboat to Navy pinnace. Do you copy? Over.'

Gilmore leapt for the main console, though even by the time he had got there he knew the voice wasn't coming over the pinnace's systems. Which had of course been disabled. It was coming from his own suit radio.

'This is the pinnace and you bet your life we need assistance,' said Donna behind him. 'Who are you? Over.'

A pause.

'This is Boon Round of the First Breed. I can hear you very faintly. You are barely in range.' The lifeboat had the power to send a clear signal as far as the pinnace, but not vice versa. *'I have been in touch with Pathfinder and they tell me your main comms unit has been disabled. Please look under the pilot's console and open the right hand access panel . . .'*

Two more minutes and the pinnace was back in touch with civilization.

'I will rendezvous with you in four hours,' Boon Round said.

'Is Joel Gilmore with you?' Gilmore burst out. 'Is he alive?'

'He is with me, alive and . . . yes, he is here. Four hours, Commodore.'

The lifeboat and *Pathfinder* had picked up each other's transponder beacons almost simultaneously, and had made contact. Nguyen had told the lifeboat to divert to intercept the pinnace on its course. Four hours later, Gilmore and Donna put their helmets on, took one last and not very regretful look at Device Ultimate, and stepped out into space.

It wasn't quite the joyful reunion either had expected. They looked down at Joel, curled up on the couch nearest the flight deck. Donna detached her armour glove and reached down to touch his face, brushing it with her fingertips. He didn't stir. Gilmore had a sudden flashback to the boy as a toddler, fast asleep in the flatline way that only very small children can manage. And the feelings that coursed through Gilmore's heart as he studied his sleeping son were very similar to the feelings he had had twenty-three years earlier when he held his baby for the first time. His vision was blurring.

'Thank you,' he whispered to himself. To God, to the universe, he didn't know, but thank you someone that my son is alive.

'He's asleep,' Boon Round said from the flight deck. 'He suffered a lot on the Dead World and it took it out of him.'

'Suffered? Will he be all right?' Donna said in alarm.

'He should be. We're both responding to antirads and he didn't lose much blood.'

337

'*Much* blood?' Gilmore demanded. Boon Round ignored the question.

'Ready to fire per your orders, Commodore.'

'Oh, yes,' Gilmore said. He gazed out of the viewport at the pinnace. 'Fire.' The port darkened automatically as the pinnace erupted in a ball of white flame which quickly dwindled away to nothing. Bye bye, Device Ultimate.

Donna yelled and Gilmore spun round. 'Oh my God . . .'

He knew what the thing coming out of the aft compartment was. He had seen pictures, recordings, images. Close up and in the flesh it was even worse. Those teeth, those claws . . . How had the lifeboat been boarded this far out? Why hadn't they been detected?

'Boon Round,' he said quietly, quickly, 'stand by to seal the flight deck and evacuate the main cabin. Lieutenant, help me with Joel but don't make any sudden moves . . .'

'I see you've met our passenger.' Boon Round trotted back from the flight deck with an aide in one grasper. 'This contains the translation program so you can introduce yourselves. We've weeded the probabilities out and it works colloquially now. Her name is Oomoing. She's asked us to take her back to SkySpy, because she wants to have words with her Marshal of Space.'

'She's a . . . friend?' Donna said, looking at the XC with a horrified fascination. She could fry the thing with her suit lasers if it so much as . . .

'An ally,' Boon Round said. 'She kept us alive on SkySpy.'

Gilmore glared at the XC. It was a glare meant for all members of the XC race. Gratitude for Joel's preservation wasn't going to change his more deeply rooted feelings.

'Well,' he said, 'I would also like to have words with her Marshal of Space. There's the little matter of an unprovoked attack on SkySpy.'

'Oh, Oomoing has a theory about that,' Boon Round said. 'The Marshal of Space didn't order an all-out attack on an extraterrestrial base because she had no idea there was an extraterrestrial base there in the first place.'

Gilmore frowned at Boon Round, at Oomoing, at Boon Round again. 'So what . . . ?' he said.

And then the emergency signal came through from the flight deck. It was the Commonwealth standard Mayday call, and it came from *Pathfinder*.

Twenty

Day Twenty: 22 June 2153

Three . . . two . . . one . . .

The attack commenced.

Outlander engineers, suited against the vacuum, were working in the rent in the side of their ship. They had been individually targeted by Barabadar's forces. As the countdown reached zero, each attacker opened fire on his assigned target. The engineers died, their suits torn apart and their helmets ripped open. The assault squad jetted into the open area.

'*Area secured,*' said their leader. '*Entry point located.*'

'Sappers, go,' Barabadar ordered.

A sapper squad blazed away from the assault craft, carrying a portable airlock module between them. They navigated it into the secured area and settled it against what the assault squad had identified as the entry point into the rest of the ship. Meanwhile the hull defence teams moved into position. In the last battle, the outlander troops had come streaming down from the prow of the ship, both between and outside the hulls, and Barabadar wasn't going to be caught that way again. The ring of defences now being erected, between the hulls and around the external entrance at the prow of the ship, would detect and fry anything that moved. Another team was patrolling the hull on the lookout for any other entrances that weren't so immediately obvious.

Barabadar was where she should always be; at the head of her troops. She was poised outside the airlock module. The outlander ship was pressurized and breaching the hull would result in a hurricane of escaping air, blowing back against her and her men. They needed the portable airlock to gain entry. But it had been a minute. How long before the outlanders noticed that their repair team was out of contact?

'Seal established, Martial Mother. Ready to make entry.'

'Go, go, go,' Barabadar ordered. The inner door opened and she charged.

The ship's gravity caught them the moment they were through, but she had expected that. It was a little lighter than Homeworld; not unpleasant, if she had had the time to enjoy it. Some exclamations in her headphones told her that some of the troops had forgotten the briefing. An outlander, one of the two-legged kind, came around a corner up ahead. It stopped in its tracks when it saw her; it opened its mouth and she shot it.

'Locate the flight deck,' Barabadar ordered. 'Implement attack plan.'

The wailing sound of an alarm penetrated her helmet. The outlanders had noticed her presence. So, the attack had really begun.

It had taken over a day to cross the gap between the

rock and the outlander ship. A day, with as many of her people as she could spare crammed into the two surviving assault craft. They had been designed for a covert attack – space-black, radar-invisible, engine outlets shielded as much as possible to avoid flares – but even so, they would have been spotted if the outlanders had actually bothered to keep a visual watch . . . which, of course, they hadn't. *Their* ship had crossed the gap in minutes; naturally it wouldn't occur to them, in their technological arrogance, that the primitive XCs could, or would, do likewise, just taking a bit longer. Barabadar had sat in the command couch of the lead craft and watched the ship creep closer, closer, closer, until it seemed near enough to touch . . . battle hormones raised her nerves to screaming pitch . . . surely, *surely* they would be noticed . . .

There had been that heart-stopping moment earlier when a small vessel left the larger one and shot by, almost within pouncing distance. But it didn't seem to have noticed them and it had vanished into the depths of the inner system. She had wondered what it was for.

And now they were in.

'Move, move, move!' In the absence of their officers, one dead and the other missing, Sergeants Cale and Quinlan were in charge of the marines. The two platoons rushed to pull on their armour as the alarm rang out and the depleted Able Platoon ran to the boat elevator, taking up position as it began to move up towards the ceiling of the hangar. The more numerous Charlie Platoon hurried to the elevator that would take them to the lower decks. The XCs had gained entry to the ship; it was already too late to repeat the intra-hull manoeuvre of last time.

Sergeant Cale tensed as the elevator moved up into launch position in the boat bay. His hands tightened their grip on his gun.

'Set thrusters to—' he began.

Laser fire tore into the marine next to him. The space entrance was rimmed with XCs and they were all firing. Able Platoon fell on their fronts and returned fire instinctively. There was no cover in the passage; both sides just had to take it, and the marines were much more exposed than the enemy.

'Withdraw the elevator!' Cale shouted. 'Withdraw the elevator!'

It seemed to take an age before the platform began to sink back towards the hangar again. Three of the XCs broke cover and charged at them on full thrust ... and crashed to the deck as they entered the grav zone. They were killed in an instant, and their bodies provided cover; only a fractional amount but much needed and enough to last the marines before the elevator had withdrawn out of gunshot.

'Hangar control, put the field over the entrance,' Cale ordered. He looked up. An XC was standing framed in the entrance above. It raised its gun and fired straight at him.

The fire flickered against the field and the energy dissipated.

Unfortunately the same field meant Cale couldn't fire back.

'Stay in your suits,' he ordered. 'Control, depressurize the hanger.'

It was only a matter of time before the XCs began to cut through the hull. Able Platoon would be ready.

The attack spread throughout the ship. Andrew McLaughlin staggered out of his cabin to see what the racket was. He bumped into his marine sentry and she caught him as he staggered.

'What the . . .'

'Sir! Get back!' The marine had her weapon drawn. 'We're under attack from—'

Three XCs came round the corner of the passageway, and they and the marine opened fire at the same time. The charred remains of the marine, McLaughlin and one of the XCs dropped to the deck.

The observers watched in horrified fascination as the laser cut through the door to the granny annex. Slowly, but with a grand and ghastly inevitability, the hatch toppled forward onto the deck, landing with a mighty clang. Two XCs leapt into the room, weapons raised.

Nothing happened. Some of the observers opened their eyes again. Four more XCs had come in and were keeping them covered with their guns, but that was all.

Rhukaya Bakan glared at them. Well, were they going to open fire or weren't they?

*

Barabadar had never actually captured any kind of spacecraft, let alone an outlander one, and would sneakily admit to having enjoyed the planning almost as much as she enjoyed the actual experience – the challenge of pitting her low-tech strategic instincts against the high-tech reality of the outlander vessel, which was quite unlike any she had seen before. What tactics made strategic sense? Obviously, all key areas to be secured, and the outlanders who actually knew how to run the thing to be kept alive, at least until it was established whether Sharing was possible between the two species.

So, outlanders gathered in groups in what looked like an operational centre – and she had, reluctantly, to trust the imagination of her troops in guessing what probably was and was not an operational centre – should be taken prisoner. Individuals, or even twos and threes, caught out in the passageways were to be disposed of – they would only hinder the advance. Anyone from either category that offered resistance was to be shot on the spot.

'*Martial Mother, Squad the Fourteenth. Outlanders have attempted to leave ship. Have repulsed them.*' Squad the Fourteenth was one of the external squads, the one posted to defend the large entrance up at the bow.

'Do you need reinforcement?' Barabadar asked.

'*Negative, Martial Mother.*'

Even so . . .

'Squad the Twelfth, assist Squad the Fourteenth. The outlanders might try harder next time.'

'Affirmative, Martial Mother.'

'Squad the Fourteenth, how many of them were there?'

'No more than twenty, Martial Mother.'

There had been many more than that who had attacked the rock, and who had defended the ship after it was rammed. So, somewhere on board was a large complement of fighting troops who were almost the equals of her own. They too had to be dealt with. But everything was secondary to capturing the command centre, and she thought she had it. A very solid-looking hatchway, a pair of large steel doors, secured against her, and it was where she would have put the command centre if she had designed this ship herself – almost slap bang in the centre.

'First Son, Squad the First to my position,' she ordered.

'Martial Mother, Squad the Third. Engine room . . . we think it's the engine room . . . secured.'

'Prisoners?' Barabadar said. Inside her helmet was a rough outline of the ship. They had counted the number of exposed levels in the damaged area, and from that estimated the number of levels in the entire vessel. A spot appeared on the thirtieth level from the top, ten below the entry area, to mark Squad the Third's success. Other spots were appearing as more and more squads reported a successful capture.

'Still alive, Martial Mother.' The squad leader sounded slightly reproachful that she could think otherwise.

'Martial Mother, Squad the Seventh. Armed opposition moving down from the bow. Request reinforcement.'

This spot appeared five levels from the top of the ship. So, the rest of the troops had made themselves known, coming down inside the ship to where the fighting was.

'Squads the Eighth through Tenth, assist Squad the Seventh.'

Messages of acknowledgement came through but Barabadar was distracted by the arrival of First Son and the rest of Squad the First. She pointed at the sealed steel doors.

'Open them.'

Two sappers pulled out cutting lasers and set to work.

'Martial Mother, Squad the Sixth. We have captured a room full of the four-legged outlanders. I can't see what operational purpose the room itself serves, but your orders about outlanders grouped together . . .'

'I understand.' Barabadar thought. 'How many of them?'

A pause. *'About fifty.'*

That decided her. 'Prisoners,' she said. Even if the room they were in didn't serve an operational purpose, fifty of the ship's crew wouldn't be gathered together for no reason. Once again, she wished Oomoing were here.

'Acknowledged, Martial Mother.'

Barabadar checked the diagram in her helmet. It was speckled with spots. The ship was almost taken.

'How are you doing?' she said.

'Almost through, Martial Mother,' said the lead sapper. 'There.'

The doors were too heavy to be kicked aside. There was a further delay while lifting equipment was brought in. Up at the front of the ship, Barabadar's squads and the troops seemed to have reached an uneasy stalemate; the outlanders were securely dug in and it would have been costly to send in her people to flush them out, though she could have done it. The problem was, it would cost lives and out here beyond Firegod orbit, reinforcements were in short supply.

The equipment came; cables attached to the severed doors strained and the doors fell away. Nothing on the other side offered fire. Barabadar walked through, gun at the ready.

'My Mother!' First Son protested. She ignored him. If this was the command centre then she needed to be the first in, the one to take it. Yes, it was bad security and she should have sent others through first to check it was secure. But this way was more fitting.

Two-legged outlanders stood around. They were all in the same dark-blue clothing that the one back on SkySpy, Oomoing's friend Long, had worn. Some had gold stripes on their shoulders. None was armed. Some sat at consoles, others just stood and looked at her.

And yes, this was the command centre, no doubt about it. There was a large central console with several seats scattered around it. More around the edge of the room. Screens, information displays, data feeds everywhere.

Barabadar removed her helmet and sniffed the air. She was amused; a strong smell that could only have been fear. Oomoing had theorized that the outlanders retained that primitive feeling. The rest of Squad the First filed in behind her, guns at the ready.

'I am Marshal of Space Barabadar, you are my prisoners,' she said. She looked around her. 'Well, I spoke to *someone* on this benighted vessel; one of you motherless runts must have some means of understanding me.'

One of the outlanders made a move; its hand went slowly to its belt, pausing when every gun in the room swivelled towards it.

'Hold your fire,' Barabadar said. The outlander showed no signs of continuing the movement now that it had the attention of every Kin present. Barabadar stepped forward, removed the device from its belt, handed it to the outlander. For all she knew, the outlander was triggering the scuttling sequence, but she had to take the risk. She did need to talk to the creatures.

The outlander spoke into the device, then held it up.

'Speak into this,' said a neutral voice. 'It will translate your words.'

Barabadar took the device in one of her feeding hands, studied it. Impressive.

'Very well,' she said. 'I am Marshal of Space Barabadar. Who is in charge?'

'Captain McLaughlin was killed.'

'Then I repeat the question.'

A pause. 'I am. 019323 Nguyen, Karen, Lieutenant, Commonwealth Navy.'

Much of that was just noise. But the word 'lieutenant' was familiar – one who acts for a superior, presumably in this case the late captain – and Barabadar could guess what a 'Commonwealth Navy' was through sheer common sense.

'First, order the soldiers at the front of this ship to lay down their weapons,' she said.

The lieutenant reached for the device that Barabadar still held, thought better of it, and crossed to the central console. It pressed a control and spoke. It had a conversation with a deeper voice at the other end, which seemed to grow quite heated.

The lieutenant turned back.

'They refuse.'

'Refuse!' Barabadar bellowed. Such ... such insolence! Had these creatures no sense of battle honour *at all*? She would have strong words to say to their mothers, were they ever to meet.

'Explain the situation,' she said tightly. They *were* only outlanders ... 'We have captured the key areas of this ship. We have captured you. We have captured most of your crew, two- and four-legged. They can die with honour, or they can lay down their weapons and live.'

The lieutenant had another conversation.

'They are complying,' she said.

A quick conversation with the leader of Squad the Seventh confirmed this.

'Good. Now, stand still,' Barabadar said. She

walked around the lieutenant and took hold of the outlander's head in her feeding arms. She felt the creature trembling. A short mane covered the head, again similar to Long's, though darker. Barabadar ran her fingers through it. Then she pulled back the outlander's collar and peered down the back of its neck. Just smooth skin. Absolutely nothing that even looked like it just might be a Sharemass.

So how *did* these animals Share? This was going to make life more complicated.

Perhaps their Sharemasses were internal . . .

She walked round to face the outlander from the front again.

'What is the largest open area on this ship?' Barabadar said.

'That would be the hangar deck.'

'Then here are my instructions. Those on board who are actively involved in the operation of this ship are to remain at their positions. Everyone else is to report to the hangar deck at once. You will designate someone to show my First Son here where this hanger deck is. And now –' the crunch! – 'can this ship move?' Barabadar said.

A pause. 'We have limited mobility. We haven't yet tested the repairs.'

'Can you get us back to the rock?'

'The rock?'

'The asteroid!' Barabadar said impatiently. 'The secret base. The one you attacked.'

'The one *we* . . .?' The words through the translator were flat and unemotional, but from the sudden

351

volume and the increased smell in the air, Barabadar guessed outrage, surprise. 'Yes,' said the lieutenant. 'We can probably return there.'

'Then we will do so. Pass on my instructions to the crew and also inform your engineering staff that my engineering staff will require a full briefing on the operational principles of this vessel. And, of course, your clever method of opening holes in space.'

She suspected the lieutenant would dispute the point, so she turned away before any argument could be entered into. Of course, the creatures would want to hang onto their superior technological secrets – who wouldn't? – but, one way or the other, she would get the secrets out of them.

And the best of it was, she no longer had to worry about preserving the bodies so as to placate the outlanders. The outlanders had come, they had been duly challenged, they had fought, and they had lost. The dead were hers to do as she liked with.

'First Son,' she said, making sure she wasn't within range of the translator gadget. 'I want volunteers to consume a couple of dead outlanders. They must have a way of Sharing and I can't guess what it is. Try eating their heads first of all; there may be something inside that I can't see.'

'Very well, My Mother.'

'And if it doesn't work on the corpses,' Barabadar added, 'try it on a couple of live ones.'

Twenty-One

Day Twenty-One: 23 June 2153

The lifeboat came to within 30,000 miles of SkySpy and stopped.

'Think they've detected us?' Donna said.

'Almost certainly.' Gilmore scowled at the display on the flight-deck desk. They weren't making any effort to hide. At this range, there was no harm in letting the XCs see them.

Pathfinder had fallen silent soon after the Mayday went out, leaving them with hours of speculation fuelled by their worst fears. But then the ship had started moving and now it was almost back at SkySpy, which was encouraging. The XCs couldn't have worked out so quickly how to make the ship move; therefore, a large part of the crew must still be alive.

'We are receiving a signal from *Pathfinder*'s step-through generator,' said Boon Round. 'It seems to be on SkySpy.'

'*On* SkySpy?' said Gilmore.

'Definitely somewhere in the asteroid,' Boon Round confirmed.

'Could we fire it up at a distance?' Donna said. The point had already occurred to Gilmore. Open a point, rush in on full, skip back to the Commonwealth and bring reinforcements.

Except that . . .

'It needs to be connected to the ship for the power,' he said.

'Does this lifeboat have enough power?'

'Probably. But we'd have to get right close to it and . . . hey, stay back!'

The XC, Oomoing, had come too close for his liking. Donna whirled round and her shoulder lasers clicked into position, targeting the creature with pinpoint accuracy. She was still wearing her armour, minus helmet and gauntlets, for just that reason.

'I just wanted—' Oomoing said, via the translator aide.

'We're having a crisis and you're not involved. I said, and I meant, stay away.'

The XC retreated to the far end of the cabin, still clutching the aide.

'D-Donna?'

It was a faint whisper from the couch at the front of the main compartment, nearest the flight deck, but they all heard it. Joel had woken up. He was propping himself up on one elbow and looking blearily about him. His eyes focused on the small group.

'*Dad?*' He looked from one to the other. 'What are . . . how are . . .'

Gilmore and Donna stepped through the flight deck hatch together and jammed. Gilmore's unarmoured ribs crunched as Donna's armour rammed into him. He gasped and staggered back into the flight deck, and Donna seized the moment to squeeze through and reach Joel first.

'Hi.' She knelt in front of him, took his head in her hands gently, ran her fingers through his hair. 'How are you?'

'Still . . . still a bit . . . what are you *doing* here?'

'I came to get you,' she said simply.

Gilmore had finally caught up. 'We both did,' he said. 'Boon Round's been telling us about your adventures.'

'Boon Round . . .' Joel said. The Rustle had stayed in the flight deck. 'Hi, Boon Round. Thanks for everything.'

'My pleasure,' Boon Round said.

'I hope you are better, Joel.' The unfamiliar voice came from the translator, again. Oomoing was standing a safe distance away.

Joel grinned and pushed himself into a sitting position. He swung his legs down to the deck and stood up, unsteadily. Donna supported him.

'Oomoing. Yes, thanks, much better. You've met my dad?'

'Indeed, though trust has yet to be established. It might help if you were to tell him how I think I could help get your ship back.'

Barabadar had brought *Pathfinder* back into a parking orbit around the asteroid. The assault ships wouldn't be back for hours. Still, the outlander lifeboat prudently came to a halt on exactly the other side of the asteroid.

Marshal of Space Barabadar gazed up at it through her helmet visor. Such effortless movement. Such grace. Such power.

'Are you ready, Martial Sister?' said the voice that she really hadn't expected to hear again. Let alone to hear blackmailing her. Meet the outlanders, unguarded and alone, or face having the half-facts that Oomoing already knew – which were still too much for Barabadar's liking – broadcast throughout the system.

'Ready, Learned Sister.'

'They say you may come up.'

'How very gracious. I'm on my way.'

Barabadar's thrusters carried her up to the lifeboat and to its airlock. She stepped through, removed her helmet and gave the Bow of Equals. 'Learned Sister.'

Oomoing returned it. 'Martial Sister. Face to face, may I first present my condolences at the death of your Third Son. He was a loyal ally, son and friend, and he died most worthily of your family.'

The words tore into Barabadar but she didn't let it show. 'Learned Sister, I have long since reconciled myself to his death without Sharing. I had to when these creatures here so thoughtfully removed him, and you, in this ship.'

She let her gaze sweep over the assembled outlanders. One of them was in the same kind of space armour that the outlanders who had attacked the asteroid had worn, and she suspected that the things on its shoulders were weapons attachments which were trained on her.

'I see you found two more,' she said. 'A clever feat. We've unearthed quite a nest of them ourselves, but we seem to have dealt with them.'

Oomoing wasn't letting her duck the subject. Now Barabadar heard the anger crackling at the back of her voice. 'Martial Sister, you said you would Share. I suggest we do it now. Did you bring—'

'Of course I brought it.' Barabadar opened a pocket and pulled out a small, thin box which she handed to Oomoing. 'Will you please do the honours? I'd rather not trust outlanders to get it right.'

Oomoing bowed again. 'My pleasure, Martial Sister.'

She opened the box and took out the Sharing scalpel and bowl, then walked behind Barabadar. The Marshal of Space felt the Learned Sister's fingers probe the Sharemass at the back of her head.

'There,' she said. Then a slight sting. Oomoing wasn't an experienced Sharer; she had dug deep with the scalpel and Barabadar would probably bleed.

Oomoing came back into view with – sure enough – the bloodstained Shareberry in its bowl, its skin inexpertly peeled back. She handed the bowl to Barabadar; a redundant piece of ritual because Barabadar held it back out to her.

'Learned Sister, take this Sharing of myself as your sacred duty,' Barabadar said. Oomoing reached out and lifted the Shareberry up.

'Be very careful, Learned Sister,' Barabadar added.

She felt a perverse satisfaction. Oomoing had black-mailed her into coming out here; now this was payback. 'Not every Sharing is worth it.'

Oomoing paused, then popped the Shareberry into her mouth and shut her eyes.

There was knowledge and there was sorrow.

Oomoing had already guessed the gist of it. Over a hundred years ago, near the end of the Era of War, scientists had finally made the correlation between the transit of the Dead World and the waves of battle lust that swept across Homeworld. The old legends were right, but the Dead World didn't get its name from any malevolent deities. Probes were dispatched there and the signals beamed back clearly showed a civilization in residence. An outlander race. Sentient life somewhere else in the universe.

The news was closely guarded. Very closely guarded. The scientists passed it to a few select politicians, the politicians passed it to their counterparts in the other nations of Homeworld. We need not fight. Something up there is making us do it.

A peace conference was called. It was partially held. A great spirit of optimism. We can do this. We can break free from the past. We can . . .

Then the orbits of the two worlds brought them together again, and war again swept the planet. There was no stopping it. Even those who knew the truth found themselves giving the orders that would cause yet more death, yet more destruction.

When the war was over, the survivors reconvened.

Every one of the Kin who knew about the Dead World was brought into the conspiracy.

Because conspiracy it was. They would destroy the race on the Dead World, and if that didn't break the cycle then nothing would. But how can you go about attacking an enemy like the unseen forces of the Dead World in the proper way? What rituals do you use? How do you judge the winner? How do you keep your honour?

You don't.

The details of the xenocide, Oomoing already knew from Joel Gilmore. Now she got to see it from the inside. It culminated in a united, manned mission to the Dead World — a technological triumph that had to be conducted in total secrecy — to finish the job. When it was all done, every member of the attack fleet committed suicide. Their ships were destroyed in Dead World orbit so that their crews could never Share again. Those who were left behind had agreed to die Unsharing. Knowledge of the xenocide would vanish from the Sharing pool of the Kin, passed on instead only in highly classified, written records.

Because a few still needed to know. The Kin were spreading out into space; it was inevitable that someone would end up on the Dead World. The satellite shield had to be implemented, a space watch maintained. So the first Marshal of Space, Barabadar's predecessor by three, and a small, select circle of senior space staff knew. So did their counterparts in other nations. As did their successors today. It was understood that when they eventually died, they too would go Unshared. Their knowledge would vanish from the pool and the secret would stay hidden, passed on only by word of mouth.

Until the outlanders turned up. Outlanders who had witnessed and recorded the whole thing.

Oomoing opened her eyes. Barabadar was staring at her.

'You . . . would do that?' Oomoing said. She felt the tearing sorrow within her. To be unremembered, Unshared. To have nothing but genetic progeny to pass down through the ages. In times gone past, it had been the ultimate disgrace – a punishment for criminals. And to save a proud and honourable people from the knowledge of such a crime, Barabadar had taken it upon herself.

'I told you that you might not like it, Learned Sister. The Era of War is over! A liberal like you should be glad. Now you know how it was accomplished, how glad are you still?'

'I . . . am humbled, o Most Worthy Sister.' Oomoing hung her head.

'As long as we know where we stand.' Barabadar turned her attention to the outlanders. 'Now, introduce me to your new friends and we can work out where we go from here.'

'Your ship is mine,' said the voice from the aide. 'It came uninvited, it was challenged, it was captured according to all due protocol.'

Gilmore looked across the table at the Marshal of Space. He suppressed a shudder at the sight: the blank eyes, the flowing mane, the shark teeth. If

Barabadar decided to lash out with the talons of her hunting arms then he would be dead before he even noticed.

Fortunately the aide didn't translate body language.

'The crew—' he said.

'Is also mine. It was captured along with the ship and my Learned Sister assures me that Sharing between our species is impossible; therefore, we must be taught how to operate the ship according to your own methods.'

Gilmore breathed a sigh of relief that Oomoing had got in touch with Barabadar *before* she had started Sharing experiments with live humans or Rusties. 'But we've already agreed you can keep the base,' he said.

'How very kind of you. A redundant, empty base on the outskirts of the solar system with no real practical purpose any more.'

'SkySpy's original purpose—'Gilmore began.

'A telling choice of name, isn't it?' Barabadar interrupted. 'Sky. *Spy.*'

'I didn't choose it,' Gilmore said through his teeth. 'I was saying, yes, its *original* purpose is now redundant. You know about us. But it would be a good, neutral centre of operations for our two species to meet and mix and ultimately form diplomatic relations. It's in your territory, so clearly it would be best for you to administer it.'

'And why would we want to meet and mix, Worthy Sister?' said Barabadar. She would not consider the possibility that he was Joel's father; speaking to anything less than a mother would have been demeaning for her.

'Because you know about us and you can't hide us. Accept us as friends instead.'

'Why?'

'Because otherwise we'll come to blows.'

'Stay away from our solar system and no blows will be necessary.'

'Sooner or later you'll leave your solar system. And we intend to study the natives of the Dead World, help them if we can. We won't let them misuse you as they used to—'

'How do you intend to stop them?' Barabadar said.

'But we can't let them go on as they are.' Gilmore knew that she knew he had ducked the question.

'Why not?'

'Because.'

At the back of his mind was the ever-present awareness that he was making promises he couldn't guarantee would be kept. But he was Arm Wild's official observer; surely that gave him ambassador status here. And if not, he was sure he could talk Arm Wild into it when he got back to the Roving. An opportunity like this would never arise again, and even a bad deal struck now was better than no deal at all.

Of course, he had no training in negotiation and he could already sense that the talk was going all over the place. He wanted, in order of priority: the crew back, *Pathfinder* back, and clearance to investigate the

Dead Worlders. He had tried to start with the first matter; now they were discussing the last. How did the pros managed to concentrate on one subject?

Barabadar squatted back on her haunches and looked at him in a manner which Gilmore suspected was thoughtful. 'They have something you want. And that something could conceivably be ... telepathy. Does it work at light speed or is it instantaneous? And if it is instantaneous, what is its range? And if its range is large enough, can it be used for instant communication with your homeworld? Or between ships, perhaps?'

Gilmore put his hands on the table, palms up. 'That could possibly be a reason.'

'You have a high opinion of your capabilities. Supposing you *can't* work out how it works?'

'Supposing you can't work out how *Pathfinder* functions?' Gilmore countered, bringing the conversation at least back to the middle-ranking subject.

'Oh, I think we can! It will take time, but we will set every scientist on Homeworld to study it. It is a machine, machines can be disassembled and put back together. A little different from telepathy, a subject that is brand new to both our races.'

'We have to try,' Gilmore said.

'So, you intend to come and go in our system as you please?'

Back to the Dead Worlders again ... 'If that's what it takes.'

'Would you allow us to do the same if we discovered a similar race in your own system?'

'Probably not.'

'What a conveniently flexible code of ethics you have. And while your Navy is reaping the benefits of telepathy, what about us? If your First Son is correct, once a sufficient number of Dead Worlders have reawakened, they will again be able to do to us what they did for hundreds of thousands of years. We can't allow that. How do you intend to stop them? In short, Worthy Sister, what is in it for us?'

Gilmore had to accept that they were going to finish off the subject of the Dead World first. *Then* he could talk about the crew. He swallowed, because this was the tricky bit.

'Look,' he said. He leaned closer, hoped Barabadar would recognize the body language for sincerity. Leaning closer to those teeth and claws required an internal adjustment of attitude, but he managed it. 'I propose we define an exclusion zone around the Dead World. You don't come within it – that's your present policy anyway – and everything within it is ours. And you'll have to acknowledge us, because step-through points can be detected with your present technology and you won't be able to keep us quiet to your people.'

He sat back and held the Marshal of Space's gaze. He had already established that human and XC body language at least had that much in common; prolonged eye contract meant trust, conviction. Or challenge, depending on context. He hoped the context was right. And he remembered what Oomoing had told him about the whole SkySpy attack. It was only a theory but Oomoing strongly suspected she was right.

Marshal of Space Barabadar was an unlikely looking peace merchant, but that was her intent, and always had been.

'For most of our recorded history,' Oomoing had said, as the lifeboat headed back to SkySpy on maximum power, 'the Kin fought one another. I for one have always been grateful I was born since the end of the Era of War. Yes, there is still tension, there are still skirmishes, but nothing like the holocausts of old. As a scientist, I've always felt it a wonder that any kind of scientific progress was made at all amongst the Kin, with the blows dealt to civilization on such a regular basis. We developed weapons that could destroy nations, we developed rockets capable of delivering them, we fought world-wide wars to that effect . . . and then the Era of War was over. It seems too good to be true, but true it is.'

'You still fight,' Gilmore had commented.

'We still fight, but that is only right and in our nature. We have the Rituals of Combat to limit the carnage to a manageable level.'

'But the knowledge must still be there,' Gilmore said. 'Weapons don't uninvent themselves.'

'Of course not! The Kin knew how to make those weapons, and just because all the nations had signed the convention limiting their proliferation, that was no guarantee they had all been destroyed. Every decade or so came a new theory which said that they *hadn't* all been destroyed and were in fact stored at some new location. These rumours were always investigated and as candidate locations on Homeworld grew ever fewer, the rumours moved out into space.'

'But if this arms dump exists at all,' said Gilmore, 'it was built before you had any decent space technology.'

'Exactly,' Oomoing said. 'Therefore, unlikely to be far out in space . . . but only if it was defended and maintained by Kin. Kin would need relieving and resupplying and the spaceships would be spotted. But that wouldn't be so if the crew were servors.'

'Servors?'

'Air-breathing robots,' Boon Round explained. He had heard the story already.

'Servors could have built a base anywhere in our solar system,' Oomoing said, 'with all the time in the world at their disposal. And of course, to attack a base defended by them, you would let the air out. Do my Martial Sister's tactics start to make sense? Not to mention her dishonourable lack of a challenge?'

Gilmore shut his eyes. Oh, God. How much of this whole business had been one mistake, one error after another? 'So when she discovered something on the asteroid was putting out heat, she put two and two together . . .' he said.

'And made five. We have a similar expression,' said Oomoing.

And now, Gilmore sincerely wished he did have

something more concrete to offer Barabadar than vague promises.

'Your confidence amazes me.' The aide's tone suggested more sarcasm than honest amazement. 'You have the whole future neatly mapped out to your benefit and we get nothing . . .'

A communication tone came in from her people on the outlander ship at almost the same time as Gilmore's aide began to chime for attention.

The chief XC on *Pathfinder*'s flight deck – the Marshal of Space's son, no less – raised his gun menacingly. Karen Nguyen ignored it as she strode across the deck to confront the small group of Rusties.

'Look,' she shouted at Sand Strong. 'There's no need. We can work this out . . .'

'I am sorry.' It wasn't Sand Strong who spoke. When it became obvious that the Device Ultimate ploy had failed, the pride had locked itself away in the ship's Commune Place and undergone the quiet, bloodless, consensual revolution that happened whenever the First Breed fell out with themselves. The new pride leader was Day Red; Sand Strong was just one of his juniors. 'We came close to doing a terrible thing. We betrayed the trust of the Commonwealth and we endangered billions of innocent lives. This is the only way we can make amends.'

'Haven't you guys heard of a simple apology?'

'Lieutenant Nguyen, in the days of the Ones Who Command, it was customary for clans to exchange prides from time to time. It enabled understanding and the growth of alliances, and it was a way for losing clans to make restitution to the winners. This is our way. Please respect it.'

'But . . .' Nguyen said helplessly. She looked from Day Red to the XC, and back. There were so many reasons this couldn't happen. It would give the XCs superior technology. It would give them a victory. It just plain *hurt*. It . . .

'There are enough humans on board to make repairs and to get *Pathfinder* back home,' said Day Red. 'You don't need us. Please don't worry about us, Lieutenant – we've changed masters once, we can do it again.'

Day Red turned to the XC and activated the XC translator. His words came out simultaneously in Standard English and the chirping percussion that was XC-speak.

'Please inform your mother that the First Breed on board *Pathfinder* are hers to command.'

Barabadar and Michael Gilmore looked at each other again across the table top. Gilmore wondered if he was just imagining the waves of satisfaction that seemed to flow out of her.

'Well,' Barabadar said, 'it appears we do get something out of this, after all. An entire – what was the word? – pride of your servants should certainly placate my government.'

'They are not servants,' Gilmore grated. 'They were created servants for the Ones Who Command but in the Commonwealth, they're equals. We work along-side each other.'

'In your Commonwealth, are they free enough to declare themselves not free if they so choose?' Barabadar said. Gilmore didn't answer. 'Then here is how it is. I will release the human half of your crew, and ... yes, I will release *Pathfinder*, and your step-through device, as a gesture of goodwill to foster further relations between our species. In return, these First Breed remain with us. They'll be very well treated, I give you my word about that.'

Gilmore could believe it. Barabadar wouldn't look ... actually, she probably *would* look a gift horse in the mouth, just to be sure, and give it a full medical into the bargain, but she certainly wouldn't abuse it once she found it was indeed sound and healthy. And this gift horse was in the form of a pride of First Breed, bursting with knowledge about step-through, starship mechanics and quantum energy sources.

'Accepted,' he sighed. 'And as for—'

'With one further condition,' Barabadar inter-rupted. 'I don't have resources for looking after or transporting a whole pride back to Homeworld. We keep this vessel too.'

Gilmore shut his eyes, groaned quietly. The XCs Would Not Get Commonwealth Technology – that had been the basis for the entire mission. But he really didn't have a choice, and he could see Barabadar's point – she needed to transport fifty Rusties, somehow.

'Accepted,' he said again. 'And *now*?'

'As for the matter of the Dead World, I think I can speak favourably to my government and to the League of Mothers about your requests. This unexpected bonus will incline them to be reasonable.' She stood to leave. 'Goodbye, Worthy Sister; I'm sure we'll be seeing more of each other.'

Another farewell at the lifeboat airlock.

'I can only echo my Martial Sister's words,' Oomoing said. She was fully suited up and ready to depart. 'I'm sure we'll be seeing more of each other.'

'I hope so,' Joel said with a grin.

'Thanks for looking after him,' Donna added. She and Joel had their arms around each other's waist.

'I did my best,' Oomoing said. 'I didn't know about *chocolate*.'

Joel gagged. 'Never again. Please.'

'Will you be involved further with the Dead World natives?' Oomoing asked.

'Probably.' Joel pulled a face. 'I mean, I'm the only one who can talk to them at the moment. Why?'

'Because I would like to study them more closely too, if a means can be found of doing it safely. We have a lot to find out. Perhaps we can do it together. There are matters that need clarifying.'

Gilmore Senior had come up behind them. 'One of the first contact ships spent a week on the surface of the Dead World,' he said, 'and they reported no survivors. So yes, there's a lot of misinformation to sort out.'

The rude noise Oomoing made wasn't translated

by the aide. 'They spent a week looking and found no-one; Joel and Boon Round landed at random and found a whole community. I'd question the competence of your original informant.'

She reached for the door control, paused. 'I confess I still have certain reservations about your physical form,' she said. 'So consider yourselves *kissed*.' The door slid shut.

'We have control, lifeboat,' said the voice. *'Rendezvous in five minutes.'*

'Acknowledged, *Pathfinder*,' said Boon Round. 'You have control.' He removed his graspers from the control desk. It continued to operate without him. *Pathfinder* was bringing them in on remote. 'Five minutes,' he said unnecessarily to the humans with him, who had heard the announcement themselves.

'Great!' Gilmore rubbed his hands together. 'Boon Round, could you give me a hand aft?'

'What with?'

'Just . . . please?' Gilmore turned and ducked through the hatch. Boon Round paused for a moment, then followed him, muttering something about humans who needed help with everything, what was the use, why did he bother . . . ?

Joel and Donna were alone on the flight deck, at long last.

'Well, *he* read the signals,' Donna said. 'Can you?'

'Huh?'

They looked at each other. Joel knew she wanted *something*. But what? It wasn't a kiss. They had already kissed. And apparently they had been left alone for a purpose. The only thing that came to mind other than kissing didn't usually take place on flight decks, it should certainly last longer than five minutes and he didn't think his dad would be quite so cold-blooded about it.

'Look,' she said quietly. 'We won't see a lot of each other when we get back. I'm in charge of the marines now.'

'Yeah ...' He swallowed. And he suddenly realized. She wanted to *know*. She had come this far on sheer faith, and she still didn't know for sure it had been worth it. Once back on board *Pathfinder* she could throw herself into her duties and wean herself off him, or ...

He reached out to her, took her hand. 'I ...' He swallowed again. 'I still can't believe you came all this way for me.'

She was still looking into his eyes. He wanted to pretend there was no bottom, no end to her gaze; he could fall into those eyes and lose himself for ever.

He felt fingers twining with his own. He looked down at their clasped hands, then back up at her.

'I never told you ...' he went on. He felt his face warming up; he knew he was blushing like a teenager on a first kiss. 'You know I grew up on Luna?'

'I know.'

'Well, boys and girls there ...'

'The same as anywhere else, surely?'

'Yeah, but ...' He swallowed. 'Mum was, um, odd. She joined the Post-Socialist Collective and there the boys and girls are *exactly* the same. We play together, grow up together ... I mean, baths and showers together! And then you're expected to join a group marriage when you're older and ... So anyway, we're, um, not exactly strangers to each other and we're world-class experts on the, um, physical differences between boys and girls but ... when it comes to, well, you know, finding *one special person* who's more important than anyone else, we're, well, we're not so good at it ...'

Throw me a line! he wanted to cry. 'Donna, having to leave you was the cruellest bastard trick that ever got pulled on me, because I knew we were this close, *this* close –' he disentangled a hand and held it up, thumb and forefinger a bare millimetre apart – 'to clicking, to making it work, and I thought of you every moment from the time I left the Roving, and I ... Look.' He freed his other hand to activate his ident bracelet. The faintly exasperated expression on the holo exactly matched the faintly exasperated expression on her face now. 'You were this close to me all that time.' He switched the bracelet off, tentatively pressed that wrist against his chest. 'And I want you closer. This close. Al—'

He had been going to say, *always*, but that was when she finally moved forward and kissed him. Into that kiss went all the pain, all the fear, all the heartache of the last few weeks; it evaporated away into nothing. They drew apart and the universe consisted entirely of Joel Gilmore and Donna McCallum, gazing with adoration into each other's eyes.

*

Pathfinder's docking tube extended out to the lifeboat's airlock. There was a clang, a bump, a hiss as the two met and sealed and flooded with air.

Boon Round operated the hatch control, and inner and outer hatches opened.

At the far end of the tube was *Pathfinder*, and framed in the big ship's airlock was the vanguard of the defecting pride. They were the first First Breed that the prideless Boon Round had seen in the best part of a month, and he had wondered how this moment would be. To his surprise, he felt very little. These creatures had defected. They had put themselves outside the First Breed nation.

In effect, they were the First Breed's first colony in space.

'Well, here goes,' said Michael Gilmore, and he stepped forward. Boon Round paused for a moment, then followed him, with Joel Gilmore and Donna McCallum bringing up the rear.

Out of the corner of his eye Boon Round noticed Joel taking a final look back at the lifeboat. Well, it had served them well . . . but Boon Round was all too keen to put it behind him. The lifeboat was in the past. Boon Round lived in the present and looked forward to . . . ah yes, the future, he thought as the other pride approached him. The future was also something he had no desire to linger on. It had XCs in it. The Commonwealth was going to work with them. Work with them, be nice to them, be nice to those forsaken creatures who had kept him and Joel Gilmore . . . alive. They wouldn't have *needed* keeping alive if the

XCs had just left SkySpy alone, but the fact was, the creatures had gone out of their way to look after them. Eventually.

Madness, he thought gloomily. But so had been handing over leadership of the Roving to a whole new species four years ago, and by and large it seemed to be working.

So he would go along with this new policy because this was how it was. But he didn't have to like it and he would request integration into a pride on the Roving that kept him well away from the beasts.

Now they were walking through the defecting pride. Their bodies jostled, the blessed smell of the First Breed filled his nostrils. It was difficult for a single First Breed to walk one way while a whole pride walked another. Without even thinking about it he slowed, missed a step, and Michael Gilmore glanced down at him. Was the human worried? Did he think Boon Round would join the flow?

Joel would probably have said something. Michael Gilmore did not. The man trusted him, Boon Round, to make his own decisions. So Boon Round kept walking.

Twenty-Two

9 July 2153

'There she blows,' Gilmore said. A dark mass had appeared on the horizon, drawing closer as the Roving's Western Ocean blurred beneath the aircar.

A solid plug of rock rose out of the waves; dark cliffs, unassailable shores.

Joel was subdued at the sight and Gilmore knew why. The Roving's St Helena had been given the name of its Earth counterpart for a good reason – a final place of exile, somewhere that the centre of attraction would never leave alive. The difference between the St Helenas was that visitors to this one didn't just witness the end of a short-lived empire, they got to meet the last of an entire species.

'You're sure he'll see us?' Joel said.

'He'll see us,' Gilmore promised grimly as the aircar banked for its final approach. They were on autopilot and Gilmore's authorization from the Admiralty for this trip was taking care of the frequent requests beamed at them for identification.

'I just understood he refused all your requests for an appointment . . .'

'That's why I stopped requesting.'

'Ah.'

The aircar was slowing, the noise of its engines rising. They were over the cliffs and suddenly St Helena looked much more attractive – a verdant plateau, plentiful plant and bird life, a sparkling lake at the centre. A complex of low, white buildings spread out from the north shore; the organic, curved shapes of classical Roving pridehalls. The aircar landed on the clear strip of grass between the water and the main building.

The doors winged open and they climbed out, wincing in the bright sunlight and the heat. They slipped their shades on, and stood and looked at the dark glass front of the building. It was shadowed by an overhanging roof and nothing could be seen through the plate glass windows.

'You think he's in?' Joel said.

'He's certainly not out visiting the relatives, and that's the main residence. Come on.'

Gilmore took three steps forward and the ground at his feet erupted in a burst of fire. He staggered back.

'*Go back*,' an amplified voice boomed. '*You are not welcome here*.'

Gilmore raised his voice, careful not to let it shake. 'I have authority from Arm Wild,' he called.

More plasma fire, a line of exploding turf that snaked quickly towards him across the grass. Gilmore swallowed his pride and jumped behind the aircar, for whatever shelter it could provide.

'*We know you have authority from Arm Wild. We do not recognize Arm Wild's authority. Leave here.*'

'Do you see them?' Gilmore muttered.

'Uh-huh. There's at least two of them, in the bushes, either side of the entrance.'

Gilmore frowned at the unattainable entrance lobby, barely a hundred feet away.

'OK. Get in.' He raised his voice again. 'We're leaving! Don't shoot!'

They stood, slowly, tensed and ready to duck the moment shooting broke out again. Nothing happened. They stepped into the aircar and the doors shut over them. Gilmore powered up the engines.

'So now what? We leave and come back with Donna and her friends?' Joel said hopefully.

'Damn,' Gilmore muttered. 'Sorry, Joel. If I'd known it was dangerous I'd have left you behind.'

Joel gave a nervous laugh. 'Well, I've faced worse.'

'True,' Gilmore growled, and the aircar shot forward across the grass. Joel yelled and covered his eyes as the glass front of the hall loomed, and then the aircar had smashed through and was skidding to a halt in the lobby.

The doors flew open again. Joel sat in his seat and gibbered.

'Come on!' Gilmore snapped. He glanced back outside; armed Rusties were jumping out of the bushes and running towards them.

'Which way?'

'Forward.' Gilmore hauled him out of his seat and

through the nearest door.

They skidded to a halt in the room beyond, because there was the one they had come to see.

March Sage Savour was surrounded by its life support bubble. It lay, frail and withered, on a couch within the bubble, with a clear view of everything around it. A small control unit rested by its head.

It was looking straight at them.

'That was unnecessary,' it said. 'I had already given the orders to let you through, once I saw who you were.' The words were forceful, coming straight out of a translator unit; they belied the feeble appearance of the speaker.

'You thought we were an assassination squad, didn't you?' Gilmore said.

'I've often wondered when my First Breed will lose their patience with my continued existence. But they wouldn't send you, Michael Gilmore, the man who had power and gave it away.'

'Just can't wrap your brain cells round that one, can you? But you're right. I'm not here to kill you. You'll die soon enough anyway.' Gilmore walked up to the bubble. 'I'm not even here to charge you with treason, though God knows you deserve it.'

'Treason?' Life-support equipment began to beep gentle warnings. '*Treason?* I once ruled this planet! How could I commit treason against it?'

King Charles the First, Gilmore mused, had probably said something similar.

'Treason against the Commonwealth,' he said. 'Conspiracy against it.'

'What do you mean?'

'Rhukaya Bakan,' Gilmore snapped. 'That woman just didn't add up. No-one, not even a loyal servant of the Confederation, could have been quite so paranoid as she appeared. She didn't honestly believe the XCs would get the step-through generator working so quickly. But, she did believe she could engineer a situation in which *Pathfinder* committed xenocide and returned home with that amount of blood on its hands. The Commonwealth would split wide open and an obstacle to the Confederation's expansion into space would be neatly removed.'

He put his face to the bubble and jabbed a finger at March Sage Savour.

'And *you* gave her the wherewithal. That's conspiracy to commit treason. You're a traitor, March Sage Savour.'

'An interesting theory,' March Sage Savour said. The tones of the One Who Commands' translator unit had gone flat; always an ominous sign of extreme emotion. 'Have you put it to her?'

'No. She took the next ship home. But I did send a note to her superiors by separate ship. They'll know she's been blown, they'll know she failed. I don't think her career prospects are good.'

'I see.' Tone began to return again as March Sage Savour switched subject. 'Now, the one with you is Joel Gilmore. I recognize his image from the reports. I deduce you wish to discuss the recent events.'

Gilmore stepped slowly back from the bubble, but continued to glare at the One Who Commands. 'You commanded the ship that surveyed the Dead World and reported no survivors,' he said. 'You can't have drawn a blank. Why did you lie?'

'Oh, we landed on the Dead World,' March Sage Savour agreed. 'We weren't well received, but we helped as best we could and eventually they came to trust us.'

'And?' Gilmore shouted. 'And you just left them to stew? You can't have been that scared of the XCs. They were Atomic Age. They'd only just got to grips with spaceflight. You could have—'

'The decision wasn't mine. It belonged to Sigil Measure Lantern, who was in charge of the whole mission, and his seniors on the Roving backed him up. But I concurred with it.'

The bubble turned, glided away from Gilmore. It headed for a small pedestal where a single data crystal gleamed.

'You're right,' March Sage Savour said. 'I'll die soon and then I won't be able to prevent you from getting this. It's all in the archives anyway, spread out and distributed here and there to make it hard to find. But this is the full data gathered from our expedition.'

A grasper slid slowly out and operated a control by its couch. The lights dimmed and a holo appeared between the One Who Commands and the two humans. Two abstract, spiralling shapes, side by side.

'Item,' March Sage Savour said. 'On the left, DNA taken from a Dead World native. On the right, DNA taken from the body of one of the crew of the XC suicide ships. There is a close match. Like ourselves and the First Breed, they have a common ancestor.'

Father and son took a moment to absorb this.

'Unlike us,' said March Sage Savour, 'their relationship is almost symbiotic. Joel Gilmore, you were correct in your supposition that the Dead Worlders somehow sap the sentience from the XCs. What you didn't realize, and what they didn't know either, is that they don't need to go so far. They *do* require the sentience from an XC to energize their own minds, but they can get all they need from a single Shareberry. When you go back to their system, you could let them know this. I imagine there will be some mutual relief in the knowledge.'

'But . . . why?' Joel frowned. 'There must be some point in that relationship. How did they evolve, what was—'

'They didn't evolve,' Gilmore murmured. 'Any more than the First Breed did.'

'Exactly.' March Sage Savour almost sounded pleased. 'The reason for the relationship? That would be known only to the ones who carried them across space in the first place. When they stopped, the supply of Shareberries dried up and the Dead Worlders needed to resort to their more drastic methods.'

Another pause.

'How recent would that have been?' Gilmore asked.

'Not for many thousands of years. We looked but found no evidence of spaceflight on the Dead World.

Nor is there any evidence of it in the legends and mythology of either world. It was a *long* time ago.'

'But now we know there's someone else out there,' Gilmore said. 'Whoever set this whole thing up.'

'Or was,' Joel added.

'Indeed,' March Sage Savour agreed.

Joel shrugged. 'So, a vanished alien race. What about it? That still doesn't explain why you lied. And why you actually wanted to use Device Ultimate.'

'Did you ever wonder,' said March Sage Savour, 'how we found Earth?'

'It's ... it's easy to find,' Joel said, baffled. 'Step-through to Sol system. It's the one with the big moon.'

'But why should we step-through there?' said March Sage Savour. 'It's over a thousand light years from the Roving. There are dust clouds between us; your sun isn't even visible in our sky. We can see the XCs' sun from here and we could deduce the existence of at least one inhabitable world by simple astronomical observation. Why should we seek out a world around a sun that we can't even see?'

'Go on,' Gilmore said carefully.

March Sage Savour's head moved slightly; another holo picture appeared.

'This is exactly the size of the original,' March Sage Savour said. 'We found it in one of the Dead World's astronomical centres.'

'Seen it,' said Joel. He and his father moved forward to study the image. It was a circular, concave bowl of stone, pitted with small dots and faded patterns. Here it stood on its edge but the last time he had seen it he had had to crane his neck back and stare at the roof. 'This was on the ceiling at the top of the tower on the Dead World.'

'Stars!' Gilmore said. He had finally worked it out. 'It's a star map.'

'You are both right. One of these was in the ceiling of each of the astronomical towers we visited,' March Sage Savour said. 'Now look more closely.'

Points of light appeared on the carving; yellow holo circles surrounding some of the stars.

'Our astrogator recognized it as a star map,' said March Sage Savour. 'But it could not possibly have been carved by the Dead World natives. You might notice there are a great many stars – many more than would be visible to the naked eye from the Dead World. Now, look at these yellow circles. These particular stars are all marked with a certain symbol. We matched them with our own records and we found that each of these stars that we already knew about has at least one Roving-type planet. We are one of them. There were also a lot of them that we didn't already know about, and one of those –' one of the holo circles began to blink, towards the edge of the slab – 'is Sol. Earth's sun.'

The two humans stood and stared at the map, taking in the implications.

'They knew about us,' Joel said.

'You humans fondly believe you are the solution to every problem. Absolute masters of your own destiny,' March Sage Savour said. Even through the translator unit there was disdain. 'Just as we believed we were the rulers of the Roving. So let me tell you this. We had our supremacy on this world, and you on yours, because whoever carved this map let us. Once there was a race who spanned the stars in an empire a million times greater than your precious Commonwealth could ever be. They left behind their legacy on the Dead World and the XCs' homeworld like a child might discard a toy. Now, do you see why I wanted to use Device Ultimate?'

'No?' said Joel, making it a question.

'Yes,' Gilmore said quietly. 'I do.' Joel looked at him, hands held out, eyebrows raised in supplication. Gilmore nodded at March Sage Savour. 'This one here was a fairly typically unpleasant member of an unpleasant race. They were the masters of the Roving, they had their own ready packaged slave race in the form of the First Breed, they had it all. Then they realized that there was someone much greater, much grander out there and, like any bully, they feared it because it's stronger than them. They put their own motives into the strangers' heads. March Sage Savour's instinct is to rule and control anything weaker than him, so obviously, that's what these strangers would want to do too. When the SkySpy thing blew up, March Sage Savour knew that if we landed on the Dead World, or got too involved with the XCs at all, we might find out about the strangers. And he knew we would go looking for them.'

Gilmore grinned. 'And he's right. The only difference is we're not afraid of them. He thinks we'll stir up a hornet's nest, bring them down on top of us. I don't think they'll care.'

'You've seen the size of their rule!' March Sage Savour said angrily. He flicked a grasper at the map. 'As they grew in size, so they must have grown in power . . .'

'Or wisdom,' Gilmore said quietly.

'Why did they grow at all? Why not stay on their home planet? Because they wanted more. They wanted to take, to conquer . . .'

'To explore,' said Gilmore. 'To spread out. To witness the wonders of the universe.'

'Your own words condemn you.' March Sage Savour's tone was translated as a furious hiss. 'You talk about the wonders of the universe while this race could wipe you off the face of the galaxy.'

'Yeah, right. So could the first technologically superior race that my species encountered, if it wanted, but it didn't want, and the Commonwealth was the result. March Sage Savour, I've had the First Contact experience and it doesn't scare me any more.'

'Then you are a fool,' March Sage Savour said.

'No,' said Gilmore, 'I'm just better than you. Come on, Joel, we're leaving.'

'You know what really makes me angry?' Gilmore said as the aircar skimmed across the ocean. He held the data crystal in two fingers, twirled it, peered into its depths. 'His paranoia became official policy, and we just inherited it without asking. I could have looked deeper and changed it, but I just took it for granted and carried on in the old way.'

'He, um . . .' Joel said. Gilmore looked away from the crystal and at him. ' . . . could have a point?' Joel finished.

'The mysterious strangers,' Gilmore said. 'Mystical and benevolent beings of power or crazed imperial galaxy-smashers? Well, which do you think?'

'Maybe neither.' Joel looked straight ahead. 'But if they're still around, and if they wanted to stay in touch, they'd have done it. It's like . . . look, if I dump a girlfriend then as far as I'm concerned, it's over. I don't want her turning up on my doorstep again and I won't necessarily be friendly to her if she does.'

'You dump your girlfriends, do you?' Gilmore said with a grin.

'Stick to the point, Dad! You don't know that looking for them will be a good idea.'

'No,' Gilmore admitted after a pause. 'I don't.'

Joel sighed. 'But you're going to anyway, aren't you?'

'Is it that obvious?'

'When do you leave?'

Gilmore chuckled. 'I can't just set off into the blue, Joel. There's plans to make, research to do. First stop has to be the Dead World. See what other clues there are. And *then* set off into the blue.'

Joel gave a weak smile and didn't say anything for a while. Then: 'When you get back, do you think the Commonwealth will still be here?'

Gilmore didn't answer immediately. 'We uncovered a lot of tensions in this mission, and they won't just go away,' he said. 'But the Rusties need us and we need them . . .'

'But we don't need them,' Joel said. 'Not any more. They gave us their tech. Supposing we decide to drop them?'

'You're quite right,' Gilmore agreed. 'Except that we wouldn't drop them. We'd turn on them instead. Enslave 'em. Make them second-class citizens. If we humans ever get aggressive and imperial, the Rusties will be the first to know it.'

Joel looked appalled. 'And that's a good thing?'

'Yup. Because as Boon Round showed, the Rusties won't stand for it. They want us as leaders but they can also stand up for themselves. They'll always be a constant check on us. We'll have to work together, or not at all.'

'Unless more prides, maybe even whole clans, start going over to other alien powers?'

'Which is always a possibility,' Gilmore admitted. 'So, to answer your question, I think there'll be something called the Commonwealth for a long time. Other than that . . . I can't say.'

The aircar flew on. After a while, Admiralty Island appeared on the radar.